HUSH-A-BYE

It was odd, really, that lack of recognition, given the parallels in their lives, the many fugues and echoes, each of them undermined by a loss of country, of parent, of sibling. Odder still, given that two of them were later to marry, that two – a different two – would becomes lovers, that three would end up as close friends, that one would cause another the deepest of agonies, that one would die – out of season, violently.

Oddest of all that no premonition attached to their casual converging there on the pavement, islanded against the traffic, considering how closely the ribbons of their lives were later to intersect, to plait themselves into braids of such intricacy that only death could untease the tangle.

But perhaps not. If an infinite number of monkeys sat down at an infinite number of typewriters, we are told that they must eventually produce the works of Shakespeare. And yet, just as we are also told that Shakespeare did not in fact write Shakespeare, so it is perfectly possible that the monkeys would produce nothing more than an infinite amount of nonsense. In the same way, there should be no looking behind that random crossing of paths for a plan, for part of a universal design.

It happened. That ought to be enough.

And yet . . .

SUSAN MOODY

Hush-a-bye

CORONET BOOKS
Hodder and Stoughton

Printed and bound in Great Britain for Hodder and Stoughton, a division of Hodder Headline plc., 338 Euston Road, London NW1 3BH, by BPC Paperbacks Ltd, a member of The British Printing Company Ltd.

British Library C.I.P.

A CIP catalogue record for this title is available from the British Library

ISBN 0-340-59440-3

For Peter Lavery
Editor and friend

There was just the white dusty road curving away out of sight, ragged grass at the cliff's edge, a stretch of low railings around the rough-mown green. A few houses stood to one side: a clump of cottages engulfed by hollyhocks and clematis, a white-rendered house set among roses and, a little apart, something more substantial, stone-built, with a handsome lintel over the door and blue-flowering rosemary guarding either side of a low-slung garden gate. Above, the sky was immense and clear, reflecting back the light from the sea.

Benches had been placed at intervals around the green: they were occupied at this afternoon hour by young mothers with push-chaired toddlers, women carrying bags on their way home from shopping, a couple of old men reading newspapers. On the bench nearest the houses sat a woman with a scarf around her head, reading a magazine. A percipient observer might have noted the tension of her posture, the way her glance moved between the watch on her wrist and the stone house where a path of York stone led between untidy bushes to the front door and the pram parked to one side of it.

But then again he might not, this observer, have noticed anything particular about her at all. She blended in, could well have been one of the people who occasionally crossed the green from the street of houses set back behind the church, pausing briefly before trailing down to the beach or town for the afternoon.

How long had she been there? How old was she? Why had she come? It was hard to say, impossible to guess. In any *case, these were not questions anyone would have thought to ask. There was nothing remarkable about her, even when she opened the bag which sat on the seat beside her and took out an object which she held loosely between her hands, staring into it as though seeking something from it: coolness, comfort, reassurance? Anyone close enough would have seen that what she held was oval, made of swirling sea-coloured glass — a paperweight perhaps, or just a bauble.*

And then, from the square church tower just visible behind trees, came the sound of a bell striking the hour. Seconds later the door of the house opened. A woman appeared, grey-haired, her figure going — if not already gone — to seed. She carried a child in her arms, which she set in the pram and strapped in, talking to it as she did so, laughing.

Finally, she wheeled the pram down the path to the gate. As they passed the rosemary bushes, she picked one of the spiky leaves and crushed it between fingers which she then held under the child's nose, urging it to smell. 'That's rosemary,' she said. She smiled.

Unhurriedly, the woman on the bench put the paperweight — if that was indeed what it was — back into her bag and picked up her magazine, which had fallen on the grass. As she did so, she watched the child with avid eyes. There was a rapacity about her, a hunger, as though she had been starved for years and was now within sight of a spread table and plentiful food. Her long mouth — broad, generous even — opened slightly as she concentrated on the two in the garden, her arms clutching her body as though she were in pain.

There had been wind earlier; now the only sounds were those of mid-afternoon: the lazy chat of birds, a hum of busy insects — indeed, a late bee staggered against the wind-screen of a nearby car and halted momentarily before flying off, leaving a yellowish blur of pollen behind — and the faint but persistent drone of the sea.

What did she want, this woman with the bright-scarfed hair? The way she had waited for the hour to strike from the church suggested that this was not the first time she had lingered there on the bench, pretending to read; and that she had, in the past, marked the rhythms of the people in the house and already knew that at three o'clock the woman and the child would appear.

She watched as they walked slowly down the road away from her, past clustered bushes of hawthorn and blackberry. Dust from the road sifted gently over the feet of the woman pushing the pram, and rose to the hem of her long, unbecoming skirt. A drift of rosemary-scent clouded the air. She disappeared around the bend in the road and all that was left was a puff of chalkdust, like magician's smoke.

The woman on the bench rose. Slowly she pulled off her concealing scarf and shook her head so that her hair flew out on either side of her face. She walked slowly towards the house with its exuberant rosemary bushes, scanning its blank windows as she went, then picked a sprig and held it to her face. Perhaps she breathed in its perfume before moving towards the cliff edge; perhaps she merely wished to hide the tears which had filled her eyes and begun to overflow.

PART ONE

PART ONE

Their paths had crossed before, of course.

It would be satisfying to record that as they approached each other, that first time, each felt a tug at the heart, a premonition of future entanglement. In fact, on that windy afternoon in Oxford, they passed without commitment, coming variously up Beaumont Street, down St Giles, crossing over from the Cornmarket and along the Broad, to meet and converge by the Martyrs' Memorial, smiling vaguely in the way that strangers forced together by circumstances acknowledge each other before disappearing again.

One of them did stare boldly, *foreignly*, at the others. His eyes lingered for a moment on a particular face before he continued on his way. Curiously enough, later, when the two involved in this unacknowledged stare did actually meet, the one would not remember; though the other, seeing that gaze again, was to experience a moment of enquiring recognition which was fleeting and never resolved.

That afternoon they were unknown to each other. At least ... that is not strictly true. Two of them had once been friends; two others, it would later turn out, had spent the same summer fortnight in the same seaside town on the northern coast of France. But not expecting, not aware of the other's presence, they passed without a second glance. In the broad reach of St Giles, new-hatched leaves drummed and spun against the speeding air, and the cold clouds of spring hurried across the sky as the four of them came together, passed, and continued unheeding on their separate ways. Was there something symbolic about the conjunction at that particular place of historic martyrdom, some prefiguration, a foreshadowing of events to come?

It was odd, really, that lack of recognition, given the parallels in their lives, the many fugues and echoes, each of them undermined by a loss of country, of parent, of sibling. Odder still, given that two of them were later to marry, that two — a different two — would become lovers, that three would end up as close friends, that one would cause another the deepest of agonies, that one would die — out of season, violently.

Oddest of all that no premonition attached to their casual converging there on the pavement, islanded against the traffic, considering how closely the ribbons of their lives were later to intersect, to plait themselves into braids of such intricacy that only death could untease the tangle.

But perhaps not. If an infinite number of monkeys sat down at an infinite number of typewriters, we are told that they must eventually produce the works of Shakespeare. And yet, just as we are also told that Shakespeare did not in fact write Shakespeare, so it is perfectly possible that the monkeys would produce nothing more than an infinite amount of nonsense. In the same way, there should be no looking behind that random crossing of paths for a plan, for part of a universal design.

It happened. That ought to be enough.

And yet ...

Would it be a good idea to take that afternoon, four or five years before this story opens, as a starting point? Or should we move forward to some time just before *now*? And if we do, with whom should we begin?

With Christina, the achiever? With Stephan, dendrophilic and rootless? Or should we move in on Harriet's life, a place made violent by possibilities of disaster, set about with hazards to be circumvented, with dreads which jutted through the surface of her existence like rocks at a harbour mouth — Harriet whom circumstance forced into strengths she had not known she possessed?

What about Tom, vulnerable intruder from another country, from a different life, whose destiny was to take such an unexpected turn that he thenceforward had no choice but to advance without protection into the future?

There is Conor, of course: catalytic Conor, unimportant, only a bit player, yet in many ways the one who could be said to have precipitated everything that was to follow. We could always start with him.

But let us go with Harriet. She is, after all, the root cause of all that happened, the matrix, literally the womb from which sprang all the rest. So yes, let us dive, plunge, into the *now* of Harriet's as yet unresolved world.

Harriet's mother had died when she was a baby. The fact of being an orphan had not, Harriet believed, affected her, apart from imbuing her with a spurious kind of glamour both in her own eyes and those of her schoolfriends. Most of these possessed the requisite number of parents; in other respects their lives and Harriet's were almost identical, their houses similar, the strictures placed upon them by adults the same. Growing up in a leafy, well-heeled London suburb, the loss of a parent by death was almost the only evidence any of them had seen of the misfortunes which could befall unluckier souls than themselves.

Harriet's father was a remote figure. Passed on the stairs of the big old house, he would nod in a friendly manner, sometimes even speak. Though for the greater part of her childhood he seemed aloof, preoccupied with other things, she was aware of his love for her; it lay beneath the surface of their relationship like a coral reef, invisible but solid. As a small girl she had sat on his knee: she would always remember the feel of the bristles in his chin at the end of the day, and the outline of lips on her face when he kissed her goodnight. He kissed wetly; she often wanted to raise a hand and wipe the place where his mouth had been, but did not like to do so in case he thought her ungrateful. The kiss would dry slowly on her cheek; she imagined it glistening silverly like a snail-track, sequinned on her skin. He was a grey man — greying hair, grey eyes — made greyer by the black jackets and striped trousers in which, as a barrister, he habitually dressed.

In his chambers was a battered oval box of red-painted tin inside which lay the curled white wig he wore in court. Once, at her request, he had lifted it out and put it on; immediately he became for her another person, someone authoritative, public. For years after that, whenever she thought of her father, she saw him in his wig, grave and powerful, with the little white tail at the back hanging down over his collar.

Her dead mother had always been unreal. Insofar as she existed for Harriet at all, it was at the edge of her consciousness. Children adapt: she was not aware of anything missing, accepting the life she lived as the one she had been given, as the norm — only differing in this one respect from those of her friends. There was never any material lack, and her father's want of overt warmth was more than compensated for by the steady affection that she and her brother Matthew received from Maggie Burns, the housekeeper.

Even when Matthew went away to his public school, the routines laid down for Harriet precluded loneliness. School — travelling to and from it; the friends she made there; the extra-curricular activities associated with it — necessarily occupied a great deal of her time. Sometimes she wondered why she too had not been sent away to boarding school, thus freeing Mr Arden-Smith from his paternal role. It would be years before she appreciated the answer to this question.

Every summer, while Maggie Burns went to stay with her sister, Harriet and Matthew spent a month in Cornwall with their paternal grandparents; and for a fortnight their father joined them there. He was different in his parents' house at the top of the cliff, looser, somehow, more brightly coloured. He wore sweaters and open-necked shirts, even jeans; he lounged in the corners of the chintz-covered sofas and left newspapers lying about on the floors. He played with them — cricket, Monopoly, hide-and-seek — which he never did in London. They would walk along the beach together; there were dogs to run with, a small boat to sail up into wooded estuaries; quayside pubs where Harriet and Matthew sat outside with their legs hanging over harbour walls, eating crisps and swallowing yellow or red fizz while their father and grandfather drank half-pints inside.

The house in Cornwall smelled different from the one in London: shinier, cleaner. Harriet's grandmother spent her time arranging flowers picked from her garden, polishing the furniture, filling the days with small routines, doing what she had done yesterday and would do again tomorrow. The lavender-scented sheets on their beds were starched and made of linen; there were starched napkins at meals too, with monograms in one corner. She did things in due season: made marmalade, collected windfalls, stirred Christmas puddings, cut the stalks of lavender and sewed the scented grains into sachets of lace and ribbon. Things were done at prescribed times: milk drunk at eleven, a walk at three, the radio switched on at 5:54 for the weather forecast before the six o'clock news. Even as a child, Harriet was aware of order maintained against the odds, of things continuing as they always had, of her grandmother in some sense holding out, clinging to the lifebelt of what she knew in a drowning world. Adolescent, reading Eliot, reading 'The Waste Land' — *These fragments I have shored against my ruin* — Harriet recognised immediately her grandmother's small desperations.

In Cornwall the three adults would drink gin and tonics every night before dinner. There was something young and touching about her father on those evenings, as though he had reverted to the boy — she knew from her grandmother's photograph albums — that he had once been. Seeing him fastened there to the black pages, dressed in white flannels or long grey shorts, grinning from bicycles, held aloft in his own father's arms, she was aware of other lives, other childhoods, of the sharp poignancy of not being able to live any other life than her own. That boy who had once been her father survived here still, just out of sight, out of reach. Many of her grandmother's sentences began with 'I remember when you ...' as she passed food around the table: local butter, home-made apple pies, eggs brought to the kitchen door by a farmer in a van. Looking at his handsome adult profile, Harriet longed to remember him too.

On holiday the stricter routines of home were relaxed; even so, it was often still light when she was sent off to bed. From her window she could see the front garden sloping towards low hedges, and beyond them the village green. To one side the view showed her trees and the square of the church tower, to the other the silver line of the sea. The smell of herbs reached her from the still-warm garden, elusive in the greenish evening air: lavender, rosemary, sage. There was peace here, and she treasured it. Below, in the drawing-room, the voices of the grown-ups murmured comfortably through the evenings. Sometimes she overheard her mother's name.

The revelation that her mother had not, after all, died in a car crash was intensely shocking.

Arriving home from school on the afternoon of her fourteenth birthday, her father called her into the dining-room. It was her least favourite room in the house, full of cold polish and the echoes of faltering conversations. He sat on the far side of the table. He did not meet her eye, staring instead at the knuckles of his left hand and the thin gold band on his fourth finger. Above his head were two large gilt-framed portraits: one of a grim fortyish woman in black with a little lace collar, the other of a melancholy man. The woman had her hair scraped cruelly back from her face and wore a small diamond watch pinned to her shoulder. There was no ring on either of her large hands, which left an exciting ambiguity about her relationship with the man, whose abundant facial hair and outthrust lower jaw lent him a vaguely simian air which could not have been intentional. For most of her childhood, Harriet had supposed this couple to be Great-Great-Aunt Alice and Great-Great-Uncle Montague, their double greatness adding an almost aristocratic quality to the lines of kinship which stretched between herself and them. Matthew had disabused her of this notion when she was ten or so.

'Dad got them in a shop in Shrewsbury,' he said, fourteen and contemptuous. 'He told me once when he was taking me back to school. He saw them in the shop window and decided to buy them as a joke.'

The idea of her father making jokes was so strange to Harriet then that she could think of no reply.

'Ugly old things, aren't they?' Matthew went on. He put his head on one side. 'The artist hadn't the faintest idea how to handle paint.'

'Hadn't he?' Harriet, who was eating breakfast at the time, examined the paintings more closely. It seemed to her that the artist handled paint well enough: had he not reproduced all the detail of the woman's dress, the man's beard, the silver watch, the gold ring? Sitting opposite them most mornings of her life, she had often studied his effects and the techniques which achieved them.

'No,' Matthew said decisively. 'He was probably an amateur.'

His condemnation was comprehensive. Harriet did not try to explain that up until now the paintings had represented a solidity in her life which she had always found reassuring. The reassurance was still there but, looking at them with an eye made suddenly critical, she could see that perhaps they were ugly, the brushwork crude. Their lack of aesthetic value nonetheless did not diminish them.

However, though she had been reluctant to part with her supposed relatives, that disillusion was one that she was easily able to encompass. This greater one, this information about her mother issuing so calmly from her father's unsmiling mouth, had about it a more damaging air.

She stared at him. At a single blow, not only was the central core around which she had constructed her personality destroyed, but the disturbing possibility had been opened up of a mother who was somewhere in the same world as Harriet herself, instead of inhabiting a lost and unimaginable region of the dead.

'What?' she said. She had been rehearsing the part of Rosalind in *As You Like It*; she still — a girl in boy's clothes, banished from her uncle's court — floated within the bubble of illusion which the play engendered. She frowned at her father, though he did not lift his gaze. 'My mother's alive?'

'I didn't say that, Harriet. I said that she wasn't killed in a car crash.'

'What difference does it make?' she said, trying to keep impatience from her voice. It was her birthday; her two best friends were having a surprise party for her that evening, and it would probably take several changes of costume before she found the one best suited to being surprised in. 'I mean,' she added more gently, realising for the first time that he must have come home early from his chambers in order to tell her whatever it was he was trying to say, 'what difference does it make how she died or anything?'

'She didn't die,' her father said.

'What?'

'She left me.'

'Left you?'

'For another man.'

Harriet carefully placed against her legs the red canvas bag from the Amnesty International catalogue, which she was currently using to transport her books to and from school. 'Why?' she said.

'She walked out on me,' her father said. It was not an answer to her question. He lifted his head and looked directly at her and she saw something in his eyes which shocked her. Not grief. She could have handled that, though she was still young enough to be embarrassed by adults displaying strong emotions. What she saw was something which in the moment of seeing it changed her attitude to him more irrevocably than any revelation which was to follow. As a romantic teenager, she could have assimilated the stricken father, could quickly have adapted from her current role of moderately rebellious adolescent to that of devoted, self-denying daughter, his little helpmeet, her sweet ways compensating in some measure for the tragic loss he had suffered so many years before.

But instead of pain she saw arrogance, affront, a still-festering anger.

'Why did you tell us she was dead?' she asked, looking away from him.

'I thought it would be easier for you not to know the truth.'

'Then why are you telling me now?' She spoke aggressively to hide the fact that her throat was thickening with tears at the sharp knowledge of his imperfectibility, for certainly he meant it had been easier for *him* if she did not know the truth.

'We agreed — your mother and I — that I would do so on your fourteenth birthday.'

Harriet could tell that her impregnable father, a man capable of lowering a room's temperature by the merest lift of an eyebrow, was acutely uncomfortable. Fleetingly she wondered if he felt safer behind the table, if he perhaps even saw her as a danger, liable to spring at him, do damage.

'She thought you would probably be mature enough by then to understand,' he continued.

'Are you saying that my own mother asked you to lie to us?' She still had the adolescent's rigid regard for truth, not yet having learned the comfort of an occasional lie.

'No.' He shook the handsome head that had earned him so much in the way of both income and reputation, and moved his lips in a brief smile. She found herself viewing him from a new perspective, no longer as a child and therefore in some way subservient or dependent, but as a presumptive adult on an equal footing. She noted, with the thin cruelty of the young, the enlarged pores around the curved wings of his nostrils, and the row of short stiff hairs which marched across the tops of his ears like pig bristles.

'What, then?' she asked coldly.

'When she said she was going to leave, I said I would tell you and your brother she was dead.'

'Why on earth ...?'

'At the time I felt it would save explanation.'

Save explanation? She could hardly believe what she was hearing.

'In fairness,' he added, 'she did not agree with me. In the end we compromised, which is why I am telling you now.'

· 15 ·

There were so many things she wanted to know, so many questions to ask, so many accusations she felt like hurling at him, that she could not find a point at which to begin. After a moment she said: 'That means Matthew's and my whole lives up till now have been lies.'

'You're being unnecessarily melodramatic, Harriet.'

'Well, it's true, isn't it?'

'Nonsense. This part you're playing in *The Crucible* —'

'That was last term.'

'— is that a lie? Is your relationship with your brother a lie? Or with Mrs Burns? Your school work, the holidays we have together, all the things that make up the person you are, the way you've been raised with some regard to duty and responsibility, none of those things are a lie.'

He was right, of course. Yet she felt that she ought to be allowed some melodrama after hearing news so momentous: news which, when she had had time to examine it further, was absolutely bound to change her life. 'They weren't,' she said loudly. 'But they are now.'

'Don't be ridiculous.'

'Does Matthew know?'

'Yes. Like you, he was informed on his fourteenth birthday.'

'Why didn't he tell me?'

'Because he was asked not to.'

'But that means the two of you have gone round for the past few years leaving me out of a family secret.' Harriet's voice was beginning to wobble out of control. Hot tears filled her eyes.

Her father looked at his watch.

This infuriated her to such an extent that she leaned across the table and grabbed him, surprising them both. In her tight grasp, the bones of his wrist seemed unnervingly frail. She found she was shaking with rage.

'Is that all you can say about it?' she demanded. Childhood dropped away from her like the shell of a shattered egg. 'You tell me that everything I've always believed is not actually so at all, and then you look at your watch as though I was a — a client taking up too much of your valuable time or something.'

Pulling himself away from her, he stood up and brushed at the sleeve of his dark barrister's jacket. 'Perhaps we should discuss this later, Harriet, when you are in a less emotional mood,' he said.

She hated him for his coolness. She wanted to hurt, to get under the outer layer of him to the vulnerable places beneath. 'Why did she leave, Daddy?' she asked.

'I beg your pardon?'

'Why did my mother run out on you?'

'Her personality was not suited to marriage and motherhood,' he said.

'Really?'

He started to shrug his shoulders, adopting a whimsical expression of rueful ignorance, as though hoping to gain her sympathy.

Before he could complete the gesture, she went on: 'Or was it because she could see what an arrogant bastard you are?'

For a moment the air seemed to have been sucked out of the room, leaving both of them facing each other across a vacuum. Between them the enormity of what she had just said hung suspended. She had never defied her father before, never spoken to him with anger; certainly never dared to use the word bastard, even in her own imaginings, let alone out loud — and to an adult. Although she had never in her life been beaten, she waited with tensed body for the crack of a stick across her shoulders, the bite of a whip on her skin, knowing exactly how they would feel, knowing they could scarcely be severe enough punishment for her temerity.

Her father's black eyebrows shot up his forehead as his face registered consternation and anger, before something much baser took their place. The pleasurable anticipation of destruction gleamed for a moment in his eyes as though he were a spoiled child on a beach about to smash another child's sandcastle. His expression grew hard and cold.

'What makes you think she only ran out on *me*?' he said softly, before he turned and walked out into the hall, leaving her alone to register the merest whisper of emphasis he had placed on the final word.

Where is she?

The question haunted Harriet. Even if her father knew the answer — and from the way he had spoken, she somehow assumed that he did not — she could not have brought herself to ask him. Not after glimpsing that alien, inimical, unparental gleam.

If I had a child, she thought, I would be on its side, not ranged against it, not willing to hurt it for my own satisfaction. I should see it as possessing its own rights, quite separate from mine.

Matthew had always been the person to whom she could turn, though she could never rely on him to see things her way. Now he had been alienated from her by what she had learned. For four whole years he had known something as momentous as the fact that the two of them were not motherless orphans, as she had always imagined them to be, but were in fact owners of the requisite number of parents, not very different from any of the other families they knew where the parents had split up, though they were still the only ones living with father rather than mother. Yet he had not shared this tremendous secret, and by not doing so had shown himself to be on the other side of some invisible line from her. She found this far more painful than anything her father had said or implied about his vanished wife. She looked at her friends and their families with newly-opened eyes, aware that from now on nothing would ever be simply as it appeared. What secrets did *their* normal-seeming parents conceal? Adoptions, adultery, hidden wills, black sheep? Her father's announcement had made it clear that anything was possible.

In the end she went to Maggie.

'Is my mother alive?' she asked, watching Maggie peel potatoes. She did not offer to help: because no one in the household had ever asked for her assistance in anything, she assumed they considered her too incompetent. In the past she had sometimes asked Maggie if she could do whatever was being done — cake-mixing, apple-coring, pastry-making

— but Maggie always told her she didn't need to bother herself with such things. It would be years before Harriet realised that this must be the result of some directive from her father. Yet she would have enjoyed taking the skin off the potatoes, gouging out the eyes, washing them under the tap and watching the dirt slide away down the sides to reveal the clean dense ivory of the flesh.

'Sorry?' Maggie clattered the metal peeler against the side of the waiting saucepan.

Harriet knew she had heard. 'My mother — is she alive?'

Maggie's eyes turned towards the kitchen door, as though she hoped reinforcements might any moment burst through and save her from assault. With Matthew away at school and Mr Arden-Smith not expected to return for at least two hours, it was an improbability. She said: 'Why would I know anything about her?'

From her tone, Harriet was immediately positive that she knew something. 'Of course you do.'

'I only work here, you know.' There was the knowledge of indispensability in Maggie's voice; the certainty of love given and received.

'Come on, Maggie. Tell me,' Harriet said.

'I can't tell what I don't know.'

'Why did she leave?'

It was obvious that whatever facts Maggie possessed, she knew which side her bread was buttered. Not only that, she was well aware who was paying for the butter. She shook her head. 'Your father's not a man to confide in people,' she said.

'But you've been part of the family practically since I was born,' said Harriet.

'True enough,' Maggie said. 'And look at me now, a poor old thing fit for nothing more than the knacker's yard after rearing you two.' She surveyed the solid front of her pinafore-covered body and added: 'Who'd have thought I was once the prettiest girl in the village, with a waist no more than eighteen inches wide and hair as black as pitch?'

Harriet refused to sidetracked. 'Why aren't there any photographs of her?' she demanded.

'How am I supposed to know?'

'There must have been some. Wedding pictures, something like that?'

'Ask your father,' said Maggie.

But that was something Harriet could not bring herself to do. 'You must have heard something about her leaving,' she said.

There was a pause. Finally Maggie said: 'Went off with somebody else, didn't she?' Long curves of potato skin curled in the wake of her speeding peeler.

'I know *that*. But who was he? Where did she meet him? Where do they live?'

'Don't know.'

'Oh, Maggie. Go on. It's my mother after all. I've a right to know what's happened to her.'

Seeming to see the force of this argument, Maggie put both hands down on the table and leaned on the knuckles, poking her head towards Harriet and shaking it slowly from side to side. 'I don't know the answer to any of your questions, young lady. But if you promise not to ask me again, I'll tell you the one thing I do know.'

'Yes.' Harriet waited expectantly.

'You haven't promised.'

'I promise.' Harriet pulled her right forefinger across her throat. 'And hope to die.'

'His name — the fellow your mam ran off with — was Anthony.'

'Anthony what?'

'That's all I know — his first name. I never heard the second.'

'That's not much.'

'Maybe. But it's all you're getting.' Picking up another potato, Maggie began to flay it, biting her lips together as though there were words imprisoned in her mouth which she was determined to prevent from escaping.

Anthony. The name was ordinary enough yet Harriet, suddenly sensitive to the sound of its three syllables, began to realise that it was not a particularly common one. How, without asking her father, was she to find him, and, through him, her mother? Perhaps if he died ... She started looking through the obituary notices in the newspaper after her father had finished reading it. Although she was up and dressed each day at least half an hour before he was, she never dared to soil the pristine pages by opening them before he appeared at the breakfast table. She had done so once, many years earlier and been intimidated by the cold displeasure with which he asked her not to repeat the offence.

Now, as soon as she arrived home every afternoon, she grabbed the paper and searched through it for dead Anthonys. It was a useless task, she knew. With no more information to go on than the single name it was impossible to determine whether the *ARMITAGE, Anthony James, died peacefully in his 91st year* might be the man her mother had fled with, any more than the *LAVALLANCE, Anthony Marcel Pierre, tragically, while on holiday in Spain, aged 54, sadly missed by all who knew him.*

Eventually, she grew more discerning. *Adored husband of Gillian*, for instance, was unlikely to be the right man, since her mother's name had been — still was, undoubtedly — Helen. Nor was it likely, if her mother had married this Anthony no more than eleven years ago, that Anthonys recently deceased, however sadly missed by loving wives and children, could also be loving grandfathers, or even Gramps, Grandad or Nandy to Charlotte, Lucy and Toby, or, as it might be, to Harry, Damian, Caroline and Mark.

Eventually it dawned on her that if the man for whom her mother had left husband, home and children was approximately the same age as her father, he would, barring accident, be unlikely to be dying just yet. Not only that, it was entirely possible that if he was, any notice of his demise might well appear in a paper other than the one her father took, in which case she would miss it. Having included in her search women of her mother's age named Helen, and found almost none — and those few usually grandmothers if not greatgrandmothers — it was gradually borne in on Harriet that, on the whole, people die at their appointed time, peacefully in their 91st year, or aged 72 after a long illness bravely born. If she was going to catch hold of her mother's death or the death of the Anthony she had left Mr Arden-Smith for, by scanning the obituary notices every day, she might just as well postpone the search for twenty years or so.

None of which answered her question: *where is my mother?*

· 2 ·

A part in a new play at school, the onset of her GCE exams, removal into the Sixth Form, being made a House monitor, her first kiss, her second kiss, her third and all subsequent kisses plus the accompanying opening of blouse buttons, touching of breast tops, tugging at zippers, moistening of parts, these soon took over from the compulsive newspaper searches.

Yet the thought was never far away, occasionally stalking on shivery feet into her mind as she read or listened to her tape recorder, surprising her with its gentle persistence as she studied for exams or sat crosslegged on counterpanes in the bedrooms of her two best friends, quite different ones from the best friends she had in the Fourth Form.

Is she dead?
If not, where is she?

She began to spend long periods of the holidays abroad. 'Europe will become a nation like the United States one day,' her father told her, in one of his rare conversations with her. 'You must learn to speak some of its languages.' She went to Spain, and to Italy; she learned their languages.

When she was sixteen she went for six weeks to the family of a French lawyer in Paris, a colleague of his. The first two weeks were spent in Paris; dutifully Michèle, the daughter of the house, showed her the sights — the Louvre, the Sainte Chapelle, Montmartre. She found their family appartement *too* ornate for her tastes, too airlessly grand; she saw no parallel between her father's housekeeper, Maggie Burns, and the austere couple — a man who waited at table in white gloves, his wife who did the cooking — that ran the lawyer's household.

She preferred to walk around Paris by herself, sitting at café tables with a *citron pressé* in front of her, staring for hours at the paintings in the Picasso Museum, drinking in the tapestries in the Musée de Cluny: The Lady with the Unicorn, the woven fields of flowers, the banners sewn with the word *A mon seul désir*. What did it mean? *My only desire*: there were so many of them, so many things she desired that it would be impossible to choose just one.

One evening the lawyer's elegantly thin wife announced they would be removing to the northern coast, where they kept a holiday home. Harriet would have preferred to stay in Paris; the seaside resort held little of interest for her and Michèle's friends were not to her taste. There was a bicycle in the small yard behind the house; she pumped up the tyres and cycled out into the fields beyond the town with a book. One afternoon she looked up from the page and saw, across the Channel, England lying golden on the horizon. It moved her less than she might have expected. I am a citizen of the world, she told herself, and returned to her book.

The Parisian lawyer kept a small boat in the harbour which lay to one side of the town. Because his wife and daughter did not enjoy sailing, he commandeered Harriet as crew. She was too well-mannered to refuse to join him or to show any sign of how much she disliked the experience. A sense of peril filled her each time they eased between the two arms of the retaining walls and out into the wilder sea beyond, where the wind snapped at the sails and the waves crashed over the bow. She could not rid herself of the knowledge that fathoms of grey water lay just below the thin hull, dropping away endlessly to the distant seabed. Commanded to take the tiller while the lawyer pulled on ropes and tightened sails, she did so reluctantly, conscious always of drowned sailors hanging in the opaque depths beneath her feet, their hair floating upward, fleshless jaws agape, while fish angled in and out of their empty eye sockets or slipped between the staves of their ribs.

*

At the end of the summer, prior to her entering the Upper Sixth, her father asked if she was likely to be in for dinner the following Friday. Since during term-time she was normally in on every day of the week except Saturday, according to the rules he himself had laid down, she was surprised by the question. In fact she was amazed that he should have spoken to her at all. Since the day he had passed on his momentous information, and had allowed her to see something she was sure he normally kept hidden even from himself, the two of them had adopted a more formal manner towards each other. For what seemed like months, if not years, they scarcely saw each other, let alone exchanged much conversation.

She often told herself she did not mind the peculiar circumstances of her home life. As a matter of fact, she had turned them into a rather romantic deprivation. She projected herself as a *princesse lointaine*, a Mariana locked into her moated grange by the cruel exigencies of being a minor, with her father as an absentee gaoler. Only sometimes did the surfaces of her heart ripple as she wished that occasionally he would notice her.

Now, when she asked why he wished to know about that Friday, he looked at her over the tops of his glasses and turned another page of his book, saying 'Because I've invited a few people to dinner that evening.'

'What?' Harriet was flabbergasted. Though dinner parties were the sort of thing that the parents of her friends frequently gave or attended, they were certainly not something she associated with her austere father. She could hardly remember the last time there had been visitors to the house. 'How many people?'

'Ten. Mostly colleagues and their wives.'

'Do you want me to help Maggie, or something? Is that why you want me to be in that evening?'

He put his book down. 'I want you to be there as my daughter,' he said firmly. 'You will be acting as my hostess, if you don't mind. Maggie is perfectly capable of organising whatever extra help she feels she needs.' He gave his brief smile. 'I have a surprise for you.'

*

The surprise turned out to be called Anita.

Anita was tall, — taller than Harriet's father, and also wider. She was, according to Mr Arden-Smith as he introduced the two of them, a professor of jurisprudence in Rio de Janeiro; they had known each other for some time. She was currently in London for a sabbatical term during which she would be delivering a series of lectures to law students in various parts of the country.

Anita had black hair pulled back into a bun, rather like the pseudo Great-Great-Aunt Alice's and she was, in fact, dressed in similar fashion, in high-necked black with a small diamond brooch pinned to the shoulder. The sartorial resemblance ended there: Anita's frock was made of taffeta ornamented with tight rows of black sequins which began just below the bosom and continued dramatically down her body to the above-the-knee hemline so that, seen entire, she somewhat resembled a shiny black mermaid. The privilege of an overall view had not been vouchsafed to Great-Great-Aunt Alice, caught for all time from the waist up only. Harriet was fairly certain that, however amateur the painter, he would have been able to make it obvious if her dress had been made of sequins.

Harriet, kept late at school by a play rehearsal and therefore leaving herself barely time to change into a flowing crimson skirt of crushed velvet which she had bought in the Oxfam shop, and an Edwardian blouse of cream silk with a double row of tucks down either side of the placket, considered Anita's dress a little over the top for a dinner party at home. She herself had put on the long pearl earrings her father had given her for Christmas that year, and piled her irrepressible hair on to the top of her head. The doorbell rang and two couples arrived, laughing and exclaiming about the coincidence of meeting on the doorstep. Harriet could not see where the coincidence lay, since they had both been invited to the same house for the same time. She felt like a stranger among these people who seemed to know each other well.

Her father made a good host. She was surprised at the urbanity with which he filled glasses, chatted to his guests, smiled at people. When introducing his daughter, there was something very like pride in his face. Harriet was astonished. If anyone had asked her if her father loved her, she would have found the question curious: of course, he loved her, just as she loved him. He was her father, wasn't he? That he might also be proud of her had never crossed her mind.

'My God, Noel,' one of the wives exclaimed, drinking gin and tonic in the drawing-room, and reaching for a salted almond as her eyes settled on Harriet. 'She's the absolute image of Helen.'

Her father raised his black eyebrows. 'Do you think so?' he asked, his voice austere. 'Tell me, how did you like the Monet Exhibition?'

Helen. The word clanged across the room like a bell. It was the first time Harriet had ever heard her mother's name mentioned. She looked at herself in the mirror above the little walnut escritoire which had — according to Matthew — once been their mother's and would one day be hers. She saw an undeniably pretty girl, her grey eyes shining, her warm complexion set off by the cascading pearls in her ears and the cream blouse of lace and old silk. She saw a girl whose long fair hair had golden Botticellian glints in it, whose broad mouth smiled, whose right cheek held the hint of a dimple. Nobody had ever commented on her looks; she was astonished that her own reflection was so pleasing — astonished and a little guilty at finding it so. Was that what her mother — what Helen looked like?

The doorbell sounded again and a further couple arrived, propelling before them a son some three or four years older than Harriet herself. He seemed very immature to her, despite being — she later learned — about to begin his final year at Bristol. His hair was swept straight back from his forehead, and his teeth, like his eyes, were very large. His name was Clive. Under a loose tweed jacket Clive wore a white shirt buttoned up to the neck, but worn without a tie. It was obviously a statement of some kind, though the statement itself was unclear. Burningly it dawned on Harriet that he had been invited so that she herself should not feel out of place.

Above the low buzz of conversation in the room she heard Anita laugh as she put her hand on Mr Arden-Smith's sleeve. The sight sent a painful premonitive shot of envy through Harriet's heart though she would have never imagined herself to be particularly possessive of her father, he having allowed her so little of himself to possess. Nonetheless she was aware of old orders changing, and was afraid it could only be for the worse, especially when Anita, throwing back her fine head with its heavy knob of hair, cried: 'Oh, Noel. Always you are a so amusing man.'

The so-amusing man seemed complimented by this remark, though what its foundation could be Harriet was not able to imagine. She was quite prepared to believe that her father was highly competent as a barrister, and even at the top of his profession. But as far as amusement went — either his ability to partake of it or to provide it — she would have placed him very low on any list of the thousand most amusing barristers in central London. Yet here he was, undoubtedly laughing, undoubtedly making others laugh. It was suddenly obvious to her that her father had another life entirely separate from the one he conducted in this house, and that other was a life in which his role as a parent was minimal or even non-existent, a life in which beautiful women laid their hands on his sleeve and distinguished men listened when he spoke. Jealously she saw him moving around London in white tie and tails, laughing over bottles of champagne set in silver buckets, or handing long-stemmed roses to girls with bare shoulders. She wished her brother was there, so that she could share some of her consternation with him but Matthew was spending the long vacation in Australia with some friends from university.

When they sat down to eat, Harriet found herself at the foot of the table, with Clive on the one hand and the younger of her father's two colleagues on the other. Anita sat on her father's right, the diamond brooch shining discreetly when she moved, the sequins muted by candlelight. Her face was that of someone already in possession. On his left side, sat Clive's mother; for most of the subsequent meal she watched her son with narrowed eyes, as though she judged and found him wanting. Despite his teeth, Harriet almost felt sorry for him. She remembered that his father was a clergyman, her father saying how much he admired him for changing careers in mid-life, how he wished he too had the courage of his convictions.

There were other dinner parties that year. Although the other guests changed, Anita remained a constant. Clive's parents were frequently invited; sometimes the mother came alone, making disparaging remarks about her absent husband. She was thin, blonde, very chic. There was something unpleasant about the curve of her mouth, something soured. Watching her across candles, Harriet thought: I bet she has a secret — a lover or an abortion, an illegitimate child, something no one would imagine. She found the notion intriguing. Sometimes, as Clive's mother's gaze rested on Noel Arden-Smith, her expression brooding and intent, Harriet wondered whether the two of them had once had an affair — or were still having one.

She applied to various universities. She would like to have studied art or drama; pushed by her teachers she decided instead to study modern languages. She did not discuss her choices with her father, mostly because he had never asked about them. When she told him she had been provisionally accepted by a northern university for the coming autumn, he seemed surprised, even disconcerted, as though time had left him stranded.

'Good Lord,' he said, putting down his newspaper and surveying her. 'I hadn't realised. You're eighteen now, aren't you?'

His expression might have been that of a prisoner unexpectedly released from a life sentence.

Harriet spent the summer after she left school travelling with friends. They bought student passes and took trains across Europe; they visited sad countries. An awareness of people living under restraint struck them all. They realised for the first time the extent of their own privilege, of freedoms they had hitherto taken for granted. In Prague one of them laid a flower near the spot where Jan Palach had died; they were frightened by their own daring, knowing that others had been imprisoned for the same offence. The high medieval buildings loomed above them, glinting with gold. In Warsaw, they were caught up in a protest march demanding something; they never found out what. Recently a dissident priest had been tortured and brutally killed by servants of the State: the girls' shoulderblades winced as they anticipated their own arrests. It was a relief to reach Turkey, Greece, Italy, places where all of them had holidayed at different times with their families, where the menace was openly sexual and therefore within the range of their experiences. Raised in a capital city, they were competent to deal with insistent invitations to fornication in a way that they could not apply to lack of liberty.

University bemused Harriet. From her father she understood the importance of training, yet all too soon she felt that her courses would, in the end, train her for nothing. She joined things: the wine-tasters, the ramblers, a choir. She became a member of a dramatic society. Here, she learned that, whatever else she had once thought, she had neither the will nor the temperament to be a professional actress. While she enjoyed drama, she had no wish to be perpetually on show, to subsume her own personality in those of invented characters. She could see that writing plays fulfilled some creative urge; acting in them did not, for her, do so. She wanted to play the leading role in her own life, not in some fictional other's.

After the years of directed learning, the examinations to be worked for, the homework assignments that had to be completed, she felt herself aimless, drifting. Making friends, she visited their homes and marked the contrast with her own. Her lost faithless mother seemed sometimes to hover in the air above her head, watching and judging. Why had she left her father? She fantasised about a mother wise, strong, fearlessly outside the bounds of social convention, driven away by her father's coldness, but the images refused to take on substance. What sort of a woman left a child behind — left a baby? Was it solely for love that she had gone? Could any love be worth abandoning children for? Had she simply not cared?

Harriet wondered how different she herself might have been had there been a maternal presence around. She realised that she did not possess enough of her mother even to hate her for her rejection.

She took to walking long hours along the river which ran through the city. She spent most of the vacations with friends in Scotland or the nearby Dales, walking the high hills, rejoicing in the smell of cold wind in her face and the ache of exhausted muscles. She felt a pressing need for loneliness.

Just before the end of the summer term, she spent a weekend backpacking with a friend. Walking between trees somewhere high and windy, her friend exclaimed; coming towards them was a man she knew. 'Stephan someone,' she whispered, 'Absolutely brilliant!'

His hair was red-gold like melted sovereigns; he wore corduroy knee-breeches, thick-soled shoes, a loden jacket. He was quite unlike anything she had ever seen before, exotic and un-English. His eyes, almost hazel, not quite brown, met Harriet's and took root somewhere in her heart.

They passed the last few days of the semester inseparable. With arrangements already made, they had to spend the summer vacation apart, he working in the United States, she as a courier ferrying tourists across Europe to Spain. She burned for him, her body raw with longing; the Mediterranean heat turned love into a fever, so that at night she murmured his name into her pillow, while outside the open window guitars pumped automatic flamenco and zithers strummed.

Back for the autumn term, they raced into bed. He was her first lover; entering her he gasped, as though he'd been given something long-yearned for. She floated through that semester, and the next, lost in a haze. He took her home for the weekend; his parents ran a guest-house on the edge of the Lake District. She liked the mother, a serene, fair woman, but the father was intimidating, his eyes cold and faintly mad. Sitting in the kitchen talking to Stephan's mother, she saw him come into the room as though acting in a cops-and-robbers movie, sidling through the smallest possible space, edging round the room with his back up against the wall. The sight disturbed her. Stephan seemed ill-at-ease; she was glad to leave.

At Easter they were again separated. Harriet found herself unable to concentrate on anything. The summer term shone like El Dorado; the days inched by. Then suddenly, shortly before his finals, Stephan told her he was sorry but it was over.

She gasped. The agony was physical. 'Why?' She leaned forward to ease the pain. 'What have I done?'

'You have done nothing, Harriet. Nothing.'

'Is there ... someone else?' Her mouth and jaw ached: getting the question out was almost too much of an effort.

'No one else.'

'Why, then? *Why?*'

'I have to work for my finals. When I am with you, I cannot do so.' His hands reached for her, then remembered themselves.

'And that's all?'

'It is enough, isn't it?' His mouth quivered. She wanted to kiss it, to feel it kissing hers. She wanted the subsumation of herself in him.

'More than enough.' Somehow she got to her feet, walked to his door, left. She must not make a scene. She knew from Matthew that women must never make scenes. She felt as though she were bleeding, as though all meaning had been leeched from her life. She spent the rest of the term bemused and out of joint. Reading the lists of exam results later, she felt a stab of realisation, maybe even of understanding, on seeing that he had got a First.

In her final year, things at last began to make sense. Acting assumed a deeper significance. She played Ophelia. She played Nora in *A Doll's House*. She knew, now, about love, about heartbreak, about stiflement. Although she slowly recovered from Stephan, she could not forget him entirely. Other men tried to involve her with themselves, but without success.

When she went home, her father was never there. These days he seemed to be spending the greater part of his time abroad. Maggie still kept house but talked increasingly of leaving; with the house mostly empty there was no longer any need for her to run it. It was a wicked waste of money to employ her to live there, she told Harriet, and besides, she had better things to do with her time. By this she meant the small cottage near Inverness which had been left to her when her sister died. Mr Arden-Smith wrote occasionally, but his letters said little. Vaguely Harriet saw him, bewigged and dark-jacketed, in Sri Lanka, in Sydney, in Rio de Janeiro. She spent hours at the National Gallery, at the British Museum, involved in a wider heritage, no longer simply Harriet but part of England, part of history. On those lonely walks, she sometimes felt as though she was trapped behind a glass wall, trapped in a shell, invisible. Stephan occupied her thoughts.

Just after her finals, Matthew telephoned the house she shared with friends, reversing the charges. His degree had been in fine art; since leaving Cambridge, he had spent a year with Sotheby's, concentrating on furniture, and two further years working his way round the world. 'My *real* education,' he called it on the few occasions when he and Harriet caught up with each other. He told her now he would be back in September, ready to take part in the ratrace. Meanwhile he had fetched up in California and wanted her to join him there.

'I'm working in a nursery,' he said.

'With kids, do you mean?'

'No, idiot. With flowers. Dahlias and things. You ought to come over, I'm sure they'll find you a job, too.'

'I don't know the first thing about dahlias,' objected Harriet.

'It's not the work. It's the life out here. You should try it.'

'But —'

'Just for a month,' Matthew said.

'I ought to be looking for a proper job.'

'Come here first.'

'Don't I need a work permit?'

'I'll organise it.' There was a silence. Then Matthew said delicately: 'Actually, Harry, I quite miss you.'

She smiled. 'What about the fare . . .?'

'Ask Pa for the money.'

'He's never around these days. Besides . . .'

'Tell him it's educational. Anyway, it was him who fixed up this job for me in the first place — he knows the people who run the place. I'm sure he'd love to do the same for you.'

Harriet dialled her father's chambers. They told her he would be back at the end of the following week. When she saw him, there was no need for persuasion. Noel Arden-Smith seemed only too willing to pay for her ticket to California. He had concerns of his own.

In California — more specifically in Bellamonte, the little town south of Los Angeles where Matthew was staying — Harriet found herself opening as though she were a door to which she had only just found the key. She was drawn by the high fine light of the West Coast, the insouciance, the sense of gaiety, of fun always about to break through. Although these made her uneasy at first, having been reared in that Protestant tradition which insists that adversity and difficulty are somehow more character-forming, she soon fell in with all of it.

Matthew was working for a commercial florist. As he had predicted, the owners raised no objection to taking Harriet on for a few weeks. The summer was a busy time and they were happy to employ her at the reception counter; her job was to assist customers in finding what they were looking for and, if they were not sure what that was, in making up their minds for them. Occasionally she and Matthew were invited to barbecues by the manager, a big man called Benny Costello. Despite his surface joviality, Harriet did not like him much; there was something hostile in his attitude towards her which she was at a loss to account for. His stepmother, Lydia, owned the place; a sad-faced widow, she took a particular liking to Harriet.

'I knew your father once,' she said. 'Did you know that?'

'My brother told me,' Harriet said.

'He was a young man then, of course. But so handsome, so distinguished.'

'He still is.' Harriet viewed her father differently now, mellowed by life, made more tolerant. She wondered briefly whether Mrs Costello and her father . . .

'He has always kept in touch with us,' the older woman said. She reached out one thin tanned arm along which jangled bracelets of silver and jade. 'My daughter's hair was just like yours, you know.'

In the Californian sunshine, Harriet's abundant hair had bleached almost white except for the golden lights which lay along each strand. 'Really?' said Harriet, bred into courtesy. 'Does she live locally?'

'No.' Mrs Costello picked up a catalogue and looked at the front of it, her face pulling into itself. 'No, she does not. She — uh — she lives abroad now. It's been a long time since I last saw her. Far too long.'

'Where abroad?'

'In England, as a matter of fact.' Patting the seat beside her, Mrs Costello said: 'Tell me about England. It's been one of my greatest regrets that I never visited Europe.'

'Why didn't you?' Looking at the luxurious surroundings, Harriet thought it could hardly have been from lack of money.

'I should have done,' Mrs Costello looked at Harriet. 'My husband . . .'

'You mean he stopped you?'

'Not exactly . . .' Her gaze moved from Harriet's hair to the mountains which formed a backdrop to the view from her windows. 'It simply seemed more . . . *fitting* not to go.'

There were old emotions here, fattening the simple sentence. Harriet said quickly: 'Surely he wouldn't have stopped you, would he?' The notion seemed inconceivable.

Mrs Costello smiled slightly, shaking her head. 'Of course not. The decision was entirely mine. It was my choice. You've obviously never been in love.'

She was wrong.

Matthew and Harriet were not the only temporary staff taken on for the summer. Nor the only foreigners. One of the others was called Conor Pearse. Meeting him for the first time between benches piled with spilling flowers — fuchsias and begonias, tiny pinks embedded in silvery leaves and, stacked behind them, white lilies, thick-fleshed, biblical, their stamens spilling a golden powder in each immaculate throat — Harriet thought him apocalyptic. Black-haired, dark-eyed, his strong black beard emphasised the energy with which he vibrated. Approaching her along the narrow path of the greenhouse, his face changed colour, reddening under its Californian tan. Later, she would learn that this was the way he demonstrated extreme emotion.

'You're English, aren't you?' he said.

'Yes.'

'So am I — more or less, anyway.' His accent lilted with Ireland. 'How do you like California?'

'It's great.'

'You're Matt Arden's sister, aren't you?'

'Yes.' Harriet wondered when her brother had dropped the unnecessary 'Smith', and decided she would do the same.

'How long are you here?'

She told him. The next day, he sought her out. 'Some of us are driving out to the beach,' he said, cloaking himself in the presence of others so successfully that for the moment she merely assumed he had been detailed to round up as many people as possible to make the party go. 'Why don't you come along?' His eyes were fierce, ready to challenge the world.

She was wearing cut-offs and a faded pink T-shirt. It was

his voice that rounded him off, she decided. Without it he would have been just another goodlooking man; with it he was something extraordinary. Not merely angelic, but archangelic. Remembering their meeting among lilies, she thought: just so must Gabriel have appeared to the innocent Mary, great wings golden, face ablaze, voice trumpeting.

'Fine,' she said, casually. She turned away and felt the backs of her knees burn where his gaze rested on them.

He was an ecologist, he told her. His first degree was from Dublin, and he had then gone to Berkeley to get a PhD. He was working here for the summer — Benny Costello's late father was related in some way to his grandfather — after which he would begin to battle with the ecological disaster that South America was fast becoming. 'And the United States, too,' he said, driving her in a small orange sports car very fast along the freeway. 'Everywhere. We're destroying our environment permanently. Look what's happening in the rain-forests. Look at Sweden — acid rain ... the Mediterranean's no more than a cess-pit ... the Great Lakes ... industrial waste.'

Although she would not have been able at that time to define it, Harriet was meeting head-on one of the most attractive of all physical attributes: enthusiasm. Irresistibly, she found herself swept along on the tide of Conor's eloquence. As he spoke, forests faded in front of her, grasslands withered, lakes and seas turned to acid, entire species groaned their last, poisoned by Man's excesses. Conor turned the world suddenly dark, filled it with hazard, with death and hopelessness.

He dazzled her. Arriving at the beach, whose gritty sand was still warm from the day's heat, she watched the Pacific breakers rolling in, turning in a curl of phosphorescent, firework green, mercury white, falling into a glitter of flung-up spray. When he took her hand in his, she felt total and unrestrained happiness for what, afterwards, she decided must have been the very first time. She knew she would sleep with him if – *when* — he wanted.

*

One weekend the two of them travelled down to Mexico, driving across endless sun-baked hills through villages which smelled of kerosene and dung. They ate sparingly, bought a cheap silver ring in the shape of a snake, swam on a deserted white beach. A net of sparks seemed to have been dropped over her. There was poverty here, and disease, but through the shine which surrounded her she could not see it. At other times they camped out in the desert, or in the forests which lined the northward hills; they drove to San Francisco and on up to Yosemite; they hiked through the forests and across rocks; they took sleeping-bags and slept out on the beach. Remembering those weeks later, Harriet realised that the sense of music she felt, as though they had been accompanied everywhere by an invisible orchestra, had in fact been Conor's honeyed bardic voice.

At summer's end, she delayed going back to England. Their father had written saying that he had put the house in Richmond on the market and had an offer for it. He intended to buy a smaller flat as a base for Matthew and her, but meantime was taking indefinite leave of absence from his chambers and moving to Brazil. He was going to marry Professor Rodriguez. It took Harriet a while to realise that this was Anita.

'The crafty old devil,' Matthew said. 'I knew he was bonking her, but I never thought it would come to this.'

'What?'

'Marriage. I didn't think he'd go that far.'

'You mean, all this time he's been . . .'

'Screwing around with her? 'Course he was. They've been an item for years — everyone knows that.'

'I didn't.'

'I can't say I blame him. Did him a power of good, I should think.'

'But surely . . .' Harriet stopped. She wanted to say '. . . at his age,' but did not. It sounded naive to say that she could not imagine her father in bed with Anita, with *any* woman — his flesh and hers moving across and above and behind in the lovely ways that she herself had learned during the summer.

'After all,' Matthew went on. 'He's been very discreet. I suppose he was just waiting for you to finish at University before he took off. Decent of him, really.'

Harriet realised that Matthew had an entirely different relationship with their father from her own. Her brother saw him as a person, a man with desires similar to his. She could only see him as a parent, distant and unapproachable. He was no more than fifty or so: for the first time that did not seem immeasurably old. 'Has he ever talked about our mother?' she said.

'Not really.' Matt looked at her thoughtfully. 'I don't suppose you remember anything about her, do you?'

'Not really.' There was a presence, a warm lap, a pair of arms, far back in the past. They could as easily have belonged to Maggie as to her mother.

'You read about these kids always remembering a beautiful face,' Matthew said, matter-of-fact. 'Or her soft voice singing a lullaby in the evening sort of thing. I can't say I remember anything like that.'

'Anything at all?'

He shrugged. 'She had fair hair, like yours. She wore it tied back. I remember some green earrings that I liked playing with. Very sparkly: I suppose they must have been emeralds. I remember going somewhere with her and her holding my hand across the road, stuff like that. I even remember her pregnant with you, her making me feel you kicking around inside her stomach.'

'I've never felt particularly deprived, not having a mother,' Harriet said.

'I have.' Matthew turned away from his sister. 'I often have.'

'You never said.'

'No, well, one doesn't really, does one?'

There was a pause. 'I wonder where she is now,' said Harriet.

Matthew did not answer.

Finally she went back to England, to the flat in Richmond,

restless, incomplete. She applied for jobs, visited friends, wrote letters. She joined an evening class in oil painting, thought about going to Paris for a time. Conor, for whom she ached as winter settled down over the drab roofs of the city, had not contacted her since her return from the United States. His silence should have made him undesirable; instead, he seemed to her more than ever archangelic, swift and ruthless as a sword.

He turned up two months after she had left the States, the morning after she had accepted a job teaching languages and art in a girl's school near Plymouth. Opening the door to him, she felt as though her whole body had burst into laughter.

'Harriet,' he said.

'Why didn't you write?'

'I lost your address,' he said.

She sensed it was a lie. If so, she did not wish to know the truth. Taking his hand, she led the way to her bedroom. In bed, naked together, his hands lingered over her body.

'I was so afraid you wouldn't be as beautiful as I remembered you,' he said. Gently he opened and entered her. She felt herself melting, fusing with him, the old Harriet burned up in orgasmic flame. She knew, with a strange kind of terror, that he could ask her anything, anything at all — acts terrifying, acts unspeakable, acts criminal or even murderous — and for him, she would do it.

In the event, all he asked was that she should marry him. Now. Straight away.

'I'm working with the World Conservation Fund,' he said. 'I'm off to the Amazon basin next month. Come with me.'

'But I just accepted a job myself ...' She felt reluctance beneath her wild delight. There had been challenge presented. She hoped to learn more about painting by teaching it; she had felt excitement at the thought of passing on, explaining her own enthusiasms.

'Harriet, I seriously don't think I can live without you, and that's a fact.' He poured words over her, gilding her like the leaves of a missal. Her hair felt stiff with gold; lilies swam just out of vision, and somewhere was the slow remorseless clap of angelic wings. 'But of course if this job is more important to you than I am ...' His face dropped.

She saw the Amazon basin, little crop-haired natives holding poles, pot-bellied babies, huts on stilts. She saw Conor among them, moving like a god, and herself here in England, alone beside the canals, alone on the windy moors.

'I'll come with you,' she said. Even as she spoke, she feared it was a mistake. She thought that if only she tried hard enough she should be able to break the curtain of the future and see what lay in store for them both.

She had been married for three years before she thought she understood what Mrs Costello had meant. Love blinded, love manipulated. Unhoneyed by its sweetly treacherous droppings she would never have taken the same decision, would not, therefore, have set her feet on the path towards terror.

· 3 ·

The wedding was fixed for Harriet's twenty-second birthday. Maggie Burns came down from Scotland to help out, but made it clear she did not approve of a marriage entered into so hastily. Nor did she care for Conor. Harriet ignored her hostility; disapproval was part of Maggie's stock-in-trade. Besides, in the flurry of organising the wedding, she had no time to ask what exactly in Conor Maggie had taken against. There were announcements to make, invitations to order and send out, letters to answer, gifts to thank people for.

Not that this was always possible. All too easily presents seemed to become separated from their accompanying letter or card, and though between them Maggie and Harriet eventually matched most of them up, there was still one gift which remained unaccounted for. It was wrapped in thick white paper and tied with gold cord, a kind of packaging which Harriet associated with Paris patisseries and bonbons. There was even a loop to hitch over a finger for easy carrying, though the package was far too heavy for that.

Maggie was vexed by the loss of the giver's name. 'There's someone who's going to go to their grave thinking you can't be bothered to thank them for their gift,' she said, clicking her tongue in annoyance.

'Perhaps there's a card inside.'

'If not, it's me they'll blame for not bringing you up right.' Her face was flushed as she looked at the parcel sitting anonymously on the table.

'They probably know what weddings are like.'

'Hmmm.' Maggie was not convinced. 'Go on, then. Open it.'

Tearing off the white paper and lifting the lid of the stiff cardboard box inside, Harriet found an ostrich-sized egg of swirling green glass.

'Oh,' she said. It sat heavily in her hands. 'Isn't that beautiful?'

'Does it say who it's from?'

'No.'

'There you are. Now you'll never be able to say thank you.'

Privately, Harriet thought that the giver — some colleague of her father's, she guessed — would not need thanking. Whoever had sent such an unusual gift must have chosen it knowing how much she would love it. Peering into the heart of it was like looking into the reflection of leaves in water under a changing sky, diaphanous and secret, yet away from the light it was solid, polar, like the earth viewed from outer space, a thing of shifting clouds and atmospheric layers.

'What's it for?' asked Maggie.

'It just *is*. It's lovely.'

'You could have done with some more sheets,' said Maggie. She had other weightier matters to disapprove of, too. Because Mr Arden-Smith had not been given sufficient time to make suitable arrangements to fly from Rio, he would not be attending the wedding. He wrote instead, offering formal congratulations, expressing the hope that she would bring her new husband to visit some time. There was no indication of love; she tried not to mind. In his place, Matthew would give his sister away. Maggie did not consider him an acceptable substitute. If people would just wait instead of rushing into things ... she set her lips in the cramped way that had become habitual and continued sewing the hem of Harriet's hastily-bought wedding dress.

Two days before the wedding, Conor telephoned. There had been a hitch somewhere: the organisation for whom he would be working had decided that they could not after all, afford to fly non-working wives out to the Amazon. His voice blazed with indignation.

'Why not?' asked Harriet. The vision she had built of her

future broke and scattered like images on a radar screen.

'They just don't have the funds, the man told me over the telephone.'

'Couldn't I pay my own way?'

'There's an idea. I'll ask them.'

He telephoned again — they would not allow her to join them, though the reasons he gave seemed less than compelling. Anxious to be a good wife, to be the kind of wife — although this was only secretly acknowledged to herself — her runaway mother had not been, Harriet did not argue, nor even show more than a proper amount of dismay. She did not wish to fuss. Yet the thought of being left behind terrified her. All her life she had been shown or told what to do: with Conor gone, she would be an oxymoron of a wife, married yet not married, possessing status but without it. If she had known, she could have taken the teaching job after all. It was too late now, so what was she to do?

'How about doing a secretarial course. Or word-processing?' Conor said next time they were together. He folded her against him, not seeing her sudden anger.

'I don't want to,' she said, mutinous, childish. 'Besides, I'm not good at that sort of thing.'

'It's supposed to be useful,' said Conor, kissing her hair. 'My mother says it's something women can take up or stop when they like, between having babies and looking after husbands.'

Harriet was privately appalled. Quite apart from feeling that Conor's mother had no place in such a discussion, at a deeper level she felt the start of panic. This beautiful man was a stranger; his views opposed to hers in the most diametric of ways. While not a rabid feminist, she had always been encouraged to view herself as the equal of her male counterparts. Conor's casual denial of that equality, or, more accurately, his assumption that the part she was to play in their joint future would be subservient, was shocking. There was not even the suggestion of an alternative or concurrent role. They had never discussed such matters. Clasped to his broad chest, smelling the rich scent of his hair, she realised they had discussed almost nothing. Conor had talked, magnificently; she had simply listened.

For a luminous moment, she knew decisively that she should break things off, stop the wedding now. *If any of you know cause or just impediment* ... weighty words, terrifying words — but what, after all, did she really know of either cause or impediment? And having set up the machinery of formal-ised matrimony, it seemed too heavy for her to dismantle it now. She let it go.

Conor's parents, over from Ireland, were a surprise. His father was big and fair, silent. His mother, small and grey-haired, was at first insignificant. It was only when she spoke that her eyes came to life; the fire in them was that of a fanatic. Part of her fanaticism lay in her feeling for her son, her only child, she told Harriet with her burning eyes on Conor, though there had been a sister still-born. Watching the two of them across the table in the Richmond flat, Harriet wondered by what alchemical transmutation the mother's faded greyness had become Conor's splendour. Mother and son never stopped arguing; the sad politics of Ireland, the ways of the world, religion, money, the environment were tossed back and forth between them. Occasionally Harriet smiled at the father; he smiled back, nervous under his moustache, darting looks at his wife as though unsure whether he was allowed to like this unknown girl who was to be his daughter-in-law.

She learned something then. She realised for the first time not only that there are those who talk and those who listen, but also that she herself enjoyed taking an active part in any discussion. There were things she wanted to say, *would* have said, given half a chance. She found herself resenting Conor for not giving it to her. But it did not seem worth forcing her way into the conversation. Conor, she knew, did not like raucous women — did anyone? — and to break into that stream of eloquence, she would have had, momentarily, to be strident.

After dinner, the mother bustled herself and Harriet into the kitchen, leaving the men to sit. 'Such a shame you'll not be joining Conor,' she said. She made it sound as though the decision not to do so had been Harriet's.

'I know. I'm terribly upset about it,' Harriet said.

'There's modern marriage for you. Where will you live?'

'I don't know. We haven't really discussed it. I could stay on here, I suppose ...'

'There'll be babies soon enough,' said the mother. 'You've a fortnight before he flies out, haven't you?'

Harriet felt herself invaded by the remark. Lovemaking with Conor was far more to her than impregnation; her face reddened with embarrassment. Glancing at the other woman, she was taken aback by the hostility she caught sight of in the mother's answering gaze.

Two weeks later she drove Conor to Heathrow. Watching a jet roar up into the skies above London, not even knowing if it was his, she waved, feeling tears on her cheeks. At the flat in Richmond she found a letter from her father. There was money, quite a lot of it. She was to buy somewhere to live for herself and her new husband — a house if she could, if not, an apartment, a wedding present from him and Anita.

The letter contained no word of warmth; she wept again. *Daddy, I want you to love me*, she thought. She was twenty-two and love was something she felt she had not had her due share of. The entire world stood before her and she was afraid to grasp it, uncertain in which direction to turn. She stood at the long second-floor window holding the glass egg in her hand. Her life seemed as amorphous as its subtle colours of wind and water, which ran into each other and out again as she shifted it about to catch the light.

A house. How was she supposed to buy a house on her own, knowing nothing of property or prices, of market values or the state of drains? How could Conor have gone off, leaving her behind, unroofed, alone. She rang Matthew.

'Find an area you want to live in, and look there,' he said. He had recently bought a property in Yorkshire, and with a partner set himself up as an antique dealer.

'But I don't *know* where I want to ...'

'Do you know where you *don't* want to live?' he cut in, impatient with female uncertainty.

'Not an inner city. Not London, even if I could afford it.'

'A village? Somewhere rural? Up north?'
'The Dales,' she said.

She looked at pretty stone-built cottages, at converted barns on the edge of the moors. She investigated magazine-cover villages, the air heather-scented, the long bare slopes rising behind them. She tried to imagine Conor there when he returned from South America, and failed. It occurred to her that her new husband was restive, unlikely to roost anywhere for long. She foresaw an endless succession of packing-ups, of discomforts endured, of goodbyes. She thought: have I made a mistake? — and refused to answer her own question.

Whatever she bought would have to be within reach of London, she could see that. She drove back to the South, reluctant to leave the hills and the shining air. A small house in a pleasant town was what she needed, somewhere he could commute from if he needed, a haven for him in between his — *their* — wanderings. Without precision she saw chintz curtains at diamond-paned windows, herbaceous borders, polished oak, inglenooks. She did not have the habit of domesticity, nor of happiness. She thought: now is when I should be learning both. Instead I am alone, unhusbanded.

She drove to Oxford.

What did it remind her of? Shutting her eyes to the modern commercialism of the place, she walked between grey stone walls, listened to chanting bells, saw old gardens behind wrought-iron gates. Roofs and arches reassured her, proclaiming centuries of hope, of learning, of Man's achievements. The city's mediaeval quality, something sad which filled odd corners or peered out of ancient doorways, reminded her of those European cities she had passed through in the summer she left school.

She had been in the city before, years ago, visiting Matthew when he was an undergraduate here. She booked in at a small hotel in St Giles and registered with estate agents. She was driven to outlying villages, to housing estates, to the Thirties developments which ringed the city.

'No,' she said. 'Something more central.' She had already decided to buy a bicycle.

'It'll be expensive,' they warned, looking at her untamable hair, taking her for an undergraduate.

'Just let me see what you've got,' she said firmly. She placed both hands on the desk, letting them see her wedding-ring.

They showed her pleasant Victorian houses on four floors; they spoke vaguely of taking in students to fill spare rooms, of recouping investments. They showed her a new development of cramped flats right in the heart of the city. None was what she wanted. 'There must be something in between these two,' she said.

One man took her to a flat in a tree-lined street leading off the Banbury Road. It was raining, and the rooms were dark. 'I know it's shabby,' he said, apologetic. 'But it's roomy.'

'It's also very expensive,' she said. She was finding herself more ruthless than she knew. 'See if the owners will come down on the price.'

She did not say that she would have paid whatever they asked, that the place — the lower half of a house originally built for some clergyman don with excessive numbers of children — was precisely what she wanted. The house was set back behind a circle of what had once been gravel and was now sandy earth. Shrubbery curved towards the street where mottled trees grew lopsidedly out of the pavement. It was private, contained, down-at-heel. At the back a wet garden flowed, green and overgrown, leaves pushing at the French windows so that the flat was full of emerald gloom. Melancholy cowered in the corners; the front door was of stained glass which cast muted colours on to the tiled floor of the hall. It would be a good place to wait for Conor to return.

The owners, a childless couple who had already moved out to a house in the country, rejected her offer. She increased it a little; reluctantly they accepted it. She telephoned Matthew. 'I've bought a flat,' she told him. It came to her that she had never before made so positive or so important a statement.

'Where?'

'In Oxford.'

'Nice. I'll help you move in, if you like.'

'I must buy some furniture, a bed, carpets. We haven't got a thing.' Once again, she wondered at Conor for leaving a young wife so rootless, so unsurrounded by anchoring possessions.

'I'll bring down a couple of nice pieces for you. I owe you a wedding present.' He added: 'You've got money, haven't you?'

'Yes.'

'From Dad?'

'Yes.'

'Good old Pa.'

She was struck by the incongruity of the phrase when juxtaposed with Noel Arden-Smith's grey elegance. On impulse she said: 'Do you think he loves us, Matt?'

'Of course he does.'

'He doesn't show it much.'

'He doesn't know how,' Matthew said. 'But it's there.'

'Is it?' While not certain that he was right, Harriet was nonetheless warmed by his male perceptions, by his lack of condemnation.

She furnished the flat in greens and blues. She would never have said that she chose the colours to suit the glass egg, though in the end she came to realise that that was what she had done. The egg sat on a large square table in the centre of the room, glowing when the lamps were lit at night, catching what gleams of sunlight sifted through the leaves which clamoured at the windows. She sat on pale blue linen with green cushions. When the night outside became too dark, she drew the curtains she had made from a silky material the colour of spruce-pines. She thought: although I have often been alone, I have never before been lonely.

She pushed through the waist-high grass of her garden and found a sagging shed under a lilac-tree. She could see the outline of a flower-bed against one wall; it was like *The Secret Garden*, exactly like. She half-expected a dark-eyed ragged boy to appear, and with him a train of small creatures.

She had feared that time would move sluggishly for her, would weigh her down. It did not. Every day she wrote to Conor. She described for him her — *their* — flat, the possessions she had purchased in their name, the cheval glass Matt had given them together with the exquisite little Pembroke table which stood in the hall, the hopes she had for their future together. As though propitiating him, as well as herself, she bought cookery books and followed recipes that she would later cook for him; she cleaned and polished, learning gradually a domestic rhythm, learning, without a husband, to be a wife. She felt vaguely that it was necessary to do these chores in order to earn the right to the long hours she spent in the Ashmoleum Museum studying the paintings there. Not sure of Conor's plans, she dared not take a long-term job in case she found herself letting people down. She enrolled in a painting class, found herself a job in one of the many bookshops, advertised extra coaching in French, German, Spanish. Because these things were far less than she was capable of, she found herself full of anger. Conor should not have left her here alone, in limbo.

She walked a lot, learning the city; the colleges, the churches, the botanical gardens near Magdalen Bridge, the alleyways between ancient houses. She even took pleasure in watching hefty female undergraduates with sweatbands round their foreheads lob lacrosse balls to each other in the University Parks. There had been girls at school like that, massively thighed; watching them surreptitiously in classrooms and science labs, she used to marvel without envy at the evidence they showed of swifter, more physical worlds than her own, based on agility and movement, on the formal relationship between hand and eye.

She developed her own routine, clearing out the abandoned shed in the garden, buying new paints and brushes, canvases. My Studio, she called it, half laughing. In oils, she found increasing satisfaction. She tried to paint Conor from memory and photograph, and was pleased with the result.

She made a friend.

*

'You bought our flat, didn't you?'

'Sorry?'

'Our flat. Off the Banbury Road. I'm Chris Crawford.'

'Oh, Hello. Harriet — uh — Pearse.'

The woman — thin and dark — grinned. 'Aren't you sure?'

Harriet smiled back. 'It's just that ...' She explained briefly about Conor, about the Amazon, about the funds which had dried up, leaving wives beached as cuttlefish in their native countries.

'The beast!' Chris cried. 'Fancy leaving you all alone like that. Come and have a cup of tea. Saturdays are our days for being domestic. Sundays we usually slob around, have people in for drinks.' She pulled Harriet towards a café, ordered tea and scones.

'But it's Friday ...'

'I know. I sometimes stay at home on a Friday — I've got a terminal at home so it's not as if I'm completely out of touch with the office, and I can get twice as much work done without all the interruptions.'

'You sound incredibly high-powered,' Harriet said.

'My dear, I am.' Chris laughed. 'I'll probably be burned out before I'm forty.'

'How long is that?'

'Would you believe five years from now?'

'No,' Harriet said honestly. 'I wouldn't.' The other woman's small taut body, eager face, boyish crop of hair, could have belonged to someone ten years younger.

'Aren't you sweet.'

Harriet learned more. Chris's husband Denis was an economics don at one of the colleges, as well as a leading financial expert much in demand as a consultant all over the world. They had no children; didn't want them, thank you very much — being a career woman took all Chris's time as it was, and being a good wife to Denis in what was left over was as much as she was capable of. 'So you can see, my dear, we're absolutely coining it, in spite of the taxman.'

Harriet *could* see. Driving five miles out of town to Chris's new house in a pretty Cotswold village, the evidence of minor wealth hung about the place, thick carpets, fresh paint, antiques, expensive furnishings, good pictures on the walls. There was a lot of heavy glass and formidable silver. In a small room to the right of the front door, Chris showed her a collection of Victorian dolls with delicate china faces and clothes of silk and hand-made lace.

'My mother started me off when I was about ten,' she said. 'I've been collecting ever since.' She picked up a teething ring of ivory and silver. 'Exquisite, really. Can't you just see some fat Victorian baby chewing on that?'

Her dark eyes rested idly on Harriet. 'What about you? Do you *do* anything? Or are you . . .' Although she did not finish the sentence, she managed to fill it with nappies.

'No,' Harriet said quickly. The thought terrified her. 'We've hardly had time . . . I mean' — she remembered beds in which she and Conor had tumbled, the feel of sand against her shoulderblades, smells of crushed pine needles, the rubbery scent of a groundsheet — 'we've had time, of course, but we need to get to know each other first.'

'Not awfully easy to do that with hubby off and away, is it?'

'No.'

'Come to lunch on Sunday.'

Harriet went and met Denis. The two of them welcomed her into their lives. She was grateful to them.

When Conor telephoned her, telling her to join him in Lisbon where he had been sent by the organisation to take part in a conference, she was reluctant, feeling him to be a stranger and she herself changed from the girl he had married. And what about her job? Nonetheless, she sorted things out, bought airline tickets; she was his wife. The night before she left, she dreamed of Stephan. Waking, she wondered where he was, who he was with.

Conor was at the airport to greet her. Seeing him, all her doubts vanished. The air about his head seemed charged, his eyebrows and beard darker, more prominent than before. His arms closed about her. 'My wife,' he murmured. She wished she felt safer.

'There's a session I ought to attend but I'll give it a miss,' he said, smiling, as he led her across the lobby of the hotel where he was staying. 'I'd forgotten how gorgeous you are. That hair ...'

In their hotel room he twined it round himself, tendrilling his fingers and hers, his insistent member. She wanted to go slowly, to look at him with love, to relearn him; but he was impatient. 'God, I've missed you ...' he said, over and over again. The richness of him clouded her mind like incense. There were things she wanted to tell him; he stopped her, devouring her body, his black eyes possessive, his mouth crushing the words back into her. 'Later,' he said, 'later,' groaning over her breasts, touching the fair hair at her crotch, 'God, I've missed you.'

She wanted to say; not me, not the Harriet I am now. You miss another Harriet. But the words died stillborn. He pulled her up from the bed, sat her upon himself, gazed hotly into her eyes as he worked himself inside her. She felt panic, terror. I am tied for life to a stranger, she thought. Feverishly she tried to hide the fact that though the things they were doing together were pleasurable, they lacked the layer of love — adoration, even — that had given them such lustre before their wedding. She cried out, feeling nothing. He was gratified. It was the first lie of their marriage. Or was it the marriage itself which was the lie?

'You obviously missed me as much as I missed you,' he said. She smiled at him as her eyes slowly filled with tears.

They walked about the town, ate dinner, talked. She told him about the flat she had bought, about the furniture, Oxford, Chris and Denis. She was aware that this was trivial surface stuff; there were much more important things to be said, promises to be made. She made him order a second bottle of the local red wine, and drank more of it than he did. It was easier to respond to him when they returned to the big curved bed. In the middle of the night she woke him and he made love to her again and then again. This time when she cried out it was with all the old tenderness. She saw the future shine ahead for the two of them.

· 4 ·

Conor came home for three months' leave, tanned, energetic, beautiful. Secure in the background she had made for them, Harriet found again with him the delight he had taught her in California. Not knowing what he wanted, she suspended her own routines, ready to be at hand for him, ready to be his wife.

They travelled together to Ireland, to the ugly little town where his parents lived. His mother's eyes rested constantly on Harriet's body, rapacious as wolves. Harriet tried to like her but could not. She made no attempt to include Harriet in her conversations with her son, ignored her when Conor was not there. When he was, her eyes burned; talking to him, she would lay her hand on his arm and look at him with the expression of someone much younger, someone infatuated.

Why, Harriet thought in amazement, coming across the two of them unexpectedly, she's in love with him, with her own son. He is the only thing we have in common. She wondered whether their failure to like each other was her fault.

Back in Oxford, she invited Christina and Denis to dinner; it was the first time they had met Conor. The two of them — Conor and Christina — made a natural pair: both so alike, both quick, both dark, both so vivid as they sparked and fizzed through the evening. Harriet was happy, seeing the roots of the relationship grow a little deeper. When the Crawfords suggested that the four of them fly out for a long weekend at their flat in Alicante, she was delighted; normalcy was asserting itself at last.

She dragged him down to the end of the garden to her shed

— her *studio* — to show him the painting she was working on. He seemed startled when he saw it.

'You did this?' The expression on his face was indefinable and, somehow, dangerous. What could she see there? Contempt? Hostility? Or something stronger: admiration, perhaps, pleasure, even? And how odd, that after nearly two years of marriage, she should still not be able to say.

Dreading his scorn, she said hastily: 'It's something I've just started, so it's not —' but he had cut her off.

'It's terrific. I didn't know you went in for this sort of thing.' He looked at her consideringly, head slightly to one side, dark eyes hooded.

'I don't.' Her breath fluttered in her mouth. 'Not usually, I . . .'

She longed to draw him into her mind as she used to. She wanted to explain, to say that she had begun to feel a stranger to herself, that painting gave her a freedom she had only recently begun to feel she needed. The Conor she thought she had married might have understood; this one she felt would not. But perhaps there was no difference between old and new, only a difference in herself.

'Conor,' she began — but he had turned and was walking back across the tangled garden to the house, looking up at the sky as he went. Without apparently noticing it, he avoided the small stone figure — Pan, was it? She had never known — set up by the lilac tree, skirted the edge of what had once been a flowerbed, stepped up on to the brick-paved area in front of the French windows of the sitting-room, which served as a sitting-out place. Conor, sure-footed and sure-minded; sometimes she wondered if she had only married him in the hope that some of his fine certainty would attach to her. Was he angry? It seemed strange that she could no longer tell. Turning back to look at the painting on its easel, she had thought, chilled: *is there someone else?*

She knew she ought to tell him that someone was watching her — except that he would probably laugh and tell her she was being silly. She wished he would take her more seriously although she was aware that it was necessary that he did not, if the balance of their relationship — he supposedly the protector, she the protected — was to be maintained. Besides, if for once he did, if he asked her *why* she thought someone was spying on her, she would have no real answer for him. It was just that several times lately she had seen someone standing under the heavy chestnut trees across the road from the house. Rationalising, she knew it could have been someone exercising a dog or waiting for a friend, someone lighting a cigarette or simply pausing to catch a breath, waiting to use the telephone kiosk opposite the house. Anything, really.

But she did not believe that. Whoever it belonged to, the figure seemed too aware somehow, too stiffly purposeful.

On top of that, last time she had walked into the centre of town, she had been absolutely certain she was being followed, yet, when she turned to look, there was only the usual midday ragbag of sauntering elderly, of dog-walkers, of young mothers pushing strollers, or undergraduates biking towards pub or lecture or games-field.

Why was she so convinced that someone was tailing her? Analysing her reasons, they came to little more than a feeling. Only afterwards, repainting the picture in her mind, had she decided that one of the figures behind her had been too rigid, too unnatural to be casual. She was not even sure whether it was male or female. In the end she had nothing much to offer in support of her theory. Plus the fact that this was not the first time. Often, in childhood, she had had the same sensation, the feeling that just out of sight someone watched, a whisk of a coat around a corner, reflections half-caught in shop windows. Intangibles. And Conor, so sure of things, did not like intangibles.

And those telephone calls which had begun after she bought the flat; should she tell him about them? They occurred perhaps once a week, nothing ever said, no obscene suggestions, no sounds of breathing, simply the presence silently there on the other end of the line. It was not that they alarmed her; it was the intrusion she resented, the sense of tranquillity disturbed, of someone trying to force themselves into her life.

At first she had simply slammed down the receiver. When they continued, she began to wonder if Conor's mother was responsible. 'Who's there?' she had cried, more than once. 'Is that you, Mrs Pearse? The line's awfully bad,' Giving her the chance to respond if she wished.

Now she sometimes listened in silence, outwaiting the caller, willing him to hang up first. One evening she had spoken, asking what he wanted, why he bothered her, and heard a sharp indrawn breath. Once, behind the silence, she had heard music softly in the background. Because it was a string quartet that her father had always been fond of, she had recognised it, hearing it on the radio the following morning. She was struck with the roundness of things, the patterns.

Conor would be pragmatic about it all if she told him. He would suggest she ring the exchange and have her calls monitored, get an answerphone, all with that glint of indifference in his eyes that increasingly made her feel as though she were a nuisance to him — an obstacle. Perhaps that was why she had so far said nothing.

Five weeks after his homecoming, the doctor confirmed that Harriet was pregnant. The prospect terrified her, though she did not say so. She was not sure that she wanted a child yet, certainly not convinced that she would be doing right by a new life to give it such an uneasy pairing as parents. Yet Conor seemed delighted.

They were to spend Sunday with Christina and Denis. On the way they suddenly began to quarrel. It was the first time they had done so. Harriet could not even identify what the apparent reason was, but suddenly the two of them were shouting vicious words at each other, screaming accusations, lips taut with anger. Conor pounded the steering wheel with the side of his hand, then smashed the hand against her upper arm. It was like a blow from a mallet. Already queasy with early pregnancy, she cowered away from him, feeling sick, then loosened her seat-belt to reach into the glove compartment for something to suck, a boiled sweet, or some codeine. Suddenly, as they rounded a bend in the narrow country road, they nearly ran into the back of a bus stopped to pick up passengers, and he braked violently, flinging her against the open door of the glove compartment with such force that she thought she would throw up. The door cut into her belly; her head smacked against the windscreen with sickening impact, and pain shot through the tops of her thighs.

Conor managed to pull the car into the hedge, then leaned across to cradle her against his chest. 'My God,' he said, 'I'm so terribly sorry. That sodding bus — are you all right?'

'I don't know.' Hariet felt shaky, nauseous. Her body pounded. She felt deeply, internally bruised.

'Would you like to go home? I'm sure the Crawfords would understand.'

'No. I'll be all right.'

He drove the rest of the way as though she were made of glass.

The row of hemlocks at the end of the Crawfords' garden, dark against the bright sky, gave off a hot piney smell. The four of them were sitting under a rustic arrangement of bark-covered poles over which green-fingered Chris had trained clematis and honeysuckle. She told them it was a gazebo.

'Uh-huh,' said Conor.

'What do you mean, uh-huh?' Chris asked indignantly.

'Can't be a gazebo.'

'Why on earth not?'

'A gazebo,' Conor said, 'is like a belvedere in that it requires to have been erected on a small prominence if it is to justify the name.'

'So what?'

'It requires a *view*, do you see. And delightful though your garden is it can hardly be said to constitute a view.' His mellifluous voice ended on a note that Harriet had leaned to dread, a combination of superiority and indifference.

'View or no view,' Chris said crossly. 'Anyone wishing in the future — or this afternoon, even — to sit out in my gazebo, let alone drink my booze or gorge themselves on my food, had better watch his tongue.'

Where is she?

The thought intruded with the sharpness of a switchblade, so solidly clothed with words that Harriet involuntarily straightened. It was years since she had wondered about her mother; she had been adolescent then, obsessed. She remembered the obituaries she used to read, the need to learn what she could about the woman who had left her behind. But events had moved on, and she with them; the thoughts had died down. She glanced round at the others, but only Christina, sensing that something had disturbed the post-luncheon placidity, opened her eyes and smiled sleepily, eyelids drooping. We could almost be in Spain, Harriet thought, settling down again; that place in the hills above Granada, when I was in love with Stephan, when I was younger and happy.

In spite of the festooning leaves, the sun's warmth settled heavily against her lids. The subtle innocent odour of her own skin underlay the smell of hot suntan oil. She heard the clink of ice-cubes as Denis sucked noisily at a Pimms, and the faint squeak of starch in his shortsleeved cotton shirt as he slumped back in his garden chair. Beside her, Conor yawned. Idly she rested a hand on her stomach.

Like a reflex, the thought returned.

Where is she?

Behind it came another, the one she had long ago persuaded herself was the best response: *Who cares?*

The one used to answer the other. It did not do so now. *She* cared. As a teenager, she had always assumed that her mother must be dead. Death provided the kindest solution, for, although it did not provide an answer to why a woman could walk out on her baby, it did explain the subsequent neglect and indifference. Death smoothed away the hurt of what could not otherwise be seen as anything except rejection. But, growing older, Harriet had begun to see that there was no reason why she should be dead. Not given the relevant dates and ages. And if she was not, then where was she, what was she doing, who did she spend time with — who, if anyone, did she love?

Harriet turned her head to look at her husband. He lay on

the chaise next to hers, half-asleep, mouth slightly open in the dark tangle of his beard, face dipping sideways so that she caught him head-on, like the Dali painting, confronted by his thick seraphic hair. The first time they met, she had thought him the most beautiful man she had ever seen. She still did. Even in sleep, he vibrated with energy, as though each nerve was separately charged with electricity. His thick eyebrows crackled with it; so did the little hairs on the backs of his wrist.

He opened his eyes and met her gaze. For a moment she saw in his face what struck her, with terror, as dislike. More, even, than dislike. Yet not hatred. Something more complicated than that. And even as her face changed, he winked at her and smiled. His hand moved up her body towards her breasts, touched one of her nipples, slid down again to her hip.

Another woman ...? Or was she being irrational? It would not be odd, given the time he had spent away from her, the weeks and months they had been apart. Why should he not have met someone else, someone more congenial to him, someone more intelligent than she, perhaps, or involved in the same kind of work?

'Anyone want their drink sweetened?' Denis said, grunting himself to his feet. He stood over his wife. 'How about you, sweetheart?'

Christina looked up. 'Just tonic water, darling. Slimline, with lots of ice and a slice of lemon.'

'I don't call that a drink.'

'You could if you persuaded yourself that the gin was lurking around at the bottom. Darling, you really ought to cut down.'

'I will, sweetheart. Promise.'

'When?'

'Tomorrow. Swear to God.'

Denis's drinking was such a constant source of mild bickering between the Crawfords that Harriet scarcely listened any more. It did not seem a very serious problem; in the two years that they had been friends, she had never seen Denis anything more than mildly jolly. Besides, if Chris was really concerned, she would have made more than a token protest. Being the energetic, efficient, don't-let-the-grass-grow-under-your-feet sort of person she was, by now Denis would be a member of Alcoholics Annonymous at the very least, if not enrolled in the Betty Ford Clinic as well.

It was true that sometimes Denis's face flushed alarmingly, but that was because he was intolerant of heat. Harriet half-opened her eyes and watched him through her lashes. He was a pale stocky man, overweight, with thinning hair and an undistinguished mouth. Not a handsome man, certainly, although a kind one. Harriet was always amazed that not only was he married to someone like Christina, but he had been married to her for eight years with no sign of discontent on either side.

'What about you two?' he said. 'Conor? Harriet?'

Conor murmured some negative. Harriet shook her head. 'No, thanks.'

'I suppose you feel you mustn't,' Christina said. 'Poor you.' She eyed Harriet's belly. 'How many months is it now?'

'Nine weeks.'

'He'll start moving soon,' Conor said. 'Start kicking away in there.' His hand stroked her belly-button, already beginning to protrude.

'God. The whole thing's so ghastly.' Christina shuddered, caressing her own small breasts under her skimpy yellow top, then added hastily: 'Not for you, love, of course. I mean, it's absolutely marvellous, and you know how thrilled we are for you.'

Harriet laughed. 'It's OK, Chris. You don't have to apologise for loathing babies. Hard as it is to believe, some of us actually don't need to be career women to prove ourselves.'

'How are the ante-natal classes going, Harriet?' Denis asked politely.

'All right.'

'I think they're great.' Conor opened his eyes. 'Amazing stuff you learn about women's bodies.'

'Conor has a marvellous time,' said Harriet. 'He and the

other mums-to-be discuss nipple cracks and episiotomy stitches and things like that.'

'Nipple cracks? For God's sake, Conor.' Christina shuddered theatrically, her black hair swirling briefly round the delicate outline of her skull before settling again.

'Harriet's the one who's got to go through it,' Conor said. 'The least I can do is learn what I can about the subject.'

'You know how he always throws himself one hundred per cent into any project that takes his fancy,' said Harriet. 'So far he's read at least half a dozen books on childbirth. What he doesn't already know could probably be scrawled on the head of a pin.'

'A nappy pin.' Conor laughed and closed his eyes again.

'And what do you do at these classes, Harriet?' asked Denis.

'Conor does all the exercises. I just lie there, trying not to fall asleep.' She yawned. 'I get so tired at the moment.'

'Goodness, how ghastly.' Christina looked at her husband then leaned remorsefully towards Harriet. 'Sorry, love, but it really does sound too gruesome for words.'

'Only to you,' said Harriet. She said it pleasantly, in case Christina took offence at her tone, though she felt that if anyone was going to take umbrage it should by rights be her. Increasingly the others — well, Conor and Christina, certainly — had begun to talk about her as though she were some breeding animal, dumb and fecund, fulfilling an instinctive function that required no more thought or care than breathing. She decided that if anyone mentioned milch-cows or brood-mares, she was going to go straight home.

Not that Denis would. As always, he was kind. Like her he lived quietly, somewhere a little back inside himself, while the other two lived on the surface. Perhaps that was why they made such a good foursome, two stars, two satellites — yet it was a role she felt did not become her, for which she was not trained.

Perhaps aware of her feelings, Conor dragged himself into a sitting position. From the gazebo's paved floor he picked up his still half-full glass and raised it. 'That was another terrific lunch, Chris.'

'Our pleasure.'

'And here's to your trip to Spain.'

In turn, Denis raised his own glass. 'Sorry you can't be with us this time, Conor.'

'Yes. Last time was fun, wasn't it?'

He stared at Harriet. Was she imagining it when she saw accusations in his eyes? Did he blame her for in some way ruining the smooth-running of their lives by getting herself pregnant? She started to answer denunciations not yet made, then stopped herself. Conor always told her she was too ready to accept the blame for things she had not even thought about, let alone done. Well, being pregnant was one she was certainly not going to feel guilty about.

'This sun,' she said. 'It's wonderful.'

'Do you think it heralds the start of a new golden age?' Denis asked lazily. He tilted his Panama further over his eyes. 'I'd say we were about due for another, wouldn't you?'

'Ah!' Conor sighed luxuriously. 'Think of it. We should all become kindly, courteous and learned once more. The patricians would dispense justice and wisdom, the plebs would revert to being a happy laughing breed who knew their place, instead of milling about in town centres, swilling lager and spitting at passers by. How blissful.'

'You, of course, being a patrician,' Chris said. She leaned across and flicked the dark skin of his leg with her thumb and forefinger.

'Naturally.'

'There has to be more to it than good weather,' said Harriet. 'People who already enjoy a climate like this aren't exactly noted for wisdom and justice. Iran, for instance. Central America.'

'We're talking about Utopia,' Denis said. 'When there'll be no more crime, no more sin ...'

'Nobody wailing or gnashing their teeth,' said Harriet.

'...quite — and the leopard shall lie down with the lamb.'

'If there're any leopards left,' said Conor.

The afternoon drifted. Harriet listened to the others chatting as the sun turned in the sky above them, wheeling towards another evening, towards another night of heat and restlessness, of cool cotton sheets and the sound of Conor breathing beside her while inside her body an alien put out fresh tentacles to grab and hold on to her.

She dozed.

Where is she?

With the recurring thought came discomfort. Not nausea, nor pain, but an uneasiness which alarmed her. She sat up. Denis and Conor were at the bottom of the garden, looking at a flowerbed. Christina lay asleep, her face curved in a smile, as though she remembered another golden age, or dreamed of love.

Harriet put her hand on her stomach. Upheaval, movement, a silent clamour which called for attention. Even though her body had been taken over, was no longer entirely her own, she still recognised its pleas.

'Christina,' she said.

'Hmmm?'

'I think —' Pain tore at her, at something deep inside her. It was out of her control. She must have screamed: she saw Conor turn, stare, come running. Even as she surrendered to it, flowing into the slippery wheels of pain, feeling hot blood bitter between her legs, she thought sadly: something has happened between us; we are not what we used to be.

And further thought, before pain whirled her away: I will never forget what I am seeing on his face as I lose this baby. I will never ever forget that he is relieved. But why?

· 5 ·

Time passed. Harriet mourned the lost baby; Conor returned to South America. We have made our own lives, separately, almost from the moment we were united, Harriet thought. It seemed odd. If we had remained lovers, would we now be together, she wondered; he working on his projects, me living nearby in some shabby concrete town, teaching English to the native children, painting fierce skies and wild colours, perhaps visiting my father and Anita? And instead we have grown worlds apart, my husband and I.

She sold a painting at an exhibition. The local paper did an interview with her; a photographer took a romantic picture of her in the garden, looking serious and artistic. Studying it, she thought: is this how others see me? Is this what I really am?

The pupils she had coached passed their examinations and recommended her to others. She found herself increasingly occupied, so that she had to cut down the time she spent at the bookshop. I am frittering, she told herself. None of this is long-term, a career; I am in limbo. Yet, while she remained in her current situation, there was nowhere else for her to be.

Then Conor came back. His contract with the conservation trust came to an end, money dried up, he and his colleagues were told they could either wait in the hope of further funding or else look for other jobs.

Meeting him at the airport, searching for his energetic face in the crowd, Harriet's feelings were mixed. Anticipation and love were overlaid by a large measure of apprehension: they had been married for nearly four years but, apart from his three months of leave, this would be the first time they had spent any length of time together.

His parents arrived for a visit. His father was still silent. His mother talked with a kind of seething intensity about the Pearses back in Ireland, about family, about roots — subjects to which Harriet could contribute nothing. One afternoon, she followed Harriet into the kitchen and asked without preamble why she was not pregnant.

'I don't think it is any of your business,' Harriet said bravely, not used to rudeness. Looking at the pointed intense face of her mother-in-law, she felt distaste.

'Certainly it is. Conor is my son, my only child. His son will be my grandson.'

'Or granddaughter,' Harriet said.

'Isn't it time? You have been married for a long time now.'

And never together long enough to learn each other, to find each other. Harriet thought. She said: 'I *was* pregnant. About two years ago.'

'Was? *Was?* What happened?'

'I lost it,' Harriet said shortly.

'A miscarriage.' Mrs Pearse said nothing more but she nodded as though her worst fears had been confirmed, her face expressing both scorn and dislike.

Harriet could have added that the fault might very well have been Conor's; had he driven less recklessly, had she not been flung so violently about as the foul words came pouring out of him, if he had not struck her, perhaps this woman would have her grandchild by now.

Harriet had assumed that they would spend time with the Crawfords, but when they were together Conor spoke only to Denis, listening, when Christina said anything, with an air that fell just short of contemptuous. Christina responded either with silence or with little cutting comments which made Harriet burn with embarrassment. She was miserable at the sudden antipathy so tangibly sparking between two of the people she most loved. Given that the four of them had spent time together before, it seemed incomprehensible. Was it possible that, with Conor home for longer, each saw the other as a rival for her own affection? She could think of no other explanation.

Conor was rude and irritable. During the day he sat around in sullen silence, waiting for letters, waiting for telephone calls, scarcely speaking to her. He ate the food she lovingly prepared for him without comment; she had hoped they would have time to visit friends, go to the theatre, explore, but he refused to go anywhere in case he missed some vital summons. At night he paced about the sitting-room, unable to sit still, then would leave the flat when she was ready for bed, saying he must walk, run, anything, he must have exercise; sitting there with her was stifling him.

She tried to excuse him to herself — he was restless, unsettled; no man could be expected to enjoy forced inactivity, joblessness — nonetheless there seemed little excuse for his bad manners.

She could tell herself that his indifference no longer affected her, but it would not be true. That indifference of his was like a bell-jar dropped over her. Sometimes she saw herself inside the vacuum he could so easily create, herself beating at the glass sides, trying to get through to him, tiny and desperate, impotent to reach him from inside that soundless prison. She infinitely preferred the blizzard of his rages, fierce though they were, to such chill withdrawal of his emotion.

As the weeks went by, there was in him a sense of something wild in captivity, of locks ready to give, of bars about to crumble. The flat was too small for so much barely-contained energy; unharnessed, it poltergeisted their existence together. She grew used to finding broken crockery lying on the kitchen table and smashed glassware stuffed into the dustbin. Lack of an outlet made Conor clumsy, she told herself, sad at the minor destruction, until coming quietly into the kitchen one morning, she was in time to see him quite deliberately pick up a small lustreware jug he knew she loved and dash it to the ground.

'Conor!' she cried.

He was startled. 'Sorry,' he said. 'It slipped out of my hand.' She knew it had not. Such lack of control frightened her.

She longed for the telephone to ring, for Conor to be offered another job, a new contract which would take him away from her again, anything so that he might once again be happy. Lying lonely in the bed she had bought alone, she pictured him walking in moonlight along Oxford pavements, passing under the shadow of ancient walls, clamoured by bells, and wanted to say: Why did you make me marry you?

Only sexually did they still seem to find accord. He is a stranger, yet my husband, she thought, responding despite herself to his hands, to his mouth. They never used to make love with the lights out; now it seemed he could only find arousal in the darkness. Again she wondered if he had another woman somewhere far away, whether that was why he appeared to be so angry, why he almost seemed to loathe her. She listened for another woman's name on his lips as he reached his climax, groaning into her, straining for a love that she would gladly have given him though she sensed he no longer wanted it from her. She longed to confide in someone, in Matthew possibly, but it seemed unfair to burden him with her troubles. Perhaps she was merely immature; perhaps this was a stage any marriage might go through, given similar circumstances.

Once, she almost told Christina, but found herself intimidated. Always ebullient, Christina had recently started on a regime of pills and creams — 'something Swiss, my dear, and *madly* expensive' — which, she declared made her feel like a teenager again. Her eyes were bright; her hair shone with a cruel gloss. Looking at her own limp goldspun, Harriet saw how unhappiness can affect the body. She felt herself to be heavy, clumsy, a drayhorse beside the neat body of her friend. Pride would not let her speak.

It was nearly seven months before Conor was offered another contract abroad. The relief which swept over Harriet was so overwhelming that she realised she would not be able to go through this again. Next time the work ended and Conor came back to wait, she would go away, she told herself. She would find somewhere else to live until he had gone again. It was not that she did not love him, simply that she could not survive the damage he was able to cause.

She tried to tell Christina when it was over and Conor was safely back in some threatened rain-forest, but Christina was ill and it seemed unfair.

Summoned, Harriet sat instead by her friend's bed, reading to her.

'Dickens,' Christina had cried. 'Read me some Dickens. He always makes me feel . . . safe.'

'What's wrong with you exactly?' Harriet asked.

'I don't know. A general malaise. Perhaps those pills I was taking . . .' She lay back on the embroidered linen pillow-covers and closed her eyes. Tears rolled slowly from beneath their delicate lids. Harriet could see the faint lines around her mouth and even — for the first time — a glint of grey somewhere in the shiny dark mop.

Poor Christina, Harriet thought, not knowing quite why. She read *Nicholas Nickleby*, using skills she had forgotten about to give the characters life. Christina was right: Dickens was safe. Whatever terrible thing happened, you knew it would all come all right in the end.

She wished she could be certain that life was like that.

'I've got to go to Paris for a conference,' Christina said. The two of them were sitting in her bedroom, Harriet lounging on the bed along with various dolls, Christina darting about like a bird. She put her head on one side. 'Why don't you come too?'

'Oh, Chris, I'd love to. But it's coming up to A-Levels — I can't walk out on my pupils . . .'

'It's only for a week, love. We could share a hotel room. You'd love it, wandering round the museums and art galleries, while I slaved away with all the other boring computer experts.'

Harriet remembered it so well, her adolescent self staring for hypnotised hours at the curves of a Rodin marble, the overlapping textures of Monet, the strangeness of being almost adult and alone in a foreign city. 'Don't tempt me,' she said. 'I can't let my students down.'

'So conscientious.'

'Maybe another time ...'

'Absolutely, darling.' Christina, now completely recovered from whatever bug had laid her low the month before, suddenly hugged Harriet and whirled away.

There was the shiny hardness of some brilliant beetle about her. It was new to her, unusual. 'Have you got a lover?' Harriet asked.

'What did you say?' Christina narrowed her eyes; it made her look dangerous. 'Have I got a *lover*?'

'I just wondered.' Harriet picked up a rag-doll in a checked gingham dress and smoothed its yellow hair. 'All this ...' She indicated the carrier bags from expensive shops which spilled over the big bed: a pair of scarlet shoes, a lacy half-slip trimmed with rosebuds, a matching bra.

'Darling Harriet, how on earth do you think I've kept Denis happy for all these years? Lingerie is the foundation of a good marriage.'

The thought of Denis and Christina in steamy embrace had always seemed bizarre to Harriet. The sexual antics of friends are always improbable, she thought, always unimaginable. She said nothing, thinking of Conor, his mouth on her breast, his fingers weaving among the softness of her nerve endings, bringing her to efficient completion.

'All that stuff about the way to a man's heart being through his stomach is nonsense,' continued Christina. 'When you get right down to it, the way to a man's heart is and always has been through his crotch.'

'Conor and me ...' Harriet started to say, and would have gone on to explain about Conor, to say that apart from their sex-life there seemed to be nothing left of their marriage, to ask for advice or reassurance, but Christina interrupted her.

'Anyway, I've never once been unfaithful to Denis, nor have I any intention of being.'

'Sorry I asked,' Harriet said. 'I didn't really think you —'

'I should bloody hope not. I love Denis. Besides, it's always seemed to me that lovers are an unnecessary complication.'

'Why?'

'Oh, Harriet, come on. All that surreptitious phoning, and yearning, and finding places to be together where you won't be recognised. All that passion for something that you both realise is doomed from the start.'

'If you've never had a lover, how come you know so much about it?'

Christina picked up the new shoes and swung them back and forth on the tips of her fingers. 'I've heard enough of my friends talking,' she said. 'From the way they go on, it's always struck me you'd have to be pretty unhappy to want a lover. Which I am not.'

I am, Harriet nearly said. *I don't want a lover — at least, I don't think I do — but I'm pretty unhappy.*

Christina came back from Paris. She drove over to see Harriet and give her the gloves she'd bought as a gift: long thin gloves of leather so fine it felt like silk.

'You look wonderful,' Harriet said.

'I do rather, don't I?' Christina looked at herself in the glass, burnished and elegant. She smiled reflectively, spreading both hands across her flat stomach, touching a finger to her lower lip. 'Yes, I'm doing rather well, considering my age.'

Six weeks later, Conor rang to ask Harriet to join him in Rome. 'A conference,' he said, 'I miss you, darling. You can't imagine how much.' He began to tell her what he particularly missed, how he planned to make up for their separation.

Harriet booked a return flight. She went into the town and spent money on underwear. She had her bright hair restyled. As she was leaving, the postman arrived with letters which she stuffed into her bag. At the airport's duty-free shop she bought an expensive bottle of perfume and dabbed her wrists and neck, aware that these were false measures, that whatever the way to Conor's heart might be, she did not wish to find it, for Conor's heart no longer had relevance for her. I think my marriage is at an end, she told herself, if, indeed, it ever began.

*

The hotel he took her to was narrow, squeezed between tall houses in a dingy backstreet. Once past the reception desk, however, it expanded into marble halls, columned and be-mirrored, with doors of carved mahogany opening into high-ceilinged rooms, grandiose but shabby.

'It's beautiful,' Harriet said. It reminded her of the little resort in northern France where she had spent a summer fortnight. The same melancholy lingered among the cushions on the sofas and the plants which stood tiredly against the pillars.

'I chose it specially for us,' said Conor. His black eyes gleamed. His hand clutched hers.

'Isn't it the conference hotel?'

'I thought you'd prefer to be away from the rest of the ecologists and their boring wives,' he said.

'Of course.' She smiled at him.

'Besides, I want you to myself.'

They sat late over dinner in a small restaurant where candles flickered and the house wine was cheap. Climbing the wooden stairs which were bowed in the middle from the passage of many feet, Conor clutched her to him and kissed her passionately. She could feel him thicken and swell as his tongue caressed her mouth; she wished she could feel an answering passion. A door opened and an old man in a buttoned woollen vest looked out at them. Laughing, Conor pulled her after him up the stairs to their room.

He took his own clothes off and lay naked on the bed to watch Harriet get undressed. 'Hurry up, darling,' he said, staring at her hotly. The bedside lamp shone behind his head and gave his hair a tint the colour of dried blood.

A huge reluctance filled Harriet. Already he was primed and ready for her; it scarcely seemed the time to speak of separation, of divorce, but in all honesty she felt she could not let him make love to her thinking that all was well between them. 'Conor . . .' she began.

'My mother says you must be over the miscarriage by now,' he said. He scratched at the dark fur between his thighs

Harriet felt entirely cold. Slowly she undid the buttons of her blouse. 'Your mother?'

'She knows about these things,' he said.

'I don't see why she should. She only had one child,' Harriet said. She was suddenly afraid.

'For Christ's sake, Harriet, get a move on.' Conor's voice was rough; there was unpleasantness about the line of his mouth.

Harriet felt herself dry up, wither, the fruitfulness ebb from her womb. The vindictive gaze of her husband's mother seemed to rake across her half-naked body as he stood up and came towards her, huge in the shadows of the big dark room, threatening. He put one hand on the back of her head and said: 'Your hair is like a shower of gold.'

Classical images swam in her mind as his voice wrapped her in reassurance. 'I'm not ready,' she said, trying to evade him.

He seized her hair in his hand then picked her up suddenly and carried her to the bed. 'I am,' he said. 'More than.'

'I don't want to,' she said, twisting away from him.

'I love you.'

'That's something else,' she said. She was aware that she was caught in a situation over which she had no control. 'Listen, Conor. I don't think we can go on like —'

'Look at me,' he said.

Unwillingly she made herself meet his eyes. Did he know what she was trying to tell him? Was that why he would not let her speak.

'I love you,' he said again, insistently.

'You had no right to discuss me with your mother.'

His grip on her arm tightened; the colour drained from his face, leaving it white. 'She simply asked if it wasn't time we had a baby.'

'It's nothing to do with her.'

'Don't talk about her like that,' he said roughly. His hand grabbed hard at one of her breasts.

'Don't do that; it hurts,' she said, her voice rising.

'Does it really?'

She realised that he was fairly drunk. She spoke reasonably, keeping her voice down: 'Conor, why don't we just go to sleep and talk about it in the morning?'

'And not screw, you mean?'

'I don't really want to, actually. I'm tired, I've been travelling all day.'

For answer, he held her shoulders down so she could not move. 'You may not want to, but I do,' he said, straddling her. He was not smiling.

She held her legs together. His mouth grim, he kneeled on top of them until pain forced them apart. Unprotected, she was afraid. She said: 'Not like this, Conor. Please ... not this way ...' But he took no notice. he seemed bigger than she had ever known him, full of feral blood; behind him she saw the face of his mother, urging him on. She opened her mouth to scream and he put a hand across her face. She saw how the violent action inflamed him, rippling beneath his skin like a jolt of electricity. Above her, his eyes shone as he forced his way into her body, tearing into her through the dryness — laughing.

Under his restraining hand, she said 'No, no,' twisting and whipping beneath his weight, trying to bring her knees up to stop him while he pistoned into her, violating, destroying, his body slapping against hers with the insistent clap of wings. She wept, partly with pain, partly because the wings were no longer those of white swan or golden angel, but leathery, fox-furred, devilish.

When he had finished, he held her close and stroked her hair. 'I'm sorry, darling,' he whispered into the side of her neck, licking the tears which fell down her face to the bed. 'It's just, it's been so long, and I love you so much. I'm truly sorry.' Then, pushing himself up on his arms to look down on her, he added: 'Didn't you enjoy that just a bit?'

She did not bother to answer.

'Your husband wanting you so much that he couldn't wait for you?' he said.

'Is that how you see it?' Harriet said.

'That's how it was. That's *all* it was.'

'Was it?'

'I said I'm sorry if I hurt you.' She turned over on her side, away from him. Her body throbbed; the tender tissues felt raw, as though they bled. *What shall I do if he has made me pregnant?* she thought. She wondered if his mother had told him what to do. The bed moved as he got out on his side. She turned her head and saw through the tangles of her hair that he was looking at himself in the full-length mirror on the wall, admiring. She hated him for what he had done to her yet felt obscurely that she was in some way to blame.

She left the next day, while he was attending a conference seminar. She did not leave a note: her absence was explanation enough. On the plane, she opened her bag and found the letters. One of them was in a hand she recognised; remembered love made her feel weak.

> *I shall be in Oxford shortly*, Stephan wrote. *I'll ring you. Perhaps we could have dinner together. I would so much like to see you again.*

She could imagine him lingering over the choice of words, screwing up the first version of his brief message and trying again — *I'd love to ... it would be nice to ... I would like to* — and in the end settling, without even realising it, for the combination which most emphasised his not-quite-Englishness.

Conor she would not think about. She had loved him — she still did — but she could not remain married to him. Knowing his anger, the hidden streaks of violence which he could display, she dreaded the thought of telling him. He would come back to bully and harass and persuade; perhaps she should write him a letter and then go away, perhaps she should give up the flat and find somewhere else to live. She imagined his mother would be glad about the break-up.

She arrived home in the late afternoon; the telephone was ringing. By the time she had opened the front door it had stopped. She imagined all the people it could have been on the other end of the line: Christina in her elegant sitting-room full of shining objects; Matthew calling from the tiny book-lined house in Yorkshire from which he conducted his antique shop; Conor repentant, one of her students, the anonymous caller ... Lilac leaves leaned like a bower against the French windows; the sitting-room was full of tender light. She picked up the glass egg and looked into its sea-green depths. Its message seemed very clear: although chaos swirls at the heart of all things, there are shapes, patterns, immutable and solid as those the glass contained. She remembered Stephan crosslegged against some landlady's bedhead, reading Eliot to her, *These fragments I have shored against my ruin*, and thought of her grandmother's peaceful house.

It seemed strange that the past should exist so easily alongside the present, always there, superimposed, under-pinning, its impressions and feelings no less real than those of *now*. She decided she would travel to Cornwall, back to the time before chaos, where the imposed patterns maintained order, where breakfast was unchangeably at eight o'clock, and at three you walked for an hour before tea.

An hour later the telephone rang again. It was Stephan. Hearing his voice after so many years, kind in a way Conor's had never been, she wanted to weep, 'I just got back,' she said.

'Where from?'

'Rome.'

'You sound sad.'

'I think I am.'

He paused, then said: 'Have dinner with me tonight. You could, if you wished, tell me about it.'

'All right.'

He brought her back. She did not ask him in; he did not even try to kiss her cheek, as though realising such privileges had been forfeited. She leaned into him, however, before shutting her front door, eased from agitation by his big strength; he sensed possibilities in her. Over dinner they had discussed not the present but the future. She told him she was married, but little else. It was obvious that she was not happy but he did not probe, knowing her well enough to realise that she did not wish to talk about it.

Near midnight, Harriet put out the bedside light. Almost immediately the telephone cheeped. When she picked it up, nobody spoke. She lay with the receiver close to her ear on the pillow; behind the silence there was music. Vivaldi, very far away. For a long time she lay there, not speaking, perversely comforted. In a world of broken dreams and shifting landscapes, the stranger who so wordlessly connected with her was at least familiar.

When the movement ended, she quietly hung up.

Nothing is more dead than a dead love, but what about a love which has been snapped in two, like a bone broken? Is it possible to put it together again and make it new? Certainly Harriet found that she and Stephan slipped without difficulty back into the ease together they had once known, even though there was no longer — on her part at least — any physical spark between them. Was it love? Of course. Though the thought had not expressed itself before, she became aware of something she must always have known: that there are many kinds of love.

She found herself needing this old, unthreatening relationship. She spread it like a balm across the wound that Conor had become. He did not contact her. In the week after her return, she went with Stephan to the theatre, to a concert in one of the college gardens, to restaurants, and found some peace.

Home after seeing an undergraduate production of *Medea*, the telephone began to ring as she made coffee for the two of them. About to ask him to answer it, Harriet changed her mind. If it were Conor, he would be hurt and angered to find a man replying. Although it was arguable that he deserved no better, she nonetheless shook her hair away from the side of her head and spoke into the receiver.

'Mrs Pearse?'

'Yes.' It was a long-distance call; she could hear the echo of oceans washing along the cable.

'This is Mike Potter — you may remember me from the conference on river pollution in Eastern Europe ...' He paused, giving her time to recognise him. When she did not do so, he went on: 'I'm — uh — Conor's — your husband's supervisor on the Amazon project.'

Something was wrong. Tiny hammers began to beat inside her body. Why else would Conor's boss be ringing her? What had happened? She started to speak but he was talking again. Through a dark cloud she heard words and tried to connect them one to another: '... accident ... fallen tree ... appalling ... did what we could· but ... so very sorry ... no one really to blame ... sorry ... unforeseen ... sorry ... sorry.'

'He's dead?' she whispered. She wondered if her voice would carry all the way across the mountains and the seas to the camp in the heart of the Amazonian basin, or whether all that would be left of it by the time it reached Mike Potter was the echo of a sigh.

'I don't know what to say, Mrs Pearse. I can't begin to tell you how dreadful ...' He was off again.

'A tree?' Harriet said.

'Yes ... pinned him down ... day's journey from base ... might have saved him otherwise. Terrible. As I said, we did what we could but it was hopeless. If it's any consolation, he can't have had time to realise what was happening.'

She saw Conor in her mind's eye, stretched upon a forest floor, foxy-red against the clinging greenery — lianas, hibiscus, huge Rousseau-like leaves — which crowded around his crushed body. Would there be blood? She saw large-eyed monkeys staring down from orchid-laden branches, a panther guardedly peering through creepers, overhead a condor. It seemed ironic that the very environment he had tried to save from destruction had, in the end, destroyed him.

She said: 'Thank you,' and put the telephone down on more words '... be in touch ... British Consulate ... sorry ... sorry ...'

Would his face be damaged, reduced to a pulp of bone and

ruined flesh? She stared at Stephan and ran from the room as her stomach heaved with loss and regret and horror.

'Hold me tight,' she said. They sat together on the blue-green sofa. In front of them, next to the glass egg, was a bottle of Remy Martin.

Stephan put his arm around her and pulled her close. She had drunk a great deal of brandy; he could smell it on her breath. He hoped she would soon fall asleep, anaesthetised by the strong spirit.

'I can't believe it,' she said for the twentieth time. She turned her head to lean against him. 'I can't take it in.'

He murmured at her. There was nothing he could say.

'I wasn't even sure I loved him any more,' she said. 'Our marriage was — it was a mess. And the last time I saw him, he —' It seemed disloyal to speak of the rape. Instead she said: '— we didn't get on at all. Oh, Stephan. I even wished he would die. But I didn't mean it ... I didn't really mean it ... not die, not like this.'

Death should be anonymous, quiet, peaceful, a relinquishing of life, not trees crashing down, not blood and splintering bone and pain. She began to weep, the slow tears suddenly turning to sobs which were cries of anguish. 'I loved him so much,' she gasped. 'Oh, God, I loved him.'

'I know you did.' Knowing no such thing, Stephan patted and soothed her wet face lying against his shoulder.

'I loved him terribly,' she said again, mouth contorting with the hurt of it. 'The dreadful thing is that it wasn't enough.'

'Yes.'

'However hard I tried, somehow it just never came right.'

'Mmm.'

She rocked back and forth for a while, uttering little cries. 'Love's not enough, Stephan,' she wept. 'You think it is, but it's not.' After a while, she said: 'I'd better go to bed.'

When she tried to stand up, she staggered and fell back. He pulled her to her feet. 'Come on,' he said. 'I'll help you.'

He undressed her, as he had done many times before. He told himself he felt nothing for her but protective affection.

Nonetheless, the sight of her pale body stirred him. Lying in the big double bed, she looked up at him, eyes drooping. 'Stephan,' she whispered. 'Please stay with me. Please hold me. I feel so ... lonely.'

He hesitated, wondering what was best. Matthew would be arriving in the morning but perhaps she ought not to be alone. She said in a small voice: 'You don't have to,' and turned over on her side, away from him.

'Shall I call your friend Christina?' he asked.

She shook her head. 'Stay with me.'

He lay down awkwardly on top of the bed, bemused by death, by grief. She said: 'Not like that. I want to feel you. I'm so cold.'

In the end, he undressed and got in beside her. She was shivering, her face still wet. When she turned into his arms her nipples brushed against his chest. He thought of another woman, one whom he had not yet touched, and found the thought rousing.

'Conor,' Harriet said, her lips warm against him. 'Oh, Conor, my darling ... don't be dead.' She moved closer, putting an arm around Stephan, pulling him towards her, on top of her. 'Love me, the way you used to.'

She was soft under him. And familiarly sweet.

Not knowing to whom she spoke, Stephan was never afterwards able to feel any guilt.

Conor's mother came to Oxford to collect her son's body, which would be buried in Ireland, beside his ancestors. Grimly she went through Conor's things, removing shirts and jackets, a knife he had owned since boyhood, one or two of the wedding presents which had come from her side of the family. Harriet did not try to stop her.

She stared at Harriet, her face rumpled with grief, full of rage. Had she been able to, she would have blamed Harriet for the death, might even have flown at her, shredded her with hands turned into claws. But she had no cause. As she walked among the rooms, her eyes appraised the younger woman's hips. Harriet shivered: were she pregnant, she felt sure the woman would have drawn the embryo out of her body with the sheer force of her hatred. Behind her, Conor's father hovered like a shadow; he did not speak to Harriet.

Once, when the telephone rang, Conor's mother picked it up. 'Yes,' she said. 'This is Mrs Pearse.'

The dislike she felt flowed through Harriet's bloodstream like untreated sewage. Coldly she took the receiver which the other woman held out to her. 'In this house,' she said, 'I'm Mrs Pearse.'

The days passed in a blur. Later Harriet would recall Matthew's shocked expression; Christina pale and weeping, her face drawn, almost ugly; Maggie dry-eyed; a handful of Conor's associates who appeared separately or together at the flat, looked at her with consternation then patted her hand and went away again.

Once the necessary arrangements had been made, life resumed its course. It was callous but true to decide that a Conor dead was very little different from a Conor not there. His absence did not make any visible difference, though turmoil often shook Harriet, leaving her weak with a mixture of sorrow and relief and guilt. Scar tissue formed over her emotions. Not again, she told herself, will I give myself to someone else. Twice I have loved someone, and both times I have suffered. I will never ever again allow myself to be made vulnerable by love.

She was not surprised to find that emotional upset affected her physically; she ignored it. So it was more than three months after Conor's death when the doctor confirmed that she was pregnant.

Much too late by then to do anything about it.

Already Harriet could imagine Christina's reaction to this news: the commiserating twist of the mouth, the dark eyes full of sympathy while the swift brain calculated the best way out of the problem, the one which would make the fewest ripples, leave behind the least repercussions. And then, blanking all that out, the sudden realisation that what to Christina would seem disaster might to Harriet appear something quite other. That would not stop her from presenting the arguments which Harriet had already endlessly debated for herself, pointing out the advantages of one course of action, the follies of the other, but once she had realised that Harriet's mind was firm, there would be the warm smile, the congratulations, the excited questions as to when and where.

The most important question — *who?* — she would not think to ask.

It was the *who* which stopped Harriet from saying anything. Explaining would be awkward — more than awkward. Explaining would add a dimension of something negative — shame? embarrassment? stigma certainly — which, however hard she told herself that this was the end of the twentieth century, that she was a modern woman, capable, efficient, self-supporting, she would not be able to avoid attaching to herself, *What? Slept with another man the night she heard that her husband was dead?* She thought: no one who has not experienced it can realise the compulsive need to assert in the face of death the continuity of life.

She realised that there was no need for her to explain, no need to say anything at all. The assumption by everyone would be that the child was Conor's. Perhaps because she did not wish it to be, Harriet felt she could not go through another six months without offering herself the possibility that it was not.

Postponing the announcement was not, in the end, to make any difference. Since it would only be a week or two before she *did* tell Christina, did make public the private facts of which, she was only just certain, the time lapse was not in any way to change the events to come; nor could Harriet, by overcoming those prejudices which were not even her own, have altered in the slightest all the nightmares that were to follow.

Getting up, she watched the two Crawfords, their faces lit by the lamps of early evening. How strange, she thought, that though they are my closest friends, they are entirely unaware of the inner seething me, the hopes, the terrors, the excitements bursting like electrical impulses within my mind. As I, conversely, know nothing of theirs.

'It's been a lovely day,' she said, 'But I really must go home.'

'So soon?' Denis began struggling upwards.

'I've been feeling awfully tired recently.'

'Of course.' Denis put a hand on her arm. 'It's only to be expected, my dear. A natural reaction to losing Conor like that. Are you sure you'll be all right on your own?'

'Quite sure.' Harriet smiled at him. I'm strong, she wanted to say. Stronger than I used to be. I've changed.

'You've certainly been looking a bit peaky,' Chris said. Her eyes were shrewd. For a moment they darted across Harriet's body, secretive, suspicious almost. She herself did not look well.

Driving back to Oxford, Harriet said out loud. 'Shall I tell him?'

She imagined his sharp-drawn breath in the darkness, the way his hand would pause on the curve of her hip, the warmth of his breath on her shoulder.

'*Are you sure?*' he would say. '*Are you absolutely sure?*', his voice breaking slightly on the word '*absolutely*', the way it always did.

And she would explain, give her small proofs of time and place, make him see that it was fact, unstayable, irreversible, that it was not just imagined. 'You have too much imagination,' he had once told her gravely. 'People talk about not seeing the woods for the trees but you, Harriet, you see not only the woods, not only the trees, but the leaves on the branches, the separate twigs, the owls in the hollow trunks, the small bugs under the bark.'

'Yes,' she said. It was true.

'You must train yourself to see less and then you will see more.'

'Yes,' she said. 'Maybe.'

He was probably right. Later, looking back, she would realise that at that time she had not yet learned to cherish her own unique vision, nor to have faith in herself.

Shall I tell him?

But suppose he started to plan. Suppose he tried to organise her. Once she might have let him, seeing herself as a floater on life's stream rather than a swimmer. Would she now?

Grasping the wheel tighter, she drove between high hedges from which the autumn winds had stripped the leaves. Through them she could see the fields beyond, bare now, ridged with ploughing, the earth rich as chocolate. Along the lanes the grass had died away to brittle yellowness; the roadside ditches brimmed with rainwater.

She decided this was something she would have to handle herself. She did not tell Conor's mother, though aware that, sometime in the future, she would have to. Not yet, though. Not until she could be sure. It was entirely possible that the woman might have no blood-claim on the child at all. If it had not already been too late, she often wondered what she would have done? Would she have kept the child? She could not feel anything for it; she felt it rootless inside her, unfathered, untethered. A *fait accompli*, she thought. A *fate accompli*. She had no choice.

She did not tell Christina for another month. By then she was beginning to show, her waistbands tight, her breasts assuming a personality of their own, as though aware of their future role.

'A baby?' Christina stared, as Harriet had known she would. Something dark flickered at the back of her eyes before she managed to control it, to smile and take Harriet's hand and ask if she was sure about it.

'I'm sure,' Harriet said.

'You must be delighted.'

'I'm not,' Harriet said honestly. She did not want to go into that last encounter with Conor, not delve into the guilt which surged at the thought that she had left him without saying goodbye, not knowing that only a short time later he would be dead.

'Don't you want it?' Christina seemed genuinely shocked.

'Would you?'

'Would *I*?' Christina's mouth twisted.

'In the circumstances, I mean.'

Christina bent her head so that her hair fell across her face. 'Perhaps not,' she said. 'I wish you told me earlier. How far are you gone?'

'About four months.'

'So it's due at the beginning of the summer?'

'Yes.'

'Darling, if you need anything, you know we're here,' Christina said. 'Both of us. We'll help in any way we can. We were both so fond of — of Conor.' Harriet was acutely aware of the polite lie. 'And you know we love you. Promise me you'll tell us if there's anything at all we can do.'

'Of course. But I can — I think — cope, in spite of what's happened.'

She did not add, then or later: 'in spite of what *is* happening right now.' The phone-calls, for instance, in the middle of the night after she had fallen asleep, the strange wild laughter which echoed round the receiver held to her ear. And the footsteps. Sometimes, sitting among her sea-green cushions, she knew she had heard footsteps outside, the swish of someone walking through the dead winter grass of her garden; once, even, hands fumbling at the window. Yet whenever she went, heart thumping, lights switched out behind her, to check, she could see nothing, nothing at all except the unleaved trees and the outline of her studio.

Sometimes she woke, sweating with fear, starting up against the pillows, not knowing what had brought her out of sleep; she felt the force of some maleficent thing somewhere out there in the darkness, waiting to pounce and drag her down.

Not given much to demonstrative affection, she nonetheless put her hand over Christina's and gripped it tightly. She wished her friend did not look so haggard. 'Thank you. And vice versa ... if there's anything I can do ...'

Denis came in. 'God, it's hot,' he said. He wore a panama and a crumpled linen jacket. He took both off and poured himself a drink. 'Anyone else?' He waved the gin bottle at them.

'I do wish you wouldn't drink so much, darling.' Christina said. She grimaced at Harriet.

'No one could describe a couple of gin and tonics before dinner as serious boozing.' Denis said. He laughed. 'After the day I've just had, medicinal would be nearer the mark.'

'No, but you do drink too much,' persisted Christina. 'You should cut down. Alcohol can be dangerous at your age. Do you know how many braincells die every time you swallow that stuff?'

'Rubbish, woman. I'm practically a teetotaller.'

When he went upstairs to change, Christina said: 'I really do worry about him, you know.'

'I can't imagine why,' said Harriet.

'He's drinking more and more these days. It's not just the drinks before dinner, it's wine with it, and a couple of whiskies before bed.' Her small face was screwed up with anxiety. 'All in all, he manages to put away a hell of a lot each night. As for the weekends ...'

'I'm sure you're worrying about nothing.'

'Maybe.' She gave a great gusting sigh. 'That's not all. You know the girl who comes in to clean?'

'Tracy? What about her?'

'I'm going to have to give her the sack.'

'Why? She seemed very efficient to me.' Harriet glanced

round guiltily at the sparkling room. In her own flat, there was dust on the mantelpiece, coffee-cups from the night before still on the table, a vase of almost-dead flowers. 'Perhaps your standards are too high for ordinary human beings.'

'It's not that. Actually she wasn't bad. But stealing — that's a different matter.'

'Are you sure?'

'I've suspected it for a while. I mean, nobody minds the odd jar of jam out of the store-cupboard, or a couple of apples. Not even the odd item of underwear.'

'Come on, Chris. You're not telling me she took your knickers.'

'Somebody did.'

'It was probably Denis,' Harriet said, laughing.

'You're being ridiculous, Harriet.' As always when annoyed, a touch of Gallic severity crept into Chris's voice, a hint of the mother she had once told Harriet was French. 'But it was the shoes which really annoyed me.'

'Which shoes?'

'Those red ones. Remember? The ones I bought just before I went to Paris? We have the same size feet, as it happens. Anyway, she took them.'

'Jolly difficult to be sure, I'd have thought.'

'I caught her strutting about in them once, when I came home early. Admiring herself in my bedroom mirror, if you please. And now they've completely disappeared. Which is why I shall simply have to tell her I won't be needing her any more. God, I hate doing things like that.'

'I can imagine.'

'Now, love, are you sure you're OK? Taking proper care? Drinking tons of lovely milk to make bones for the baby?'

'For heaven's sake, Christina . . .'

Her friend's face was momentarily wistful. 'I know it's silly but I almost feel I ought to get pregnant too, just to keep you company.'

'You'd hate it,' Harriet said. 'Maybe not the getting pregnant, but certainly the being it.'

'Maybe.'

'Definitely. But it's a very sweet thought, especially when I know you can't imagine anything worse than the thought of losing your figure the way I've already done.'

Not, she might have added, after all the work that had gone into that figure. Though it was more than that. The idea that Christina would willingly give up her highly-paid job as a financial consultant to an Oxford-based marketing firm was equally untenable. She had heard Chris's views more than once on the subject of babies and what they did to the careers of ambitious women, and she remembered with amusement how her friend's face had drooped with horror when she first announced her news, before she managed to mask her dismay with a smile of congratulation.

As the spring turned slowly to summer the sun began to burn down from a sky so palely blue that it was almost colourless. Early mornings with the texture of pale velvet gave way to bright ferocity as the sun climbed. At night the scents of honeysuckle and roses trailed across suburban gardens long after darkness had fallen. But as tans rivalling those available in the cheaper Mediterranean countries began to cause discontent among those who had expensively booked holidays the previous December, as farmers voiced concern over rain-thirsty crops, as Government spokesmen talked sonorously on the early-morning radio shows about reduced water-tables, and building societies discoursed on the danger to house foundations in areas where the soil had dried out, the nation, at first disbelieving, then ecstatic, had now grown sick of the endless heat. The pundits spoke of global warming, warned against the increase in melanoma; fair-haired people began keeping an anxious eye on their moles.

Too much of a good thing, people said, shaking their heads and staring up at the sky. Sinister, if you ask me; drains the energy right out of you. Give me a nice downpour any day.

The English, Harriet reflected, were not good at handling hot weather. In her student days, dragging across Europe with endless coach parties, she had seen how efficiently other nations tackled heat, conserving energies, moving into a lower gear, minimising effort. Her own countrymen had the wrong temperament. The wrong figures, too. For herself, the lethargy generated by the high temperatures seemed no more than a necessary interim between one stage and the next. Seed-time and harvest, she told herself as the summer days spread into summer weeks. Seed-time and harvest; and, in between, germination and growth.

Stretching her legs out in front of her and contemplating their immaculate sheen, Chris said: 'Guess who I saw in the super-market today.'

'Don't be irritating,' said Harriet. She looked across at Denis, lying on a chaise in the gazebo, his panama over his eyes. 'How can we possibly?'

'Just one guess.'

'Salman Rushdie?'

'That's silly,' Chris said severely.

'I don't know. Tell me,' Harriet said, reflecting that, as a conversational opener, Guess-who-I-met-in-the-supermarket was invariably a loser.

'I was standing in front of the vinegars when this woman stretched past me in such a rude fashion that I was about to say something nasty, until I saw who it was.'

There was a pause. 'And who was it?' asked Harriet.

'Tracy Wotsit.'

'On balance, I'd have preferred Salman.'

'You know. Tracy ... Marling, wasn't it? The girl who used to clean for me. You remember.'

'Vaguely.' And indeed Harriet could put together a picture: short hair, shorter skirts, lots of lipstick, a bosom confined in a too-tight bra.

'I didn't think I could just ignore her, even if she was probably the worst cleaning lady I've ever employed, so I said "Hello" and she told me she was pregnant.'

'It sounds an unlikely exchange,' Harriet said. 'A says "Hello", and B says "I'm pregnant".'

'Obviously there was a bit more to it than that. What

happened was, I thought she was looking a bit peaky and she told me she was going to have a baby.'

'I suppose you asked her who the father was.'

'Of *course*.'

'Honestly, Chris.' Sometimes Harriet wondered if her friend had any sense of humour at all.

'Well, I knew she wasn't married. At least, she wasn't three months ago, when I —'

'Kicked her out,' Denis said, muffled, from under his hat.

'Let her go.' Chris said with dignity. 'Dammit, the girl was stealing my Janet Reger knickers.'

'You never had any proof, did you?' asked Harriet.

'That's what I told her,' Denis said.

'How's she going to cope?' said Harriet.

'Oh, all unmarried mums get council houses and social security and things these days,' Chris said airily. 'There's no stigma attached to illegitimate babies any more. Good thing, too, I suppose. It could happen to anyone.'

'Was there some point to this story?' asked Denis sleepily.

'Yes, actually. The thing is, Harriet might meet her in hospital. She's nearly six months gone, she told me. Just like you, Harry.'

Two weeks later, Christina said, her voice high and excited: 'We've decided to dash over to Spain for a week. Denis has some holiday due to him. It seems a good chance to go.'

'Lucky you.'

'Do you want to come too? We'd love to have —'

'You know perfectly well I can't,' Harriet said. 'I've got more work than I can cope with at the moment.'

'And the baby?'

'What about it?'

'It's all right, is it? And you? Everything's ticking along in good order?'

'Absolutely.' Harriet tried not to smile, knowing how distasteful Christina found the whole subject of pregnancy. She put a hand on her belly, feeling the tiny mound of her distended navel, remembering the way her nipples had darkened and spread over the past weeks. Christina would hate all that. 'Have a good time in Spain.'

'Oh, we will.' Christina lowered her voice. 'As long as Denis can keep away from the booze. Honestly, you've no idea what he's like these days. It's playing havoc with our sex life, I can tell you.'

When the telephone rang early one morning a few days later, Harriet had no premonition of disaster. 'Chris!' she said sleepily. 'Did you come back early?'

'I'm still here ... in Spain.' Christina's voice sounded odd, as though it had been stretched very thin. 'Harriet, it's too terrible.'

'What's happened?' Alarm brought Harriet wide awake. She sat bolt upright; the baby kicked in protest at this sudden upheaval. 'What is it?'

'Denis. He had — he fell ...' Christina broke off. Harriet heard the sound of wild weeping.

'Christina, what is it?' she said.

'He fell over the edge of the — of the balcony,' Christina said, her voice wavering. 'He must have been — he'd been drinking all evening — I went to bed — I didn't know anything about — they banged on the door — woke me up — someone'd found him on the — on the ground.'

'Is he all right?' Even as she asked, Harriet knew what the answer would be. The Crawford's flat was nine floors up; the ground beneath was tarred over and set with huge concrete tubs from which flowered wildly profuse geraniums. It was unlikely that anyone could have survived such a fall.

She felt sick. In her mind's eye, Denis lurched across the marble-floored balcony while the lights of Alicante twinkled in the warm Mediterranean night and harbour smells floated upwards. She saw him stumble, grab at the rail, miss, go plummeting over ... She squeezed her eyes shut, not wanting to visualise the final hideous sound as he hit the ground. Again and again he stumbled and plunged, limbs loose, the glass in his hand flying from his fingers to smash beneath him. Or would it reach the ground after the heavy body? She could not remember: *If you dropped a pound of feathers and a pound of lead from the top of the Leaning Tower of Pisa . . .*

'He's dead,' Christina's tiny voice said in her ear.

'Oh, God . . .'

'Dead . . .' The voice swayed, as though its owner had turned away from the telephone.

'Chris —'

'You, of all people, can imagine how I feel.' She sounded suddenly very clear and matter-of-fact.

The sense of malign fate hovering above her was very sharp; Harriet heard the slow black beat of devil-wings and knew it was her own blood pounding. 'What's happening to us, Chris?' she said, suddenly frightened.

'I don't know.' Christina gasped and wept. 'I just don't know. Oh, Harriet, what am I going to do without him?'

'Do you want me to fly out? I will, if it'll help.'

'No. Don't do that. There's police and things I have to deal with. Then I'll have to come back with him — with the . . .' She could not finish the sentence.

'Let me come and be with you.'

'No. I'm all right. And flying's not good for the baby.'

Putting down the receiver Harriet lay back and closed her eyes. She was trembling. Why us? she thought. Both of us widows, so unexpectedly, so young. Out of all the world, why us?

There was no answer that she could have given; not then.

'I can't stay here,' Christina said, immediately after the funeral service. She avoided Harriet's glance. 'I'm sorry, but I simply can't.'

'You shouldn't make any sudden decisions,' Harriet said. 'You should give it time.'

Christina glanced round at the room. 'Everything in here reminds me of him. I want to get rid of it all and start again.' She looked at Harriet with painful eyes and said: 'I know Denis and I seemed an odd combination but we were happy together.'

'I know you were. I know.'

'I don't want to desert you, with the baby and everything, but I shall have to move away, find somewhere that doesn't scream Denis at me every time I turn my head.'

'He'll still be with you wherever you go,' Harriet said gently. 'You can't expunge him entirely. Any more than I can forget Conor ...' *His white back with the freckles laid like flowers on the skin, his black Irish hair, the fine strong sound of his voice, oh Conor ...*

'I don't want to forget him,' Christina said. 'I just don't want to be reminded of him all the time.' She broke down, resting her head on her thin brown arms, her shoulders shaking. 'I've resigned from my job, by the way,' she added.

'Do you think that was wise? You ought to keep busy, take your mind off things.' Strange, thought Harriet, how the clichés rise so easily to the lips in time of stress. Why should Christina keep busy? Maybe long hours brooding was the best form of therapy, maybe keeping her mind on things was the best means of surviving her loss.

'I've got to get right away,' repeated Christina.

Her pretty Cotswold house sold quickly. 'Where will you move to?' Harriet said. She did not speak of her own loss, the rising panic that the thought of losing Christina induced.

'I don't know. To the West Country, perhaps.'

'That's right. Didn't someone leave you a cottage there?'

'Denis's aunt. But we sold that. Didn't I tell you?'

'I don't think so.' Harriet tried to recall what was said when the subject had come up during the fierce storms of two or three years ago. Christina had said something about a rare tree and the aunt having registered it with Kew Gardens. A gecko, or something similar. Gingko? Bulky now, Harriet was too engrossed in the events within her own body to make much effort to remember.

'I might even look for somewhere on the south-east coast, where I grew up,' Christina said. 'The countryside inland is pretty down there.' She was packing glass efficiently into a box, already planning ahead. 'I'll start looking round on Monday. It'll do me good to drive about, give me something to do.'

In the end, she went northwards. 'What do you think?' she asked, visiting Harriet, and showing her a photograph of herself standing outside a stone slate-roofed cottage with wooden trim. Behind lay the smooth line of moors. There was the edge of an estate agent's board, a large tree to one side of the house. 'A pear,' said Christina. 'According to the agent, it produces tons of fruit every year.'

'Where is it?'

'Somewhere called Whitemoor. That's how they pronounce it, anyway, although it's spelt Whitmoor. It's only about three hours' drive from here. Once I'm established, I can easily drive down to see you.'

'Are there other houses around? It looks kind of lonely.'

'Plenty. It's a village — a small town, almost. Lots of nice people there. There's a solicitor living on one side and a headmaster and his family on the other. Couldn't be more respectable.'

'You'll probably enjoy it up there.' Harriet held the photograph at arm's length. 'It looks nice.' She heaved herself up from the sofa and headed towards the kitchen. 'Very nice. I should go for it.'

Christina did. 'It needs a bit of work done to it,' she said. 'I shan't be able to move in until they've done it. I'll have to rent somewhere nearby so I can keep an eye on the workmen.'

'Poor things, you'll nag them rotten.'

'Of course.' Christina looked smug.

The man standing on the doorstep wore jeans, a checked shirt, work-boots and a donkey-jacket. His face was tanned by long exposure to the sun.

'I'd like to speak to Mrs Pearse,' he said. He made some attempt to smooth down unkempt sun-streaked hair; his glance skittered about her swollen body, in an effort to avoid settling on her belly.

'I *am* Mrs Pearse.'

He seemed surprised. 'Mrs Conor Pearse?'

'Yes.'

'Oh, I see.' Hesitations passed behind his eyes; but he came to some decision. Awkwardly he held out his hand. 'I'm Mike Potter,' he said. 'Your — uh — Conor's former boss.'

'Who — oh, yes.' She recognized the voice now. Conor seemed a hundred years ago, in a different life on another planet. 'Would you like to come in?'

In the sitting-room he remained standing. 'I'm just back from the Amazon. I wanted to come and tell you personally how dreadful I feel about your husband's death.'

She sat on the edge of one of the sofas, knees pressed together, staring down at her palms. 'You're very kind,' she said softly. 'It all seems so long ago now, and with this to occupy me . . .' She touched the front of her dress.

'Of course. I didn't want you to think that we had simply forgotten him. He was a marvellous colleague, tireless, enthusiastic. We really miss him. His death . . . the accident was a terrible shock to us.'

'It must have been.'

'Naturally, as his boss, I feel in some way responsible, although nobody could possibly have foreseen . . .'

There was a small pause. She knew he wanted her to ask for more details but she did not wish to ask for them, knowing that once she had received them she would be condemned to keep them in her mind, endlessly re-running footage of Conor, the falling tree, the pressing green jungle. She got to her feet. 'Would you like something, Mr Potter? Coffee? A drink?'

'No, thanks.' Awkwardly he fumbled in his pocket and pulled out a card. 'If you need to call me at any time; if there's anything further I can do . . .' He put it on the mantelpiece, behind one of her jugs.

'You're very kind,' she said again. Conor was gone; that stretch of her life was over now. She could not imagine any circumstances in which she might need to call on Mike Potter. Nonetheless, she thanked him.

She drove out to help Christina with the last pieces of

packing. 'We all accumulate so much stuff,' Harriet said, surveying Chris's closets. 'It's embarrassing, when you think of people who've got nothing.'

'I know. And, believe me, I'm embarrassed.'

'Where shall I start?'

'You could take those things off their hangers and stick them in the cases on the bed,' Christina said. 'I'm going to more-or-less live out of suitcases for the next month or two, otherwise I'd leave the whole lot for the movers to pack.'

Harriet folded silk, wool, linen, suede. Nothing but the best for Christina, she thought wryly. And with that kind of financial investment in clothes, it would be highly uneconomical to get yourself pregnant and risk having to buy a whole new wardrobe afterwards.

Bending, with difficulty, to the floor, she began to pick up shoes and stack them in cardboard.

'Honestly, Chris,' she said. 'You've got more shoes here than Imelda Marcos.' She turned, with a pair of yellow and mustard sling-backs in her hands. 'These are gorgeous.'

'They are rather, aren't they.' Christina looked up. Her face changed dramatically and she got up from the edge of the bed, where she was wrapping gloves in tissue paper. 'Heavens above, darling, let me do that. You can't possibly pick stuff up off the floor with a tummy like that.'

'I can manage — just.' Harriet reached further into the closet.

'No. Absolutely not. I insist. Here, take my arm and I'll help you up.' Chris stood over her. 'I'll take over here.'

Later, sitting with mugs of tea in their hands, Harriet said: 'I'm going to miss you dreadfully, Chris.'

'And me you, love. You know that. But I'll ring you all the time, though it'll have to be from a call-box until the telephone's installed.' She eyed Harriet critically. 'How much longer now?'

'Three weeks.'

'You will take care of yourself, won't you?'

'Of course.'

'Is that foreign chap still around?'

'If you mean Stephan, yes, he's around. But he's not really foreign. And we're not' — Harriet felt herself flush — 'lovers or anything.'

Although we share a bed sometimes, she thought, and perhaps might be lovers if I was not so huge, if I felt that way about him, that surging sickening joy I knew with him once; that I knew with Conor. Sometimes she wondered how Stephan would behave if he suspected that the baby might not be Conor's but his own.

'Make him look after you,' ordered Christina. 'I'll send you my telephone number the minute I have one. I'll drive down to be with you as soon as anything happens.' She took Harriet's face in her hands. 'And forgive me,' she said quietly, 'for running out on you like this.'

STEPHAN

· 7 ·

The woman in the seat next to his was panicking. It was obvious from her brightness, the over-controlled manner in which she reached into her airline bag and brought out a small pile of books; the way she then carefully aligned them on the pull-down table attached to the back of the seat in front. As she fumbled around with her seat-belt, she caught his eye, and he saw in hers a terrified recognition of imminent death.

He wanted to take her hand in his and soothe her. He wanted to explain, as he would have done to his mother Helena, that the chances of their plane coming down were almost non-existent, that every day, all over the world, millions of people arrived safely at their destinations, that statistics were in their favour; that anyway if there was a bomb on board, death would be quick and unexpected; and if they crashed into the side of a mountain, she would be too busy screaming to feel anything before that final moment of obliteration.

He said none of these things. To do so might give substance to fears carefully held in check. She was a stranger, older than himself; she would have her own protective mechanisms. Besides, she might not understand his desire to calm, to enfold; or, if she did, might suspect it to be something other than it was. Outside the ovoid windows, Los Angeles wheeled away from them as the pilot banked, turning into his scheduled flight-pattern towards the East Coast.

Over the Rockies, the FASTEN SEATBELTS sign lit up as they hit a patch of turbulence. The plane shuddered. Stephan's neighbour blinked, biting her lower lip. Then, seeing his glance on her, she said: 'I simply hate flying.'

'It's the safest way to travel.' Stephan prepared to give her statistics, thinking: English, middle-class, decisive in a way that showed she was used to authority.

'And it can't be much fun for you to have me sitting next to you having forty thousand fits for the next six hours or so,' she went on, as if he had not spoken.

'From what I can judge,' he said, 'having you next to me looks as though it will be a great pleasure.'

The compliment made her smile. He saw her hands relax. 'Well, now ...'

He indicated the stewardess trundling a trolley up the narrow aisle. 'When she gets here you must let me buy you a drink ...'

'There's really no need.'

'... medicinal, of course.'

She laughed. 'Alcohol does tend to dull the apprehension.' She had a pretty smile. He watched her assess him — big, fair, nearly half her age — and find him unthreatening. He guessed her to be fiftyish; beneath the unkindnesses of time, it was easy to see the girl she had once been. He reflected that for older women this must be a perpetual source of grief.

The plane lurched again and he lightly patted her hand. Impervious to the possibility of disaster, a girl across the aisle was laughing at something her companion had said. Looking at her, Stephan felt the familiar involuntary jolt of potentiality that, he supposed, most men experienced at the sight of an attractive woman. At base, we are all sexual creatures, he thought: all prisoners of our own biology. The girl was tanned, her hair — yellow streaked with gold — tied back with a piece of flowered cotton. Firm-skinned, clear-eyed, she reminded him of Harriet: the same flowing hair, the same air of someone still half-asleep, still unaware of the power simmering inside her.

Lovely Harriet. Was she ever reminded of *him*? The echo of wrong done sounded along the corridors of his mind. With Harriet he had behaved badly; he had been younger then, impatient, ambitious, unwilling to commit himself at that stage in his life, unwilling to settle for one woman when there were so many still to discover. Above all, too cowardly to tell her about the one he had most recently discovered. At the time he had excused himself with the thought that she needed someone older than he, someone steadier; he hoped now, as the flight attendant wheeled the drinks trolley towards him, that she had found him. Looking back, he was appalled at the flimsiness of the rationalisation with which he had permitted himself to cause her pain. For most of his final year at university he had been in ferment over her. He knew his feelings were reciprocated, yet he had brutally expelled her from his heart when it became necessary. Remembering he felt uncomfortable: he did not see himself as a brutal man.

Harriet — there had been a parent missing, had there not? A father who had died when she was still a child, was it? No. He pushed at his memory and it came back to him with a rush. Unusually, it was a mother Harriet had lacked, a mother who had absconded, leaving her and a brother. He had met the father once. He was a man full of a hard-to-calculate charm: it had been difficult to decide whether it was surface only, assumed for the occasion, or whether it extended as far as the heart.

Once more the plane staggered in the sub-zero winds outside; the yellow-haired girl laughed again, putting a hand on her companion's arm. Beside him his neighbour tensed. He felt a tenderness for her, a wish to comfort and sustain that the blonde girl — young, assured, desirable — did not inspire. He glanced across the aisle and saw she was leaning forward, trying to see out of the window next to him; catching his eye, her face immediately gathered in to itself, repelling the possibility of invasion before it was even broached. He looked away.

He was fascinated by the diversity of women. Or, rather, by the fact that however diverse, they all had in common the burden of their own vulnerability. Each one carried it around like an extra hand, like a hump, inseparable from themselves: a precious egg that must be always protected from breaking in case it produced some monstrous, life-threatening force.

His neighbour ordered a martini from the stewardess; he had whisky. She would not let him pay, but clearly felt that she owed him for the drink he had not needed to buy. Politely she made conversation:

'Will this be your first visit to England?' She spoke like a well-behaved little girl, coached in courtesy.

'I *am* English,' he said.

'You don't sound it.'

'Oh.' He was put out. 'I've been living for some time in the States — I've probably picked up the accent.'

'No. There's something definitely ... European about your voice.'

'My parents are not English,' he said.

'Where are they from?'

'Czechoslovakia.'

'Ah.'

'And you yourself, you are English?'

'Absolutely. Born and bred.'

'And where do you live?'

'Here and there. Mostly Hampshire,' she said. 'Near Winchester. And you?'

'In the Yorkshire Dales.'

'Beautiful country. I used to walk there a lot.'

'Not now?'

'Not recently.' He saw enlarging sentences gather in her mouth and then, as she decided she might be boring him, dissipate. She tipped her glass at him and opened the first book on her pile.

And I cannot tell her that she would not bore me, Stephan thought. I cannot say that, to me, all lives are extraordinary, that I, acutely, am aware of how extraordinary those who appear ordinary can be.

She was reading *The Cherry Orchard.* Was she teacher, academic, actress? She was the right age to play Madame Ranyevskaya. He glanced sideways again but her profile remained unfamiliar. He tried to remember when he had last seen the play performed — he never failed to feel sick at the ominous thud of the axe in the final scene. Perhaps for him its echoes rang too loud.

He closed his eyes.

It was hard to know where his own memories ended and those of his parents took over. The tanks, for instance. Had he really heard them rumbling over the cobbles, tireless and inexorable, or had he merely seen them do so on film? It seemed unlikely that as a small child he would have been out on the streets of the city, even in such stirring times. Yet he distinctly remembered the smell of them, oil and metal and something that must have emanated from the men inside: tobacco, sweat and a distillation of fear. He could still hear the grind of them if he cared to listen; he could still feel the way his scalp had tightened as one of the long gun barrels slowly swung around to focus on the silent gathered crowds, had searched blindly for a target, had found — or so it seemed to him — among the many the single terrified one who was him. He could still remember, if he tried hard enough, exactly how his cap had felt on his head, its weight there yet somehow lifted. Later, coming across the phrase in a book, he had decided that his hair must literally have been standing on end.

On the other hand, his father always insisted that they were not in Prague when the Russians came.

'What do you know?' he used to say when Stephan argued the point. 'You were just a child.'

'But I remember it so clearly.'

'We were at the weekend cottage. We could not have been there.'

'We were.'

'No.'

'*I* was.'

Reluctant to relinquish his memories, Stephan had come to believe that this denial of his father's was simple expedience. After the years of repression, it must have become automatic to establish one's absence from any trouble-spot. One never knew when events would overtake one, and, as trouble-spots went, Prague in the spring of 1968 was among the worst.

*

Looking back, Stephan felt his life to have started off badly. Tears, sombre voices, men banging tables, women weeping quietly together, knocks at the door in the middle of the night, terror. Mostly Helena's: it had permeated their flat, powdering the furniture, the curtains, the plants on the windowsill, even the food they ate, with a thin dust of despair. Several times his father, a professor at the university, had been taken away. Each time he returned, the space in the tall rooms had grown more clogged with his mother's fear, more palpable, anticipating the next time or the time after that. Sometimes Stephan felt that it might choke them if any of them took too deep a breath. Young though he had been, he had registered and been moved by the fragility of her, the ease with which he sensed she might disintegrate if pressed too far. Often, the droop of her head as she listened to the radio returned to him, and with it, his own urgent, impotent desire to comfort her.

The radio had determined the patterns of their lives. Its scratchy voice provided a background to everything they did, heeded more particularly when the news bulletins came on, but nonetheless omnipresent, imperious. One of Stephan's abiding memories was of hearing Dubcek's voice as he told of the results of his visit to Russia. Stephan had not understood the full import of what he said, but he would never forget the choking emotion with which he spoke, the sighing, desperate catch of his breath.

Invasion. Tanks on the streets, impassioned speeches, flowers and bayonets and death. Listening with his mother to the news bulletins, his own forehead had mirrored the frown on hers, though the news had meant little to him then.

His father had come home from the university to tell them he was dispossessed, jobless. Helena had cried. For Stephan, his father took on a new identity, the way a snake emerges from its old skin; indeed, he saw him in his mind's eye as wriggling and slithering out of the grey suits and white shirts he used to wear and assuming the clothes of a different man — sweaters, old trousers, a cotton scarf instead of a shirt. At first his father held seminars in their apartment: his former students came, easing through the front door with the flimsy solidity of ghosts, backward-staring, faces drawn with the tension of defying the edicts of the state.

Stephan listened to their voices, subdued, hopeless. He heard his father declare: 'This system is iniquitous. It forces us to lead two lives, to become two people, to do one thing and feel another, to say one thing and think the opposite.'

There were murmurs of agreement:

'The system is too inflexible.'

'Designed for second-raters.'

'It encourages only those who do not wish to exert themselves.'

His father said: 'We shall end up as a nation of self-perpetuating mediocrities.'

The police came for him yet again: the thump of his big body being dragged down the carpetless concrete stairs of the building sounded like — might even have been — blows. Stephan and Helena stood on the top landing, listening. Apart from the thuds receding down the dim-lit stairwell, there was only the hiss of rasping breath and the occasional grunt of effort. Afterwards Stephan was to wonder at the fact that there had been no word spoken by either captors or captive. Close behind him he could feel his mother's rigid body and the trembling of her hand on his shoulder but could think of no way in which to assuage her fear except to pat it with his own, as he had seen his father do.

Later his father found himself a job as a night-watchman at the very university where he had once taught. Later still he moved his wife and son out of Prague to the weekend cottage in the country.

The radio spluttered. A voice spoke, not Czech but English, telling of a student burned to death in protest at the invaders. Stephan's father, explaining what had happened, had wept. 'We must leave,' he said. 'I can no longer remain in a country where such things can happen. We must leave.'

'Where are we to go?' Helena said.

'I don't know.'

'Will they let us go?'

'If not, we must escape.'

'Exiles?' Stephan's mother said. 'Refugees?'

'We shall run right across Europe, if necessary.' There was a kind of satisfaction in his father's voice.

'My sister,' said Helena. Stephan would never forget the lightening of her face. 'We could go to my sister in America.'

His father shook his head. 'No. It is too far away. I need to stay in touch with people here.'

'There are letters, aeroplanes, we could —'

'No.'

Watching his mother's drawn, resigned face, Stephan learned the powerlessness of women.

In the end they had crossed Europe with only the clothes they stood up in.

'And a pack of food,' Helena said. 'All I was able to put together before we left.'

'What did we have?' Stephan asked, knowing perfectly well.

'Oranges,' she said. 'I saved them for weeks. Oranges, a few rolls, chocolate.'

Although he could not remember the oranges, they assumed for him the sacred aura of communion wafers; they hung in his mind, special, bright as ornaments. The chocolate, eaten in stealth, the rich dark smell of it, the sense of something strong and warm in the middle of confusion, remained with him for the rest of his life.

'We held your hand,' his mother would say, coiling her hair in front of the mirror. It was his favourite story. 'We stayed in the woods all day. You were drugged, sedated, in case you cried out.'

'What happened when it got dark?' He knew already. She only had to provide the cast of characters: he had seen enough films to be able to set the scene for himself, to place barbed wire, guard dogs, floodlights, in appropriate positions.

'When it got dark, then we ran. Faster and faster, across the border. We had you between us, each one holding a hand.' She laughed, looking at her own placid beautiful reflection. 'I don't think your feet touched the ground once.'

'Did anyone come after us?'

'No.' Helena, safe now, the anxiety of those days and nights long since faded into the past, remembered how it had been. The dark clear night, smelling of pine-trees, of moss, of some pungent leaf crushed under them, of the urine they had necessarily passed during the day, of orange peel; the glow of a town far on the other side of the border; the absolute, integral silence. There were guards somewhere near; during the day they had watched them pass back and forth a quarter of a mile away. Josef, as always, had read, leaving her to watch over the child. It ought to have felt dangerous; but it had not. Not after the past year, the abuses, the harassment, the corruption, the gradual erosion of self-respect. 'No one came after us,' though there had been a dog which barked, and male voices much closer than either she or Josef had expected. 'No, we ran through the night for a while. We sheltered under a rock until daytime. In the morning we found someone to help us.'

She makes it sound so matter-of-fact, Stephan would think, hearing the story again and again through the years of his growing up. So *ordinary*. And yet it is extraordinary. This whole life we live is extraordinary, given what it should have been, given the way it started out. Europe — the concept rather than the actuality — possessed a meaning for him that it could not possibly hold for the other children in his school. Falling asleep, he could picture himself so clearly, dangling between parental arms, the three of them running, running across a giant map, across country after country, across borders: Austria, Germany, Yugoslavia, France, the names streaming behind them, banners in the wind of their escape.

The past, extraordinary, made the ordinariness of the present that his parents constructed all the more emphatic. Once they had settled in the north of England, his father was seemingly content to work as a gardener. His mother, who had trained in Prague as a librarian, now ran a boarding-house. Her elder sister wanted them to come and live with her in the States; his father refused. He spent his spare time writing polemical articles for little newspapers and journals; occasionally he disappeared to London to speak on the BBC World Service.

His parents seemed sufficient unto themselves, anxious to blend in, to shrink back into the landscape, to go unnoticed. They spoke only English to each other and to Stephan. When the stirrings of adolescence made him consider them in the act of making love, he was to wonder what language they used to each other in intimacy. They listened assiduously to the radio, mouthing phrases which took their fancy; watching television, they repeated sentences aloud, trying to catch the English intonation. They worked hard at being unremarkable, as though afraid of being discovered.

Yet at the same time, under the ordinariness, there was always a seam of excitement, a constant quivering on the edge of momentous happenings. News, always bad, punctuated his growing-up: police brutality, Charter 77, Laterna Magica, friends imprisoned, friends beaten, friends unable to work, friends whose books were banned, whose positions at the university were taken away, letters telling not so much of atrocities as of bleakness, resignation, despair.

The guest-house was remote, standing on a slope overlooking a lake. Its purchase had been made possible by a gift of money from Stephan's aunt and her husband, the wealthy owner of a chain of shoeshops. Because it stood on the edge of walking country, its rooms were always filled with hikers. Cagoules hung like brilliant parrots in the dim spaces of the hall; mud-encrusted boots stood tidily in the spacious porch. Strangers ate his mother's cooking.

The garden of the house was large and L-shaped, outlined by dry-stone walling. Beyond rolled the moors. In winter they ran up to the cold sky; in summer the view of their rounded contours was interrupted by a huge willow tree which stood at the far end of the garden. Its fronds hung right down to the grass, like a skirt under which he could hide. Inside, it was green, peaceful, unsuspected. Sitting there, behind the ropes of greenery, he could hear people talking, see people — hikers — lounging in garden chairs, doing up bootlaces, rubbing ankles with wintergreen.

The tree was his place. He spent hours, in the summertime, lying on his back, watching the long leaves shift against the sky. When the wind blew, the whole tree shook.

He had reached puberty before he became aware of a more sinister thread in his life. Getting off the school bus with a boy who lived nearby, he invited him in for tea. In the big warm kitchen they found Stephan's father sitting at the table, staring at nothing in particular. Instead of greeting them, he seized one of the cooking knives and held it in front of him.

'Who is this?' he demanded.

'Paul Chambers.' Stephan thought his father must be playing some kind of game. He laughed.

'Why have you brought him here? What does he want?'

'He's come for tea.' Embarrassed, Stephan looked at his friend.

Josef began circling around the table, fixing his gaze on the two boys, the knife poised in front of him. His breath hissed through his teeth; he seemed to grow even larger, as though he had put on extra flesh, extra menace. Stephan did not know what to make of this red-faced staring man: his father, yet unknown. As Josef reached the door leading to the rest of the house it opened and Helena came in.

Hardly pausing, she took the knife from her husband. 'You have been asleep, Josef,' she said as she passed in front of him. Stephan recognised that the statement was both explanation and cover-up. He did not understand for what.

His mother smiled. 'Hello, Paul.' She produced cakes, scones, jam.

The scene was never referred to between them; it was to be years before Stephan brought anyone home again. It is ironic, he used sometimes to think, that this house is always full, and yet it is with strangers, not with friends.

A school trip was planned to Prague. Excited at revisiting the place where he had once known a sort of terror, a place where he had lived, he told his parents, assuming his participation would be automatic.

His father, pale, stood up. 'No,' he said. His broad face shook back and forth. 'You must not go.'

'Why not?' Stephan looked from one to the other of them. 'Why can't I?'

'You could be arrested ... imprisoned ...' Josef sank back into his chair and buried his face in his hands.

It seemed absurdly theatrical to Stephan. He found himself obstinate, determined. 'I'm a schoolboy,' he said. 'They wouldn't arrest me.'

'You have no idea what they might do.' Josef slapped at the newspaper beside his plate. 'Every day there are stories, people taken away and never heard of again. I have letters from friends ...'

'It would be best to listen to your father,' Helena said. She too was pale as she looked at her son.

'It's ridiculous,' said Stephan. A tall ochre-painted building, a bridge lined with black statues, suddenly came into his mind: where was that? 'You can't stop me going back to my own country.'

'This is our country, Steffi,' his mother said gently. She seemed sad.

He saw his past being snatched from him; he saw his own roots, white and tendrilled, suddenly begin to shrivel. For the first time a sense of nationality filled him, though lightly. 'You won't be able to stop me when I am older,' he said rudely.

'Perhaps, when you are older, you will not wish to go,' Helena said.

News broke of the murder of Georgi Markov, a prominent Bulgarian dissident and one of Josef's colleagues on the World Service.

'That is the end.' Josef threw down the newspaper.

'What do you mean?' Stephan looked at his mother, but she was busy shaping loaves out of the dough she had prepared earlier in the day.

'I can no longer go to London,' said Josef.

'Why not?'

'It could be me next. Look at this.' Stephan saw a grainy photograph of a pellet with three holes in it. 'Murderers.'

'What is it?'

'Poison.' Josef's prematurely white hair seemed to shake with indignation. 'Injected with an umbrella tip. They are devils — fiends.'

'Why would anyone want to kill you?'

'As a lesson to others back home.'

'But he was from another country.'

'Nonetheless, it is intended to make all of us toe the line. And as a warning to me.'

It seemed absurd. Stephan nonetheless accepted it. One does not, after all, suspect that one's father may be mad.

As a child, he had seen the hikers, the overnight guests, as a diversion; at school and university, they became an intrusion, distancing his foreign parents even further from his own understanding of the country in which he had grown up. He had been denied his roots. Assimilated, almost-English, he resented the fact that these hearty people in socks knitted from coarse parti-coloured wool, had more in common with him than his own parents had. He disliked being on the same side as strangers, while his parents stood on an opposite shore.

Looking back, he was better able to understand why Josef had acted in the way he did. At the time it seemed merely an act of capricious cruelty. Looking at the devastation his father had caused, Stephan had wanted to ask why. Instead, he had simply turned away.

· 8 ·

Next to him, the woman let out her breath as the aircraft took off from JFK. Apologetically she said: 'I'm not so nervous once we're off the ground ...'

They had touched down in New York. New passengers had embarked; the girl who looked like Harriet had gone, along with her companion. Watching her hair recede down the aisle, Stephan wondered briefly how Harriet was. It might be interesting to look her up when he was settled: he had six months in England before taking off again for Brussels. Since leaving university he had spent hardly any time in England and consequently, apart from his parents, knew the whereabouts of almost none of his former friends. As an adviser to the European Economic Community on ecological problems, liable to be sent all over the Continent whenever an environmental issue raised its head, it was a pattern that was likely to repeat itself over the next few years. He thought wryly: my patterns were established long ago. At twenty-eight I'm still running across Europe, but now the names of disasters stream in my wake: Chernobyl, Romania, the Rhine, the North Sea ...

'... shortly passing the northern tip of Maine before ...' The captain's voice sounded above the engines' hum.

He craned to look out of the window. Spangled against the night sky, the northern seaboard glittered. Odd to think that he had been a boy down there, once, looking up as planes passed overhead ...

'You are to spend the summer with your aunt,' Helena said. Her eyes veered away from his. She was hulling strawberries picked from the garden. He knew she was about to say something that was incomplete, that was as close to lying as she was capable of.

'My aunt in America?'

'Yes.'

'Why?' The ripe berries lay richly in a cut-glass bowl, each one snowed with a sprinkle of caster-sugar.

'Because she has never seen you and would like to. She has sent the money for your ticket. You will enjoy it.' During their early years in England, Helena had favoured short sentences as being less likely to drop her into semantic pitfalls. Now they had become habitual.

The reason given for the visit was insufficient; having watched his mother's anxiety about his father increase with the years, he could guess what had been left unsaid. 'I am to go alone?'

'Yes.'

She was probably right — he would enjoy it. Stephan enjoyed almost everything, even the vast shaking sorrows which from time to time overwhelmed him. Nonetheless he thought it prudent to object.

'But my aunt has no children. What am I going to do for weeks and weeks on my own?'

'Perhaps she will find someone for you to play with.'

'I'm too old to play,' he said. When had he ever been young enough?

'To do things with, then.'

'What things?' Stephan thought it unlikely: his favourite pastime was reading, and it was not an activity which could be shared. On the other hand, someone who — for instance — enjoyed T.S. Eliot, for whose work he had recently conceived a passion, someone who might possibly have read the complete works of P.G. Wodehouse, someone even who was as moved by Dylan Thomas ... 'Who? Who will she find?'

'I really don't know, Steffi. But I'm sure you'll have fun.'

He would like to have said that fun was not something he had ever really had — not since he had left Prague. Sometimes he was sure he remembered that forest where they had cowered, could feel again the sense of danger which must have sparked between the three of them like electric currents, charging the air with a hot dry energy. After such an experience, how could anyone be content merely to have *fun*, especially in the sense his mother meant it? He saw her brow crease, the two small lines gather between her eyebrows, apprehension darken her eyes. Letters must have passed between the two sisters. He thought it probable that Helena had requested this invitation for Stephan to visit, had perhaps even mentioned her husband's increasing mental instability.

Thinking this, his eyes went involuntarily to the window. He could see the stump at the end of the garden, all that remained of his willow tree; beyond it the moors spread smooth and lonely under the sky. It was a view he could not enjoy, remembering what it had been like in spring when the yellow-green shoots first appeared, the fronds catkinned and delicate; or, on summer days, lying inside the tent of long dark leaves; remembering, too, the thud of the axe, the thick smell of sap, the devastation.

He wished he could still love his father. He had been horrified at the murderous rage which had seized him at the sight of the severed stump. Almost he had grabbed the axe from his father's hand and brought it down on his head. It had been impossible for him to disguise the loathing he then felt.

Not having siblings himself, he was intrigued by the dissimilarities between his aunt and his mother. That they should share so many quirks of behaviour — the tilt of the mouth, the sudden snickering sneezes, the voice — was expected. That the one should be so fraught with problems and the other so carefree, so happy, seemed somehow unnatural. They came from the same womb, he told himself, picturing the womb as something mysterious, crimson and secret; they are filled with the same blood, how can they be so unalike? He had not until now thought of Helena once being a child; here, with her sister, he was able to visualise the two girls as they must then have been. He saw them in frilled pinafores, hair loose, running through meadows of flowers towards blue mountains, an image shaped by illustrations in the books of his childhood brought by exiled friends.

Susanna, his aunt, was smaller than Helena, trimmer, her face tauter. She laughed freely, showing white teeth.

'Goodness,' she said, meeting him off the plane at New York. 'You're so large. I hadn't expected someone so big.'

He grinned at this new relation, embarrassed.

'Helena talks about you as though you were still a child,' his aunt said. 'You look more like a man, to me.' There was admiration in her eyes. He enjoyed that. He felt masculine and brave.

She led the way to a car, a long shiny Mercedes. As they drove northwards, she talked.

Nothing she said was of much consequence. Nonetheless — or perhaps because of that — he fell completely in love with her, and, in so doing, wished he could take the same uncomplicated pleasure in his mother as he did in his aunt. He followed Susanna about the house, rejoicing in the way her dark hair fell around her shoulders, in the bright colours she wore, in the smell of her soaps and creams, the glitter of the cut-glass scent bottles on her dressing-table. She never did any housework yet the house never seemed dirty. Where Helena wrestled with recipes, kneaded dough, whipped eggs, poured cream, Susanna seldom cooked anything more complicated than roast chicken, joints, steaks.

He loved the superfluity, the sheer lavishness of her. The house was full of objects, duplicated, heaped, overflowing: televisions, soap, cushions, knives — all objects that Helena would buy only one at a time and use thriftily until finished or worn out. There was a bounteousness about Susanna that thrilled at the same time as it slightly alarmed him, as though he were party to some minor crime. But what he liked best about her was her ability to enjoy herself. Previously he had taken as the norm the gravity of the existence his parents led. Now he saw that there were other ways to approach life; hedonism enveloped without overwhelming him. Susanna would look at him across the breakfast table — muffins, orange-juice, pastries; a far remove from the sober breakfasts of porridge or cereal that he was used to — and say: 'I feel really sinful this morning, don't you?'

Stephan, who had never consciously felt sinful in his life, would nod. Yes, indeed, as far as he was able to encompass sinfulness, he was ready to sin with his aunt in whichever way she ordained.

'Let's go and spend *lots* of money!' she would cry, and off the two of them went to do so. She bought him clothes: jeans and running shoes, baseball caps, striped shirts with button-down collars, jackets of a tweed that passed for English but would never have been worn by an Englishman, T-shirts displaying iron-on messages of various kinds which she invented and had made up on the spot. None of it could be worn when he returned home: nonetheless he treasured each item, wore them to accompany her up and down the aisles of department stores and supermarkets, stored them up against the future.

'I just *have* to have a new blouse,' she would say, or 'I really need a sweater,' though he knew that she already had racks of blouses, drawers full of sweaters. Passing displays of china, of lingerie, of jewellery, she would pause in front of the window, drawing in her breath in a sigh of pleasure before rushing in to buy. Stephan felt that the whole of America was one giant shopping-mall designed specifically to tempt his prodigal aunt into spending money.

In the food market she would move unseeing past the dull bags of flour or sugar, the jars of olive-oil and workaday bottles of vinegar. Not for Susanna were such grocerial mundanities. 'I want something luxurious, don't you, Stephan?' she would say, and he would agree, knowing that she *always* wanted something luxurious, that luxury for Susanna was a necessity. He loved the way she always included him, always asked for his opinion.

'Smoked salmon? Chocolates? Caviar?' She offered him the prodigal world, assuming his familiarity with it, and he took it from her with outstretched hands. At lunchtime the two of them would gorge on salt-beef, pastrami, avocados, chili —

things he had never heard of, let alone tasted; even if such esoterica existed in England, or had percolated through to the small market town where Helena shopped.

On the way back to the house they sometimes drove past the harbour to pick up boiled lobsters, half a dozen of them at a time; their hard red bodies banging together in a brown paper sack, the claws bound with black rubber bands.

'I don't like to think about them dying,' Susanna said, her strong teeth crunching the claws, squeezing out the pink flesh, dunking it into a large bowl of garlic-flavoured mayonnaise. 'Poor things. Such an agonising death.' Her face would register sympathy, disgust, regret before she looked across at her husband, Richie. 'But *sooooo* delicious!' And she would smile, showing dimples similar to those which sometimes appeared in Helena's cheeks.

Susanna's house was large and raw, as though its red brick and fake Corinthian pillars had been planted on the bare soil only the week before. Had he been older, Stephan might have called it brash. Everything sparkled, everything seemed still to possess the stamp of newness, as if the price tags had just that minute been removed. In the evenings Richie and Susanna indulged in what Stephan, used to the steady application of his parents, could not help regarding — at first — as a shameful waste of time. They watched television, played games, went to the cinema, ate out. The television was huge; Susanna and Richie would lounge in front of it on one of the vast sofas with which the house was filled. The two of them sat entwined; during the advertising breaks they would give each other noisy kisses. At first, Stephan was embarrassed by their uninhibited pleasure in each other. When Richie's large hands fondled Susanna's breasts under one of the soft fluffy sweaters she wore, he looked away, clearing his throat, or picking up a magazine. However, as the summer progressed, he came to see such caresses as natural, as ordinary, and his own parents' careful avoidance of contact with each other — at least in front of him — as perverse. He learned, too, that what his parents would have scorned as time-wasting was in fact quite the opposite. Susanna and Richie filled their time with each other.

Susanna had other disturbing habits. There was a pool to one side of the house, blue as a kingfisher. Here she lay for an hour each afternoon, before plunging into the water to swim slowly up and down a dozen times. Sometimes she lay topless; sometimes she removed her costume altogether. She had a sturdy body; to Stephan, surreptitiously watching the sweat break out beneath and between her dark-nippled breasts, it seemed entirely beautiful. He had never seen his mother naked, never even glimpsed breast or thigh: his aunt's strong nudity was to be for years his exemplar of female perfection.

Long afterwards, he was to wonder whether Susanna was aware of her effect upon a boy just breaking in to manhood, whether she had hoped for something more from him than mere glances, whether she dreamed of his body and hers, one so dark, so contained, the other golden, flowing, still undiscovered. Perhaps, displaying herself to him, she had wanted him to touch her, engage with her. Certainly there had never been anything overt either said or done, though the swell of his groin inside his bathing-suit was sometimes almost unbearable.

He did not ask why there were no children in the house. He was old enough, sensitive enough, to realise that somewhere there was a grief which had been dealt with, a neatly-packaged pain put away in some emotional closet. Susanna's eyes sometimes rested on him with an expression he found hard to interpret; catching his glance, she would smile and busy herself with other things. Although he would not have been able to articulate the feeling, it was obvious to him that she mourned for something she did not have; that however many things she purchased in the shiny shopping malls, however much she spent, she would never be able to fill her inner void. Brought up in a household where emotion had been deliberately dispensed with, he had not, until now, understood that adults were capable of experiencing the same storms of feeling as he himself.

Adolescent, clever, he had been prepared to patronise the clumsy uncle who had, as he frequently told Stephan, left school without any formal qualifications at all. It proved, however, impossible to patronise Richie, even supposing Stephan had continued to wish to do so. Stephan came to see that intrinsic worth is not measured in academic qualifications, that a man who was able to generate the happiness that Susanna enjoyed, possessed a gift that no amount of formal training could guarantee. The knowledge changed the boy's perspectives.

'Steffi doesn't want to hear all that old stuff,' Susanna would say indulgently, proudly, as Richie told her how he had forged his own way in the world without any help from anyone, an unashamed self-made man.

'I do,' said Stephan. 'Honestly I do.'

Richie fascinated him. Josef's insistence on scholastic achievement was perceived for the first time to be wrong: Richie was living proof of that. Stephan saw him making his own way, the Candide of the shoe industry, shouldering his way forward through a thicket of cured skins on his long journey from apprenticeship to salesman, from manager to owner of his own place.

Richie took him to see his first shop, the starting-point of the chain which eventually became his empire. It was a tawdry space squashed in between a dry-cleaning establishment and a shop selling sports equipment. Tall wooden shelves, stacked like a library and crammed with open boxes of shoes, filled its small area. The smell of leather was intoxicating.

'Quality,' Richie said, 'that's what you gotta remember, son. Quality's the key to success.'

'Right.'

'You can always tell a lady by the quality of her footwear,' said Richie. 'Remember that. Look at my Susanna: never puts anything on her feet that ain't a top-notch grade-A shoe.'

His big face grew soft, thinking of Susanna. Stephan walked behind him down the narrow aisles, breathing in the hide-scented air. His uncle pulled out shoes as they went, calling on him to note their craftsmanship, their quality: here a thonged sandal from Greece, there an English brogue or a ridge-soled walking shoe.

'And this,' Richie said reverently. 'This is craftsmanship for you, kid. Quality. Take a good look.'

Stephan did, seeing a pair of Italian-made court shoes in sage-green leather as soft as a scarf, with a toe-cap of darker green inset with a tiny motif like a spreading oak. It was lined in palest leather; the waisted heel reminded him of the Court of Versailles. He wished it were possible to become temporarily female so that he might wear them himself.

That night, he dreamed of Susanna, naked except for the green shoes.

The big brick house had no formal garden. Instead, rough grass ran behind it into a forest of pine trees. If the willow had been a room, a tent, these woods were like a cathedral, sweet-scented and silent. Looking up, Stephan could not see the sky. One windy afternoon, walking soft-footed on pine-needles between the thin trunks, he came suddenly, unexpectedly, upon the sea. Huge flat-sided rocks lay tumbled together as though spilled from a giant box; between them the water moved tempestuously. Hitherto, the watery places he had encountered had been placid, grey or brown or green, lapping the foot of stone scree, nibbling at reeds or the roots of willows. He had only seen the sea in books and expected a flat expanse, blue, a boat moving picturesquely across the swell. This sea was all power, flinging itself up against boulders, grabbing at the land and falling away, only to crash forward again. He stood there, entranced. Behind him the pine trees tossed, lashed by a summer storm; in front the sea roared. For a few moments he felt himself to be no longer an inhabitant of his own earthbound body; shaken by an access of yearning, he became elemental, primordial. Briefly he knew the thrill of otherness. Whipped by the wind and the spray, he could not quite catch hold of his own essentiality: it was a moment of pure happiness.

After that he often walked through the trees to the edge of the sea, though after that first time it remained as he had expected it to be, flat, calm, interrupted only by sail and bird, and — once — by seals.

One afternoon, in thin drizzle that turned heavier as he walked, he came out of the wood on to the boulders and heard, above the nose of the rain, a human voice. Turning, he saw further along the shoreline a boy of about his own age; he stood on one of the granite boulders, his face lifted to the sky, his eyes closed, chanting some strange song. Rain had plastered his hair down on his head and ran down his white face like tears. He was naked.

Knowing the boy believed himself to be alone, Stephan melted back into the shelter of the trees. The chant followed him through the woods.

Shopping with Susanna, they met a neighbour.

'My nephew, from England,' Susanna said. 'He's spending the summer with me. Stephan, this is Mrs Seaton.'

The neighbour was thin, patrician, older than Susanna. She had a distant voice. From her look, Stephan suspected that she disapproved of his aunt.

'My grandson is home,' she said. 'Perhaps Stephen would like to come over and visit some time.'

'Is this the boy whose —' Susanna lowered her voice and dropped her eyes as though they were in church '— whose parents —'

Mrs Seaton interrupted firmly before she could finish. 'Yes. How about tomorrow or the next day?'

Stephan, conscious that in his baseball cap and messaged T-shirt he cut a figure somewhat less heroic than he wished, was not enthusiastic but Susanna accepted for him, assuming a graciousness that he had not seen her use before.

'A very good family,' she said as they drove homeward. 'You'll like the boy.'

'How do you know? Have you met him?' asked Stephan.

'Well, no. But he's sure to be nice, coming from that background. Besides, he's probably lonely, poor little kid.'

'Little?' Stephan said, appalled at the prospect of an afternoon with some seven-year-old.

'He may be little, he may not,' said Susanna. 'The thing is, his parents — that's Mrs Seaton's son and daughter-in-law — were drowned recently while sailing just off the coast here.'

Stephan tried to visualise what he would feel if someone told him that Josef and Helena had drowned, had died. A world without them would be unimaginably bleak, insofar as he could visualise such a world in the first place. His feelings for his father were undeniably mixed, but not to have him there at all ... The thought brought tears to his eyes.

'Yes,' Susanna said, seeing them. She took a hand off the wheel and put it round his shoulders. 'It was terribly sad. They were such a nice young couple. A real tragedy.' She shuddered. 'They never did recover one of them — Ellen, the daughter-in-law. The other body was found right on the foreshore, the other side of our woods. The sea had thrown it up on the rocks there.'

He stared at her. The information invested the boulders with fascination. In his mind's eye the flat granite surfaces melted, re-formed, solidified; he knew he would never think of them again without the addition of a body, face-down, spread-eagled, limp. His feet had stood where a dead body lay — the thought somehow unnerved and at the same time extended him; inside his sneakers his toes curled.

Mrs Seaton's grandson was called Tom. Stephan recognised him instantly as the boy who had stood naked on the seashore. He did not mention it. He wondered whether he had been calling somehow to his drowned parents. Looking into Tom's brown eyes, he thought: *the fog is on the briar rose*. He felt suddenly old and very accustomed to death.

Travel is supposed to broaden the mind. Stephan feared that it had merely narrowed his. Returned to England, he found that the layers of tolerance with which he had hitherto regarded the undoubted eccentricities of his existence had, as though they were silver or copper, been beaten to an almost transparent thinness. Particularly, after two months of exposure to Susanna's warmth, he was aware of the chill at the centre of his home. It had not always been like that, he was sure. Once the big fires which burned in the reception rooms, the Aga in the kitchen, had offered comfort; they failed to warm him now. The house full of overnight guests had never seemed cosy; now it seemed positively alien. At night he lay on his back in bed, thinking of Susanna, of her warm brown body languid beside the pool, of her breasts, of the tuft of hair at the divide of her legs. Maine became set for him in a series of scenes: the slabbed rocks by the sea, the columned pine forest, the pool itself growing, as time drew it further away, bluer and more scintillant in retrospect than it could ever have been in actuality. He wished passionately to return to what he perceived not as a different life, but as another world. The thought of Susanna filled his mouth with juice, like an overripe plum.

Like Susanna's, Mrs Seaton's house was big and square. It was covered in white weather-boarding and its windows were flanked by green shutters; the front door, brass-decorated and fan-lighted, imposed. Stephan knew instinctively that despite the shabby paintwork, the worn rugs, the small cobwebs which sat intricately in the corners of the broad window-sills, this was a place of quality and permanence, something which Susanna's house almost deliberately eschewed. The rooms here were shadowed, the windows kept shrouded with heavy drapes to deny entrance to damaging sunlight. There was a great deal of fine plain furniture and, on its slightly dusty surfaces, quantities of glass, porcelain, ivory and carved wood. In the big living-room, silver objects — teapots, sugar bowls, candle-snuffers, vegetable dishes — sat piled together on a tarnished tray on a table by the door.

'It's worth thousands and thousands of dollars,' Tom told him. He rubbed a forefinger over the tray's streaked patina. 'My grandmother carries it upstairs every night and hides it under her bed.'

'Why?' Stephan's eye lingered on chasing and filigree, on engraved initials and heavy leaf-encrusted adornment.

'It's a custom round here.'

'But *why?*'

'So it won't get stolen, I suppose,' Tom said.

'Wouldn't thieves look upstairs as well as downstairs? Maybe even under your grandmother's bed?' Stephen had a vision of somewhere dark and creaking, of dustballs and tired slippers, maybe even a chamberpot, flower-sprigged.

Tom seemed to think this unlikely. 'All her friends do it, too,' he said.

Given that it was common knowledge, Stephan did not say that unless the thieves were from out of town, or extremely stupid, the very first place they would look would surely be under the bed. Thinking of those burglarious hands groping, he glimpsed the danger and impermanence that the ownership of possessions bestows. At the same time he took aesthetic pleasure from the worldly goods which filled the Seaton house.

In particular, his fingers lingered over the fronts of tallboys and breakfronts, on chiffoniers and secretaries and the backs of chairs. He was entranced by the swirls and patterns of the different woods; questioning Mrs Seaton, he learned gradually to distinguish burr walnut from hickory, rosewood from yew, each as individual in its markings as fingerprints. She told him of other lovely woods: amboyna and amaranth, cedar and sycamore. They sounded to him like poetry. He imagined walking through thickets of mahogany, forests of sandalwood, stands of calamander and myrtle and olive, all polished and grained, aromatic, beautiful.

He asked Tom what sort of tree produced rosewood — such dark flamboyance could not have come from the bushes his mother grew back in England — and what a hickory looked like, but Tom did not know the answer. Tom did not know much about anything, in Stephan's opinion. He had never read any P.G. Wodehouse; he professed not to have heard of T.S. Eliot, though Stephan did not see how that could be possible. He put Tom's ignorance down to the effects of trauma, accepting that it might be difficult to read while one's mother still floated like Phlebas the Phoenician, somewhere out on the deep sea swell.

Instead, he sat on salt-spumed grass, or in the lower branches of a giant cedar which swept across the small area of lawn in front of the house, reading aloud, offering Dylan Thomas, Yeats, Eliot to the silent boy at his side. Tom never said, but he seemed to enjoy these long afternoons.

Occasionally they were joined by Tom's cousin, Amis, a large pale boy with a high forehead and big glasses, who lived some miles away. Amis was impressed by the fact that Stephan came from England.

'We're sort of English, aren't we, Tom?' he said.

'Very sort of.'

'Grandfather Seaton came from somewhere near Oxford,' Amis said importantly. He looked at Stephan as though for approval and Stephan perceived that there were situations in which being English was considered a bonus. He did not add, therefore, as he might otherwise have done, that though he came from England, he was in fact not English; like a silent film, the tanks rolled briefly across the backdrop of his mind and the long arm of a gun swung slowly round. He felt like Peter denying his Christ. Guilt nibbled at his psyche, as though he had deliberately tried to destroy something precious.

The three of them talked occasionally of women. Amis, a

couple of years older, alleged that a girl had kissed him on the mouth last Christmas vacation, and that he had put his hand up her skirt.

'What for?' Tom asked.

'What for? Because that's what you do with girls, dumbo,' Amis said. Stephan could tell he hoped not to be questioned more closely on the matter; he deduced an ignorance as total as his own.

'Have you ever seen a naked woman?' he asked.

'No,' said Tom. His eyes looked into a distance that Stephan imagined to be occupied by his lost mother.

'Why?' Amis said. 'Have you?' He stared hungrily from behind his glasses, ready to absorb whatever information was about to be offered.

Stephan hardly hesitated. Loyalty to Susanna, a desire to keep her for himself, made him shake his head. 'No.'

'I wonder what it's like to have a baby,' Amis said.

'Weird, I should think,' said Stephan. 'Fancy having another person growing inside you.'

He had not thought before of himself inside Helena. For fear of rousing the misery which he sensed dozed inside Tom, he changed the subject. He did not wish his friend to remember his mother and be grieved.

He could not help but wonder whether it would have helped if the body had been found. Perhaps, in some secret corner of his mind, Tom still hoped that she was alive somewhere, had been cast up on some alien shore, amnesiac, helpless, had been taken in by kindly fisherfolk, like Shakespeare's Perdita, or a benevolent vicar, and absorbed into a new culture, never realising that it was not her own. Enlarging the fantasy, he speculated that perhaps she — Ellen — lived even now only a few miles up the coast, oblivious of her mourning family, though it was unlikely: there would have been search parties, police enquiries, identity checks. Nor, in that case, would the society have been alien. Though his knowledge of geography was small and his grasp of wind and tide considerably less, even Stephan could not seriously envisage the forever un-knowable Ellen floating undetected all the way down the New

England coast and on past New York and Maryland, across the Chesapeake Bay, past Cape Hatteras and the Carolinas, surviving past Palm Beach and Miami, to end up snagged on the Bahamas or the West Indies or even, having evaded their white beaches and palm-fringed lagoons, tossed starfishlike onto the rocky coast of Colombia or Venezuela.

The night before he left New England for home, a storm blew up. He heard it tearing at the roof, whistling through the screens which covered the windows. Above the noise of the wind he heard a huge groan, the sound tugged up from somewhere deep and painful. When he looked out into the night, it leered greyly back at him from the other side of the glass, tangible, thick with sea mist. Tatters of it still hung in the pine branches when he went out the next morning to take a last look at the places where he had felt so happy. He discovered that one of the trees had been blown down and now leaned in the arms of its fellows, exposing its roots. It seemed to him unbearably sad and yet, at the same time, fitting, as though nature had chosen a suitably dramatic gesture with which to mark his departure.

His parents seemed to have diminished while he was away. Embracing them on his return, he felt the thinness of his mother's body, the hard shape of bones under her clothes. Had she been so eroded when he left for the States, had his father been set so close to the ground? He was ashamed to realise that he could not remember. Time prior to the visit to the States assumed an attenuated air, misted by distance: reality was now, reality was the baseball caps in the new suitcases Susanna had bought him, reality was his broadening stretching body, his strength opposed to his parents' weakness.

They were such frightened people; he often thought that their confrontation with guns, tanks, flight, ought to have reinforced, not weakened them. Judging, he found them wanting. Their past was, he supposed, heroic; they themselves were not. He wanted always to assert his difference from other people; they had assimilated, determinedly, doggedly, muting accent and habit until a stranger meeting them would never have known they had not always been part of where they now were.

And yet, despite all their efforts, they had not been able to slough off their essential foreignness. Their own childhoods still clung to them, redolent of things not known in the Dales, or else long forgotten: of swineherds and goose-girls, of deep forests where witches prowled, of talking trees and princes imprisoned in the bodies of toads, of castles where long-haired maidens languished. His own childhood, on the other hand, seemed peculiarly English, furnished with an endless display of anthropomorphic creatures, Poohs and Piglets, hedgehogs, moles and, above all, rabbits.

School started again. Assembling with his fellows on the first day, he breathed in the familiar smell of polished wooden floors, new wool, lunch and cloakrooms, and was aware of being quite other than they were. He felt he had undergone some rite of passage which none of them could possibly have experienced, though he could not have said precisely what. Strong and sure in his adolescence, bronzed and bleached by the summer sun, he criticised. He thought: my parents live with anxiety; it covers them like a sheen of perspiration. Opened up by Susanna, exasperated, he asked his father what he was so worried about.

'Nothing,' Josef grunted. He sat on the edge of his armchair, holding the brass poker lightly in his hand. There was new weight around his waist; his skin was pasty. His eyes moved continuously, watching the room.

'Then why are you always so tense, Dad? Why can't you relax?'

'Relax? Why should I relax?'

Because you fill the air with tension, Stephan wanted to say; you make it impossible for anyone else — for *me* — to be at ease. On the other side of the hearth, his mother knitted, staring into the logs which burned in the first fire of autumn. There was a small ineradicable frown between her brows. What did she see there, in among the corpses of dead trees? Danger, death, the menacing faces of alien soldiers come to conquer? He tried very hard to imagine it. His mother had been in her twenties then: what had she felt when the tanks rumbled in? Invasion must have been a nightmare come true. He imagined a people in terror, scuttling between doorways, scavenging for scraps, strong shadows cast upon rain-slicked cobbles.

He had always been a good scholar; now he found it hard to concentrate on his books. Bent over them, images of the summer past intervened. The people he had grown up with, with whom he had never had a lot in common, receded as though sucked away from him into a time-warp. Gone into some kind of spatial overdrive, they glittered behind him like dying stars in the darkness of the time before. *When I was but fourteen or so, I went into a magic land* ... He missed Tom Seaton; despite Tom's silences they had become friends, united by the adversity of upheaval.

He went back again to Susanna's house when he was sixteen, just before entering the Sixth Form of his grammar school, and the long grind towards university.

Nothing much had changed, except Stephan himself. The mystery of the place still called to him, the confluence of sea and land, of tree and water, was as heart-stopping as before. This time, however, he looked at his aunt with the sternly austere values of committed youth — Camus-reading, Green-peace member, anti-fur, left-wing — and felt that she failed to live up to expectations. He still loved her, as a parent loves an erring child, but despite the lift he felt at the sight of her smile, he could not admire her materialist, sybaritic values.

Tom Seaton was home that summer. The two years since they last met had changed him. He was still serious, still aura-ed by his loss, but he laughed now, looking forward to what was to come rather than back to what had been lost.

Some evenings he and Stephan sat on the swing seat on the verandah which enclosed the back of the Seaton house and talked about the future. Tom was to go to Yale, where Amis was already a student; it was a family tradition. He would read law, like Amis; when he graduated, he planned to take a year off, go to Europe, visit all the places that he had heard about — Paris, London, Vienna. He would bum around, find a garret and wear a black beret, maybe, though maybe not because of his glasses. Not so much your bohemian, is it? he said; a beret and glasses is more your total wimp. He grinned at Stephan. The two of them rolled about with laughter while the white net curtains of Mrs Seaton's drawing-room billowed towards them, and music from her piano dropped into the quiet night, sweet as lime.

'And you, Stephan?' Tom said, when they could speak again, though the image of Tom in his beret kept intruding, sending them back into giggles. 'What are you going to do?'

'The people at school think I could easily get in to university to study English literature,' said Stephan. 'But I don't know. Maybe not.'

'You used to read a lot of poetry.' Tom said.

'I still do, but it's not *real*, it's not' — he wanted to say *important*, *caring*, but it sounded prissy — 'it's not relevant enough. Maybe I'll do something to do with ...' He looked around at the dark swell of the woods where the grass sloped away. 'Something to do with ecology, maybe. Be a forester, or an environmentalist of some kind. Maybe even a writer.' He shrugged, as though it did not matter, though they both knew that it did, having had it impressed on them enough by their families that the decisions they made at this stage in their lives might have to last them a lifetime.

They bathed off the rocks. Stephan, plunging into the chill water from the edge of a rock, felt a momentary spasm stiffen his body, as though afraid he might find himself knee-deep among the coral bones of Tom's drowned mother or, bursting upwards through the waves to open air, find pearls in his hands that had once been her eyes.

Did Tom feel the same worry? I ought to ask him, Stephan told himself, and not leave this matter of such importance unspoken of. One day I shall do so. I might even tell him that I once saw him naked among these boulders, throwing his misery back at the sea which had caused it. The possibility that the two of them might meet infrequently or never again did not occur to him. Nor, apparently, to Tom.

'When I come to England, I shall stay with you,' he said, stretched out on the warm slope of the boulders. He was skimpy; his hips jutted across the top of his red bathing suit. Water dripped from shoulders half as wide as Stephan's.

'Not if you're wearing that beret,' Stephan replied, determined that Tom should never see the boarding-house, the walkers, the madness of his father's eyes. It was not that he was ashamed of his home, simply that he did not wish his two worlds to overlap, to concentricate.

'I'll take it off in the house. Promise.'

'But I shall know it's in your pocket or somewhere. It wouldn't work. It would haunt me.'

They laughed. 'Let's keep in touch,' Tom said.

'Of course.' Stephan immediately saw letters flying from the nib of his pen to lie on Tom's tables: witty, barbed letters which Tom would keep and which would some day be discovered in a sandalwood box tied with pink tape, to be published with footnotes and reverential glosses by some literary biographer of the time.

'We could even do the trip across Europe together, if you like,' Tom said generously.

'Moscow,' Stephan said. 'Leningrad.'

'Rome. Oxford.'

'Prague.' Stephan's eyes widened at the thought.

Though both of them knew there would be other intervening friends, the thought of this older friendship, predating those not yet formed, gave them a sense of security they scarcely knew they needed. They looked at each other with Europe in their eyes: castles, cathedrals, old stone, Old Masters.

Tom could drive now. They went in Mrs Seaton's Cadillac or Susanna's compact to little seaside towns along the coast. Away from the busy shoreline of these places they found villages that might have come out of an idyll, picket-fenced and shady. One afternoon they visited Tom's aunt and uncle, parents of Amis, brother and sister-in-law of Tom's father. The uncle — Jack — was a lawyer in the little nearby town, a one-man firm handling the affairs of family it had cared for over generations.

The house was dark inside, lined with wood. Bare floors of thick pine planking were spread with hooked rugs, wooden stairs led up from a panelled hall, a round cherrywood table held beech leaves and chrysanthemums arranged in a chip basket. Spare pieces of furniture stood against the walls. Two ladder-backed rocking-chairs stood on either side of an empty hearth. There was a museum-like sense of peace, almost of spirituality, about the place. It was very quiet.

'It's a beautiful house,' Stephan said. He touched the surface of a chest of drawers, feeling the smoothness, knowing that someone had worked to keep it so unadorned.

Elizabeth, Tom's aunt, nodded. 'Yes. I had very little to do with it, of course.' She offered them iced tea in tall glasses, and put a plate of homemade cookies on the table. The underside of the plate gleamed in the table's surface.

'What did you think of my son's collection?' Mrs Seaton said when they returned to the clapboard house. She was drinking white wine on the verandah, fanning herself. The swing seat creaked back and forth; the smell of the sea was strong.

'Which collection?' Stephan wondered what he had missed, but could remember nothing. Apart from the furniture, the house had been plain, almost barren.

'He has one of the finest collections of Shaker furniture outside a museum,' said Mrs Seaton. 'Surely you realised.'

He had not. He shook his head, feeling foolish. 'Nobody said.'

'You do not wait to be told such things, Stephan. You should enquire.'

'It would never have occurred to me to ask,' he said, stung by the unspoken reproof.

'My daughter-in-law Elizabeth is a typical close-mouthed New Englander. It would never have occurred to her to tell.'

'But why not, if —'

'It would have sounded as though she were boasting.' Mrs

Seaton spoke as though she thought the trait admirable; Stephan was not convinced that it was.

He hoped they would go back, but they never did. It pleased him to think of the sober industrious people who had made their furniture as sparely as they could, and of the present-day owners still using it, and finding something in it more than mere practicality.

After a while, the rocky headland faded from the forefront of his mind, though it was always there, ready to be brought out like a photograph album, to be savoured and relived. Reality became school work, exams, university interviews. He tried for Oxford; at his interview he sensed antipathy between his own values and those of the dons who engaged him in discussion. Though offered a place, he decided, for reasons he could not explain to his teachers or parents, nor entirely to himself, against taking it up, aware that he was deliberately interfering in his own destiny. Instead he went to Durham. Perhaps he felt that having grown up in the North, he would be more at home in a northern university; perhaps it was simply that the elitism he glimpsed while sitting the Oxford entrance examinations repelled him rather more than the mediaevalism of the city attracted him. There was no question that he felt tugged: in Oxford, walking down cobbled alleyways between colleges which had been there for hundreds of years, he felt as though something was calling him home.

The school heaped prizes on him; the university offered special grants. His future seemed set fair, triumphant. He felt further divided from his parents by his success. It was the triumph, he knew, which alienated his father; Helena, without understanding it, nonetheless gloried in it, but Josef found it bitter that his only child should succeed so effortlessly in a culture that was not his by birthright. Watching them in the evenings, sometimes, Stephan wished fiercely for them that they might return home one day. It was a time that he feared would never come; their — his — country seemed too deeply mired beneath the boot which had flattened it.

Sorting out the possessions he wished to take to university with him, he searched for his exam certificates, books presented as prizes, a pewter tankard he had won in the county chess-championships. They had vanished. He frowned, sure that he had not moved them from the drawer in his desk. His mother denied all knowledge of them. His father watched him, a slight smile on his face. The image of the murdered willow-tree rose in Stephan's head and he turned away, terrified at himself, at the anger which ate at him. I could kill him, he thought with cold surprise: truly I could kill him.

At the end of his second year he went on a field trip with some of the other students in his department. They walked between tree trunks, marking, recording growth patterns. It was a piece of work which carried on from one generation of undergraduates to the next, without ever seeming to reach any scientific conclusions.

Coming back to their lodgings at the end of the day, he saw two women approaching, their path joining his. One of them he knew vaguely from attending the same lectures. She was with a friend, a girl whose hair reminded him of the nests of golden birds, of spun sugar, of madonnas. How like an angel, he thought.

The first girl smiled. 'Stephan!' she said warmly.

He nodded, trying to remember what she was called. Sheila, was it? 'Hello, Sheila,' he said, keeping his voice low in case he had her name wrong.

'Do you know Harriet Arden-Smith?' She indicated her friend.

'No.' He held out his hand.

When she took it, smiling directly into his eyes, it was as though winter had been banished.

· 10 ·

His summer plans had already been made. He would be working in the States for the Forest Service on a project to replant some of the acres devastated by the eruption of Mount St Helens. The work was dirty, absorbing, exhausting, sometimes dangerous. Ash flew and danced with the least movement, choking the throat and clogging the eyes so that the wearing of breathing masks became a matter of survival. Sometimes he imagined he could actually feel the grey dust coating the delicate inner tissues of his body. During the day he scarcely had time to think but at night he lay listening to the wind, eerie in fire-scarred trees, holding Harriet in his mind like an egg made of glass, carefully, afraid of breakage.

When the project finished for the summer, he telephoned Tom and flew to New York. Seeing him again, a man now, as he was himself, Stephan was surprised at the rush of feeling which swept through him. Briefly they embraced.

Stephan said: 'So when's the trip to Europe coming off?'

Tom looked embarrassed. 'I've met this girl, as a matter of fact ...'

'You too?'

Over dinner at an Italian restaurant which Tom swore he would love, they talked antiphonally. 'Rebecca ...' Tom said. 'Harriet ...' said Stephan.

'Perhaps the two of us'll make it over to your side next year, when I graduate,' said Tom.

'We'll look after you when you come,' promised Stephan. He was warmed by the pronoun, the sense of future sharing. 'We'll show you round.'

Smiling into each other's eyes, they realised how easily they could lose each other for love's sake.

*

Back at university for the beginning of his final year, Stephan took Harriet into his arms and thought that nothing in this life again would be as exquisite as this moment. He touched her closed eyes; when she opened them and stared into his, he knew what the poets had meant when they talked of drowning. He filled her hair with kisses as though it were a net and they were butterflies: briefly he saw them flying, golden and delicate, in the delicate net of her hair.

He felt that life was complete; he had taken root at last.

The following Easter, plans made early the summer before bore fruit. He was going to Czechoslovakia, going back home at last, attached to a group studying the effects of industrial waste on the forests of eastern Europe. After some thought, he decided not to tell his parents.

'It's extraordinary to be returning,' he said to Harriet. 'To my ... fatherland.' The word felt good in his mouth, solid and inspiring, very European. He wondered if she understood just how important it was to him, or even if he himself did.

'Is that how you really see it?' she asked seriously.

He considered, sensing in himself something of his father's streak of melodrama. 'Perhaps not. Not entirely. Perhaps I'm just curious about the place. After all, it's been years, practically my whole life,' he said. Yet it was more than that; he knew the feel of the country under his feet would be more significant to him that merely stepping on to different soil.

'After all,' Harriet said, 'you're English, really, aren't you?'

'Am I? I suppose I am, to all intents and purposes. Most of me, anyway.' But, he thought, I could so easily not be; I never have been entirely.

The group travelled across Europe by bus, borders, checkpoints, countries left behind in blue-grey diesel fumes. 'I am retracing my steps,' Stephan told himself. 'Running across Europe again. Going back.' A tremendous excitement filled him. As they crossed into Czechoslovakia, emotion thickened his throat and caused his eyes to fill with tears. He had not understood until now how deep his sense of dispossession had been. As they drove towards Prague, he searched his memories but retrieved only fragments: a bridge, tall buildings, statues outlined against grey sky, the forest where they had lingered on their final day. Yet everything they passed was exquisitely familiar to him. He kept his face pressed against the window and hoped nobody would speak to him. He could not have answered without weeping.

In Prague they were allocated to students of their same age with whom they would stay overnight before setting off for the south. He found himself taking the Underground with a girl called Elvira Hacek. 'I am your interpreter,' she said. Her English was as good as his.

'What subject are you studying?' he said carefully. Names of stations passed incomprehensibly; he realised just how thoroughly his parents had clean-slated his own language from him.

She shook her head. She had soft fair hair, pale as moonlit water. 'I'm not a student,' she said. 'I am a — a freelance.'

'A freelance what?'

'Painter. Artist.'

He smiled at her. 'That's good,' he said, and wondered afterwards what he meant by that.

He was fascinated by her eyes. They were light grey, the colour of ice, arctic ice from beneath the polar cap. Looking into them, as the train rushed beneath Prague, he thought: ice is too cold; not ice but ... vodka. He smiled; she smiled back and looked away.

By English standards her home was unluxurious. She lived at the top of a shabby villa set on a hill among leaves; on the second floor lived an uncle with his family. Her parents, who seemed to be away, occupied the ground floor, where he was shown to a bedroom. Wishing him goodnight, Elvira touched his sleeve and disappeared up unvarnished wooden stairs. It was much less than he had hoped for.

His room was sparsely furnished with a cheap wardrobe and hard no-nonsense bed. He slept poorly; in the middle of the night he woke and remembered her face. Thirsty, he got up and tried to find his way to the kitchen but, opening a door, instead found himself in a sitting-room. In the light from the street, he saw a piano, a music-stand with a flute lying across it, furniture of the sort that in England would only be found in student lodgings. There were pictures on the walls of magic things, a world of nursery rhyme: mice with paintbrush tails, princesses in fishnet stockings, birds with beards, a schooner whose masts were elongated arms spread to hold wide the sails. They reminded him of the drawing which hung in one of the bedrooms in the guest-house. Were these Elvira's work? He saw many photographs: old people, faded houses, children in elaborate pinafores. Time was caught here, and held. He supposed that if you had no future, if, like these people, you were held in a limbo not of your own devising, with hope and initiative stifled, you would, of course, cling to the past as a reminder of the fact that things could happen. He had to remember that he himself was one of *these people*.

In the kitchen the refrigerator was tiny; the fittings were old-fashioned, from the Fifties. Searching for orange juice, he found tins of it with curious faded labels. He realised with a sense of shock that things he took for granted were luxuries here, though he was not looking at poverty, only at unavailability. He drank from the tap, hoping the water was safe.

On the bus the following morning, Elvira sat next to him. If a sun dazzled, what does a moon do? Stephan wondered. Outside the windows, Czechoslovakia, his country, passed, bathed in sunshine. He saw rust-streaked buildings, broken fences, uncut lawns that in England would have been smooth. White and yellow flowers bloomed exuberantly in hedges; the roads were narrow and untrafficked. Houses needed painting; nothing glittered. He felt at home here. He felt that he belonged.

He mentioned an exiled Czech writer. Elvira turned her cool eyes on him and said: 'Who?'

He did not believe she was ignorant of the name; in front of her a man he had not seen before turned round and stared at him intently from under a soft black hat, as though memorising his face.

Elvira's hands were long and narrow, the nails faintly mauve. He looked at them, wanting to touch her white skin — and remembered the flute. 'Do you play an instrument?' he asked. It sounded brash.

'Yes. My parents are both musicians,' she told him. 'We are a musical family.'

'What instrument?' He wanted to see her under moonlight, a high gold crown on her head, the flute raised to her lips while dogs and cows leaped across arching moons, and dishes painted with flowers rolled down gentle hills.

'Me?'

'Yes.' He smiled at her. 'You.'

She turned away to stare out of the window; in the line of her jaw he thought he saw an exquisite melancholy. Her hair had come loose from its restraining combs and he almost reached out to touch it. 'My father is a composer,' she said. 'My mother teaches piano and flute.'

'And you?'

'I do not teach anything,' she said.

'But what do you *play*? What instrument?' Harp, he thought suddenly. She should play the harp. Clearly he saw her in a silver gown, delicate fingers plucking the strings of a harp fantastical, seated on a three-cornered stool in a meadow while moonflowers leaned over her long bare feet.

'The accordion,' she said.

'What?' His vision blurred, gave way to beerhalls and round-faced burghers banging mugs down on scrubbed tables while a red-cheeked jolly *Fräulein* swayed to some coarse melody, pumping a squeeze-box in and out.

'Yes.' A dimple appeared in her cheek. 'And sometimes the flute.'

'Ah.' Had she understood his thoughts? He flushed, feeling clumsy and foolish.

He woke in the middle of the night; they were bunked down in an ugly concrete building set deep in a forest. All around them leaves stirred. He could smell resin and, between feathered branches, see the moon.

'Elvira,' he whispered: it was a silvery name, a moonlit name. There were stars, high and clear through a dirt-smeared window. I am home, he thought; I am happy — not sure if it was true.

The forests were huge and green. Every day the bus travelled for miles down unmade roads, bumping across rutted paths, startling deer. Apart from themselves they saw no one, though each day they were joined by a couple of silent men in dark clothes, not always the same two, whose eyes were never still. The leader of the Czech students lectured them, showing maps and diagrams to indicate prevailing winds, the composition of anthracite and its waste products, the clustering of industrial centres. Elvira translated fluently; as she spoke, her hands moved through the air like willow fronds, like wings.

Stephan took in little of what she said, finding the way her mouth shaped syllables, pronounced consonants, of far more interest. She wore no make-up. Her face was very pale and rather long, not at all pretty. *She walks in beauty, like the night* ... the line rushed back to him from the past.

He could not stop thinking of her, nor keep away from her. He felt idiotic, as though he had reverted to the awkwardness of adolescence each time he manoeuvred to sit next to her or stand at her side.

One evening a bonfire was built. They all sat around it, the English on one side, the young Czechs on the other. The forest surrounded them with a hush so huge that they spoke to each other only in murmurs, glancing sometimes over their shoulders at the immense blackness behind them. There was beer in heavy pressure-capped bottles; there was vodka, strong and cold. Suddenly a thin clear voice began to sing, rising up through the trees towards the stars. Was it Elvira? Stephan could not see clearly in the darkness, but beyond the flames he thought he saw her face surrounded by its pale hair, and her mouth open. The line of melody rose like smoke that thickened as other voices softly joined in. What did it say, this song? It could have been anything, but Stephan told himself she spoke of love and happiness and freedom. Tears came to his eyes. He welcomed them, seeing them as proof of the romantic streak which surged through his own long-denied Slavic blood.

'I love her,' he thought, cold vodka heating his veins. 'Not just her, but everything here. My country ...'

He got up and walked around the fire, staggering a little, not caring if anyone sniggered, feeling its heat on his face. He made his way towards Elvira and took her hand. He raised it to his lips and she turned her silvery eyes on him, laughing. Her fingers brushed his; she held them loosely. He thought: What kind of man am I? How can I love this girl I scarcely know when I am in love with Harriet? Yet I do, I do ...

Above his head, the trees spread out their arms, magic, mysterious. Elvira's hand was cold.

Returning to Prague on the first leg of the journey back to England, Elvira sat with someone else. He watched, ripped apart with jealousy. She wore earrings of some soft silvery colour; they hung like moons on either side of her face. Once she turned and smiled at him and he felt sick, knowing that after tomorrow he might never see her again. Which left tonight — could he separate her from the crowd, take her out, walk across the Charles Bridge with her, look up and see the castle crouched on its hill? Could he kiss her?

It seemed not. They went to a student drinking-place on the edge of town; everyone danced and drank beer. At least I shall have her to myself later, he thought, thinking of the underground, the walk from the station to her house. But even that was denied him; someone else was allocated to Elvira, and he went home with a boy who smelled of stale sweat.

But she kissed him. 'Maybe I shall see you one day in England,' she said, her eyes smiling at him. She cupped her hand round his chin, and he pulled it towards his mouth, pressing his lips into her palm.

'Or here,' he said. 'I shall come back.'

'Yes,' she said coolly. 'I'm sure we shall meet again one day.'

She did not mean it — though he did. 'I'll telephone you. I'll come ...' he said, but she was gone, to kiss someone else.

Compared to Elvira's paleness, Harriet now seemed too brassy, too golden. He made love to her without enthusiasm, wondering how Elvira would look naked. Guilt seared him; it was a situation he could not handle. He began to talk of his final exams, of the pressures to do well, the need to stay at home and study. Finally, too cowardly to talk of love or to hint that there might be someone else, he told her they must stop seeing each other. He loathed himself when he saw her fighting to be understanding, to retain her dignity.

He was to leave for graduate work in America almost immediately after his finals. He went back to his parents' house, realising that he no longer thought of it as home. He expected the pair of them to be pleased with his First. His mother exclaimed with shining eyes, patting him, constantly touching him as though to reassure herself, or him. She produced champagne and the three of them toasted each other. In doing so, he realised that they were toasting more than their son's success; they were celebrating their own arrival, the fact that they had won through. He was disconcerted to see his father staring at him over the rim of his glass with eyes that were full of dislike. Yet why should they not be, he thought. I don't like him, either. He flinched from using the stronger word *hate*.

He remembered the willow tree, the painful jagged edges where it had finally fallen, the bitter smell of sap which had hung like blood in the air. It was just after his O-Level results had come through — nine 'A's and a 'B'. With a chill that iced his heart, Stephan wondered now whether the destruction had been deliberate: not induced by paranoia but by jealousy — an attempt to curb further success.

'How is that lovely girl you brought up here?' his mother asked.

'Harriet?' Stephan said carelessly. He could not unlock his gaze from his father's. Madness curdled the space between them; he wondered how his mother managed to behave as though the situation was ordinary, then remembered that ordinariness was her religion.

'Fine. Just fine.' In the first flush of passion, he had ventured to bring Harriet here for a weekend once, wanting her to see him whole, to understand everything about him. Josef had hardly spoken, his eyes watchful, his hand always hovering near weapons: knives, bottles, candlesticks, ready for what might befall.

'She has another year, I think?' said Helena.

'Yes. But we aren't —'

'Such a pretty girl. But sad.' His mother poured more champagne. 'You will make her happy, Stephan, yes?'

Did she realise that her Englishness was slipping away from her as the years of safety piled up behind them? He wrested his glance away from his father's enmity and smiled at her, seeing an echo of Elvira — of Czechoslovakia, indeed — in her pale face and the curves of her piled fair hair.

'Let's drink to America,' he said. 'And to the future.'

'The future.' His mother raised her glass, laughing.

His father tossed back his head and poured his champagne down his throat without speaking.

That night Stephan dreamed of the willow tree; revived, reinstated, its leaves swept the earth again, under a silver moon. Coming closer, parting them to step inside, he saw that each frond was a snake in a high golden crown. He woke feeling desolate and endangered.

The years in the States passed quickly. There was always so much to do, to see, to learn. He spent nine months in Nicaragua. He gave papers at conferences and seminars. He became, to his surprise, an authority. Women fell in love with him; one of them he almost married. Something held him back. Trying to analyse what it was, he finally came to the conclusion that she lacked melancholy. It seemed a strange quality to look for, yet, having made the diagnosis, he was able to see that despite their differences it was one both Harriet and Elvira possessed.

Giving a paper once in Ann Arbor, he flew on after the conference to visit Susanna. Newly wise, he realised how she too hid a profound melancholy beneath her gaiety, and how determined was her brightness. He walked through the woods to the shore and stood on the rocks where Tom's father had been flung by the murdering sea. Water foamed at his feet, eternally restless, forever entreating the land. Distantly he could hear the tired clang of a buoy. *The sound of the sea bell's perpetual angelus*, he thought, remembering how he had read to Tom on sea-breezed afternoons. He thought: Although I would like to, although I feel I should, I do not have the attribute of sadness — is this why I seek it in others? Behind him the pine trees brushed the air with whispering sounds; his boyhood seemed both immeasurably long ago and yet immediate, present.

Susanna and Richie appeared unchanged by the time which had passed since his last visit here. She still walled herself in with possessions to hide the absence of the one thing she really wanted. It occurred to him that the desire for continuity, for the small immortality which having children conferred, was as deep-rooted an instinct as the need to believe that life was something more than random. When she asked him what he wanted to do, he said he would like to buy some jeans and saw how her face lit up.

'We'll go down to the mall,' she said, busy with plans. 'We could have lunch there, too; maybe even go by the market and see if there's anything ...'

Inside the artificial air of the mall, she gained reality. 'Come on,' she said. 'Jeans. And maybe some running shoes — I heard somewhere they're much cheaper here than in England.'

He followed along behind, indulgent.

I guess you're too old now for a T-shirt,' she said wistfully, as they passed the booth with the iron-on stickers.

'I guess.' He wondered what message she would plaster across his chest if he had said he was not.

She bought a sweater.

'Do you really need it?' he asked, teasing.

In all seriousness she replied, 'Oh, I do, Steffi, I really do,' and he understood now that she really did, that the need would always be there.

They stopped for lobster on the way home, and ate out on the patio. It seemed dear and familiar to him, much more so than the guest-house in the Yorkshire Dales. Afterwards, Richie and Susanna sat on the sofa with their arms around each other and watched a TV soap of some kind.

'Susanna's getting her papers,' Richie told him proudly as they sat out on the porch after dinner. 'Gonna be a real Yank, isn't that right?'

'You bet.' Susanna looked at Stephan. 'I've been hesitating for years, but I've finally made up my mind.'

'Do you feel Czech?' he said.

'God no. After all these years I've been here, I'm American through and through.'

'What took you so long to make it official?'

She hesitated, shrugged. 'I guess part of you always clings to the place where you grew up. But you can't live between two countries, Steffi; you can't divide your loyalties.' She put her hand on Richie's thigh. 'At some point you have to choose.'

Stephan walked through the woods to see Mrs Seaton. There the changes were clear: time had ravaged her. Dust sat thicker on the fine surfaces; the need for paint, for repair was evident everywhere. The kitchen was an unhygienic mess; she was beginning to let things slide. He remembered that her son, Tom's uncle, lived not far away, and wondered why she was allowed to continue in this state of dissolution. As though reading his mind, she said, seated in the old swing seat on the porch: 'They tell me this house is too big for me. They want me to give it up, but I do not wish to.'

'It's a beautiful house,' he said. 'I can quite understand why you —'

'You are far too young,' she interrupted, with the splendid arrogance of old age. 'You cannot possibly understand what it is to lose a child, as I did. This is where they left from, you know, Ned and Ellen. That's why I can't go myself.'

She turned her old eyes, still clear, towards the woods behind which lay the sea. He looked, too, through the dusk, and almost saw them himself: Tom's father Ned, and fair-haired Ellen the lost mother, both of them in deck shoes, in shorts and thick jerseys, turning at the edge of the trees to wave goodbye, not knowing that it would be the final farewell.

'If they had found her too, perhaps I would not feel so fiercely that I must stay,' Mrs Seaton said softly. 'Absurd, isn't it? But sometimes I still think she'll come back. Sometimes I think, just for a moment, that I see her there, among the trees, coming home. Of course I understand she will never come back, but because none of us *know*, do you see, we are all of us, in a way, suspended, waiting. Especially poor Tom.' She sighed. 'Am I being egotistical in suggesting that though his loss was acute, no loss can be more — more *desperate* than a mother's?'

He saw that her face was wet and started to speak, but she held up her hand.

'You see, Stephan, the act of giving birth creates a bond that only in exceptional circumstances can be broken. Mother-love can be sorely tried but almost never destroyed. Therefore nothing — ever — can compensate for a lost child. However long you live, the emptiness and the ache are always there.' She smiled faintly. 'Forgive me for saying all this, for not keeping these things to myself, but as I approach the end of my life I perceive increasingly how important it is that we older ones should display our feelings, show the young that we too are alive, can know passion, have suffered. How important, and of course how futile.'

'No,' he said. 'Not futile. Not at all.'

'Yes.'

'I think not. I shan't forget what you've said.'

'Perhaps not. Nor the circumstances: this crumbling house, the smell of the sea, the sound of the trees. But not the feeling — that has to be experienced for yourself.'

'The torment of others remains an experience unqualified,' he said.

'How percipient of you.'

'Not me. T.S. Eliot. It's a line from one of his poems called 'The Dry Salvages'. I always think of it when I stand down there on the shore. He wrote it about this part of the world.' Recalling suddenly the soaring of the white curtains at the window, he leaned forward and put his hand over her thin fingers. 'Do you still play the piano?'

'Not much these days.'

'Please play for me.' He saw pleasure in her face. 'Play that Mozart piece. I've always remembered sitting out here with Tom and hearing it through that window.'

She went inside. After a while he heard the sound of the piano, plangent, the melody faintly distorted by notes not quite in tune. He was shaken by the sadness of things.

· 11 ·

Now, returning finally to England, qualified and degreed, he
had more or less forgotten Elvira, though not the emotions she
had inspired. He thought of her as the spirit of his homeland;
he felt faintly ridiculous, even embarrassed, in doing so. Often,
as he settled himself in Oxford, set up his latest environmental
project, familiarised himself with the laboratories and equipment provided, he thought of going back to Prague, finding the
station where they had left the Underground, retracing their
steps to her house. He told himself that one day he would do
it. But first there was Harriet. First there were matters which
must be put right.

Seeing her again, his first thought was that his mother had
been right: she was sad. He suspected she always had been,
but that he had been too crass, too self-absorbed to realise it.
His earlier betrayal of her twisted his heart; he felt he owed her
something of himself. With the news of her husband's death,
he gladly took responsibility for her upon himself. Despite
what had happened between them the night that Conor died,
he told himself that he felt about her as he might have done
about a sister. Sometimes they slept together in the same bed,
but for him it was part of his duty to comfort her. When she
told him that she was pregnant, he did not once consider that
the child might be his.

He met Christina Crawford and was glad that despite the
loneliness which surrounded Harriet, she at least had a close
friend, someone older than herself who might in some

measure take the place of her mother. He found himself in the position of stand-in husband; when Christina invited Harriet to her house, it began to be understood that Stephan would come too.

Admiring the immaculate Crawford house, shiny with opulence, he was strongly reminded of Susanna: the newness of everything, a certain expression he sometimes caught on Christina's face, brought Maine sharply back into focus for him.

Tom, now working in partnership with his cousin Amis, wrote from California to say that at last the great trip to Europe was getting underway. The letter was forwarded from the guest-house; the envelope had a battered look which suggested that it had been opened and the contents read. Knowing that only Josef could have been responsible, he wondered, without really thinking about it, whether there might be repercussions.

> *The plan is to go to Paris first*, Tom wrote. *I have some important shopping to do. As you can imagine, I wouldn't dare show my face over there without a beret. What about all those places we were going to visit together? Any chance?*

Stephan wrote back. He received another note from Tom, in which he wrote:

> *Funny you being in Oxford. My grandfather comes from round there — I thought I'd see if there were any third cousins fifteen times removed I could check out. Plus there's someone else I was going to look up there, a friend of a friend. What I was thinking was I might try to find myself a place somewhere for three months or so, and use it as a base to take off from. If you know of anywhere ... Hey, in case I didn't say, it will be just great to see you again.*

Stephan drove Harriet up to the Lake District for a weekend. Remembering the visit she had made during their university days, she was reluctant to go; the hostile glare of Josef was something she still recalled in moments of depression. Stephan persuaded her: 'It'll do you good,' he said cheerfully. 'The air up there is —'

'Don't tell me it's like wine,' Harriet said. 'I'm not supposed to touch alcohol while I'm pregnant.'

He laughed.

In the years since he had last brought her there on a visit, his father had shrunk into the essence of himself, no more than a thinly ominous presence, watchful and hating. He could not help observing how Harriet tried to keep as far from Josef as possible, as though obscurely she felt that he might manage in some way to harm the embryonic baby inside her.

His mother, however, seemed scarcely to have changed. 'Harriet!' she cried warmly, as though only weeks had passed since their last meeting. 'What a treat for us that you have come to visit.'

'It's lovely to be here.'

'Stephan told us about your husband. I am so sorry.'

'Yes.'

'And now you are pregnant.'

'Yes.'

Helena's fine eyes turned towards her son. 'Is it yours, Steffi?'

'What?' Stephan stared at her in astonishment.

'This baby, is it yours?'

Embarrassed for both himself and for Harriet, he began to shake his head, then caught Josef's malevolent glance. With a shiver of inexplicable apprehension, he said: '*Of course* it's not,' and could plainly hear the unnecessary vehemence in his voice.

Showing Harriet to her room, he saw on the wall the painting which resembled those he had seen by moonlight in Prague, in Elvira's house. The name moved sluggishly through the tilth of his memories, leaving him moved, disturbed in ways he could not entirely determine. The room contained many of the books he had bought as a boy. He leafed through one he had purchased after his first trip to the States, when anxious to learn more about woods, anxious to maintain, however distantly, the links with Susanna, with Tom, with Mrs Seaton.

He and Harriet spent hours walking on the moors, and left in the afternoon of the second day, having managed to avoid Josef for the most part. He told himself that something must be done about his father; although Josef still apparently functioned perfectly adequately, had even spoken of taking the train to London or to Newcastle, he was clearly suffering some form of abnormality. Buried at the back of Stephan's mind was the feeling that he was lucky to get away from home unscathed.

Tom arrived. Picking him up at the station, Stephan asked: Who's this other guy you wanted to see in Oxford?'

'Not a guy. A girl.' Tom reached into his wallet. 'Someone called Harriet Pearse.'

Stephan opened his mouth to exclaim, to say what a coincidence, to remark how extraordinary it was that, of all people, his friend Tom should have the name of his friend Harriet in his wallet. But was it, after all, extraordinary, or was it merely so planned, so *meant* that it was not remarkable at all? 'I know her,' he said. 'We'll go and see her tomorrow.'

'There's no need. Not now you're around. She's just a name given me by someone who knows her in California — you know how one gathers up contacts when you're about to hit a strange place. Kind of insurance against loneliness, I guess. Do you know what I mean?'

Stephan did not. He perceived in his friend an insecurity not glimpsed before. 'We'll go and see her anyway,' he said. 'You'll like Harriet.'

The next evening the two of them arranged to take Harriet out to dinner. They picked her up at the flat and Stephan noted how Tom's eyes moved slowly and with pleasure round the quiet room of blues and greens which she had created. She had lit many candles.

'Electric light is so harsh,' she said. 'And so unflattering.' She gestured downwards at her figure. 'I need all the help I can get at the moment.'

'Don't say that.' Tom touched her lightly on the shoulder. 'I think you look beautiful.'

She turned her big eyes on him. 'Why, thank you very much.' She looked at Stephan and grinned. 'Why don't *you* ever say things like that?'

'I'm not just saying it,' said Tom. 'I really mean it. Really.'

Her smile faded. She poured them drinks.

Over dinner, Tom said: 'Could I stop by and visit you some time, Harriet? I'm here for a few days and I know Stephan has to work. But I have messages for you, from Lydia Costello. And for your brother.'

'Of course,' Harriet said. Stephan was aware that she felt uncomfortable, and he wondered why. 'Come whenever you like. I'm usually home in the evenings.'

Tom left for Scotland. He would be returning in a couple of weeks, he told them both, holding Harriet's hand but looking at Stephan.

'What did you think of him?' Stephan asked her later. It was a Sunday evening. They had just come back from an organ recital in one of the college chapels.

She picked up the egg of swirling glass which she kept on her coffee-table and held it in both hands. 'Very nice.' She sounded noncommittal.

'Is that all?'

'What else do you want? I thought he was very nice. A bit earnest.'

'He never stopped talking about you,' Stephan said. 'I think he fell for you in a big way.'

'Do you?' She watched him carefully as though she had hoped for a reply which would make sense of something puzzling her.

'What's wrong with that?'

'Nothing, I suppose. Except that I just don't want anyone falling for me. Nor do I want to fall myself. I've had all that sort of thing. First you, then Conor. Twice is more than enough.'

There was a current there which Stephan could not fathom. He changed the subject, spoke instead of his plans to return to

Czechoslovakia as soon as his time in Oxford was completed. Closing the doors out into the dark garden, where rain was beginning to slap invisible leaves, and drawing the curtains across, he tried to explain how he felt about the country. His voice cracked with emotion.

'Go back? For ever, do you mean?' She looked at him with wide eyes.

'Why not?'

'Get married? Have children there?'

'It's possible.' *Elvira*, he thought. Moon-pale, she rose before him; almost he thought he heard the ghostly sound of a harp.

'What would you do if — if you fell in love with someone here ... maybe even had a child?' She was looking down at her hands spread flat on her big belly. Outside rain fell hopelessly in the garden.

'I'd take it — them — with me, of course.' He laughed, picking up her hand, stroking it, remembering Harriet lying by a rocky stream in the Dales and the smell of crushed grass. He felt a huge love for her, a universality of affection which was entirely unsexual. 'It — this putative child you have wished on me — would be part of me. Of course I would take it back. My country would be its country.' It was not something he had thought about before, but he realised as he spoke that the feeling had been with him for years. He saw the curtains stir as wind shook the windows.

'I see.'

After a while, she said 'But suppose this girl — this purely hypothetical woman you've fallen in love with, had this child with — doesn't want to leave England.'

He saw that she was serious. 'It couldn't happen,' he said lightly. Her hand still lay in his as though abandoned.

'But if it *did*.'

'How can I know? My roots were denied to me by my parents. I should never want to do the same to my own children.'

'But if the mother of this child was English, the child's roots would be here.'

'Only half of them,' he said firmly. She seemed to be

working herself into agitation, though he could not imagine why. 'Besides,' he said, putting an arm round Harriet's shoulder. 'I would never fall in love with someone who did not feel as I do about this.'

'I see,' she said again. Her voice was very small. 'You can be very ruthless, Stephan.'

He thought about it; ruthless was not a word he would ever have applied to himself, yet he could see that she was — in some ways — right. His treatment of her at university hung unmentioned between them. 'Maybe,' he said, not liking the description much, not liking it applied to himself. He helped her up from her seat. 'You are a pregnant woman,' he said. 'You should already be in bed.' She seemed suddenly very vulnerable. 'You need plenty of rest.'

'Will you stay tonight?'

'If you wish me to.' Despite himself, he felt stirred. There was something immeasurably moving about Harriet's swollen body, the enlarged stomach lending an extra delicacy to wrists and ankles, the blue veins spreading across her white breasts. I shall enjoy being married, being a father, he thought. And immediately after, he wondered: is Elvira married?

Impatience enveloped him. His contract here had only five more weeks to go, but Harriet would not produce her child for another two months. He would have to wait; since despite her friend Christina, her scattered family, she was alone, he felt he had no choice; that his earlier cruelty forced this present responsibility on him. But as soon as she was comfortably settled, he would be off.

The next morning he brought her a cup of tea.

'Nice Stephan.' Her eyes were huge and shadowed. He felt uncomfortable, seeing them. Life has not been kind to her, he thought.

He went into the drawing-room and pulled back the curtains to let in the morning light. Sun streamed wetly through the lilac leaves, striking rainbows from grass blades and spiders' webs. He pushed open the long windows into the garden. The catch was broken: anyone could get in simply by turning the handle. He promised himself he would fix it for her and get the garden into some kind of order. Everything was soaked with last night's rain; the grass was ankle-deep, juicy and rich with buttercups; somewhere a thrush sang. His foot touched something. Looking down he saw, spreadeagled on the stone slab of the threshold, a doll. It was quite new, though damp with dew. Had it been there last night? Since it had been dark when he drew the curtains, it was impossible to say. The doll wore a pinafore of blue-checked gingham over a white blouse from which its pink arms stiffly protruded. His heart began a wild beat: he had seen dolls like it before, dolls whose yellow braids were tied with gingham ribbons, who wore a gingham mob cap which matched the pinafore dress. This one did not. At least ... he felt sick. Someone had stood here last night — he could quite clearly see where they had come around the side of the house and pushed through the long grass, and a stain of mud which might have been a footprint. Someone had been listening to them, he was sure of it. Someone had heard them talking, had perhaps even opened the door a crack — he remembered how the curtains had swayed — had heard them go to bed.

There was movement in the room behind him and he turned. Harriet stood there, huge in a dressing-gown of — he could not help noticing — slightly grubby towelling.

'What a lovely day,' she said. Before he could stop her she had brushed past him and stepped out into the garden. 'Everything's sparkling like diamonds. Look at it.' She stopped. Raising a hand to her mouth, she said slowly: 'Oh, my God.'

'Harriet, come in. Don't ...'

'What is it, Stephan? What is it supposed to mean?' Her voice began to rise.

'I don't know. I only —'

'Someone's trying to hurt me. To frighten me.'

'Harriet —'

'Why? What do they want?' she demanded loudly. 'Why would anyone do something like this?'

They stared at each other across the torso of the splayed doll at their feet. It lay there, limp and mutilated; its head had been hacked off and flung towards the grass. From between tangled green stems, suspended like a field mouse's nest, blank eyes gazed at them, woollen pigtails stiffly angled on either side of pink cheeks. The neck had been dipped into something. Paint, maybe. Red paint. Or perhaps cochineal. It was nothing like the colour of blood. Yet both of them knew that blood was what it was supposed to represent.

CHRISTINA

· 12 ·

'A new Golden Age ... Utopia ...'

The voices travelled towards her across the heat. She lifted her face to the canopying leaves of the gazebo and thought: *a new Golden Age? All I ever wanted was the old one.*

In her mind's eye she saw it shine again, childhood, aureate, somewhere long ago, the happy time before everything went wrong. Perhaps, if it had been a gradual process, they might — those of them left — have been able to prepare themselves for it, instead of being so suddenly struck down, forever changed by disaster. It had not happened like that; it was not a slow erosion of happiness so that one day, after it, she was able to look back and say: *then* I was happy, now I am not. It came like a thunderclap, definite and undeniable. Like the clouds which accompany a storm, it darkened the world so that it had never really seemed light since.

It was a day, a time, whose details were acid-etched on her heart, unforgettable, indestructible. And, every time she remembered, the old pain came flooding back, as though she too were drowning.

The train pulled slowly into the station and the usual bunch of them got out, glad to be home after the long school day, glad that the weekend lay before them. The train had started out importantly from London; by the time they joined it at Folkestone, it had degenerated into a little local service, ambling through cornfields in the late afternoon light, throwing up glimpses of the sea, pulling unhurriedly to a halt at places where no one waited on the platform. Christina loved that last slow meander along the coast, the stops at stations where flowerbeds bordered by sea-rounded lumps of chalk blazed with asters and chrysanthemums, the tracks from which you could look down on apple orchards and back gardens, the lazy thunk of compartment doors being slammed, the sense of a task almost completed under the wide bright sky which always heralds the nearness of the sea.

Conspicuous in their striped school blazers, the girls walked across the footbridge which straddled the railway tracks, watching the train caterpillar away from them to places whose names they knew but where they had never been: Sandwich, Dumpton Park, Broadstairs, Ramsgate. The wind from the sea caught and tugged at their round school panamas and lifted their short navy skirts. In unison they put up automatic hands to keep their hats on their heads. Clattering down the wooden stairs and out on to the station forecourt, they made plans for the weekend before parting: Sally and Anna to set off towards the solid Thirties houses along the London Road; Valerie and Liz to wait for the bus which would carry them the last mile homewards.

Christina always enjoyed the moment when she sloughed off the others — when school split away from home, and she was left neutral, suspended for a few moments between both, nobody's friend, nobody's daughter or sister, just Christina. She walked across the High Street and up to the seafront where the fishingboats sat pulled up on the shingle and bundles of netting lay about, seeded with cork floats. She breathed in deeply, smelling salt and wind and fish. And oil — soaked into the old railway-sleepers laid across the shingle, glistening on cables, blackening the winding gear which was used to drag the heavy wooden fishing-boats up from the tide-line. Gulls swooped and screamed at the end of the pier; flags snapped in the breeze which blew in off the grey-green water. A weathered fisherman sat on the bottom half of an old kitchen chair, fiddling about with a greasy part of his boat's engine.

Christina smiled at him, hoisting her school satchel higher on her shoulder. The name of his boat was embroidered in red letters on his navy seaman's sweater: *Sea Spray.* Her two brothers had gone out with him once, for a day's fishing — that was before they took up sailing, before they got their own dinghy, now kept further along the beach at the Sailing Club. Sometimes, if the shoals had run right, the varnished wooden boats would putter back, trailing blue smoke from their engines, one behind the other, to nose up on to the shingle so the fishermen could sell their mackerel straight from the sliding slippery pile heaped on the decking. They gutted and cleaned them right there, tossing the heads to the gulls, leaving the innards on the shingle for the birds to quarrel over later, while housewives and pensioners in shapeless coats waited with newspapers to take the shining corpses home for supper. Christina liked that; she liked the immediacy of it, the sharing in a natural process of harvesting the sea which reached back to the Bible and beyond.

Sometimes, on these early summer evenings, she was lucky, as she had been that particular day, not knowing that it was to be her last luck for years. Yesterday, when she had left for school, the sea had been choppy under a grey sky, full of brutal spume-topped little waves which slapped badtemperedly at the beach and the pilings of the pier. She had been carrying an overnight bag, since she was to spend the night with a friend who lived near the school. Looking out at the turbulent horizon, she had reflected that it was the kind of weather when the maroons boomed from the lifeboat station, warning that someone was out at sea and in trouble and the lifeboat crew was needed at once.

That was another thing she liked: the closeness to the elements, the constant possibility of danger; the notion that, all over the little town, men would down tools, untie aprons, drop stethoscopes or crates of oranges, leave letters undelivered and houses half built, in order to obey the great imperative of the ruthless sea. Once, she had been awaked by her mother in the middle of the night and bundled into her clothes; carrying thermos flasks, she and her brothers had stumbled along the seafront in the roaring dark to watch the lifeboat return, bringing with it the survivors from a Dutch ship wrecked on the Goodwin Sands. She had never forgotten the flickering lights, the sound of the wind screaming in from the black sea, the crash of water on shingle, the blanket-wrapped sailors being helped ashore, her mother pouring coffee from a thermos and handing it to a boy not much older than Christina herself. Looking into his eyes, she had seen in them a shocked awareness of something she had only later been able to define as his own mortality.

Overnight the weather had changed. Gleaming on the horizon lay France, a bulk of land set low on the water, on the very edge of the world. When conditions were right, it was possible to make out all sorts of detail: the grassy headlands, the perpendicular lines of the cliffs, sometimes even the war memorial and the glitter of sun reflecting off the windshields of cars. It always seemed miraculous to Christina that she could stand on the beach with the shifting stones of England under her feet and stare right into another country; could see — or almost see — a foreign town where traffic drove on the wrong side of the road, where they spoke an entirely different language, ate different food, smoked cigarettes with foreign names.

The minute she turned the corner past the pub, she knew, that something was wrong. The narrow street of mixed Georgian brick houses and pastel-painted cottages, running down from the sea, vibrated with disorder, with things not as they should be. She could not have said exactly how she knew: was it in the hang of a curtain perhaps, a door half open, a carelessly parked car?

Mrs Ashland, she thought. The old lady had been ill for a long time, had been at Death's door for weeks: had she finally pushed it open and gone through? Christina saw it clearly, that door of Death's, solid, gloss-painted, with a bold brass knocker and a handsome fanlight. The thought of Mrs Ashland, a bulky figure with untidy grey hair and suspicious spectacles, lying dead was surreptitiously exciting. From her bedroom at the top of the house, Christina could look straight into Mrs Ashland's room, across the street and one floor down. What did death look like? Would the old lady be stretched still and silent on her bed with its carved mahogany bedstead and thick mattress, never again to shout at her grown-up children or slobber over her meal-tray, or even — as Christina had once seen her — to use the bedpan which the district nurse, her face distant, held under the folds of pink nightdress? Would her mouth be open? Her eyes shut? Would her expression be peaceful, or would her face be screwed up in a hideous grimace of fear?

And what would the processes of death and decay do to her? What would her ancient 83-year-old body look like naked, stripped of nightdress and bedjacket, readied for the grave? In her biology class at school, they had been studying the human body, both male and female. Christina was particularly fascinated by the diagrams of the woman: the belly which could be pulled up to reveal womb and ovaries, like two kidneys on a plate; the breasts which lifted to show veins and muscles and fatty tissue, the rounded pelvic curves. It seemed somehow more exciting to be female: there was more there, the structure was more complicated than the male's, despite its external additions.

She had gone into the bathroom once when Peter, home from college, was standing naked at the mirror, shaving. Theirs was not a family given to shared nudity. The sight of him came as a surprise to her; the protrusion, the dangle of him from the midst of dark hair, had been obscurely exciting. She had stared, unable to take her eyes off him — and he had laughed.

'Bet you wish you had one, too, don't you?'

'No.' She had been thinking exactly the opposite, glad that she herself was safely contained within her own body, not hanging dangerously, vulnerably, outside.

''Course you do.'

'I do *not*.'

'It's a well-known fact,' Peter said. 'All women do. Freud had a name for it.'

'Freud had a name for everything.'

'Penis envy,' Peter said. He touched himself, grinning at her.

'Why should I envy you that horrible thing?' she said, unable to look away, half horrified, half amused as it slowly swelled and stiffened. 'I'd much rather be me, thank you very much.'

'Rubbish.'

'If you ask me, it's much more likely that men have womb-envy,' said Christina coolly. 'How awful for you, not to be able to have babies.' Hearing her mother's voice, she had stuck her tongue out at her brother and retreated into the passage.

Later that evening, when the five of them were sitting round the dining-table, she had said: '*Maman*, why don't you have any more children?'

Her brothers had laughed loudly and looked away from their mother, creatures already intimately aware of their own sexuality, and therefore of hers. Her mother had laid down her fork, then said in her quiet voice, 'Because I have no need of other children, Christina.'

'But didn't you want another baby?'

'I already have the children I wished to have. Not the number, you understand, but the children. I have no need for others.' She smiled round at them; Christina felt the old house swell with contentment.

That day, that last day, she rang the door bell of her own house. Her parents would be pleased with her: she had got an A in the first maths test of the autumn term; every single question right, Miss Ransome had announced, so that the other girls had turned round at their desks to stare enviously. Tomorrow she was meeting Sally and they would do something: go for a walk or to the cinema, something. She hummed with anticipation at the thought of two days off school. Maybe she could even persuade her parents to take them on a picnic on the cliffs near Dover. There would be broom and gorse up there, and birds flying out of leaves into the sky. There would be fresh rolls filled with the pâté which her father brought back from the supermarket in Boulogne, and warm peaches and wine. There would be the strong grass and tiny yellow butterflies and the smell of salt from the sea which stretched below — all the way to France.

Then the door opened and she understood that whatever was wrong was nothing to do with old Mrs Ashland. It should have been her mother who stood there above her, at the top of the three narrow marble steps which led straight up from the pavement. Instead it was Kate, who worked with her mother at the greengrocer's. There were tears on her face. And the look in her eyes ...

Absence chopped at Christina with the brutality of a kitchen knife. 'What is it?' she said, already knowing that whatever it was, her life was never going to be the same again.

Kate drew her inside the house, held her close. 'Poor Chris,' she said. Her voice broke. 'Poor little Chris.'

'What?' Chris had wriggled away from the embrace. The disaster, whatever it might be, was going to require strength if it was to be contained. It was difficult to be strong when pressed against a bosom which smelled of carrots and over-ripe fruit. 'What is it, Kate?'

Tears brimmed again. Kate began to sob. Gasping words issued from her mouth, each one containing loss, irrevocable and unencompassable. '... accident ... lifeboat ... your mother ... the boys ...'

Christina was often to speculate as to what she might have become if nothing had happened that day; if, instead of Kate it had been, as usual, her French mother there welcoming her home, giving her a hug, asking, in her funny English accent — 'just like Maurice Chevalier's' the boys used to tease her — if she had had a good day at school, drawing her into the warmth of home. Perhaps she would never have developed the need to prove herself which had propelled her towards A-Levels, qualifications, success. She might instead have been happy to settle for what her mother had: marriage, friends, family, an undemanding part-time job in one of the local shops. And if she had done that, would she ever have felt a yearning for the alternative path she had not taken, or would she have remained contented, as her mother always seemed to have been?

Impossible, of course, to say. All she was certain of, looking back, was that the grinding misery of the next few years had killed something vital inside her, as though she had been forced to dip into the reservoirs of previous happiness until they had run dry. From then on she had been like a camel ever plodding through the desert, subsisting on the water in its hump. What happens when the last drop of juice, of joy, has gone. What then? Doesn't the body of a starving man begin to feed on its own tissues? Christine was convinced that it must do. Up until then she had been round, happy, plumped out with puppy-fat; from then on, sorrow withered her.

Her father took her over to Boulogne on the cross-Channel ferry to stay for a while with her mother's parents. He wore his purser's uniform; during the crossing he did not speak to her. She watched the white cliffs pull away from them, and the thick churn of water round the propellors. As Dover receded, she saw his eyes sweep the grey sea and his mouth tremble. She wanted to shriek. She wanted to break down, to behave badly, to say: *'What about me? I suffer too. I have lost as much as you have.'*

He was a quiet but condemnatory man, much given to rage. His eyes did not soften when they rested on his daughter, though his sons had appeared to please him. Because of that, it would have been unthinkable for her to intrude into his grief; it did not seem to occur to him that she had a grief of her own.

On the other side of the Channel, her grandfather was waiting for them. He began to weep when he saw them come through customs. His white hair stuck up over his head as though he had forgotten to brush it that morning. The buttons of the cardigan he wore under his old suit jacket were in the wrong buttonholes. He put his arms round her father and the two of them stood entwined, their shoulders shaking. Christina stood apart. There was a deadness inside her: she felt as though invisible weightless rats were gnawing away her vital organs, chewing her womb, sucking the roundness from her breasts, crawling up inside her pelvis to swallow her ovaries, her uterus. She felt de-sexed, no longer female, just a husk, barely alive, breaking apart with loss.

The two men separated. Her grandfather said: *'Où est la petite?'* He came over to her. Somewhere behind the customs sheds she heard a ship's siren. Her father said, not using her name or even looking at her: 'I'll come and fetch you in a couple of weeks, all right?' His face was closed to her.

It was not all right, but to say so would have been point-less, though she sensed that for once it would not have provoked one of his sudden terrifying angers. She wanted to be with her mother, even the silent sodden wraith her mother had suddenly become. Although, since childhood, she had spent part of every summer with her grandparents, she did not now want to be here on the opposite side of the Channel, plunged from the normality of school and home into the special atmosphere of the little coastal resort where her French grandparents kept an hotel.

Much later she would realise that sending her away had been misguided rather than deliberately cruel; that her parents had simply wished to spare her the double funeral, the generalised grief. Yet it fostered in her a sense of alienation which she was never afterwards able to escape.

The resort only came alive in the summer months. For the rest of the year it mouldered gently — withdrawn, suffused with Chekhovian melancholy. Now, with the summer over and the visitors dispersed to their winter lives of schools and jobs, the promenade was deserted, stretching emptily between the mildly bustling little harbour at one end of the town to the grass-topped headland at the other. Most of the houses were owned by rich people from Paris and Lyons, and used only as holiday homes: out of season they were shut-tered, empty.

Her grandparents' hotel — Auberge Albertine — catered mainly to families, many of whom came back year after year. They left reminders of themselves when the summer was done: sand in the hallway, a desiccated starfish on a window-sill, an old sandshoe with rust round the eyelets. The building stood three-sided round a cobbled yard which was separated from the roadway by a tall wrought-iron fence, once dark blue, now paled to the green-grey of bread-mould. The stucco needed repainting; there were holes in the roof where the orange pantiles had crashed down during the winter gales. A faded green shutter swung by a rusted hinge from one of the dining-room windows; it had done so for as long as Christina could remember. Geraniums and petunias flowered in bursting wooden flowerboxes set against the walls. Hanging in a doorway was her grandmother's canary.

In the hotel kitchen her grandmother wept endlessly, wiping her eyes with the corner of her blue apron. '*Ces garçons*,' she said, her tears falling among the pans and the cutlery. '*Ces pauvres gosses.*' Coming here had previously been one of Christina's greatest happinesses; her grandmother was closer to her than either parent, more generous with her love. Now, after her initial embrace, sorrow pulled her away from her granddaughter; she bottled pears and plums for next year's summer visitors, put up *haricots verts* in jars of brine, pounded goose-livers and boiled ducks which she had bought from the market, tearing the flesh from their bones when they were cooked and pressing them into jars with rubber-sealed lids, along with juniper berries and a drop or two of orange liqueur. She was old enough to be aware that life would go on, that next season would come, and the one after — that disaster does not halt the stars in their tracks nor cause the globe to cease its spinning.

Christina did not have enough experience to be so prag-matic. It seemed unforgivable to her that the world should take no notice of her private tragedy. She walked alone on the promenade, along the deserted sands. No one else was about. Although the air was still warm from the past summer, she felt constantly cold. Sometimes, despite the autumnal sun, she shivered for hours on end, her teeth clattering inside her head, her hands tucked up into her armpits. She stared towards England, as in England she stared at France, but received no reciprocal image of home: either the light was wrong or there was a mist rolling in, floating on top of the sea. She thought obsessively about her brothers, Peter and Paul. They had been older than she, almost out of her orbit, yet she longed for them, longed for things to have been different, for opportunities that she would now never have.

She remembered Paul coming into her bedroom only a few weeks ago, as she was changing out of her school clothes. He watched her as she stood in T-shirt and pants in front of the mirror and said: 'You're going to be pretty, Chris.'

'Don't be silly,' she said scornfully. She had pulled her glossy black hair back from her face and secured it with a grip shaped like a butterfly. 'God, I wish my hair wasn't so straight. Look at it, just hanging there.'

'All our college friends will be running after you.'

'Will they?' She liked the prospect, saw herself pursued like a butterfly by a crowd of young men in boaters and white V-necked sweaters, like the ones in the team photographs which hung on the walls of Paul's room.

'Don't worry, I shan't let them lay a finger on you,' he said.

'Not like you.'

He glanced at the door as though afraid someone might hear. 'Ssh!'

'Anyway ...' Pouting, she turned sideways and looked at herself provocatively in the mirror. 'Maybe I'd like a finger laid on me.'

'Not by my friends you wouldn't. They're all rugger oiks.' He got up from her bed where he had been lounging, and stood behind her. His hand touched her breast. 'You want something much more refined than that lot.'

'Do I?'

'Certainly you do.' His hand moved; she shivered as it touched her nipple.

'Don't.' She wriggled away from him.

'You just need a bit more up top,' he said, sliding his hand over the softness that would become her breasts. 'Any minute now, I should think.'

She longed to ask how he knew, but felt uneasy. 'Go away.' She looked at his image in her mirror, standing behind her with one of his arms across her body.

'You're not frightened of your own brother, are you?' His hand dropped to the curve of her bottom, cupped, fondled.

She slapped it away. 'Of course not, stupid.' She spoke carelessly. Nonetheless it was not entirely true; she was afraid of him, of both of them, perhaps even more afraid of herself and her own feelings for them. She liked the feel of their hands, the smell of them, the way one or other of them would sometimes get into her bed, hold her, touch. She watched his reflection; his eyes were narrowed and there was a little smile on his mouth. She wondered what it would be like to be kissed by him. He and Paul were so male, so big, much bigger than either of their parents; they filled the house.

Now, alone on a lonely beach, she could only think of them as parts, not as a whole: their eyes, their big feet, a green sweater, a college scarf, their black hair and huge hands, reddened from playing hockey in the winter, or sailing in the summer.

In front of her the sea rolled endlessly, casting seaweed and crabs at her feet, but never the treasures it had stolen from her. She tried not to think about what it must have been like for the two of them, the gasp and shock of it, the feel of salt at the back of the throat, the thrust and strive, the final bursting realisation that there was no hope, that life was finally over.

She wept. She tasted the salt of her own tears. She thought: *from now on, I shall always hate the sea.*

The canary sang in its cage; her grandmother picked the dead blooms from the petunias, and boiled leaves from the geraniums with quinces for jelly. Standing with her in the kitchen, Christina sometimes reached out a finger and touched the blue strings of her apron, for comfort. When it was time to return home, her grandfather took her back to the ferry terminal at Boulogne. Her father, who had worked on the boats for years, was waiting for them by the barrier; she saw people greet him, coming up to touch his shoulder, to indicate their sympathy. He seemed different, paled and destatured. Once he was the father of two sons; now all that remained was a daughter. She hoped he might grow to be as proud of her as he had been of them. If she worked hard enough, tried hard enough, she could perhaps attain some of the goals they had reached, and, in so doing, compensate him a little for their loss.

During her stay — her banishment — in France, her brothers had been cleared from the house. All trace of them had gone. There had been noise and laughter before; now there was only silence. There had been rugger-shirts and wet towels on the bathroom floor, six pints of milk left daily on the doorstep, salt-streaked oilskins hanging up in the side passage, a boisterousness, a constant sense of revelling. Now there was nothing.

She wandered through the rooms, looking for something of them. Among her own books she found one that had been Paul's; at the back of one of the deep cupboards built into the chimney embrasure she found a scarf she had borrowed from Peter. She slept with it round her neck; it smelled of him still. These were all she could find of the brothers she had loved. She felt like screaming her rage at the unfairness of it. She said nothing.

From a bottom drawer she took a box. Lifting the lid, she put aside tissue paper and stared down at the face which lay framed in curly yellow hair. Angélique. She picked the doll up and hugged her tightly; she had belonged to her mother and been given to Christina on her tenth birthday. Her dress was of real silk; her puffed sleeves were edged with handmade lace and there were shoes of real kid on her feet. Christina loved her passionately. She had thought herself too old for dolls, but in the weeks and months to come Angélique gave her comfort when no one else even tried.

*

Winter that year was fierce. At night, she lay in her bed near the stairs and listened to the sea. It clawed at the shingle; the noise it made sounded like the gnawing of rats. Icicles hung from the roof outside her window. When she broke one off and sucked it, she could taste salt, as though it was formed from frozen tears. When the storms came, in early January, the sea leaped thirty feet into the sky and rolled down the street, leaving stones and gravel outside their front door.

Her mother sank into herself, further and further as though she were collapsing from within. Christina herself seldom spoke for fear of reminding her parents of what they had lost. She longed to be comforted as she had been when a little girl, but it did not seem to occur to anyone that she, too, mourned, that she too had lost her status within the family hierarchy; for where she had once been a girl with two brothers — the youngest of three — she was now an only child. Neglected, she learned to live alone; the house remained silent, as though shuttered and full of ghosts. Her parents seemed no more substantial than the memories of the lost boys, except for the occasional rages of her father, when his eyes would redden and the veins would fill with angry blood to lie along his temples like blisters.

Time passed, made up of terms, homework, exams. She moved up through the school — solitary, marked out by her tragedy. In the Upper Fifth they studied *The Tempest*; she had to leave the room as the English mistress read Ariel's song aloud to them. 'Those are pearls that were their eyes,' she murmured, and thought too: *This pain I feel will kill me.*

Since there was nothing else, she worked harder than ever, striving for perfection, cast down by any grade less than an A, sometimes studying through the night before staggering out into the early morning to catch the train for school. It was not enough to come top in the class — she needed to come higher than top, to achieve grades beyond perfection, if she was going to show her parents that, although the boys were gone, they still had a daughter as clever as they had been. She found mathematics soothing: in calculating odds, percentages, adding or multiplying, averaging out, she found a special pleasure in the rigorous inevitability of numbers. She liked the lack of surprises, of disturbances. Increasingly, before she undertook any project, however small, she made plans, drew up schedules. To have everything mapped out beforehand was one way of avoiding the hurtful unexpected.

Her parents seemed oblivious of her scholastic progress. Kate, visiting Christina's mother one afternoon, saw the school report left opened but unread on the kitchen table and said, 'What marvellous results you've had in the examinations, Christina. Your parents must be very proud of you.'

'I don't think they've noticed,' Christina said.

She looked at them, seated side by side at the table, still sunk in despair, her mother almost invisible, her father's face sullen and disappointed. She wanted them to be alive again; she wanted to pick them up and shake them, as her brothers used to do with her when she was little. She wanted to tell them to laugh again, to stop mourning, to see her.

She wanted to say to her mother: I am seventeen: why haven't I started my periods yet? Where are my breasts?

· 13 ·

She decided against university. Instead, she took courses in computer technology, travelling daily to the heart of Kent so that although she had left school, her routine continued as it always had. Her silent mother saw her off each morning and welcomed her back at night, though the welcome was so muted as to be understood rather than explicit. Despite the lack of communication between them Christina gradually became aware of a new element in her mother's insubstantiality. Looking up from a book, or turning unexpectedly, she would find her mother's eyes fixed on her and sense impatience, even urgency stirring that etiolated personality.

Her father seemed to spend less time in the house than formerly. For Christina this was a relief; she had no idea whether it was one her mother shared. Whatever relationship she had once had with him now dwindled into non-existence. Once, coming back from Ashford on a winter's evening, she thought she saw him on a station bench, his face turned to that of a woman beside him, but the train moved on before she could be sure, and all she retained was an impression of yellowness, of amber, the yellow glow from the lamp above them, the woman's amber hair.

Finished, fledged, Christina decided to move to London. Without much difficulty she got herself a job with a marketing company; she was prepared to accept the relatively low starting salary because she had no intention of remaining at that level for longer than six months. If, after that, the firm did not recognise her abilities, she would move on. Her mother nodded at the news, her eyes almost smiling, the colour spreading beneath the skin of her pale cheeks. She came to the station to see her daughter off. As the London train arrived, she put her arms around Christina and touched her face with one thin hand. 'Goodbye,' she whispered. 'Goodbye.'

Christina had found herself a flat in Chalk Farm which she was to share with three other girls, all strangers. They remained so: during her first week, she discovered that their lives were based on men, on the pursuit of happiness as defined by their own appeal to the other sex. Having been self-sufficient for years, Christina had no time to relearn a social code that must necessarily end in her own subservience. She felt an urgent need to get on, to go somewhere: it did not occur to her to ask herself where she was headed or what she would do when she arrived.

A week after she left home, her mother killed herself.

Riding in a car behind the hearse which carried the coffin, Christina realised this must have been something her mother had planned from the moment she learned that her sons were drowned, that she had simply waited until Christina was ready to step out alone. Bitter laughter twisted her mouth before turning — perhaps inevitably — to tears.

'Why bother waiting?' she would have said, had her mother still been there to question. 'Why stay alive only for my sake, and yet deny me what was left of my childhood? Why make *me* responsible for the burden of your last years?'

Her grandparents crossed the Channel to be there. Her grandfather put his arms around his son-in-law, as he had done before at the loss of his grandsons. Her grandmother sat dry-eyed, holding Christina's hand, she the one, this time, in need of comfort.

When they arrived at the cemetery, they were joined by a woman with yellow hair. Her eyes did not meet Christina's when she was introduced as Ellen Barker, who had worked on the cross-Channel boats with Christina's mother long ago, before she married. Christina was aware of secrets, of huge things left unsaid; she sensed between this woman and her father meetings, kisses, hands held under station lamplight, the unveiling of middle-aged bodies in chilly rooms, freedoms renounced. Perhaps, for all his inexplicable rages, her father had at least been loyal. She wished passionately she could feel something for him, but knew it was impossible; her emotions had been too brutalised. Returning to London after the funeral, she was not sure that she would ever see him again. What appalled her most was her realisation that, except for her grandmother, there was now no one in the entire world for whom she cared.

She spent her two-week summer holiday in France. There was comfort in the knowledge that her mother had been a girl here, and in the way the Auberge Albertine stayed the same: the yellow canary, the smell of simmering fruit and roasting meat, the drooping shutter. She recognised for the first time the ageless strength of a family's women, the importance of grandmotherhood, its status within a family structure. Grandmothers passed on a wisdom that mothers had not always yet attained; grandmothers could provide a needed security to the forlorn.

Over the next years, as she piled up diplomas, found herself jobs, moved higher in her field, Christina saw that, if she was to succeed to the level she wished, she would have to present at least the appearance of caring. Deliberately she set about reconstructing her persona; she drew up a plan of necessary change. She forced herself to smile more; she touched people. Moving into a flat of her own, she gave parties, cultivated friends, bought smarter clothes, joined an exercise studio, experimented with haircuts and make-up. She found herself being invited out a lot; her free evenings were the ones around which other women planned dinner parties.

It was at one of these that she met Denis.

He was sixteen years older than she was; an economist of international repute, attached to one of the Oxford colleges. They found a common enthusiasm in their intellectual appreciation of money, of numbers. When he asked her to have dinner with him, she accepted with an unusual sense of anticipation. They went to Le Caprice. She wore a short straight frock of crimson silk under a black jacket of fine wool. She liked the way his eyes lit up at the sight of her, and the linger of his hand on her arm. When he asked if she would like to come back to his hotel room for a nightcap, she refused, but only because she felt it to be politic, knowing that next time she would go. She had no doubt that there would be a next time. She drew up a plan: which clothes she would wear, the things she would say, the lingerie she would buy.

A week later, he came back to London again; again they had dinner. When he suggested a last drink at his hotel round the corner, she smiled at him, filling her glance with learned warmth. Under her slim black dress she was wearing expensively seductive underwear; she had already packed a toothbrush in her handbag, and a fresh pair of bikini pants, white lace studded with hand-embroidered yellow daisies. He was not the only man she had slept with, but the first she had enjoyed. Although not particularly skilful, he charmed her by his concern for her pleasure. Lifting her hips to his questing body, she thought she almost felt something, the echo of what it was supposed to be about.

Denis was the first man who proposed to her. Because she was nearing thirty, she accepted him, seeing marriage as a way to cover herself with a skin of normality. Yet she was painfully aware that in some way she was abnormal, as though that distant disfiguring loss had left a wound which still suppurated, oozing pus, poisoning her. Her body did not function as she guessed the bodies of other women did. Her cycles were misshapen, abrupt; she did not bleed regularly. Sometimes, catching sight of herself in shop windows or unexpected mirrors, she took herself momentarily for a boy and wondered, with a catch of the breath, if that was why Denis wanted her.

Her grandmother came to the wedding, bringing wine and bottled fruit and half a dozen fresh goat's cheeses wrapped in green leaves. Her eyes were sad when they rested on Christina standing in ivory silk among her friends. What did she want for her granddaughter? Christina did not know and dared not ask, afraid that the want might match her own.

Often, she wondered about love.

For Denis she felt something, she was sure of it — but was it love? Could she love? She remembered the invisible rats devouring her inner tissues and thought for the first time that perhaps they had eaten her heart as well. With Denis's diamond on her finger, she slept uneasily at night, her dreams heavy with clifftops and precipices and herself, tiny and unprotected, teetering on their edges. The view of France, horizoned, islanded, moved closer to her in sleep: she could see again the cars, the people, the phallic war memorial, and herself standing alone on a foreign shore, isolated from the rest of the world. Sometimes she woke with tears in her eyes and a sense of unbearable anguish while her mind still retained the tattered night-images of howling winds, flapping sails, the feel of salt at the back of her throat as she sank beneath the surface of a bitter sea.

She moved to Oxford, into the big bare flat Denis owned. The task of decorating the place, buying china, silver, sets of Waterford glass, reinforced her femininity to herself. Watching the smooth spread of pale Wilton carpet, the gleam of polished furniture, the well-chosen objects, she was deliciously conscious of appearing to be a woman like other women, instead of someone apart. Travelling daily up to London she felt her life revolving in circles, and herself a schoolgirl again, catching a train, stopping somewhere yet nowhere, not yet arrived at her final destination.

Love: she wanted desperately to love Denis, but was afraid that she was incapable of it, that her love had already been given long ago, and that she had no more to offer. When he travelled abroad on business, she worried about planes falling from the sky, about heedless native drivers, ignorant peasants murdering him for his money or his kidneys. But was it love? Each time he came back safely she took him to bed, finding reassurance in his hands roaming her, in his mouth on her minimal breasts. During his absences she read sexual manuals; in bed with him she would try new positions, new ways of arousal, that set him moaning with pleasure. Yet, though she felt she ought to, she found no satisfaction in acrobatic sex;

what she liked best was the passive role. It gave her pleasure to hear him above her, groaning to climax, to feel his seed pulse into her body, to watch him lose control.

She thought often of her brothers, of their mouths, and herself running after them, crying 'Wait for me! Wait for me!' and how they always had done, holding out their strong aggressive hands to her, lifting her up. On her thirty-second birthday she decided to get pregnant.

She had expected it to be easy, almost automatic. It was not. As the months went by, she took to examining her body, studying every inch of it: the line of her ribs, the colour of her nipples, the small swell of her belly and, below it, the sparse virginal hair. There had been girls at school whose pubic hair had jutted like a dark fountain; Sally's for instance. She remembered lying on the dunes with Sally in the summer holidays, listening to the wind rustling through the coarse sea-grasses, and wondering at the almost obscene bounty which filled and overflowed the bottom half of her friend's swimming costume, at the coarse hairs which lay atop her thighs.

In mirrors she watched her own secret enclosed body, seeded but still unripe. What was wrong with it? Why did it refuse to fulfil its function? She thought: I am a failure. I have always been one. I should have been a boy.

The doctor told her to relax. He suggested yoga classes, gave her tranquillisers to reduce tension, advised her not to think about conceiving, and simply to enjoy relations with her husband without worrying about babies. Later he asked how old her husband was and she fancied that she saw him shake his head. She took to reading magazine articles about infertility; she discovered that in the majority of cases it was the man's fault. Despite the doctor's advice, she could not relax: when she and Denis made love she was desperate to bring him to climax so that his seed could travel to its proper destination. She fancied she could follow its passage inside her body, could feel its mating with her own eggs.

Nothing happened.

Without telling Denis, she went to the Radcliffe for a series of humiliating tests. Cold instruments probed her secret places; thinking of those invisible destructive rats, almost she expected the doctors to express astonishment at the emptiness, the devoured state of her womb. They told her they could find nothing wrong, that it was simply a question of time. They advised a holiday, somewhere in the sun, perhaps, somewhere warm; they advised hot baths before lovemaking, even a glass of whisky, something to reduce inhibition.

She thought: my father was right to disregard me. I am not even able to be a woman. Need, desperation, gnawed at her.

Passing a shop in the centre of Oxford, she saw an antique doll propped up in a ladder-backed rocking-chair. The seat was made of rush intricately woven in a herringbone pattern; the frame was of oak. The whole chair was no more than eighteen inches high. She went in and bought it; she told herself it was for Angélique, her mother's doll.

'I want to move,' she said. Light flooded in through the French windows from the garden she had begun to neglect.

'Where to?' Denis, with toast crumbs on his mouth, turned the pages of the *Financial Times*.

'I don't know. Somewhere else. A real house.' Looking for formulas, she did not say that in a real house she might find herself being a real woman at last.

'In the town?'

'Outside. In a village.' She saw beams, thatch, raspberry canes in a cottage garden, a dovecot.

'What about your job?'

'I could work from home. Computers these days . . .' She let the sentence drop. He would understand about modems, about hook-ups. One of the pleasures of their relationship was the way they so easily followed each other's thought processes — and thinking this, she ducked her head, as though he might otherwise perceive through her eyes the thoughts which filled her mind.

'All right, darling, I'm game if you are.' She saw him

suppress a breath and realised that for him to move out of Oxford would mean inconvenience, upheaval, extra stress.

'It'll be fun,' she said warmly. 'You'll see.'

'I know.' He reached a hand across the yellow tablecloth and covered hers. 'With you, everything's fun.'

That night she cooked something fine and delicate; she persuaded him to open a second bottle of wine. In bed, clambering over him, stroking and sucking him, she felt her inhibitions had vanished: tonight, if ever, was the moment she would conceive. As his movement inside her grew faster she raised herself giving him an easy slide into her womb. Did she hear a secondary gasp which echoed his, as sperm and ova met and conjoined, or was it merely imagination? She lay afterwards in his arms and felt her body to be fruitful at last.

Knowing they would have little trouble in selling, she set about finding a place to move to before putting their flat on the market. She drove out to honey-coloured villages, seeing a part of England she had only heard about: a solid, satisfying, complacent Englishness which reminded her sharply that she was in fact half French. She wondered if her grandfather had yet mended the shutter at Auberge Albertine and thought: when we are settled again, Denis and I shall go there. It had not occurred to her before how unpeopled with relatives their mutual life was. He was the only child of long-dead parents and apart from her grandparents, she had lost touch with all that remained of her family.

Yes, we will go — all of us — she told herself, hardly daring to reconnoitre the possibility of being more than two. We shall walk along the promenade and drink an aperitif on the hotel terrace, looking towards England. I shall look at the sea and for once not think of my drowned brothers, of their hands clutching at the air, of the salt damming their throats, their energy stilled. Somewhere in the picture was a perambulator, a carry-cot, a pushchair.

She took Angélique from the box where she had been laid, unfolding the tissue paper to look again at the time-discoloured silk dress. The eyes were still as blue, the cheeks as rosy. She held the stiff cloth body against her breast; she pressed her lips to the unresponsive porcelain face and remembered how passionately, how desperately she had loved her once. And Paul. And Peter. Her heart ached beyond bearing. Time was supposed to heal or at least to dim, but it did not. *Oh God, why could she not forget them?* Why did the pain, the love, not lessen? She licked one of her own tears from Angélique's china face and, tasting salt, tried not to choke.

She found a house which fitted in remarkably with her dreams. Here, if anywhere, she would conceive. There was an inglenook; blackened beams traversed the unsteady ceiling, and the diamond-glazed windows looked out on a pretty cottage garden. Behind a dry-stone boundary wall ran a stream; beyond it another back-garden climbed to a similar house.

'What do you think?' she said.

Denis smiled. 'It's delightful.' The word told her everything she needed to know. Next morning she rang the estate agent and said it would not do. In the middle of the village high street there was an antique shop: she bought a Victorian glass bowl and, almost as an afterthought, an old baby's teething ring of ivory and silver.

It took another three months before she found a place which suited them both. It was less than she wanted, more than Denis had hoped for, though he did not say so. He sensed in her a desperation — he guessed, being both intuitive and kind, that she wanted something he could not give her. He was willing to wait; she would discuss it with him when she wished. Having grown up the only child of elderly parents, having learned habits of speaking when spoken to, he waited for her to talk about it. When she did not, he assumed it was because she did not wish or need to. The thought that she was terrified of having to admit the possibility of childlessness did not occur to him; because he viewed her as a successful woman, he did not understand that she felt herself to be a failure. Nor did he appreciate that for

Christina, while the subject lay unaddressed, it could remain unacknowledged. Once out in the open it would no longer be possible to ignore it.

It therefore seemed easier to Christina to pretend.

They moved without having sold the flat. Christina busied herself once more with furnishings and decorations, feeling some of her old crispness return. When the agent telephoned to say he had a buyer at last, she refused the offer, saying it was far too low. She drove into Oxford and visited their former home: long unoccupied, it had a shabby neglected air and the garden had become a wilderness. From the telephone booth across the road she telephoned Denis, suggesting that they meet for lunch. Sitting together among mirrors and potted plants with spear-shaped leaves, she considered they made a handsome couple. No one would know, she thought ... That afternoon she walked Denis back to the high-arched oak-gated entrance to his college then walked through the little streets. *No one would know* ... Near the end of the High Street, she went into a shop selling old furniture, necklaces made of seeds, bits of coloured glass, Victorian jewellery. In a flat-topped glass case she saw a baby's rattle made of coral with little silver bells which tinkled tinnily when shaken. Under a table was a maple cradle, put together on clumsily-carved rockers. She bought them both — for Angélique.

The flat reminded her of failure: she wanted to get rid of it, to clear the decks. When the buyer repeated the offer, she accepted, though aware that she was being unbusinesslike. At the agent's office to complete some paperwork, she was amazed to be told that the girl who had left as she entered was in fact the purchaser of the flat.

She can't be more than eighteen,' she said, amazed.

'Older than that,' the man said, smiling, 'but very youthful, I agree.'

Christina watched the girl recede down Cornmarket Street towards the Broad and the bulk of Tom Tower. She thought: she looks exactly like Angélique.

· 14 ·

Christina saw the girl again, a couple of months later, coming out of the Ashmolean Museum. On impulse, she crossed the road.

'You bought our flat,' she said. Close to, though young, the girl seemed less doll-like, more adult. There were the marks of time around her eyes; her mouth wore a bewildered look.

'Sorry?'

Laughing, Christina introduced herself, then dragged the girl off for tea in a café.

Her name was Harriet. She was recently married; her husband was off in some jungle or other, doing things to the environment. The surface Chris — the one she had taught herself to become — responded giddily, waving her small hands about, flicking up the curve of her short glossy hair, being amusing. But the other Chris sensed in Harriet a well-hidden confusion, as though she had not entirely grasped the point of things but did not want anyone to find out.

'Come to lunch on Sunday?' she cried, as the two of them parted.

Harriet duly did.

They became friends, easy with each other. When both men were around, the husbands joined them; they did things as a foursome. Christina found Conor Pearse difficult, even selfish. He did not take care of Harriet the way Denis took care of her. When possible, she avoided him, finding his attitude scornful, his conversation overly superior. She sensed that he despised women, that for him Denis might have some validity but she herself did not. He appeared to feel the same way about his own wife; she was appalled to realise that Harriet was not aware of it. Yet he was good-looking in a coarse kind of way; attractive even, and far more alive than Denis, for all his lack of manners. He reminded her of her brothers: he grabbed at life; he took. Although she would never had admitted it, despite herself, she found him in some way exciting. Sometimes, when Denis made love to her, she fantasised Conor's hands doing to her what her husband did, imagined Conor taking her, using her, not caring whether she enjoyed it. Surprisingly, the thought roused her, led her to heightened pleasure so that Denis, looking down at her flushed face, wondered what trigger he had found to please her, and whether he could find it again, next time.

Christina found herself wondering about Conor in bed with Harriet, what the two of them did together, whether Harriet reached orgasm. She surreptitiously examined Harriet for signs of pregnancy, though she found none. She herself declared a total lack of interest in babies. 'I have my career — and my child-substitutes,' she cried gaily, showing Harriet her by-now extensive collection of miniature furniture, the pretty antique toys, the coral rattles, the ivory and silver teething rings, a couple of new dolls.

'I've always collected,' she said, 'ever since I was a girl,' and she wondered afterwards why she had lied. Was it because she was afraid that there was something unbalanced, almost mad, about a childless woman still mooning over dolls?

'You have some lovely things.' Harriet picked up Angélique. 'Isn't she beautiful?' She touched the delicate painted cheeks, stroked the ancient silk of the doll's dress.

Christina wanted to tear her from Harriet's arms. Angélique was hers; she had never seen anyone else but *maman* hold her, and was surprised at the strength of the jealousy she felt. 'She's French,' she said. 'She was my mother's.'

'Is your mother French?'

'She was. She's dead now.' To distract Harriet, to regain possession of the doll, she added: 'My grandmother's still around though. She runs a seaside hotel.'

'How interesting. Where?'

'Somewhere near Boulogne — a tiny place no one's ever heard of.'

'Really? Harriet was about to say that she had once spent a fortnight on a French exchange in a similar place, but Christina, taking the doll away, was now showing her an antique cradle fashioned from some reddish wood.

'Isn't this lovely? It's American, made of maple. And look at this ...' She turned the cradle over. 'It was made by one of the Shakers — that's a religious sect in New England — they weren't allowed to decorate or ornament anything they made. It had to be plain and functional, but look:' Underneath, tucked into a corner by the rocker, was a mark: three tiny hearts, one inside the other, carved into the wood. 'I like to think that this was made for their first baby,' said Christina. 'And he couldn't resist decorating it just the tiniest bit. Isn't it sweet?'

'It's lovely,' Harriet said. 'Can't you just see him, big and blond with one of those pudding-basin haircuts flopping over his forehead, surreptitiously disobeying the edicts of his order?' Her artist's finger roamed over the curved end-pieces, touched the incised hearts.

'Of course I'm probably wrong,' said Christina. 'He was probably called Hertz or something, and this was just his woodcarver's mark, a kind of play on words.' She laid Angélique back in her tissue paper-lined box.

'Actually,' Harriet said. 'I think you *are* wrong. If I remember rightly, the Shakers were celibate.' She laughed. 'So much for romance.'

'Let's go on a magical mystery tour,' Harriet said one weekend.

'Where to?'

'It wouldn't be a mystery if I told you.'

'Is it going to be magical?'

'Absolutely.'

'It sounds fun,' said Denis.

Conor, sitting apart in a deckchair, snorted unkindly. 'Sounds like another of Harriet's harebrained ideas. We all pile into a car and sit for hours in some traffic-jam, inhaling carbon-monoxide fumes until we're blue in the face —'

'Red,' Christina said, hating him.

'What?'

'Carbon-monoxide makes your face go red, not blue.'

He stared at her inimically, then closed his eyes.

They got up very early. Harriet drove them. 'I've made a picnic,' she said. 'And you're to promise not to look at sign-posts.'

'Where are you taking us?' Denis asked. 'I mean, what sort of place — I know you aren't going to say where exactly.'

'It's somewhere I went with my brother and my father once. It's beautiful.'

They found themselves on a cliff-top, in an area of meadow turf. Small pines like parasols scented the hot air; there was a haze out to sea, blurring the line of the horizon. Thick tumbles of blackberry hedges and profuse elder laced with honeysuckle sheltered them from the wind which blew in from the sea, forming an archway behind which lurked the remains of a derelict army fortification. A path led precipitously down a chalk cliff to a cove of seaweed smells and slippery rocks enclosing tidal pools. Harriet was happy. She took off her shoes, found bits of driftwood, the empty carapaces of crabs, a long shell like a cut-throat razor. Along the edge of the tide were strings of black wrack, pieces of sea-etched glass, rounded lumps of coal. 'There's a seam stretching right out into the Channel,' Harriet said. 'My father told me. There're mines here, further inland.'

Back up in the shelter of the scrubby pines, she produced a basket. There were rolls stuffed with pâté, game pie, punnets of raspberries, some nectarines. 'And wine,' Harriet said happily. She poured for them all. With her hair blowing away from her and the tumbledown arch behind her, she resembled one of Dürer's madonnas.

Christina was suddenly stricken. Memories, loss, the mist hazing the blue water, the wine — she got up, blundering her way between the honeysuckle hedges to lean against the rough trunk of a tree. Paul, Peter, lost happiness made her weep. Someone came up behind her. Conor's voice said:

'What's the matter, Chris?'

'I've been here before,' she said. 'It reminded me of — of sad things.'

He put an arm round her shoulders; it was the first time she had ever seen him gentle, non-combative.

'I grew up near here,' she explained.

They were both silent for a moment. Conor said ruminatively: 'I don't really care for the seaside.'

'Neither do I.' Christina could hear Harriet's laughter, Denis's deep rumble of a voice. Above her head screamed gulls; far away a fog-horn sounded its intermittent warning of danger.

She could not say she longed, she yearned. She could not tell this unsympathetic man that love had eluded her, nor why. She forced brightness back on to her face, shook her hair, became brisk. 'Dear me,' she cried gaily, plunging back into the sheltered circle of grass. 'I do hope you haven't eaten everything — I'm ravenous.'

Harriet looked up. As Conor followed behind, Christina saw the look of concern in her friend's face. Does she really think we've been up to something? Christina thought. She could hardly explain that Harriet's husband was almost the last man in the world she would consider having an affair with. Possibly *the* last, give or take a hunchback of Notre Dame, an Elephant Man. She laughed, longing to reassure, but unable, since nothing had been said. 'Fill my glass, darling,' she said, and turned her back on the ravaging sea. Oh, Peter, she thought, Paul. My brothers — and felt her womb contract.

She considered adoption. Somewhere she had read that women who adopted often produced a child of their own shortly afterwards. It was a plan she dropped when the agencies she approached refused to discuss matters without Denis being there. 'And of course, there's your age,' they said kindly, their eyes bland.

'What about it?' Christina asked fiercely. 'I'm only thirty-six.'

'We prefer younger parents,' she was told. 'Your husband is . . .' They looked down at the pieces of paper she had filled in. '. . . fifty-two.'

'What happens if I become pregnant,' she said angrily. 'The State doesn't forcibly prevent a thirty-six-year-old woman with a husband of fifty-two from giving birth, does it?'

'Of course not.'

'Then why should you discriminate against me like this?' she demanded.

But it was not her age they were against, she could see; it was her air of desperation. She took a deep breath and smiled at them.

'There's still plenty of time,' she said.

Love, when it came, was unexpected and blinding.

They bumped into each other at a large business exhibition in Birmingham; he heard her asking knowledgeable questions of a salesman, and stood by, frankly listening. When she turned, raising a cool eyebrow at him, he asked her if she would care for a drink. She agreed. At that stage there was not the slightest indication of the whirling passionate highs or debilitating lows she would suffer because of him.

'Are you staying here overnight?' he asked.

Over her glass she stared at him. Denis moved somewhere inside her skull: kindly Denis, overweight, tamped down, *old*. It's the man's fault, she thought. It's usually the man's fault ... 'I rather think I might,' she said, and shook her short hair at him.

He looked away. She knew what he was going to propose before he said it. 'Perhaps we could save on hotel bills. After all ...'

'After all ...' she agreed. She ordered another drink for them both; she insisted on paying. The alcohol was marvellously liberating. She followed its progress through her body and felt the deep-hidden tissues soak it up, swell into life, grow fecund. She felt enormously ready.

They dined together at a Spanish restaurant, knees touching beneath an inadequate table. The food was indifferent, the wine warm and very red. Afterwards, the two of them walked back to the hotel, not touching. In the bedroom, she telephoned Denis while the man pulled her white blouse from her shoulders. He pushed her down on the pillow, he tore her pants apart, ripping the thin material between strong hands while she assured her husband that she was fine, the exhibition was instructive, she would be home the following day. His head was buried already between her thighs as she replaced the receiver. She had never in her life felt as far from her own concept of herself as she did then, lying passive while he discovered her. He wanted nothing from her except her body; she gave it totally, wanting him to have everything of her that she could possibly give. He had no interest in sexual prowess or fancy positions; he wished only to dominate, to move himself inside her according to his own physical imperatives. Once he turned her over, raising her buttocks, tilting her so that she clearly felt him probing at the mouth of her womb. She hoped he would come then, in that auspicious position, but it took a little longer. As his seed rushed towards its destination, she thought: if I become pregnant, it will have my colouring, and Denis will never know. She was happy.

In the middle of the night, she fitted herself round his sleeping body and reached a hand across him to caress him into erection again. Turning, suddenly astride, he grinned down at her, her thighs spread, her arms pinned on either side of her head by his hands. There was a savagery about him that she adored. 'Jesus,' he said. 'You really wanted it, didn't you?'

She nodded. 'Didn't you?'

'Looking at you, I'd never have guessed,' he said.

She did not say that she had fallen in love with him. She sensed that would be disastrous.

She knew his field of expertise took him abroad for long stretches at a time. When they parted the next morning, she did not ask if they would meet again.

He telephoned her. 'Look,' he said. 'Meet me for lunch.' He named a pub some fifty miles away from Oxford. She agreed.

'I'm married, you're married,' he said. 'We shouldn't do

this. Trouble is, I can't stop thinking about you.'

'Do you feel guilty about it?' she asked.

He looked away at the river which flowed past the windows. 'I ought to,' he said.

'I don't. I don't want my husband hurt, but I can't see any reason why he should be,' she said. She touched his hand and felt electricity spark between them. Inside her designer suit, her body frothed and melted. If he did not suggest they rented a room, she would do so herself. But he did. They made love again and again; with each of his ejaculations Christina felt herself swelling into orgasm, her body bucking under his. The pleasure was far more than physical.

They managed a weekend together while Denis was abroad. They stayed at a small hotel in the Peak District with views of water and stark hills. Waking her in the night to begin one of his slow savage attacks on her, he suddenly began gasping.

'What's wrong?' she whispered. She sat up against the pillows.

'I don't know.'

'Us?'

'Not us. Me. I've made a mess of things.' He laid his head against her small breasts. She cradled him, feeling his hair soft on her arm. When he turned and softly nuzzled at her nipple, she nearly screamed aloud with pleasure. This, she thought, this is what it would be like if I ... this orgasmic sharing, this bonding.

'What sort of mess?' she asked.

'Marriage. I should never have got married.'

'Why did you, then?'

He grimaced. 'I was persuaded into it.'

'By her? Your wife?'

'No, actually.' His laugh was self-condemnatory. 'By someone else, one of my family.'

'How strange. Why should someone urge you to get married when you didn't want to?'

'Reasons ... they seemed to have some point at the time.'

'Not terribly fair on her, was it?'

'I know. Poor girl ...' He brushed his hand down across her stomach and between her legs. 'That's why I feel so bad. I thought I could handle the situation, but I can't.'

'How does she feel about it?'

'We don't discuss it. But we never had anything in common but sex.'

'Still?'

'Not even that any more. Not like us, you and me. We're the same sort.'

'Total bastards, you mean?'

He laughed, in the middle of a sigh. 'That too. I just wish I could share something with her, though, the way I can share just about anything with you. She's not happy, and I don't know how to make her so. And the trouble is I don't really care.'

'That's very obvious.'

'Is it?'

She reached down and gently stroked his testicles. She felt him harden and turn in her arms. Sliding down into the bed again, she said: 'I know how you can make *me* happy.'

'You're shameless,' he said.

She was. For the first time in her life she felt no shame, no secrecy. If she could have turned herself inside-out for him, exposing glands and veins and tissues to his gaze, she would have done so. She remembered the female form in her biology classes at school, the little flaps which lifted to expose the infrastructure beneath. She remembered confirmation classes, too, the school chaplain, *all the sinful lusts of the flesh*. Even then it had seemed a ripely robust, lip-smacking sort of phrase. This, she supposed was what it meant: this complete freedom, this total giving of the body ... *sinful lusts.* What she loved most about her lover was that he expected nothing from her. Because of that, she expected nothing from herself.

She talked to him. For the first time in her life she told someone of the sea-swallowed brothers, of the shock, of the pain those two young deaths had caused her. She spoke of her mother, of the feeling of alienation she had always had. Doing so, burdens rolled away from her. Her breasts grew; her periods became more regular. She felt as though, having been merely in bud all her life, she was at last flowering.

He often telephoned, always from a callbox, to tell her methodically, in tremendous detail, what he proposed to do to her next time they were in bed together. Afterwards, she lay on the coverlet in the bedroom she shared with Denis and brought herself to climax, her body jerking while tears of forlorn ecstasy squeezed from her eyes.

Although she did not immediately become pregnant, she knew that eventually she would; that the child would be his.

Harriet invited her over for the afternoon. Christina longed to talk about it, to tell her friend about the parching passions which filled her. The words crowded sometimes at the back of her throat, salty and searing. If she were ever to let them out, they would cause untold damage. She had stopped drinking except when with her lover, afraid that wine would make her garrulous. Harriet remarked on how beautiful she was looking. Harriet herself drooped, her shoulders hunched under her thin blouse. She was sad. 'What is it?' Christina asked, but Harriet shook her head. She guessed that Harriet's marriage was in difficulties; not surprising, with a husband hardly ever there and, when he was, so rude, so discourteous, so unlike Denis.

Harriet led her through the unkempt garden to the shed. 'Look,' she said.

Christina saw canvases, a dozen or more, stacked around the wooden walls. They burned, they shouted. 'My God,' she said. 'Did you do these?'

'Yes.'

'But they're amazing.' Christina looked again, astonished by the power and energy, the brilliant screaming colours. Suddenly perceptive, she realised that inside Harriet must be a core of solid strength.

*

Her lover asked her to come to Paris for the weekend.

'There's a conference,' she told Denis. 'You don't mind, do you?' — meaning you won't mind, will you, if you find out what I'm really doing?

He looked up at her, bending over his chair, her face alight. He thought: she is going to a lover. The thought did not disturb him. Above everything else he wished her to be happy, and knew that she had not been. He wondered if she was right to be so vehemently opposed to having children. For himself he did not mind: he liked the even patterns of their life together. Clearly she wanted — needed — something more.

She bought lingerie, new shoes, stockings of real silk. She examined her body in the mirrors of her bedroom and imagined her lover's hands on her. She cupped her small breasts in her palms. 'This is the time,' she said aloud. 'I'm ready. And, surely, in the country of my mother's birth it would be particularly fitting. Surely I cannot fail, this time, to conceive.'

He met her at the airport. 'God, I've missed you,' he said. 'Definite withdrawal symptoms have been setting in.'

'We'd better do something to alleviate them, then,' she said.

'Here?' He turned a mock-alarmed face to the taxi-driver's back.

'As soon as possible,' she said. She guided his hand under her skirt to her crotch. She was not wearing panties; she was wet.

'Christina,' he said, later, as she lay exhausted in bed, eyelashes long on her cheeks.

'What?'

'Do you think ...? I mean, should we, perhaps ...'

'What? Tell me.'

'I think ...' He looked abashed, sitting naked on the side of the bed. There were red roses all round the room; champagne waited in a silver bucket, with two glasses he had bought in the kitchen department of the Galeries Lafayette. 'I love you.'

The words hit her opened flesh like a whip. Happiness cut

through her. She cried out, as she did in orgasm.

'Oh, God,' she said. 'I love you, too, more than you'll ever know. I love you, I *love* you.'

He turned and forced his mouth down on hers. 'I want to *be* you,' she cried, when he stopped. 'Make me you, make the two of us one.'

'I'd give anything, anything ...' he said. He bent his head so his face was close to hers. 'Listen. I want to marry you.'

'What about ... your wife?'

'She doesn't love me,' he said flatly.

'I do.'

'Really?'

'Really.' She started the soft scream which heralded her climaxes as her body closed round his, contracting again and again. He began to come; it went on and on, while Christina laughed softly, pinning him to her, feeling the endless life-productive stream of him.

'I love you,' he said.

Harriet's telephone call came like a holocaust. 'Conor's dead?' Christina said. 'He can't be.'

'Some kind of logging accident,' Harriet said. Her voice was soft, muted, as though tears had washed its strength away.

'No ... no.'

'I can't believe it, Chris. I can't take it in.'

'I'll come,' Christina said. Shock made her legs tremble.

'No,' Harriet said. 'I have a friend with me — another friend. Someone I knew before I ever met you.' Even in trouble, Christina thought, she tries to make sure nobody is hurt. She wondered if this could be some kind of divine retribution for her own betrayal of Denis, then realised how far-fetched that was. Harriet, after all, was innocent; why should she be punished for the sins of others?

The circle that had once been four was now three. Three was not a comfortable number. But better than one, Christina thought, remembering the three she had once been part of. She watched Harriet, concerned by the younger woman's pallor, the shadows under her eyes, her bewilderment. *Had she genuinely loved Conor?* she wondered. *Is her heart breaking?* She felt very close to her friend; she made every effort to touch, to comfort, to reassure.

It was a time of disaster. Her lover no longer telephoned; her hopes of pregnancy did not seem to be fulfilled. Her periods had ceased altogether, and Denis seemed more importunate. Did he guess what she had been up to? She felt warmth for him, and gratitude; but she did not wish to make love with him. Nonetheless she did so, just in case.

'You're not looking well,' Denis said.

She smiled at him. 'I'm fine, darling. A bit tired.'

'Why don't we go away for the weekend?'

'Where to?'

'Anywhere you like. You choose.'

'No, you choose.'

'Alicante? I could just about squeeze the time in — and the sun would do you good.'

She shook her head. 'Later, maybe — but not at the minute.'

He looked at her and smiled. 'I know the perfect place.'

He took her to a guest-house on the edge of the Lake District. It was peaceful there, watery and green. They walked gently among the rounded hills, taking the car out, finding lonely moors. The smell of heather under the slight English sun was reassuring; she began to feel safe again, as though there was at last some space between herself and Conor's death.

'I used to come here a lot,' Denis said. 'I had a lectureship at Durham.'

'I didn't know.'

'There are lots of things you don't know about me.' He smiled at her, a plain man, and kind.

'And much more you don't know about me.'

The smile moved from his eyes. 'I'm aware of that,' he said quietly.

She reached over and touched his hand.

At breakfast one morning, Denis said to the woman who ran the place, a foreigner, some kind of East European: 'What a pity to cut down that willow tree in the garden.'

The woman stared at him as though searching his words for hidden meanings. Finally she said: 'Yes.'

'What was it, rotten or something?' Denis said. He pulled the marmalade pot towards him.

'Something like that,' the woman said. She looked up sharply as her husband, an odd, shambling man, sidled into the room, his back pressed tightly to the wall. Then she walked quickly towards him, took his arm and led him out of the room.

Christina and Denis raised enquiring eyebrows at each other. 'There's something unpleasant about the husband,' she said. 'I can't make out whether he's mentally deficient or downright sinister. Or both.'

'Amazing, isn't it, how people present a surface to the world which bears no resemblance to what's going on inside them.' Denis's expression was nonjudgemental; she wondered what he knew.

When Harriet told her that she was pregnant, Christina felt sick. When Harriet went on to say she did not want the baby, Christina scolded her. 'You mustn't say things like that — mustn't even think them. The child will know. It's not fair.'

'Would you want it, in the circumstances?' Harriet said bitterly.

'Perhaps not.' Christina saw how Harriet's mouth opened, as though to confess something, then closed again. Somewhere secret and faraway inside herself, she found herself thinking: she does not deserve to have Conor's child if that is how she feels. 'We must make a plan, draw up a timetable,' she said briskly.

Harriet groaned. 'Must we?'

'Yes. Exercises for you; a proper diet. You must not put on too much weight. And you must join a class, learn how to do whatever it is pregnant mothers do — exercises and so on.'

'Christina, please.'

'It's important for the baby, Harriet.' She laughed. 'But what do I know? It's just — you had that miscarriage, didn't you? You have to be a bit careful.'

'That was Conor's fault, not mine.'

'Darling, nobody's blaming anyone here.' Christina put her head on one side. 'Mind if I ask you something personal?'

'You can ask,' Harriet said.

'Did you love Conor?'

There was silence. Harriet picked up the egg-shaped paper-weight of blue-green glass which she kept on the coffee-table in front of the fireplace. 'I don't know,' she said, after a pause. 'I did, once. I think I still did when he — when he was killed. But —'

'He was a bit of a sod, frankly,' Christina said.

'Yes.' Harriet bit her lip. 'I suppose he was.'

Looking at her, Christina thought: if you won't plan things, or get organised, then I shall.

'We're going to have a quick dash to Spain,' said Christina. 'Before ...'

'Before what?'

'Darling, I've got to be *here* when this baby arrives. You'll need someone like me around.'

'I hope you don't see yourself boiling pans of water on the stove and tearing Denis's old shirts up.'

'Don't be silly. Mine will be the calming influence. In the absence of both husband and mother, you're going to need one.'

'How silly of me not to realise ...'

Explaining on the phone about Denis was terrible. 'He fell,' she said. 'He's dead.' Such bald and naked words to describe something so momentous. *Fell. Dead.* What they meant was that she was on her own; she must learn to live without Denis. The things still left to do were logged into her brain; one by one she must deal with them, tick them off.

'Oh God ...' Harriet sounded very far away.

Christina tried to sound calm, despite the threatening

tears. It was important to keep Harriet away from hysteria, for the baby's sake. But in the end the tears overcame her. 'What am I going to do without him?' she gasped. For so long Denis had been the rock in her personal sea.

'Do you want me to fly out?' Harriet said.

'Flying's not good for the baby.'

Christina put down the telephone slowly. There was an ache in her heart, an emptiness. It was nearly forty-eight hours since she had opened the door to the police, seen the appalled face of the woman in the ground-floor apartment, heard sirens below the window. Yet the flat was still full of shocked air, the doors on to the balcony swinging open to the lights in the harbour, where Denis had been standing before he ...

She stared out at them, still holding the receiver, thinking how odd it was that she had never felt this sea to be threatening, contained as it was by the harbour wall, by the marble-flagged *paseo* and the dark green palms. What had those last seconds been like for him? Had the night air whistled past his ears, had he time to realise what had happened, before the final terrible landing? Would it have been worse if he had cried out her name, instead of descending into the blackness with the final mouthful of wine blocking his throat?

For a moment she was numb with the enormity of what had happened. She knew it would begin to bite only when she returned home to England, to the house where Denis no longer was.

What both astonished and frightened her was the fact that this latest tragedy meant so much less than the first, more than twenty years ago.

TOM

· 15 ·

As figures went, that was definitely not a bad one, Tom Seaton decided. And especially well suited to the tight black skirt which covered and, at the same time, defined it. It was not always easy to find compensations for a small-town law practice that despite strenuous efforts on the part of its two partners to remain general, nonetheless dealt with an ever-growing number of matrimonial cases. One compensation might be held to be an increasing expertise in divorce law, particularly as practised in Delrey County in the State of California. The other would have to be the number of high-quality asses stepping — you might almost say queuing *up* to step — through the door of their office.

After two years of it, Tom felt he could tell a would-be divorcée's marital history just by looking — discreetly, of course — at her butt. Sometimes, generally after a long lunch with his partner, who also happened to be his cousin, he considered asking the plaintiff — the *would-be* plaintiff, that is — not to open her mouth, just to show him her rear-end, and he would then prepare the appropriate case, without a further word being spoken between them.

But he told himself that laughing to hide the tears was one thing. Ending up on the wrong side of a civil suit for sexual harassment was quite another.

Nonetheless, over the past two years, if he'd learned anything at all, it was the correlation between the size of the backside and the size of the alimony its owner demanded. Watching this particular rear, set on top of long legs in sheer black hose and black patent shoes, stepping carefully down the three brick steps from the front door on to the herring-bone-bricked path, and moving erotically towards the sidewalk between the foot-high picket fencing, he remarked for the first time a further truth. Show me a small butt, he told himself, and I'll show you a lady asking to be screwed. In the metaphorical sense, of course. In the purely financial sense. Because he had come to the impartial view that, as a general rule of thumb, out of all the women who came and wept in his office, dabbing at their eyes with the pink tissues he kept handy in the bottom right-hand drawer of his desk, the ones with the small tight buns were basically there because they still loved their husbands and hoped that somehow he, Counsellor Tom Seaton, could put the clock back to the time when they were fresh young brides, when the bloom still lay untouched upon their marriages, when their husband had still loved them. To the time, in other words, before the said husband met the woman/bitch/floosy/tramp/homebreaker who was currently engaging his attention.

Divorce was the last thing those ladies wanted. They all held their errant husbands to be blameless, convinced that the woman/bitch/floosy/etc. had enticed him away from his happy family circle into a seething maelstrom of illicit sex and controlled substances. Not to mention spiritous and expensive liquors. Whereas, *generally*, the bigger looser ladies hated the crumbum husband who'd been giving them hell for the past ten/twenty/thirty years, and they were out to take him for every red cent they could.

Maybe there was a paper in it. Maybe he could present it at the next legal congress, which, if he remembered rightly, was set for Seattle next October. The Correlation Between The Size Of The Female Posterior And The Size Of The Female Desire For Vengeance By Way Of A Separation Agreement. If nothing else, it might liven things up a little.

He sighed. Face it, he thought. It wasn't just 'things' — whatever they might be — that needed livening up a little; it was himself. Some days he felt as if he were operating from the middle of a cloud. He sympathised with those eastern women who were forced to wear the *chador*; he'd experienced the same sensations as they must feel behind their enveloping layers. How much easier it would be if his black depressions were something he could tear off and fling away when he wanted to, instead of being attached to him like a second skin.

Down on the street, the lady in the black hose stopped under one of the two big pepper trees that shaded the building, and dabbed at her nose. Pink to match the tissue. For a moment, with the auburn hair and the high frilled collar of her white blouse, she looked so like Rebecca that his heart somersaulted. Rebecca used to wear a blouse like that. Broderie anglaise, she had told him. Hand-made in Switzerland.

'Ever been hand-made in the USA?' he'd asked her, and she'd allowed as how she never had, but there was always a first time. The blouse had emphasised the soft vulnerability which, at the time, he had not yet realised was as false as a pensioner's teeth. One of Nature's con-tricks, designed to perpetuate the species by entrapment of the unwary male.

He looked at his watch. At the same time, the door of Amis's office opened and Benny Costello shouldered through it. Big Benny Costello, his face flushed under his year-round tan, almost the same colour as one of his own dahlias — if you could imagine a dahlia in rimless eyeglasses. Benny Costello who looked as though he cut down trees for a living but was one of the shrewdest businessmen in the county, and incidentally was also, as of twenty minutes ago, the new owner of some of the primest real estate around, and thereby committed to the kind of interest rates on his bank loan that brought tears to the eyes.

Benny had plans; shopping malls, ten-screen cinemas, fast food outlets, fancy restaurants. Privately, Tom very much doubted if Benny knew an escalope from a chopping board, but then he wouldn't need to. If his financial gamble — and this was definitely *not* a good time to be taking gambles; as Amis had been far from reluctant to point out — he would be able to leave such subtleties to others.

Look at the guy. Baggy old work-pants and a blue check Pendleton shirt was good enough for the Costello Nurseries, and it sure was good enough when he came into town to see his legal advisers. No sheer black hose and patent leather pumps for Benny, even if he *was* worth somewhere round a million bucks plus loose change.

Behind Benny came Amis, trying hard to look like the Englishmen his and Tom's common grandfather had been. And failing, it should be said. For one thing, Grandfather Seaton wouldn't have given a damn about hair-loss. Might even have welcomed it as adding dignity and weight, whereas Amis always reeked of the snake-medicine hair restoratives they sold him at the barbershop. Bald is bald, Tom had told him scores of times; to which Amis always said he knew perfectly well what bald was, thank you — who better?

Lots of famous people are bald, Tom would say, and Amis would ask him to name one, just one. It was like when people asked you if you'd read any good books lately, which a surprising number of them did. Naturally, you not only couldn't remember what books you had read recently; you also couldn't remember the name of any book you had ever read in your whole life. Equally, the only famous baldy that sprang to mind was Humpty Dumpty, not much compensation for a man who was losing his hair. But when you thought about it, there had to be hundreds of others.

Rebecca, he thought, you were my compensation, for just about everything.

'Boy,' Benny said, taking in both the cousins: Amis standing by the leather-topped partners' desk, Tom over by the window still watching the neat ass sway out of sight. 'What a relief to get that signed. It seems like a hundred years since we started negotiating.'

'You have to get the details right,' Amis said, sounding prim.

'Plus Gardner sure took his time about selling,' Benny said.

'You can't afford to hurry these things along,' said Amis.

'I guess not.'

'All the same, it was a lucky break for you, his mother dying when she did,' Amis said.

'Hey, listen, you said it, not me.' Benny spread his big hands, at the same giving both of them in turn what Tom's — and Amis's — grandmother would have called an old-fashioned look, though the accuracy of the description would depend, Tom thought with surprise, on receiving the full beam of Benny's gaze, on exactly how you defined oldfashioned and to what extent you differentiated it from malevolent.

'Not wishing to sound callous,' Amis added, realising he had.

'I can't pretend I wasn't darned relieved the old lady snuffed it,' said Benny. He saw the way Amis frowned at this remark, and went on quickly, 'Look, don't get me wrong, guys. I was real sorry, old Miz Warrington going like that. But hell, come on now, I can't pretend it was some kind of tragedy: sixty-something, nearly seventy last birthday, and all. And I know all there is to know about being stymied by old gals who think we're still back in the Depression.' He looked from cousin to cousin again, then added quickly: 'Guess maybe I was kinda out of line there.'

Avoiding his gaze, Tom wiped a speck of dirt off the window with his finger. 'I still think you could be sticking your neck out,' he said. 'The interest rates and all.'

'Nothing venture, nothing win,' Benny said. 'You gotta speculate in order to accumulate.'

'I did warn you that you might be overstretching yourself,' said Amis stiffly. He touched the Phi Beta Kappa key on the chain across his chest. Tom knew he was thinking about the insurance cheque he'd signed the week before. Up by 17 per cent on last year's premium, and likely to double by this time next year. The judges were voting in such ludicrous malpractice settlements these days that nobody was safe. Not even lawyers — who oughtn't to be liable since they could only advise, not act for their clients. Unless instructed, of course.

'Yeah, well,' Benny said. 'A man's reach should exceed his grasp, isn't that right, Amis?'

Amis smiled thinly. Tom smiled too. If there was one thing Amis did *not* believe, it was that a man's reach should do anything but remain exactly where it was. Words like exceed made Amis very very nervous. Words like risk brought him out in a cold sweat. Words like unsecured loan or stock-market speculation had been known to induce minor breathing difficulties.

'Better take good care of your stepmother,' he said.

'Sure,' said Benny. 'You bet.'

'Otherwise,' said Amis, 'you'll really be up the creek, won't you?'

Benny stared at him. 'How exactly do you mean?' he said. Under the tight-stretched skin of his face, the meat seemed to harden. Tom had never realised just how steely the guy's expression could be.

Amis stared back at Benny — then over at Tom. He brushed at his forehead, careful not to disarrange the thin-spread hair which decorated the top part. It was a gesture he'd been making since childhood. A gesture of appeal. A gesture that said: for chrissake get me out of this. He pulled a watch from his waistcoat pocket and consulted it, though Tom knew for a fact that the watch hadn't worked since Amis was seventeen.

Which did not alter the fact that Amis had boobed. It looked as though Benny Costello was not privy to the provisions of his mother's will. It also looked as though Lydia Costello wanted it that way. Tom was not privy either; nonetheless, he acted quickly. He laughed. 'One thing about your Mom,' he said, false-hearty. 'She certainly isn't going to go out with a whimper. Anything ever happens to her, she'll expect nothing less than a public holiday.'

'Right,' said Amis. 'A national day of mourning. Every flag in the Union flying at half-mast.'

'State funeral. You know how she is,' said Tom.

'Absolutely,' said Amis. 'With all you've got on your plate, the last thing you want right now is to be coping with your stepmother.'

Benny's face cleared. 'See what you mean. Yeah, right. We're going to be in over our ears for a while.' He grinned. 'Jesus, I've taken gambles before, but I could really go to the cleaners on this restaurant thing, anything went wrong.'

'You could always sell up,' Amis said, 'If the worst came to the worst.'

Benny laughed. He thought Amis was joking. Tom knew he was not. Amis never joked about money. He was right about

Benny selling up. Although the acreage on which the Costello glasshouses and flower-fields stood was not large, it was prime land, especially with the Los Angeles suburbs spreading further and wider with each year that passed.

'I'm real grateful to you boys for all the hard work you put into this deal,' he said. 'It's up to me now, I guess.'

If Amis liked being called a boy, he didn't show it. Tom appreciated it. Sometimes a guy his age started to wonder what had happened to his life, particularly after a slug or two of vodka or, as it might be, slivovitz. Sometimes a guy his age started thinking about jogging in a serious way, or pinched his skin between thumb and forefinger to see how long it took to go flat again — the way he read about in a woman's magazine Rebecca had picked up from the supermarket. Sometimes a guy thought — ever so tentatively, because if he thought too hard, it might hurt — about children, and why he hadn't got any when other guys his age had been fathers for years. Guys like Amis, for instance, with his three musical daughters, and his brand-new Winnebago to take them camping in at Lake Tahoe on weekends. Tom didn't even have a *pet*.

'That's right, sir,' Amis said. 'Lots of work out there before it'll be a paying concern.'

'Right,' Benny put out his hand. 'For a minute back there, talking about Lydia, you had me worried,' he said. 'Hell, you know what could happen if anything went wrong.'

Amis said: 'No reason I can see that it should.'

'Right. Well, guess all I got to do now is to thank you folks and pay the goddamned bill.'

The goddamned *expensive* bill, he might have said. It was not just the insurance. The firm of Seaton & Seaton was good, even if it was small. No more than two guys plus a girl to handle the paperwork. It was an arrangement that wouldn't have worked anywhere but a town the size of Bellamonte. In the big city, the firm of Seaton & Seaton would probably have needed to employ a receptionist and a researcher and maybe even another secretary. Plus God knew what in rental fees, even supposing they were able to locate empty office space. Tom had occasionally suggested to Amis that they up sticks and move up to LA or one of its bigger suburbs: Pacific Palisades, for instance, or Newport Beach. To which Amis would simply point at the photograph of his three daughters which sat right there on his desk, and shake his head. 'Quality of life, Counsellor,' he would say. 'Quality of life.'

He was right, of course. The quality of life in this small tree-lined town was infinitely better than anything up in the city. Also infinitely more boring, especially if you were a one in a place where everyone else came in twos.

'No hurry on that side, Benny,' Amis said now, as he always did. He did not like discussing money. Gentlemen might *need* money, but in Amis's book, they never talked about it.

'How's about you two boys coming over to dinner tonight?' Benny said. 'Informal. We'll be barbecuing.'

'That's very kind of you,' said Amis. 'But there's a PTA meeting at the school, and Margaret and I promised we'd go.'

'You, Tom?'

'Thanks, but I'll have to take a rain-check,' Tom said. He had arranged to meet a client for a quick drink, to discuss a trust fund the client wished to set up for his children by his first and second marriages. Besides, almost certainly Benny, or rather Dale, Benny's wife, would line up some girl for him. People were always lining up girls for him, although he was perfectly capable of lining them up for himself. He just didn't want to, that was all. Or, to be perfectly honest, had not yet met one worth lining up. Not since Rebecca.

'Well, I'm off to the gym,' Benny expanded his chest so his lumberjack's shirt strained at the buttons. 'Us older guys gotta keep in shape, am I right?'

'Right,' Tom said.

The two cousins waited without speaking until Miss Roma Hogg, in the outer office, had closed the door behind Benny. Miss Hogg combined the duties of receptionist, file-clerk and secretary with an efficiency that was truly remarkable. Also, because her boyfriend, a long-haul truck driver, was frequently out of town, she was more than happy to work long hours when necessary. Which was why both partners were prepared to overlook the familiarity with which she treated one of them. The one being Tom. Though, as Tom often said to Amis, he could understand why Amis should overlook it, but he was darned if he saw why he himself should.

They watched Benny walk down the brick path, then pause between the two pepper trees and look left to catch the clock on the top of the First City Bank of Bellamonte and check it with his own watch. He rubbed his chest inside his shirt then took a leather cigar case from the back pocket of his work-pants and pulled out a cigar.

'How old do you reckon him to be?' Amis said.

'Fifty-five, fifty-six,' said Tom. 'Somewhere in there.'

Amis drew his breath in sharply between his teeth. 'Fifty-six,' he said. 'And I'll bet he's got every goddamned hair he was ever born with.'

'More,' said Tom. 'You think about the average baby.'

'Yeah.'

'Shakespeare,' Tom said.

'What about him?'

'He was bald.'

'So?'

'Just thought I'd mention it.'

'Think I should start wearing a ruff to the office?'

'It could bring in a lot of business.'

'Not necessarily the kind we want,' Amis said.

Having lit his cigar, Benny crimped himself into the big black Citroën parked at the kerb. Only when the car had pulled away did Amis look at Tom.

'Well,' he said softly. 'Life is full of surprises.'

'I'm not about to disagree with you on that one,' Tom said. 'Why, only last week I met up with some guy I'd known in college and he turned out to be none other than that —'

'The surprise *I* refer to, Counsellor, as you well know,' said Amis 'is the one Benny Costello has just given me.'

'I am cognisant of that fact, Counsellor.'

'Or was I wrong in thinking that he was unaware of the terms of Lydia's will?'

'It looked that way to me.'

'It certainly seems the obvious deduction to be drawn from his reaction when I referred to Lydia's health.'

'You'll forgive me saying so, Amis, but that was a dumb thing to do.'

'How was I supposed to know Benny didn't know what you and I are very well aware of, viz, that if Lydia Costello dies —'

'Which sooner or later she's pretty well bound to do.'

'— *when* she dies, all hell will be let loose?' Amis peered at Tom through his glasses. 'You ever looked at that will? Closely, I mean?'

'She's your client.'

'You should. It's a real dilly.'

'And guess who's going to be right in the firing-line flak when Lydia goes.'

'The executors is whom. Seaton & Seaton.'

'Frankly, I'd have called your words to Mr Benjamin Costello a definite breach of attorney–client privilege, Counsellor, wouldn't you?'

'Most definitely, Counsellor,' Amis said. 'There would be no other way to describe it.'

There was a pause during which Miss Hogg could be heard vigorously slamming file drawers shut. Then Tom asked: 'Just as a matter of interest, Counsellor, how would you describe the quick-thinking way in which I pulled you out of the shit into which you so thoroughly dropped yourself?'

Amis thought about it. 'Fucking marvellous would probably cover it appropriately,' he said.

'Would you consider that lunch might *reward* it appropriately?'

'I think it might.'

'With martinis?'

'With wine but without martinis,' said Amis. 'You want martinis, boy, you buy your own damn martinis.'

'You're on,' Tom said.

· 16 ·

Roma had been walking backwards and forwards across the floor of her office ever since she got in that morning. The noise was driving Tom into the first stages of an anxiety attack. Each time one of her cork heels hit the floor, it sounded as though a gun had gone off. Plip! Snap! Crack! With every detonation, he winced. Wincing hurt. Incapable of shouting through the closed door, he dialled her desk number.

Clip! Clap! He heard her go over to her desk. She picked up.

'Roma?'

Although he could hear her breathing, she didn't answer.

'Whatever you're doing, stop,' he ordered.

'Tied one on last night, did you?'

'Not just one.'

'Serves you right.'

'Boy, I hope I never get sick and end up with you for a nurse.'

'Fat chance.'

'What are you *doing* in there, anyway?' he said.

'What does it sound like?'

'As though you're practising for the inter-county pistol shooting championships.'

'Gee, Mr Seaton. However did you guess?'

'Well, practise on your own time,' growled Tom.

'Actually, what I'm doing is my filing. But since you made a pig of yourself last night, guess it'll have to get all behindhand.' She sighed hugely, nearly perforating Tom's eardrum. 'Where was you at?'

'That's my private business,' Tom said. He was sensitive

about such questions. He had found that they nearly always led on to a question about who he was with. He hated having to say nobody.

'Bet it was the theatre fundraiser.'

'There is absolutely no privacy in this town,' Tom said.

'That's right, Mr Seaton. Never has been, never will be. You want privacy, you got to move up to the big city.'

'I might just do that.'

'It's plenty private up there. So private up there you can get mugged or raped or murdered and ain't nobody going to notice a *thing*.'

'Yeah.'

'"Sides, who in Bellamonte's got anything to hide?"

Tom stared at his law degree, hanging on the wall next to his licence to practise. 'Good question.'

He returned to his paperwork, trying to get through it at double speed. With his European trip coming closer every moment, he was running out of time in which to reorganise his schedules for the three months he planned to be away. And now Lydia wanted to see him . . .

Last night's quick drink had led on to several slower ones, and then dinner at an out-of-town restaurant that specialised in steaks. Rather, it specialised in top-quality wines from Californian growers, and provided superb steaks to go with. It was only as they had ordered a second bottle, having enjoyed almost to swooning point a 74 Cabernet from Stag's Leap, that Tom's client looked at his watch.

'Hey, I'm supposed to be over to the theatre by nine,' he said.

'Why?' Tom said.

'They're having a fundraiser,' said his client. 'Come on, you can come with me.'

'OK,' Tom said. There was nothing else he had to do.

The fundraiser was in full swing when they got there, spilling out of the glass cage of the theatre's reception area into a patio behind. When the theatre was first built, by public subscription, the intention had been to use the patio to stage plays of the more experimental kind — things that would not come across on the conventional stage — or hold open-air chamber-music concerts given by visiting trios and quartets. The present event was an attempt to raise enough money to persuade a trio or quartet or someone — *anyone* — to include Bellamonte on their next tour, and thus raise the cultural level off the ground. Most of those present had been trying to do that for some time, without marked success. Bellamonte, as a whole, seemed rather to enjoy being culturally on the ground. Anyway, they had a perfectly good community orchestra, didn't they, which played three concerts a year, didn't it, so where was the point in bringing in strangers? Bellamonte was very insular.

Tom waved to a few people, talked to a few more. He missed Rebecca. He *always* missed Rebecca, but at gatherings of this kind he remembered her with a different kind of longing. Not a sexual or emotional one, but a throat-choking nostalgia for the sense of belonging that she bestowed. As though she had spun a web, people used to come to where Rebecca was at parties; she trapped them with her smile and her red hair, with her sparkle, just as she had once trapped Tom.

At least three of the women present were former clients. Tom saw their eyes slide sideways at him, and knew that in a few moments they would begin the casual journey that would bring them eventually to his side. Whichever got there first would look up at him and place her soft little hands on his sleeve and make it clear that she would be more than happy to continue the relationship that had begun in his office on a footing that had nothing to do with business. Tom had no illusions about his personal attractions. But he was a man on his own and they were young women on their own. Having sloughed off one man, they were on the lookout for another, even if they had not yet admitted it to themselves. He could not blame them. He knew how lonely being alone could be.

Each of the three women had discovered her husband to be fallible, and had then found she did not have the strength to cope with the knowledge. Sad, Tom thought, looking into their eyes across the room and seeing the ruined memories of things once shared; ball-games and picnics and kisses and plans, high winds and hot beaches and saved-up-for sectional couches. Sad that fooling around with a woman who was not your legally wedded wife so often led to the loss of both the woman and the wife. Sad to lose so much for so little.

Tom did not advocate fooling around. In his own marriage he had never for one moment contemplated going to bed with a woman who was not Rebecca. Nonetheless he felt sometimes that those who *did* fool around needed some kind of protective code of practice, some rules which would help them to minimise the dangers they were getting into, some clear guide to the risk. Of all the divorces he had arranged, at least fifty per cent were over a one-night stand.

He spoke for a while with J.D. Ekins. Back on Wall Street, where he had been an associate — a very junior associate — in a well-known law firm, the J.D. Ekins case would never have been considered. Here in Bellamonte it had the makings of a five-act drama. J.D. was a local merchant who had petitioned for a use-of-premises variation order so he could switch from selling embroidery silks, petit-point canvases with pictures of hollyhocked cottages printed on them, sampler patterns and wools to be knitted into ecologically-sound sweaters, to also selling the finished samplers, completed petit-point pictures and made-up sweaters. The town fathers had nothing against the samplers or the petit-point. Why people who lived in California would want to waste time embroidering a picture of the sort of thatched cottage Shakespeare might have shared with Ann Hathaway, let alone buying one that someone else had wasted time embroidering, was anybody's guess, but apparently enough of them did that J.D. Ekins wanted permission to sell them. It was the finished sweaters that was causing the problem. The town fathers were firmly of the opinion that selling finished sweaters turned J.D. from a purveyor of notions and hobby-goods, for which he had permission, into a clothing outlet, for which he did *not*; and, if they had anything to do with it, never would have. It was plainly ridiculous to see the next step as J.D. offering specials on marked-down Oxford cloth shirts or fire-sale men's jackets, and Tom was rewording the petition to make this clear. The Council was dominated by a female Mayor who had been in office for some fifteen years and, taking its cue from her, was of the opinion that if just one of the original city ordinances was revoked, they would all be trampled to death by the rush of Mexican chili-stands, soft-drink concessions and eighty-foot-high representations of Colonel Sanders or Shoney's Big Boy.

J.D. Ekins returned to his wife. Before Tom could move, the Mayor herself appeared, trapping him uncomfortably against a rough-cast bronze of an elongated man with a spear.

'I saw you talking to J.D.,' she said. 'I hope you told him we need another clothes shop like we need a plague of locusts.'

'J.D. doesn't want to *sell* clothes, Beatrice.'

'Since when is a sweater not a clothe?'

'When it's made from hand-spun, vegetable-dyed wool knitted on miniature flagpoles,' Tom said.

'That's just legal quibbling.'

'Have you ever seen one of these sweaters?'

'Yes.'

'Think about it, Beatrice. Would *you* wear one? Would anyone on the Council wear one? Would anyone in their right *mind* wear one?'

'That is not the point.'

'It is. How many people are actually going to buy clothes — even if those sweaters count — from old J.D.?'

'You know how it is, Tom. One crack in the dam, one precedent established, and we won't be able to move for planning applications. You mark my words, five years from now, Carmel will be unrecognisable.'

'Carmel?'

'By-the-sea. Where they elected that film-star as Mayor.'

'Are you seriously telling me, Beatrice, that it's going to take another Clint Eastwood running for Mayor before J.D.'ll be allowed to sell sweaters in Bellamonte?'

'More or less.'

'Even though he only wants them to demonstrate to his customers what they'll end up with if they buy one of his knitting kits?'

'Right.'

'Perhaps I'd better drive up and ask Clint if any of his friends are interested in running for Mayor down here.'

'You do that, but Tom ...'

'Yeah?'

'He'd still have to beat me in the elections, wouldn't he.'

Tom did not think J.D. had a hope in hell of getting his variance.

Across the room he could see another of his clients — and Bellamonte's self-acknowledged cultural leader — Lydia Costello. Lydia was doing her Grand Duchess number, grey hair wreathed in banks of curls around her head, white peeptoe shoes, long strings of amethyst beads cascading over a dress that could have come straight off the hangers at Buckingham Palace. She looked, he told himself, searching always for the laughs that increasingly he felt were not there, as if she'd sprayed herself with graciousness before she came out.

She saw him. Imperiously she beckoned him over. She looked considerably less imposing than last time he had seen her. Almost as if the beckon had taken up most of her reserves of energy. She must have been overdoing things; perhaps he should tell her to tone down the imperious, and cultivate a little humble. Smiling, he joined her. One of the things he appreciated about Bellamonte was the way that nothing whatsoever happened there. That was the way he liked it. It might not be very demanding, but at least it was quiet. He felt that he needed some quiet. Life with Rebecca had not exactly been a rest-cure.

Sometimes, coming back at the end of the day from his law firm, he would have to make a physical effort to smile at his wife as he saw, beyond her, sprawled across the huge cushions with which she had furnished their Village loft, Tony and Mark and Gemma and Lisa, or Jimmy or Brad or any other of the aspiring actors with whom she seemed to share such an intensely symbiotic relationship. They always had glasses in their hands; they were always plainly intending to stay for hours. Since none of them had ever seen the noonday sun over Manhattan, let alone the dawn, which was mostly when he himself saw it, getting to bed at three o'clock in the morning did not matter much to them. It mattered a great deal to him. Because the loft was in fact no more than a one-room apartment, there was nowhere else for him to go; either he sat it out, willing them to leave, or else he made himself as comfortable as he could among the cushions and tried surreptitiously to doze. What he would really have liked to do was to strip down, shower and watch something totally mindless and undemanding on the TV. With the others there, banging on about Stravinsky — or was it Stanislavsky? — and the new off-off-Broadway experimental production of *Streetcar* with the male roles played by women and vice-versa, that was quite impossible.

Looking back, he often wondered why he had not said something; not ordered them out. He could have pointed out that he was in a demanding job and needed rest and relaxation when he came home from the office, not constant partying. But to do so would have been to cause the fine frown lines to show up on Rebecca's broad forehead, and her voice to hover somewhere between incredulity and scorn. It meant her asking whether he really believed a woman should have to curtail her life merely because she is female and married.

Yes, he would have said, resting his head in his hands, trying not to think about the gin bottle in the icebox and the lovely sound of ice-cubes in a glass after a long, long day. Yes, frankly, I do, particularly when the man involved is working his buns off all day to keep the woman he loves — the gorgeous wonderful woman for whom he is *happy* to work his buns off — in acting-classes and voice coaches. Even more particularly when the woman is so busy postmor-teming the auditions she and her friends fail, and discussing the parts they intend to try for, that she doesn't even have time to fix something for supper, let alone make the bed or clean out the apartment. He could have said he needed peace and quiet in order to recoup for the thunderous day ahead, and all the ones after that. He did not much like living in New York, but accepted that if Rebecca was to make it as an actress, she needed to be where the theatres were, and the classes and the coaches and the auditions.

Now, he could see that the relationship had been based more on sex than on compatibility. He could remember being in bed with Rebecca, holding her, one hand on her back and one just below her buttocks, pressing her against him, every cell on the surface of his skin reacting to every cell of hers, every hair and nerve and fold of his drawing out the heat of hers. *With this body I thee worship.* That was what he did: he worshipped.

At weekends, when they had time to themselves, he would spread her out on the silk and velvet cushions. Looking at her. Marvelling. Feasting on her. Sometimes she stared back, eyes slowly widening, slowly reaching out to stroke his stomach, his thighs, his penis, before she opened to him, laughing, as he braced himself above her, prolonging the moment of entry for agonising seconds while he remembered all the other times and knew that no memory could possibly retain the unbearable sweetness of her flesh enclosing his. Sometimes she closed her eyes and dozed with a smile on her face, while he learned her, tracing ribs and veins, the shape of her bones beneath the white skin, committing her to memory. He liked to snuffle at her, to smell her, to touch her with his tongue, under her arms, behind her ears, the salty-sweet places between her thighs. He liked it when she moaned, when her breathing quickened. He liked her liking that. Sometimes they lay together for hours, he swollen inside her, as they felt the blood move within their mingled bodies, sharing sensation to such a heightened degree that, he had always believed, their two identities became one.

He sucked breath in suddenly. Lydia was looking at him; he tried to smile. She had told him once that she had married the first time for money, the second time for love.

'Most people,' she had said, 'do it the other way round.'

A sudden sharp pain had enclosed his eyes; he felt as though acid tears were leaking from under his eyelids. Sometimes he found himself ridiculous for still, after four years, mourning a woman who had never in the first place been what he supposed her to be. '*I* did,' he had said, keeping it light. 'Do you get a choice, the second time?'

'I can't see why not.'

'In that case, I think I'll opt for love the second time, as well as the first.'

She had smiled. 'Lucky Tom, if you can do it,' she had said.

Now, she put one of her beautiful hands lightly on his shoulder. 'Benny tells me you're off to Europe next week, on vacation.'

'That's right.'

'For how long?'

'Six months. Maybe longer. Maybe,' he said, reckless with the time ahead, 'for ever.'

'Some vacation.'

'Europe's something I promised myself I'd do right after graduating, but other things got in the way.'

Like Rebecca, he thought. The long-awaited meander across Europe had ended up as ten scrambled days in London and Paris. He had not even had time to contact Stephan, though he had managed to take a side-trip to Oxford, which he had found as romantic as he always suspected. He recalled now a girl he had glimpsed and, remembering, remembered also one of the poems Stephan had read to him as they sat in the cedar tree that endless summer in Maine when life had seemed too bleak for bearing: *I did but see her passing by and yet I love her till I die*. Romantic, he told himself, but unlikely.

'Come and visit tomorrow, Tom,' Lydia said. 'There's something I have to discuss with you.'

'Wouldn't Amis be —'

'This is not something Amis need know about. It has very little to do with my affairs, anyway. So you'll come?'

'Tomorrow? I'm not sure . . .'

'Please, Tom. It's terribly important.' She seemed desperately concerned. He looked at her fine square face and saw a translucence about the skin that disturbed him.

'Let me think ...' He would have to juggle his appointments around, skip lunch maybe. The trip to Europe was coming closer by the hour and the amount of stuff he had to deal with before he took off seemed never to diminish; all his evenings were taken up with business as it was. Lydia, however, was not only a client but a valued friend; he would swing it somehow.

'Benny's out tomorrow: come and dine with me,' she said. The shadow of her youth hung like a ghost about her face.

He thought quickly. He guessed he had to eat sometime, so why not with Lydia? 'Eight o'clock be all right?'

'Eight would be wonderful.' Her relief was disproportionate to any service that he could imagine she needed. He would not have called himself fanciful but he felt a sudden chill cross his back: what his grandmother would have said meant an angel was walking across his grave.

Around them, people moved wavelike towards the end of the room. Lydia was about to address them on the subject of money, something about which she was very knowledgeable; he recalled that she had been an investment broker in her first husband's firm. He had edged out of a side door and gone home to bed. But not to sleep.

The phone on his desk rang.

'I can see Miz Haldane coming up the path,' Roma said into his ear.

He groaned. 'I'd forgotten about her.'

'I'll bring in her file.'

'Oh Lord. I just can't cope with tears this morning,' Tom said. He brightened. 'Maybe she won't cry today.'

'Dream on, boy. She already started.'

'Darn it.'

'I'll bring in a fresh box of tissues when I come in with the coffee,' Roma said. 'Best I can do.'

The road out of town to the Costello Nurseries was lined with pepper trees. In the evening sunshine, their leaves glittered, hanging like shards of glass in the windless air. Tom found himself thinking back to Maine, to his grandmother's big white house standing between salt sea and freshwater lake. There had been wind there, blowing off the sea, carrying with it a sharpness that was altogether missing in this clear California light. He longed for greyness and the great thunderheads massing silently out to sea; he missed lifting the latch of a back door and being hit by air which, though not quite wet, nonetheless carried moisture in it.

Excitement nipped his stomach at the thought of the coming trip to Europe. He had been given a second chance; he felt immeasurably lucky. Carefully he skirted the place in his mind where he kept memories of his parents padlocked and barred. In the past, luck had been something that had better things to do than hang round Tom Seaton — and yet somehow, without any conscious effort on his part, he had won through to this point of being able to take off, to bum around without responsibilities, without having to give a minute's thought — not even a second's — to anyone else except himself. It grated to have to admit it, but perhaps there wss something in the old saying about ill winds. After all, if he and Rebecca had hung on in there, stayed married, had kids, he wouldn't now be in a position to indulge himself the way he was about to.

Six months in Europe — hell; eight months, a year, for*ever*, if he wanted — it was like breathing pure oxygen. What I found so great over there, he told himself, unconsciously pressing the accelerator closer to the floor, was the size of the place, its manageability and the lack of taken-for-granted ease. Daily living required more effort over there than it does in California, and the effort meant there was more challenge — I liked that, too.

His head filled with the lightness of — what? *The unbearable lightness of being* ... there'd been a book, hadn't there? And a film? He remembered it; slow sequences shot with a white kind of light about them, an atmosphere of not being quite tethered to the ground, of eyes not quite meeting, of passion and someone weeping just out of earshot. Yes: passion, of the sort he remembered so well. He refused to be bothered by the fact that he and Rebecca had always promised themselves this trip; after all, prior to Rebecca, he had promised it to himself.

He could clearly see Stephan, big and blond and earnest. They'd said they would keep in touch, but had done so only sporadically. And then it had mainly been through Stephan's efforts, he remembered guiltily. This time he would definitely contact the guy — he'd already called his aunt in Maine and gotten the address. He felt warmed: although they hadn't met for years, Stephan was one of the valuable things left, one of the fragments of his past to be cared for, watched over.

He recalled the white sheers of his grandmother's house, ghostly through open windows as she played Mozart on summer evenings. Maine had always been special; partly because it was home, but mostly because it was the place where he had last seen his parents. He felt close to them there; for years he had secretly cherished the hope that maybe, just maybe, his mother had survived the storm, that one day he would open his eyes and see her again in front of him, that, like Botticelli's Venus, she would rise reborn from the sea foam with her yellow hair blowing about her face, would come walking back between the pine trees, waving, and their lives would take up from where they had left off.

Growing older, of course, he understood that it could not happen, that she was gone and would not come back, any more than his father would. For months he could not look at the boulder down by the sea's edge where he knew his father's body had been found; then one day he had stripped off his clothes and stood naked on the rock, desperate to find him again, desperate to get closer to the element which had snatched the two of them away from him and left him unshelled, unprotected. It had been raining; the sea poured endlessly over the hard granite, over his bare feet, and spray had salted his body. He had opened his mouth and shouted for them, '*Mom, Dad, come back, oh, please don't leave me alone, please,*' his words whipped away in rags of sound as he repeated them over and over again, until they became a wild song, a chant, a mantra: '*Dad, Mom, come back to me, oh, come back,*' tears and rain running down his cheeks and his heart turning over and over with intolerable pain.

It would have been easy then to slip into the water and let it carry him away to where they were, yet he had suddenly been aware of the world shaking under him, of flames roaring below the earth's crust and of his own desire to live. Perhaps it had been a turning-point for him; it was at any rate the summer Stephan arrived, like some kind of healing angel, carrying his poetry in one hand and his high ambitions in the other.

Ahead of him the shadows folded themselves down the hillsides. *I'm half-sick of shadows*; where had he heard that? From Stephan probably — practically everything he knew about literature had come from Stephan. But it was sunlight he was sick of, blue skies, openness and cleanliness. He thought: living out here has been healing, an unguent smoothed over my ragged ego, but I am mended now and need somewhere with more sharpness to its blade. On his rushed visit to England, years before, he had gone to Kew Gardens — *go down to Kew in lilac time*, Stephan had intoned, *it isn't far from London* — and though it had not been lilac time, he had gone, thinking of his grandmother, and rejoiced at the severity in the air. Rain had spattered; wind had jittered the needles of pine and spruce; high white clouds had rushed across a grey-blue sky. Reaching down, he had picked up a stone and put it in his pocket. For his grandmother; for himself. Rebecca waited for him back in New York; meanwhile he was there in the small shabby country where Grandfather Seaton had been a boy. He had lifted his face to the sky and felt unbearably happy.

The turn-off into Costello's Nurseries led to a driveway which ran between neat fields of flowers bounded by greenhouses. At the end stood a facsimile of a country house, Georgian, straight out of County Cork, complete with stone pillars supporting the portico and an escutcheon over the massive door. There was a round stone fountain in front, and some plump-bellied statuary in the middle of it; water spilled artistically between ferns while a cornucopia dripped stone vine-leaves and grapes. Benny was proud of it; it had been built by his immigrant grandfather ('Supposed to be an exact copy of some big old house near where he grew up. My dad sent architects back to take photographs and everything'), but had nonetheless a few non-Irish touches such as the wide verandah which ran the length of the rear, and a covered swimming-pool.

Lydia had moved out of the place after Benny's father had died, several years ago. Now she lived in a small frame house close by. Clapboard-covered, white-painted, it always reminded Tom of the house in Maine. He parked under a tree, because of the heat, and got out. California assailed him, dry and merciless; it was draining him, reducing him to a handful of sticklike bones.

The smell of Lydia's house was nostalgic. For a moment he closed his eyes, remembering his grandmother, the dank salty feel of certain objects — iron buckets, knife handles, chopping boards — and the faint sweat from the old quarry tiles on the kitchen floor, the smell of her larder; ham and apples, cheese and the smoked sausage she loved. There had always been a bowl of oranges set on polished wood shining like a detail in a Dutch interior, and on the kitchen window-sill a jar of sea-softened glass fragments gathered on the beach. And rain.

He remembered it so well, the unyielding cling of water-proofs, rain dripping through the fir trees which surrounded the house, rain lifting earthy scents out of the ground as though by a magnet, reviving.

The world had taken on a scoured bleached aspect when Rebecca had left him for her drama coach. His grandmother had died the year after. The house with most of its contents had become his under the terms of her will, along with a substantial sum of money; but so far he had not had the courage to live there, to face up to his ghosts. The sense he had felt then of being skeletal, reduced to the bare essence of himself, had never really left him. Why had he grown so closed, so shut off from others?

Because, boy, he told himself, *every time, every single goddamned time you love someone, they go away and leave you.*

Lydia refused to talk about the matter which concerned her until they were sitting out on the porch with coffee and a glass of Benedictine. The soft darkness wrapped them both like a shawl. For a while neither spoke. Then she said abruptly: 'I used to have a daughter. Did you know?'

Tom had heard, naturally. The story was common currency in the town. The disappearance of Nell Costello some twenty-five years ago was about the most exciting thing that had ever happened in Bellamonte. Perhaps the *only* exciting thing. Even though not too many people had known her personally, it was one of those long-term mysteries that everyone had a favourite theory about; Bellamonte's answer to the *Marie Celeste*, with just about as much explanation. A woman from Cincinatti had even written a fictionalised account of the case, speculating on what might have happened and where she was now, blaming the family in large part. Sean Costello, Lydia's husband, had sued the publishers and the book was withdrawn, with Sean being awarded the token damages of one dollar that he had asked for.

'Well, I, uh ...' Tom said.

'Of course you do,' Lydia said briskly.

'It all happened long before my time.'

'Don't be embarrassed, Tom, I'm not going to break down or anything. But I've recently been thinking about ... about my eventual demise.'

Tom started to make some conventional murmur. She stopped him.

'It's a little closer than I had anticipated. In fact, considerably closer.'

He glanced quickly at her through the darkness. In the dim light from the room behind them, her profile seemed suddenly sharp, sepulchral. He thought: my God, Lydia is dying.

'The point is, I would like to know where ... how she is.' Her hands knitted together in her lap and she stared down at them as if surprised to find them there. 'I really would like just to know. I would hate to think of her somewhere unhappy and alone. I should hate that.'

'I understood that your husband had employed top private investigators to try and find her. I thought ...' Tom stopped.

'You thought that she was dead.'

'Well, yes. Didn't they find ...?'

'... her body up in the hills?'

'Right.'

Lydia shrugged. 'It's one way to close a case, isn't it?'

'You sound as if you don't think it was your daughter they found.'

'I know it wasn't.'

'How come?'

'I didn't say anything at the time — I knew why she ran away. I thought it better that she was left to find her own way for a while. Sean was a very determined man. If he had thought she was still alive, he would never have rested until she was brought home again. The police were never entirely sure about it, but for Sean's sake ... He was so broken up by her disappearance that it seemed better to leave things as they were.' She shook her fine head at him. 'I don't suppose you can understand that sometimes it's better to *know* something terrible has happened to someone you love than never to be absolutely sure.'

Tom would have said that she was wrong, that he knew all about the nightmares of uncertainty, but she went on: 'I never dreamed for a moment that I would never see her again.'

'How did you know the body they found wasn't your daughter's?'

'Because Nell contacted me. She had grace enough to telephone me when the case hit the headlines.' Lydia rose suddenly to her feet. Her arms hung stiffly at her sides; she managed to look both woebegone and authoritative.

'And what do you want me to do?' Tom asked unenthusiastically. He had a feeling he already knew.

'Tom, look for her for me. While you're in Europe, see if you can find her, or if not her, then some news of her, some trace. Please. I don't ask her to come back, I wouldn't expect it, not after all these years, but I do so desperately need to *know.*'

'Lydia, how can I possibly —'

'Please, Tom. Please.'

In her voice he heard an echo of his own sea-chant all those years ago — *come back, oh, please come back, don't leave me.* If she was feeling even half the pain he had felt then ... He had a vision of Lydia and himself at either end of a chain, with her missing daughter and his lost mother as the connecting links.

'You can't imagine how often I've wondered if she was all right. Or, rather, if she's all wrong, if everything turned out badly for her. I'd have searched for her myself when Sean died, but by then my health wasn't good,' Lydia said. 'And now, with the news I've just been given ...' she wrapped her arms round her body, holding her elbows close. 'Tom, I cannot die until I know.'

'Where would I start?' Tom said helplessly. This was not how he had planned to spend his time in Europe. Depression sagged over him at the knowledge that he would not be able to refuse Lydia's request. He guessed she had seen her doctor recently and received some kind of death sentence.

'I don't want to ruin your vacation,' Lydia said. 'Why don't you give me a week of your time. Just seven days. If you can't find anything in that time, then I must just accept that she's gone for good.'

'Why don't you call in professionals?' Tom said. 'They'd do a far better job than I could.'

'I don't want professionals involved. I want a friend, and you are the only one I can ask,' Lydia said. 'I've watched you since you came here. You have a quality that almost nobody else I know possesses — you don't judge people. Besides that, I believe you would be discreet. I think discretion may be necessary here; I wouldn't want anyone else to know the things I should have to tell you. Certainly not strangers — not even Amis, though he is, of course, my lawyer. Where are you planning to visit?'

'All over. Italy. Russia. I have a friend in Paris I want to see. Another in Oxford.'

Lydia smiled. 'Do this favour for me, and I'll give you the address of a most charming girl I know in Oxford. You two would get on together like a house afire.'

'Lydia, I don't need a matchmaker, thank you.'

'No. But if you ask me, Tom —'

'I don't.'

'— you badly need a match. Not that this could be one. Harriet Pearse, as she now is, met her husband here, working at the nurseries — he's connected with the Costellos in some vague way — and is happily married.' Her face sobered. 'I knew her father once.'

Tom ignored her. 'Even if I agreed to do what you ask, how do you suppose I'm going to pick up a trail that went cold years and years ago?'

'I have one or two suggestions to make. Just starting-places.' Sensing his vacillation, Lydia said shamelessly: 'I'm a dying woman. I only want a week. It isn't so much to ask.'

'It's a heck of a lot to ask,' said Tom.

'You have hope and happiness ahead of you,' Lydia said. 'I have nothing.' Tears gathered in her eyes. 'Nothing at all.'

'Oh, *hell*,' Tom said.

'Does that mean you will?'

He groaned. 'This is real needle-and-haystack stuff, Lydia.'

'It's not. Not at all. I've thought about it for years. It's not nearly as easy to drop right out of sight as you might imagine. Especially for an American.'

'It can't be that hard.'

'But think of the places you *couldn't* go. Nell was a woman, a white woman. To disappear effectively, she wouldn't be able to go to any Middle East country, for instance. Not the Far East, either. Nor South America. She'd stand out. To someone determined to find her, the trail would be too easy to follow.'

'If she had money, she —'

'She didn't. At least, not much; though she took the jewellery left to her by my mother. She'd have to have got a job, even though she had no skills.'

'What if she got married and changed her name?'

'That's exactly what she did.'

'How do you know?'

'She told me herself. After that first call. I didn't hear from her for five years. Then on my birthday she telephoned me and said she had met someone. She was getting married.'

'That's all?'

'Yes.'

'How can you be certain she's not in the States? It seems to me that if she really desperately wanted to disappear, she'd more or less have to choose somewhere like Canada, where an American accent wouldn't be too noticeable, or somewhere big within the United States itself. Chicago, New York, like that. Picking up the trail of an American in Europe surely wouldn't have been too difficult for the investigators your husband hired.'

'I know where she is,' Lydia said.

'Then why are you —'

'Calling on you? Because she's in England. She went originally to Ireland, she told me, but decided England was safer, in case I tried to track her down through Sean's relatives. She told me. She wouldn't say where.'

Lydia's face showed pain. Tom tried not to think of those telephone calls; the pleading desperate mother, the adamant daughter. 'Why did she go?' he said.

'What?'

'*Why* did she leave, run away, whatever?'

For a moment, Lydia hesitated. Then, filling the two small glasses again, she sighed and said: 'I'd better tell you.'

· 18 ·

'What's the matter, Roma?'

'Nothin'.'

'You sound weird.'

'Well now, you listen here, boy. Just 'cause I sounds weird, that no reason to suppose I *is* weird.'

'Maybe not, but it sure is a good reason to suppose that something's going on. You never give me that jive-talk unless you're worried. Where's Amis?'

Roma expelled a gusty breath. 'Guess you better call Miz Seaton,' she said quietly. She hung up before Tom could say any more.

What in the hell? He looked out of the hotel window on to thin rain and the rounded shape of St Paul's cathedral against the sky. It was unfair; although he had promised to keep in touch with the office from time to time, he had not expected to be intruded upon like this. He was on vacation, dammit, and wanted to remain so. From Los Angeles he had flown direct to Rome. He had given himself two weeks there, just to give himself a taste of what he had come for, then travelled by train up to Venice for a few days, before flying on to Paris to stay with a college friend. Europe had enveloped him; the Louvre, St Peter's, the Sacré Coeur, the Bridge of Sighs. As he had known would happen, he had been swept up, embraced by the past.

He had called the office from Rome, from Venice, from Paris, but Bellamonte seemed increasingly insubstantial, each time he did so, compared to the solidity of canal, cathedral, castle: history made palpable.

Now, resignedly, he picked up the telephone and dialled

Amis's house in California. He heard the burr; almost immediately the receiver was lifted.

'Hello?' It was Margaret's voice.

'Hi. It's —'

'Tom! Thank God you rang — I tried to get you at the last place but you'd already left and I just didn't see any way I was going to find you short of calling out the FBI or Scotland Yard or something and I could just imagine what Amis would have said if I'd done that — not that he could have said much about it right now, poor angel, but I'd have known what he was thinking and that would have been just as bad if not worse, oh Tom, what am I going to do?' Amis's wife, a woman who always seemed to Tom to be balanced on the edge of hysteria, broke into a high-pitched noise which he assessed as being somewhere between a wail and a scream.

'Margaret,' he said. 'Calm down, will you? I don't have the faintest idea what's going on.'

'Didn't Roma say?'

'Roma didn't say one damn thing, just told me to call you. Why don't you tell me what's happened and we'll go on from there.'

Margaret swallowed audibly. 'I knew it would be all right once you got in touch,' she said. 'You're always so calm and reliable. Like Amis — I guess it runs in the family — I guess that's why I married him in the first place — apart from loving him, of course, which I did dreadfully and still do though it takes something like this to make me realise that you don't bother to say so nearly often enough and I can tell you when he comes home from the hospital I'm going to —'

'Margaret!' Tom bellowed.

She stopped. For a moment the line hung empty between them. Then she said: 'He went back to the office after dinner the other night, to catch up on work. While he was there, someone broke in and attacked him. They beat him up quite badly.'

'How badly?'

'Broke all his fingers. Stamped on his hands. Knocked half his teeth out. Smashed him across the throat. Punched both his eyes. Poor Amis ...' Quietly Margaret began crying. 'He looks dreadful.'

'Why would anyone break into a lawyer's office?' asked Tom, frowning.

'That's just what the police kept saying.'

'Do they have any theories?' Tom said.

'Money for drugs,' said Margaret. He heard her swallow. 'They think they were looking for something they could sell quickly for cash.'

'That's terrible.' Tom tried not to think of Amis, for whom the maintenance of personal dignity meant so much more than to other men, in the hands of some drug-crazed punk. 'They sure picked a poor choice of joint to knock over,' he said. 'What does Amis have to say about it?'

'Nothing. He can't say anything at all at the moment, with his mouth swelled shut like that and his throat so bruised. They're talking about temporary amnesia, maybe even permanent damage to the windpipe. 'Oh, Tom, if you could just see him you'd —'

'How many intruders?' Tom asked hastily.

'Just one, they think. Honestly, he must have been a madman to beat up on Amis like that.'

'Was anything taken?'

'Roma says: not that she can see. It's difficult to be sure, because nothing seems to have been touched.'

'I particularly don't figure,' Tom said slowly, 'why anyone would break into an attorney's place when the attorney's sitting right there at his desk. Why'd this punk bother to beat up on Amis? Why not just get the hell out?'

'We don't know. Maybe just from frustration because there wasn't anything around he could convert into cash. Or plain meanness. Oh, my poor Amis: his eyes swollen shut and his mouth puffed up, making these terrible croaking sounds. It's dreadful. I daren't take the girls to visit him; he'd be so upset to have them see him that way.'

'At least they sound like mainly superficial injuries: things that'll heal in time.'

'I don't know how soon he'll be fit to get back to the office, though. I suppose you wouldn't —'

'Right,' Tom said. 'I wouldn't.' He thought: all my life I have obliged people, I'm through with that kind of thing. Now it's my turn.

'Not even for a month, say?'

'Sorry, Margaret. I've waited too long for all this. Roma can manage for a while. If there's anything urgent, she can farm it out. Larry Kincaid would help out. And Dee Lorrimer. We've worked with both of them before.'

'I can't blame you,' sighed Margaret. 'It's just that ... people like us, we don't come across this sort of violence normally, and when we do, it kind of throws us off balance. I feel almost as shaky as if it was me that was attacked. I keep looking round, expecting terrible things to happen to me.'

'That's normal, honey,' Tom said. 'Give the poor guy my best, and say how sorry I am.'

Showering, he tried to think when something like this last occurred in Bellamonte. The odd car stolen off the street by teenagers wanting to joyride; the occasional suspension for pot-smoking at the High School; a knife fight from time to time outside the Tavern on hot Saturday nights — par for the course ... But this ... The way Margaret told it, it sounded so deliberate. So *purposeful*. Why damage Amis's hands, for instance?

Towelling himself down, he wondered again why anyone would want to break into a lawyer's office in the first place. It made no sense when you thought about it; it was not as if there would be large amounts of cash lying about, and while the guys up in the big city might have the odd Klee or Braque or something hanging on their walls, no one in Bellamonte did, as the entire town would know. There were a couple of pieces of nice Shaker furniture which Amis had been given by his parents, but nothing else worth stealing. Either the thief had made a mistake and broken into the wrong premises, or he was after something other than money. Tom was too far from home to care very much what that might have been, but nonetheless the unresolved question continued to vibrate somewhere at the back of his brain.

*

He had another call to place. Via the guest-house in the Dales he finally got hold of Stephan's Oxford number and called it.

After his initial expressions of delight, Stephan was insistent. 'Come up here. There's a spare bed and plenty of room.' He paused for a moment then said: 'In your letter you said you were intending to find a base — why not Oxford? I've got this flat on a year's lease, but I don't want it for all that time. You could take over the lease if you like.'

'Oxford?' Tom said.

'It was one of the places you always wanted to visit.'

'And your place is up for grabs?'

'Yeah.'

'I'll take it,' Tom said. The two men laughed, both of them, for different reasons, relieved at the ease of the arrangement.

Tom got the train up from London, revelling in the views which unrolled before him as they moved out of the capital into the deeper countryside. A faint sun was shining through a thin cloud layer, softening the shadows, purifying the green. Trees stood hunched in deep meadows; rivers idled between rush-lined banks. It seemed a long way to California, to hot sun and dry soil and the fish-hooked leaves of succulents.

And Lydia's voice, relentless in the warm darkness ...

'Parents are uniquely qualified to hurt their children,' she had said. 'For that reason they have to guard particularly against doing so. I didn't. I was careless — or, rather, uncaring.'

'As a human being you do have a right to be less than perfect some of the time,' Tom said. The Benedictine coated his mouth like sweet oil; he sipped his coffee to dispel the taste.

'I told you once that I married the second time for love. It was, I should have added, my love, not his. Sean was fond of me, but he started to want someone younger than I, someone to reassure him that he was still a man, still virile. I'd have done that for him, but I didn't count.' Her piled white hair was as thick now as it must have been when she was still a girl; he wondered what colour it had been. 'Ever noticed, Tom, how after a certain age women became desexed?'

'How do you mean?' Tom felt awkward.

'They're no longer seen as sexual objects, which is the way society views the vast majority of them. They lose their sexual validity, and along with it, their visibility. Certainly, because I was the same age as Sean, he couldn't see that I was still a woman, still ...' she cleared her throat '... beddable. So we were having problems just before Nell left. It wasn't for the first time. He was having an affair and I ... well, I know I felt threatened by Nell's beauty, especially with such obvious evidence on his part that my own was not enough to keep him from straying. And then, of course, there's always the rivalry which exists between mother and adolescent daughter, unspoken but definitely there, however much love exists between the two.'

Lydia's voice was strained, her sentences coming in uneven patterns, full of pauses and sighs. Tom sensed that saying what she had was hard for her, born as she was of a generation which did not speak of personal matters, which hid so much behind conventions of courtesy, which valued privacy. Seeing her vulnerable, laid bare, he felt a pang of regret for the old armoured Lydia Costello with her grand-duchess ways.

'Then Nell fell in love with a man who I had thought ...' She looked away '... I had hoped, even, was in love with me. I was hovering on the edge of forty — I can't explain how much I needed confirmation that I was still attractive — perhaps only another woman can understand that sense of loss for something you once heedlessly possessed, and can never have again. Nor can I explain what happened except to say that it was some kind of madness. It is enough to say that I more or less threw myself at him, with the quite conscious intention of proving that I could have any man I wanted, even one my daughter was in love with.' She shook her head. 'Madness, indeed. Dangerous madness.'

'What happened?'

'The inevitable. I seduced him — it wasn't really too diffi-cult.'

'What then?'

'Nell found us in bed together,' Lydia shrugged, the dismissive gesture entirely without casualness. 'In her bed.'

'What?'

'Yes. Looking back afterwards I could see that I had intended to make my own victory complete by that heartless little refinement, though I certainly wasn't aware of it at the time. At least, I don't think so. But the look on her face when she saw us there — I suddenly remembered it all: what it was like being young, being uncertain, being in love. I've despised myself ever since for taking advantage of her. The young are so vulnerable.'

'I guess they are.'

'Nell was in some ways a difficult girl. She didn't seem to date the way her friends did. In spite of being beautiful, she didn't have a lot of boyfriends — not even a lot of friends. So I guess she fell for — for this man pretty heavily.'

'And it was after finding you *in flagrante*, as it were, that she ran away?'

'Yes. Literally. Straight from the room, out of the house, into her car. I heard it turn on the gravel outside —' She closed her eyes and drew a long breath into her lungs. 'I've never seen her since.' There was a pause. Then she said: 'They found the car, and then — much later — the body, up in the hills. But, as I said, I knew it wasn't Nell's.'

'Because of the phone-calls.'

'Yes. The body made national headlines, if you remember, because they thought it was one of the Freeway Strangler's victims, one nobody had known about. When she called, she said it was because she didn't want me to think she had died like that, at the hands of that insane ... animal. She said she didn't want me to suffer the way I'd made her suffer, so she was calling to say she was all right — not happy, but at least alive and well.' There was a long silence. Tom was about to break it when Lydia said: 'Her voice was so cold.'

'Where was she calling from?'

'Dublin. Or so she said. I begged for an address. I ...' Lydia's face grimaced with distaste at her past uncontrolled self — she who was always so controlled. 'I grovelled. But she wouldn't give me one. She said she never wanted to see me again, and that as her husband was English, she was never coming back to the States.'

'Couldn't that have been a lie, something to put you off the scent? She might have been just up the road in the next county.'

'She might. But I don't think she was. She told me that from time to time she would ring so I would know she was all right.'

'And has she?'

'Irregularly. I never know when it may be. Sometimes a couple of years go by; once she rang twice within twelve months. That was the year she got married, and then had the first child.'

'How long ago was that?'

She sensed the question behind the question. 'I guess he'd be in his late twenties now, and the girl three or four years younger.'

'Do you know her married name?'

'I know her surname. So I know her husband is not the man I . . . she . . .' Lydia squared her shoulders. 'It was a fitting punishment: one I feel I deserved. I did what I did quite deliberately. I don't ask to be let lightly off hooks. I ruined her life, and it is just that I should pay for that.'

'Come off it, Lydia. That's self-indulgent crap and you know it. Any life which could be ruined by a single setback was probably going to have a hard time making it anyway.' Tom got up and walked to the edge of the porch which surrounded the entire house, hearing the snap of boards under his feet. He leaned against the wooden surround; he could see lights, fireflies jitterbugging in the darkness, the faint shape of a tree against the sky. He felt bemused by the essential sadness at the foundations of things; the checks and balances between happiness and despair seemed precarious, their differentiation too delicate. 'Does your daughter know you're — uh — ill?'

There was a long silence. Then Lydia said, almost apologetically: 'She doesn't know anything. She hasn't rung me for a very long time.'

'How long a time?'

If he had still had any doubts about whether he would help her, they vanished as she looked up at him. In it he saw her despair. 'Years,' she said.

As the train slowed down for the entry into Oxford station, Tom saw spires, towers, pale stone flattened by rain. He had the feeling that nothing had changed since his last visit except himself.

Beyond the barrier, Stephan waited, his hair still bright but thinner than it once had been. Tom thought he seemed strained, like a bird caught in a snare, poised for flight but unable to soar. Embracing him, he felt a tightness in his friend's shoulders which had not been there before.

Stephan drove them through streets which seemed vaguely familiar. Tom sighed with pleasure, turning in his seat to catch glimpses of college gardens, arched gateways. 'You don't have any idea how lucky you are to live here,' he said.

'I wonder if you'll still say that after you've been here a while,' said Stephan.

'It's so peaceful.' Tom stretched his long legs. 'As I get older, I realise that's all I really want out of life. Peace.'

'Not much of an ambition, is it?'

'I'm not an ambitious man. Not like you. Or my cousin Amis — do you remember him?'

'Certainly do. How is he?'

'Just fine. Doing well. I guess we both are. He's beginning to think about the State legislature, politics, all that sort of thing,' Tom said. Should he tell Stephan the news about Amis? 'He's more or less exactly the same as he always was. Except for his forehead.'

'What's happened to his forehead?'

'It gets nobler by the minute,' Tom said. 'Every time he runs a comb through his hair, his forehead gains another inch.'

Stephan laughed. 'Poor old Amis.'

'He blames it all on sports, poor guy. Says his above-average college record in track and field is directly responsible for his present below-average follicle count.'

'I never heard that before.' Uneasily, Stephan touched the top of his own hair. 'I used to run at university.'

'Ah,' said Tom solemnly. 'Now, Amis has this theory about scalp-sweat ...'

He was amazed to find that Stephan did know — apparently did a great deal more than simply know — the girl whose name Lydia Costello had given him to contact if he had time in Oxford.

'Such a pretty child,' she had said. 'She and her brother worked here for a summer; it was before your time. I gave them both a job here for old time's sake ...' She coughed, heavily. 'Their father was ...' The heat of the night stifled the unspoken words, cut short the sentences; the effort of speech seemed suddenly too much for her. 'I've kept in touch through occasional letters and Christmas cards. I shall write and tell her you might give her a call while you're in England. I'm sure she'll be glad to see you, though I haven't heard from her for a while.' The lines of her face had drooped; she looked immensely sad.

'What is it, Lydia?' Tom had begun to rise from the table, but she motioned him back.

'Nothing, really. Nothing that can be dealt with. But she reminded me so much of my daughter. I think that's when I first got the idea of setting up some kind of search for Nell — but of course I never got round to doing anything about it, and now it's almost too late.'

There seemed little point in contradiction. All too plainly time was running out for Lydia Costello. 'Does Benny have any idea of what you plan?' he asked.

'None whatsoever.' An expression Tom found hard to decipher tightened the skin across her cheekbone. 'I hope he doesn't, either.'

'Wouldn't be too pleased, huh?'

'Not at *all* pleased.' She spun the stem of her wineglass between thumb and forefinger. 'You do realise that he is not my son, don't you?'

'Yes. As a matter of fact I —'

'Naturally anything that was his father's goes to him without question. Especially when he's put so much effort into building up the Nurseries. But, as you know, I have some money of my own. Some of that too will go to him — but only when I have seen to it that others with prior claims have been taken care of.'

'Such as your daughter?' Tom could not help thinking that 'some money of my own' was hardly an adequate description of the several million dollars Lydia was worth.

'Not Nell,' she said. 'She has been too ... unforgiving. But her children.' There was a look on her face which Tom had no problem in defining as steely.

'Tom ...'

'Yes?' In the lamplight she looked haunted, the eyes so far back between the bones of her face that the effect was that of a skull. Yet, amazingly, she was still beautiful.

'You probably think this is a mad whim on the part of someone desperately trying to stave off the truth,' she said. 'But it's more than that. There's a wrong to be put right here, and I must do what I can to see that it is.' She glanced down at the hands which lay tightly clasped together in her lap. 'Nell may be ... I recognise that she may be dead.'

'Why should she be? She can't be much more than fifty or so.'

'The fact that she hasn't been in touch for so long suggests it. In that case, where are those children? I don't even want to intrude on their lives, but I want them to have something of the grandmother they've never been allowed to know — even if it now can only be money. Only then will Benny get some, if not all, of what he wants. It's all in my will.'

Lydia's voice cracked on the word and Tom realised she was keyed up to an almost unbearable pitch of tension. 'She denied me my grandchildren, Tom,' she said, in a dry whisper. 'I can't forgive that.'

Nell Costello appeared to have exacted her pound of flesh several times over, Tom thought. Since Lydia was being so candid, it seemed only fair for Tom to say: 'Benny's kind of counting on inheriting everything, I guess. He's overstretched at the moment. If anything should happen to you ...'

She reared her head back the way he had so often seen his own grandmother do. For a moment the old Lydia reappeared, straightbacked and imperious. 'He acted against my advice,' she said haughtily. 'He'll have to take the consequences. If there are any.'

Shadows moved at the corner of the porch, where the lantern swung in a sudden breeze. Out in the darkness he heard a sharp crack and then another. Lydia looked up abruptly, her head on one side. 'Is there someone out there?'

'I doubt it. A racoon, prob —'

'Have a look,' she ordered. 'Quickly.'

He went down the wooden steps and on to the grass. The warm insect-crowded night surged against his face as he listened. He could hear nothing except the burr of crickets and a faint squeak as the swing-chair stirred under Lydia's weight, and the joviality of distant music stretching through the darkness like strings of spun sugar. He walked along to the corner of the house. Had someone been out there? He could see lights on in the big house, some three hundred yards away, where Benny and his family were probably finishing supper. Between the two houses the darkness moved and whispered; he realised that despite their nearness, Lydia was very vulnerable, should anyone wish to harm her.

'Anything?' Lydia called.

'Not that I can see.' He came back to her.'Why did you think there might be? Have you had trouble before?'

She shrugged. 'How do you define trouble? I've heard footsteps — or thought I did. And once or twice a car has driven in and parked out there under the trees, with its lights off.'

'Whose car?'

'I've no idea. At first I assumed it was a courting couple or something. Except ...'

'Why would anyone do their courting on private land, fifty yards away from an occupied house?'

'Exactly. It's a little eerie, I must confess. I look out of the window and see that dark windscreen staring at me, as though it was watching me. You start to imagine all sorts of horrors.' She laughed weakly. 'We've all seen so many terrifying films on TV ...' Again the sentence dragged into inconclusiveness. 'But with Benny just over the way ...'

'Would he hear if you called for help?'

'I hope so.'

'So do I.' Tom decided he must alert Benny to his mother's — *step* mother's — isolation.

Later, as he left, he saw movement on the dark patio of Benny's house, and the glow of a cigar in the dark. Benny? He raised a hand in greeting, not knowing whether he could be seen or not. A chair creaked; footsteps sounded on the wooden floorboards as the big man got up and came to meet him. He held a beer-can in one huge fist. 'Hi, Tom.'

'Hi.'

'Been visiting Mom on business?'

'Just a social call.'

'When do you leave for Europe?' Benny raised the can to his lips and swallowed.

'Couple of weeks,' Tom said.

'That all?' Punching Tom's arm, Benny said: 'Hey, I'd sure like it if you could make lunch before you go.'

'Gee, I'd love to, but I'm kind of hard pressed for time these days,' Tom said.

'I understand. But it looks like I might have to get over there myself sometime soon.'

'Is that right?'

'Some family matter which just came up. Maybe Lydia mentioned it.'

'No, she didn't.' Tom looked back over his shoulder but Lydia's house was dark, the white paint dull in the blackness.

'Well, it'd be real fun to meet up with you while I'm over, maybe try one of those fancy French restaurants or something.'

'Sure,' said Tom. He could think of a whole heap of things that would be more fun than meeting up with Benny Costello in Europe.

'Maybe you could let me know where you might be so I

could get in touch,' continued Benny.

'I'll be travelling around a lot of the time.' Tom gave a laugh which he hoped did not give away his reluctance to commit himself to anything specific. 'I might be hard to catch up with.'

'There's always American Express, isn't there?'

'Sure there is.'

Benny's broad shoulders drooped. 'Guess you'd rather be left alone on your vacation, huh?' His lower lip protruded with disappointment.

'Ring my office,' Tom said resignedly, getting into his car. The guy was like a big child. 'I'll see what I can come up with in the way of an itinerary for you.'

'Gee, thanks, Tom. That's real swell.' A delighted smile spread across Benny's face as he crunched the beer-can in his hand. 'It's kind of nice to meet up with friends when you're in a strange country, don't you agree?'

'Uh-huh,' Tom said, noncommittal. The naïveté of the man was ridiculous. Did he not appreciate that Tom himself was going away precisely so that he should *not* meet up with friends? Evidently not.

Tom had waved as he drove off, and watched the glow of Benny's cigar grow smaller until it faded into the darkness.

Harriet Pearse was a surprise. For one thing, she was much younger than Tom had anticipated: no more than twenty-five, twenty-six, when he had expected someone nearer his own age. For another, she was pregnant, heavily so, perhaps no more than a month from her term.

Seeing her, he had the fleeting impression that he had seen her once before, but the memory slipped away before he could anchor and examine it. He found himself excited by her heavy body. The thought that between her ribs lay a potential fellow human both enthralled and alarmed him; the easy way in which mankind perpetuated itself seemed suddenly dangerous. Learning that she was a widow, he could not help staring at Stephan — and found Stephan staring back, his blue eyes full of denial.

They sat down. Tom watched her move in the light of the candles she had lit and the way her shadow thickened on the walls. Her hair was beautiful, multicoloured, yellow and topaz and gold, spread around her face like a halo. The room was the colour of the sea and full of quiet; he found himself remembering some of the hymns his grandmother used to play: *Rocked in the cradle of the deep* and *Abide With Me*, tunes which had invariably brought tears to his eyes. Not now, however; not now, perhaps at last. He looked around at the curtains, at an oval of blue-green glass which stood on a low table beside an antique pitcher crammed with grasses and long-stemmed daisies, at the silk cushions, the careful evidences of someone who cared about the effect of little things. Quite suddenly he felt as though a hole had been breached in the walls which surrounded him.

As they were leaving, he asked Harriet if he could visit her again, making some excuse about messages from Lydia. She told him, not quite willingly, that he could come whenever he liked. He was surprised to feel young again, even more so to realise that he was not really that old.

Stephan had a seminar to attend in Liverpool the next day, leaving Tom alone. Nonetheless he waited two days — 'gentleman's days' his grandmother used to call them, explaining that a man should never rush a lady — before he visited Harriet again, timing his visit for four o'clock, when he understood that the English had tea. Harriet opened the door; he could see at once that she was reluctant to let him in. He should have discussed her more with Stephan; perhaps there was a lover, a fiancé, a person who had far more right to be with her than he did, and who might resent his presence. She wore some kind of loose sun-dress in bright citrus colours. Her face was tanned, thinner than it ought to have been at this stage of her pregnancy; he guessed she had been sunbathing. Shrinkingly, anticipating embarrassment, awkwardness, he followed her into the sitting-room and on out into the rioting garden where she had spread a rug in the middle of the towering grasses — but no one else was there.

She brought a tea-tray out and gave an involuntary grunt as she bent over a teak garden-table.

He jumped up to take the tray from her. There was a bowl of strawberries, home-made lemonade with slices of lemon floating on the top, some yellow cream.

She pushed hair away from her forehead. 'It's too hot for tea,' she said.

'When's it due?' he asked.

'What?' Her voice was chilly.

'For a moment he wondered if he had committed some terrible *faux pas*. Perhaps it was impolite to mention to an Englishwoman that you'd even noticed she was pregnant; perhaps she just had a very unfortunate figure and what he had taken for impending maternity was in fact the stomach of obesity, perhaps — but she was laughing, patting herself, saying:

'This, you mean? Sorry, I couldn't think what you were talking about for the moment. Sometimes I almost forget I haven't always been like this, it's been so long. Thank God, I've only three more weeks to go.' She dipped a strawberry into the cream and the sugar, then handed it to him.

'I suppose your mother or someone will be coming to stay with you,' Tom said.

She stared at him. Her eyes reflected the green of grass and leaves; in the middle of them he could see his own image, tiny. 'Someone,' she said.

'Sorry?'

'I have no mother.'

'Oh, I see.'

'But I have a good friend — Christina. She's coming down. And there's Maggie, who looked after my brother and me when we were children.'

'Oh, yes.' He wanted to ask about her father, but decided that to do so would be to be brash, American, un-European. Instead, he moved quickly on to talk of Lydia, of California, of Bellamonte, trawling among his acquaintance until he hit on someone she thought she remembered. Staring at her pretty sun-flushed face, he thought back to those events of more than twenty-five years ago, to a set of people he had never known, and wondered whether she would be interested in Nell Costello. But lawyerly habits die hard, and discretion kept him silent. It was not, after all, his story, but Lydia's.

He took another strawberry, dipped it in cream and sugar, gave it to her. She smiled and, to his mortification, he blushed. She had the sort of teeth that would have been corrected with braces back in California. One of the charms of European women was their diversity, not the homogenised size-8-A-cup-standard female product he was used to back home. Surely, he thought, I cannot, in this unlikely spot, be falling ... falling?

When her face was in repose he could not help seeing the places — where later there would be lines — which made her seem wistful, even melancholy. She was so unlike the women of Bellamonte, the sad soft-eyed divorcees laying their little hands upon his sleeve, looking up at him.

He set himself to be amusing — and succeeded. He told her about the J.D. sweater controversy, about Amis, about Roma and the game shows she was continually entering and how, during one big moment, with a split-level barbecue set and a VCR on the line, she had frozen and been unable to remember the name of any US Presidents except Ronald Reagan. 'They only wanted three,' he said, 'and all the poor woman could say was "Ronnie Reagan, Ronnie Reagan". And then finally inspiration struck and she screamed out: "I got it. Bobby Kennedy!"'

'*Bobby?*' Harriet said.

'Yeah.'

'She couldn't even remember Abraham Lincoln?'

'Especially not Abraham Lincoln.'

She laughed hugely, making a noise that seemed inappropriate in a woman with such slender wrists and ankles; she had a wide mouth, something he had always found immensely attractive in a woman. He was kind of keen on slim wrists, too, as it happened. There was blue paint under her fingernails and a daub of yellow on the underside of her arm. He leaned forward and touched it lightly. 'You're a painter,' he said.

'Of a sort.'

'May I see some of your work?'

'No.'

He reddened, trying to decide whether her refusal had been unpleasant or simply firm. He had hoped she was beginning to warm towards him, then wondered why he should care. He was a bird of passage, a ship passing in the night, nothing more than a transient. While he was in Oxford he would probably see her a time or two more, even after Stephan was gone, but, face it, she had her life to live — a much fuller life once the baby had come — and he had his.

They ate strawberries in silence for a while; she told him that the cream had come from Cornwall, a gift from her grandmother.

He told her about his own grandmother, finding it easy to talk. He spoke of the house — *his* house — in Maine, with the rocks and the sea on one side, the quiet, reed-fringed lake on the other.

'It sounds beautiful,' she said. 'Why bother to come over here?'

He was tempted to say, *to meet you*, but decided that was too bold, too sudden. 'For us Yanks, Europe is a rite-of-passage.'

'What else are you planning to see while you're in England?' she said politely. He found himself disliking the courtesy; it distanced him from her, reduced his status from friend to visitor; it denied any possibility of future intimacy.

'I'm going to do the whole tourist bit, I'm afraid,' he said. 'Stratford, Cambridge, Scotland. I'm heading for points north in a couple of days. I want to see York and Edinburgh, some of those Scottish castles, a few cathedrals.'

'How long will you be gone?'

He wanted to kid himself that she was asking because she hoped it would not be for too long, but could not quite make it. 'About ten days, I guess. Maybe by the time I get back you'll — uh — have had the baby.'

'Don't.' She stared at him with frightened eyes. 'I'm not really ready for all that. I ... well, to tell the truth, I didn't ever

· 243 ·

want this baby in the first place, and I'm just scared to death I shan't want it when it's born either.'

He touched her hand; she did not appear to notice. 'Hey, listen. That's just prenatal nerves. Everybody feels like that,' he lied smoothly. 'It's perfectly natural. I remember my cousin's wife, Margaret, demanding that we do something before it was too late.' He mimicked a high-pitched female voice: '"Do something, guys. You gotta do something, get me out of this, I'm too young to be a mother" — or did she say she was too old?' While Harriet laughed, he hoped she and Margaret would never meet, or, if they did, that this story never came up. Margaret had taken to pregnancy and motherhood with an almost sickening intensity.

'What was it, boy or girl?'

'Girl.'

'And she loved it when it arrived?'

'Like her own daughter.'

For a moment she stared at him, before smiling tentatively. He frowned. There was something odd here, something that did not exactly jive. Was it because the baby was post-humous? Was it to do with the missing mother? Perhaps Stephan would know.

He was away two weeks. When he returned, it was to find a note from Stephan stuck to the door of the tiny fridge, explaining that he had had to go over to Cambridge for the weekend. He drank a Scotch, unpacked his things, took a shower, knowing all the time that however hard he argued with himself against it, he was eventually going to find himself standing on Harriet's doorstep. To dispel any sense of obsession, he would imply — lie, even — that he had returned a couple of days earlier. He bought a bottle of chilled white wine from an off-license along the way and a huge mixed bouquet from a florist. When he knocked on Harriet's door, the pulses in his throat were thumping so painfully he was afraid he would not be able to speak.

He could hear her coming slowly along the passage. Under his shirt he could feel his heart; his forehead was hot. She opened the door and he stared at her, not caring what she thought, nor what she could read in his face.

'Tom,' she said.

'Hi.' He cleared his throat. There were dark shadows under her eyes and beads of sweat on her upper lip; her hair was damp where it lay on her neck.

'Are those for me?' she said.

'Yes.' *Those, and everything else beside ...*

'How pretty.' Slowly, as if the movement hurt, she reached out her hands and took the flowers from him. 'Come in.'

He walked behind her. 'Are you OK?' he asked.

'I feel a bit tired, actually.'

'Sit down and let me pour you a glass of wine.'

'That sounds wonder...ful.' She finished the word off in a sudden puff of breath.

He brought two glasses he found in the kitchen. He took the flowers and stuffed them into a vase which had been sitting on the counter.

'They're beautiful,' she said. She leaned forward and touched the petals of a pink rosebud, then lay back against the sofa as though exhausted. 'So beautiful,' she repeated.

Without thinking, Tom found himself smoothing the hair away from her neck. It was dark with sweat. This close, he could smell her mingled scents of talc and hot skin, of musk from her armpits and something else, something that alarmed him. He remembered a heavily pregnant Margaret at the office, Amis held up by a client out in the hills, a sharp intake of breath and Roma Hogg rising swiftly from her desk, ushering Margaret to the washroom. As the images flashed across his brain, sending an unequivocal message, Harriet reached out and took his hand, squeezing it so tightly that he almost cried out. After a moment, she let it go.

He said calmly: 'The baby's on its way, isn't it?'

She nodded.

Which was how Tom Seaton, night ship, passaging bird, simple transient, came to be on hand when Harriet went into labour, and why he was the one who signed the necessary papers, held the hand of the straining mother, rubbed her back, offered her water, listened to the deep ecstatic groans, the high-pitching wondering shrieks and, as the moment grew nearer, encouraged her onwards in the frantically hard work of giving birth until her daughter finally slid empurpled into the world.

Tom it was, too, who later tumbled out of the hospital into the darkness and wept, leaning his head against a wall while his shoulders heaved and his eyes overflowed at the mystery, the painful miracle of it all, before finding a call-box from which to make the necessary phone-calls.

PART TWO

PART TWO

· 19 ·

The telephone shrilled, dragging Harriet up from the depths of a sleep as thick and clogging as a blanket. She groaned. Trying to summon the energy to pull herself out of bed and answer it, she thought how odd it was that the slightest sound from the baby had her halfway to the nursery before she was even aware of having wakened, whereas these dead-of-night summonses seemed to take an hour to penetrate her sleeping brain.

Drugged with tiredness, she walked slowly into the sitting-room. In the shimmering dark the furniture loomed dimly, shapes of sofa and table outlined against the uncurtained windows outside which waited the quiet garden. She already knew that when she picked up the receiver there would be nobody there; it would be yet another of the anonymous calls which had been a feature of her life for so long. Once she had spoken of them to Christina, trying to convey something of the strange muted relationship she had developed with the silent caller. Chris's reaction had been robust.

'Complain, darling. You don't have to put up with that sort of thing. The telephone company knows how to deal with nuisance calls. They'll monitor everyone ringing you.'

'But they don't occur all that often,' Harriet had objected. 'Once a month — less, even. They hardly constitute a nuisance.'

'Once a month or once an hour, it's still an invasion of your privacy and you should let them handle it.'

It had seemed silly, after that, to explain that, in a weird way, whoever was making those calls provided her with a kind of stability.

That had changed. Now, keeping her from the rest she so badly needed, they held only a planned malevolence. Were they from the same person? Without any basis for the feeling, she thought not. Several times recently she had attempted to communicate with the unresponsive receiver: 'What do you want?' she had screamed one night, the baby cranky and herself almost unbalanced with fatigue. 'Leave me alone!' But, of course, there had been no reply.

Picking up the receiver now, holding it to her ear to hear only hostile silence, Harriet thought, exhaustion fogging her brain: this can't go on. I must call the telephone people tomorrow.

Unable to keep her eyes open, she fumbled her way back to bed. It had been every night for the past ten days. As soon as she had given the baby its two o'clock feed, had got her off to sleep again and was just drowsing off herself, the insistent peal began, echoing in the darkness, reverberating through her tired brain with the insistence of a fist, while she blundered into the living-room, expecting disaster. A couple of times she had deliberately left the receiver off and then barely slept, wondering whether anyone — her father? Matt? — might be trying to get through, needing help, damaged. In daylight she could see the illogicality of it; at night, when things lost their edge, grew huge and unsolvable, it seemed to make perfect sense.

I must get some sleep, she thought. I am barely getting through the days.

No one had told her how tired she would be, afterwards. Nobody had warned her that the nine-month trauma of pregnancy would catch up with her, that her body would need time to recover, that new-borns demand incessantly, even when asleep. These days she functioned on automatic hold, moved in a haze of tiredness. She found herself clumsy, dropping things, forgetting. Her days had distilled themselves into compact littleness: the baby, the shopping, the flat. She had expected to be filled with energy, had thought her life would expand once the baby was born, but lack of sleep was turning her into a zombie.

Tomorrow, she told herself as she pulled the covers over herself, Christina will be here. Then I'll be able to rest.

'Talk about to the manner born,' Harriet said. She sat slouched in an armchair watching Christina as she deftly powdered the baby and rewrapped it in a clean diaper.

'Me?' Chris peered over her shoulder, her dark hair swinging like a curtain across her face.

'You handle her like a pro,' said Harriet. 'Like the old woman in the shoe.'

'It's simply that I like efficiency,' Chris said. She handed the baby to Harriet and picked up the soiled diaper, which she dropped into a bucket underneath the table. 'I certainly don't care much for all this sort of thing, frankly, but if it's got to be done, it might as well be done right.'

'You make me feel so lazy,' murmured Harriet.

'Enjoy it, darling. I'll be off home soon and then you'll be on your own again. Except for Stephan. Or his lovesick friend Tom.'

'Lovesick? What nonsense.'

Christina gave her a sharp look. 'Perhaps you'd prefer it to be Stephan.'

Harriet shrugged. 'I'm fond of Stephan. But there's a side to him which I find rather terrifying.'

'That's because he's good at what he does,' Christina said briskly. 'I'm the same. Hard as nails under the surface charm — which you could hardly say about the other one.'

'Tom?'

'Of course Tom. It's obvious the man's besotted.'

'With the baby, maybe.'

'With you, definitely.'

'Well, I wish he wasn't. And it's certainly not mutual. And actually I think you're quite wrong about him — in the right circumstances, I think he could be as ruthless as — as Hitler.'

'I don't think I agree.' Christina plucked the baby from her mother. 'Now, since you're so keen to establish a routine, it's time for you to have a nap while I take young Wotsit — I do wish you'd hurry up and find a name for her, darling — out for a stroll round the Parks.'

'I thought it was *you* who liked routine,' Harriet said lazily.

'It does make for efficiency, frankly.' Chris opened the front door. 'I'll drop in at that health-food shop on the way back and get something amazingly healthy for lunch.'

'Chris.' Harriet caught at her friend's hand.

'Yes?'

'You've been wonderful. Absolutely marvellous.' As so often recently, weak tears came into Harriet's eyes. 'I honestly don't know what I'd have done without you.'

'Don't be silly. You'd have been fine.'

'Apart from anything else, you've given me a chance to catch up on some sleep. Honestly, with those damned phone-calls, I was beginning to think I was losing my mind.'

'It's been a pleasure,' Christina said lightly. 'For one thing, it's given me a brief taste of the joys I've missed. And for another, it's absolutely confirmed every prejudice I ever had about the ghastliness of motherhood. I mean, don't get me wrong, the baby's absolutely angelic and all that, but when I think you've got her for years — for *ever* — when I can leave at the end of the week, I go all weak and trembly inside at how close I might once have come to what, let's face it, is a species of penal servitude.' She saw Harriet's look of disbelief. 'No, honestly, darling. I really do.'

Later, over the lunch Christina had prepared for them, Harriet said: 'Are you happy, Chris? You look it.' It was true: Christina had filled out, there was more weight on her bones now, and she smiled a lot more than she used to.

'Yes.' Christina laid down her fork and gazed through the open windows at the billowing garden. 'I think I am. I shan't get over Denis for a while; I know that. But Whitemoor's very peaceful, and I like the people there. In fact —' She gave her darkly brilliant smile and ducked her head.

'What?' Harriet laughed. 'Don't tell me you've got an admirer already.'

'It's much too early for that sort of thing,' Christina said primly. 'But I must admit the barrister — remember I told you about the barrister next door?'

'I thought you said he was a solicitor.'

'Did I? I always get those legal terms mixed up. Anyway, he's been rather attentive. Especially while those wretched workmen are making such a meal of getting the alterations finished. He brought me flowers the other day and insists on taking me out to dinner or inviting me in for a drink, just to keep up my morale, as he puts it.'

'As long as that's all he's keeping up.'

'Darling, so crude.'

'I'm dying to see it all,' Harriet said warmly. 'Your house, the village. I love that part of the world.'

'I can't wait to show it to you. Just as soon as you can, you're to strap Miss Wotsit into her carry-cot and drive up and visit. Straight up the A1, turn left at Scotch Corner and keep on for twenty miles or so — you practically drive into my front garden.' An expression of consternation crossed Chris's face. 'Oh, gosh! I nearly forgot to tell you. Remember that girl who used to clean for me?'

'Stacey, was it? Casey?'

'Tracy. Tracy Marling. Well, I bumped into her when I was shopping yesterday, and guess what.'

'She's starring in the next James Bond movie?'

'What?'

'Chris, how can I possibly guess? Just tell me.'

'It's rather sad, actually. You remember me saying months ago that she was pregnant, too?'

'Yes.'

'Well, I started telling her all about you and the baby and it turned out that her own baby was born just after yours, but it died. Some kind of respiratory problem, I gather, though obviously I didn't want to be too Gestapo-like with the questions. Awful, isn't it?'

'How dreadful for her.'

Christina reached into the salad bowl and picked out a lettuce leaf. 'I hardly recognised her, actually. She looked really wild, talking on in this kind of dreadful monotone and shrugging all the time as though it didn't matter a bit, when all the time you could see how much it did.'

Harriet pushed back her chair and got up from the table. 'The poor woman,' she said. 'I can't imagine anything worse than losing your child.'

She found herself running into the spare bedroom, now turned into a nursery, and staring down at the tiny crumpled face of her sleeping daughter. Love overwhelmed her. I said I would never again give myself to anyone else, she thought. That I would never again allow myself to be made defenceless by love. But I embrace the vulnerability you bring me.

To lose her ... She found herself clutching the edge of the baby's crib, weeping again at the thought of sad Tracy Marling, who had gone through her pregnancy only to end up with nothing. The bleakness of it filled her with a sense of mourning; she found herself gasping aloud at the thought of someone else's pain. She seemed to have lost a skin or two since the baby's arrival. Everything moved her to tears these days: the plight of children in famine areas, the mothers of *los desapericidos* in Central America, the AIDS orphans of Romania. Even looking at a reproduction of the Velasquez portrait of *Las Meninas* — the innocent little princess shining among her ladies and still unaware of how soon she was to be made a pawn in someone else's dynastic plans — Harriet had found her throat thickening.

A tear fell on to the baby's cheek; she leaned over the cot and wiped it from the moist skin, marvelled at the brush of eyelash on cheek, the miniature chip of fingernail, the frail scalp. Under one of the petal-thin ears was a mark, a tiny puckering of brown skin, a mole: it only served to point up the perfection of the rest.

She heard Christina come into the room, felt her thin hands on her shoulders. 'Come on, love. These things happen. You aren't responsible. You can't take on the world's pain.'

'Suppose I lost her,' Harriet said, gulping. 'Like Tracy lost hers.'

'But you haven't.'

'But I might.'

'Of course you won't.' Christina steered her away and into

her own bedroom. 'Lie down and catch some more sleep. Take advantage of me being here. If the baby wakes up, I'll take care of it — I've had enough practice by now.'

'Thanks, Chris,' Harriet said gratefully. 'That would be marvellous. Exhaustion seems to be a permanent state just at the moment.'

'Exactly. So appreciate me while you've got me.'

'I do, Chris. You don't know how much.'

Drowsing in the shaded bedroom, Harriet thought of the past crowded weeks. Her main emotion was still one of wonder at the absolute marvel she had managed by producing a child. Millions of women back through the ages had done it before, she was well aware; that did not stop her from an almost overwhelming sense of pride, a certainty of being unique.

Once she was allowed home from hospital, Maggie, deafer now, and white-haired, had come down from Scotland to spend the first three weeks with her. Harriet had been thankful to leave everything to her. There had been cards, presents, flowers; she had enjoyed feeling important, being self-indulgent. And now Chris was here. Maggie had slept in the bedroom which had been turned into a nursery; Chris refused to do so, preferring the little hotel further up the road. 'Darling,' she had said. 'I'll do anything for you, you know that, but I really must have my nine hours if I'm going to be human the next day.'

'That's fine,' Harriet had said. She enjoyed those quiet hours of night-time alone with her daughter, learning each other, bonding — or she had done until the phone-calls started.

Now almost a month had gone by, with nothing to show for it but the small changes — an ounce here, a centimetre there — in her child. She guessed it would be like this for years: the days marked out with the child's achievements rather than her own; like a tree which had taken root in her soil, she would be overshadowed as its branches grew. It occurred to her that she might one day have to fight to retain her own self. She wondered if that was what her mother had done.

*

Her father had sent one of his rare letters from Brazil, on receipt of the telegram informing him of his grand-daughter's birth.

We are delighted, he wrote. *We are planning a trip back to see her within the next few months. However, duty calls for the moment. Both Anita and I have been working on a most demanding case — one of these unpleasant prosecutions of a drug 'baron', complete with promises of revenge and death threats, both over the telephone and by letter. Luckily the trial is almost at an end now, but we are both in need of a change and shall be taking a few weeks off to travel into the interior. For obvious reasons, we shall be incommunicado. Can you imagine us with a police bodyguard? The prospect is very far from pleasing.*

Harriet remembered again the mermaid lady in the black sequined dress and her father's laughing at the end of the table: a different man, new-made by the caressing hand of a stranger. She had met Anita no more than half a dozen times, not enough to establish much feeling for her; she had realised some time ago that her father must have waited to marry her until his children's needs and opinions no longer had relevance to his own choices. She winced at the thought of either of them at the mercy of some drug cartel; every day, it seemed, one read about members of the judiciary in South American countries being gunned down in the streets or outside their own homes.

She wondered how she would cope when Christina left, but next week seemed to exist beyond a curtain which she was too indifferent to lift. In a couple of days she and her daughter would be on their own, and she could start to manage their lives together. One thing she could hardly wait for was the chance to get out to the shed in the garden again. Images crowded her mind, tumbling like birds through her thoughts, images she wanted to trap, to set down in oil or watercolour. Her fingers itched for her sketchpad, but she was content to wait.

She stood at the front door with her daughter in her arms, watching as Christina stowed the last leather case on the back seat of her red MG sports car and slammed the door. The tall trees in the shrubbery moved restlessly in a wind which smelled of the coming autumn; a few early-falling leaves drifted across the drive.

'Lovely car,' she said without envy, kissing the top of the baby's head.

'I know. But impractical.'

'Why? It's not as if you need a family car,' said Harriet.

'The darn thing's unreliable about starting in the mornings, especially in cold weather — which I've already been warned there's a lot of up North. If there's one thing I require of my cars, it's that they start. I'll have to get rid of it before the winter sets in, I'm afraid.'

In Harriet's arms the baby stirred and opened an eye of milky blue. Harriet gazed fondly down at her. Rumpled face, asiatic eyes, a thin red rash across the cheeks: hardly beautiful, but nonetheless ...

Christina came towards her. 'Give me one more hold,' she said, reaching out her arms. She hefted the child against her chest. 'I shall really miss the two of you, you know.'

'Not nearly as much as we shall miss you,' said Harriet. Exultation welled up in her at the use of the word 'we'. I'm a double unit now, she thought, not alone any more. Never again.

Christina kissed the baby and handed her back. 'Adorable,' she said briskly.

'And how delighted you'll be to be back in your own home, away from nappy pails and baby burps and two-in-the-morning feeds,' said Harriet. 'You can't fool me.'

'Can't I?' Christina smiled. 'No, honestly, darling: I can't pretend that motherhood is my thing, but I really do envy you in a way.'

'And I you — in a way. Your work, and the new house, and the barrister-next-door.'

'I don't know about the new house,' Christina said,

grimacing. 'I'm sick to death of those workmen. It's been months now. What a luxury it will be when I can ring you from home instead of having to put on my wellies and trudge down the lane to the pub.' She put her arms round Harriet and hugged her. 'Talking of which, don't forget the importance of routine. Babies like it; I'm sure I read somewhere.'

'Thank you for the advice,' Harriet said gravely.

'And promise you'll come and visit as soon as you feel strong enough.'

'Absolutely.'

'You could get that nice American — Tom — to drive you up, you know.'

'I could, couldn't I?'

Christina grasped the handle of the car door, then turned to stare at Harriet. She opened her mouth to speak, then closed it again. Her eyes met Harriet's and glanced away. She shook back the short dark hair from her face, and said: 'I'm sorry, darling. I truly am.'

'Don't be.' Harriet smiled brightly. 'I'm happy. I've got so many things ... there's no need to be sorry.' Conor seemed little more than a memory now. Life had smoothed out, and unfurled before her.

'I'll keep in touch.'

'Let me have your phone number the minute you've got it.'

'Of course.'

That same afternoon, almost as if she had been watching for Chris's departure, another visitor arrived on the doorstep.

'Oh.' Guilt made Harriet blush. She stepped aside and let her parents-in-law walk past her into the hall.

'How's my grand-daughter?' Conor's mother demanded.

Harriet flushed even more. 'How did you know?' she said.

The other woman's mouth twisted. 'Never you mind. I have my spies.' She glanced at her husband. 'Just as well, it seems, for all the information we've been given by *you*.'

Harriet could not explain, could not tell this woman how often she had scanned her daughter's features, looking for some resemblance between her and her father — whoever he was. It was impossible for her to say, into such blank hostility, that she genuinely did not know whether it was Conor or Stephan.

Conor's mother picked up the baby and cuddled her. Harriet, watching, had to restrain herself from leaping up and snatching the child away from those possessive arms. Does she have the right? she wondered. If it is Conor's, then of course she does, and I cannot deny her. But if Stephan is the father . . .

She went into the kitchen to avoid looking at the woman crooning over the baby. She plugged in the kettle, set out cups, brought a tea-tray into the sitting-room and set it down on the table.

'It might be best if we let her sleep,' she said, despising herself for being glad of an excuse to remove the baby from the older woman's grasp.

Setting down her cup and wiping her narrow mouth with a tissue, Conor's mother straightened her shoulders. 'I've something important to say to you, Harriet, and I want you to listen before you answer,' she said. Her eyes avoided her daughter-in-law's.

'Oh?' That's the first time she has ever used my name, Harriet thought.

'I've been discussing it with my husband,' the other woman went on. 'We both agree that it would be a good idea if we brought the baby up for you. After all, we're not particularly old, even though we're settled, and you're a young girl, with your life to lead. You don't want to saddle yourself with the burden of a child at this stage in your life.'

She's mad, Harriet decided. Quietly, she said: 'I don't think of my daughter as a burden.'

'What I thought was, we could take the child —'

'You most certainly could not,' Harriet said.

'Think about it,' Mrs Pearse said. The lines round her eyes and mouth were hard. The thought of her hands touching the baby made Harriet's still unsteady emotions surge. I think I hate you, she thought, and realised how unwonted an emotion hatred was to her.

Mrs Pearse appeared not to notice Harriet's agitation. 'Yes, we've been thinking it through for some time, ever since we were told about your pregnancy and we —'

'Who told you?' demanded Harriet.

Mrs Pearse smiled thinly. 'That would be telling, wouldn't it? Now, I think you'll see that my idea has advantages. You could, for instance, do your painting full-time, without the distraction of a baby.'

'What? How do you know about —'

'I — we would even be prepared to move nearer here, so you could see her from time to time.' Mrs Pearse swept on as though Harriet had not spoken.

'I don't think you heard me,' Harriet said, shaking with mingled anger and fear. 'What on earth makes you think I would give my child up, and to you of all people?'

'I won't ask what that remark is supposed to mean, though it's fairly obvious that you don't like me any more than I like you. But we have rights, too, as the child's grandparents.'

It was Harriet's cue to deny it, to get rid of the woman for once and for all by saying that Stephan was responsible. She could not bring herself to do so. Mrs Pearse had touched the raw nerve of Harriet's feelings of guilt for not letting her know about the baby. Nonetheless, she was both astonished and dismayed at the woman's ability to deny reality, to refuse to hear what Harriet herself was saying. Conor had often done the same.

'And if you're thinking of anything like refusing us access to her,' her mother-in-law went on calmly, 'you ought to know that we've looked into it, that we have rights as grandparents which you are legally bound to fulfil.'

Harriet could feel the dislike behind the words. She got up. Although not tall herself, she stood a head above Mrs Pearse. 'Perhaps I am. I shall have to get my solicitors to look into it,' she said, hoping that none of the panic she felt was showing. Surely these people could not take the baby away from her, could they? Show she was unfit in some way? 'However, I have absolutely no obligation to allow you into my house and I would like you to leave immediately —' She found herself gasping and continued loudly: 'And until we've settled the matter legally, I'd rather you kept away from my child, too.'

'What?'

'You heard.' There was the taste of something metallic in Harriet's mouth, as bright and sharp as a sucked coin. Although she was shaking, she sensed that in this particular confrontation she was the victor. She had no doubt that there would be others where she might not be.

'Don't worry, I was going anyway,' her mother-in-law said. 'But, believe me, you'll be sorry for this.'

For a moment the anger which had begun to simmer inside Harriet threatened to erupt. She felt an urge to attack the face in front of her with both fists. In that moment, it was clear to her that in defence of her baby she would be as capable of murder as any psychopath. Her mouth shuddered; something in her expression made Mrs Pearse move nearer the door. 'Will I?' she said quietly.

'Yes. It's not the right way to behave.'

'Neither was yours.'

Mrs Pearse pulled at her husband's arm. As the two of them stood on the doorstep, she turned to Harriet. 'Just think about what I said.'

Harriet stood in the kitchen for a long while afterwards, running cold water over her wrists and taking deep breaths. Her chest felt as though it were too small for the huge heart which beat inside it. When she blinked, the world turned briefly scarlet.

That evening, Christina rang. 'God, darling, what a drive. The roads ... you've never seen anything like it. And when I got here, guess what?'

'The roof had blown away? The place has been overrun by white mice? *I* don't know.'

'Harry, you can be so frivolous sometimes,' Christina said with reproof. 'No, there was a letter from Spain, some complication to do with the sale of the flat in Alicante. I've got to go out there more or less immediately and deal with it.'

She won't like that, Harriet thought. At the back of her mind, Denis hurtled once more, briefly, falling, spinning, thudding, a clumsy shooting-star.

'So irritating,' Christina sounded subdued. 'Quite apart from the awfulness of it all, it couldn't be more inconvenient, what with the work going on here at Whitemoor and trying to get everything finally finished. I mean, I could be out there for weeks.'

'Guess who showed up just after you left.' Harriet told Christina all about the visit from Conor's parents. 'The thing I can't work out is who could possibly have told that awful woman I was pregnant.'

'Odd,' Christina said thoughtfully. 'Though since she *is* the child's grandmother, you'd have thought she was entitled to know.'

'Uh ... yes, I suppose she was. But it's a bit weird, you have to admit.'

'Yes, it is.'

'When do you leave for Spain?' Harriet asked, sensing that Christina was not entirely sympathetic.

'At the weekend. Look, darling. In case I don't have time to ring you again before I go, look after yourself and the baby, and I'll give you a call when I get back. OK?'

'Of course.' Harriet nearly added an injunction to have a good time but bit it back. 'And don't worry about me. I'm very capable.'

'I know you are. But there's the baby now, as well as yourself. Anyway, *ciao* ...'

'Goodbye,' Harriet said slowly to an already dead receiver. One by one they were peeling off. Matthew had gone to the States for an indefinite period. Her father was travelling. Christina was off to Spain. Stephan would shortly be leaving Oxford.

She was amazed at how much she was looking forward to it.

'I'll be flying out to Prague tomorrow,' Stephan said. He spread an arm along the back of the sofa, behind Harriet.

'I'll really miss you,' she said.

'I might turn round and come home, you never know,' Stephan said. 'It's not necessarily for ever.'

'All the same ... And I've never thanked you for everything you did after ... after Conor died.'

'If I did anything at all, it was not nearly as much as you deserved. I was harsh with you once; I would not like to be so again.' He smiled. 'The woman for whom I ... I deserted you ...'

'Yes?'

'She lives in Prague.'

'Elvira,' Harriet said softly.

'How do you know that?'

'I looked through your address book once, the term after you came back from Czechoslovakia. I don't know how, but I always knew it was because of her.'

Harriet's hair lay across his fingers. 'Where did you get these?' he said lazily, touching the emerald earrings she wore. 'I haven't seen them before.'

'They're nice, aren't they?' She turned her head this way and that so that the green stones caught the light. 'Someone sent them when the baby was born — I'm not sure who, actually. They must have written a letter and forgotten to enclose it.'

They were silent, then she said: 'And I haven't said how grateful I was for all you did for me while I was pregnant.

'I did nothing.'

'I would have found everything completely overwhelming after Conor died if you hadn't been there.'

'Nothing will overwhelm you, Harriet. You are a strong woman, one who survives.'

'We all survive,' she said. 'In our different ways.'

'Your way is one of the best.'

The two stared into each other's eyes. For a moment possibilities dusted the air between them: love, promises, needs unacknowledged and scarcely recognised. Slowly, slowly, they moved towards each other, towards kisses and union and a whole unknowable future. Then, in her room, the baby stirred and whimpered, and the moment was broken.

Smiling slightly, Harriet nodded. He nodded back, his mouth rueful.

'Stephan.'

'Yes?'

'Does it ever occur to you that ...' Harriet was still undecided as to whether she should tell Stephan of her doubts about her child's paternity, whether it would be fair to lay a burden on him that was only potential. She knew she should not have started this, yet, with him leaving, perhaps for years, she felt she ought at least to mention the possibility. '... that the baby might be yours?'

He moved sharply away from her. 'What are you saying?' He glanced towards the open door and the passage beyond. 'That I am your child's father?' He sounded incredulous, even alarmed.

'I didn't say that. I merely asked if you'd ever wondered about it. After all, the possibility — if you think back — does exist.'

'I never once thought such a thing,' he said angrily. 'I always assumed that your husband ...' A flush spread slowly up his face from the jawline, and his eyebrows drew together in a frown. 'Is there a genuine chance of this?' he asked.

'Come on, Stephan. You did fifth-form biology, just as I did. Of course there is — if you think back to what happened between us. Like you, I've always assumed the baby is Conor's.' She did not add that often, in the night, she heard again that final beat and clap of Conor's body on hers and the dreadful triumphant flow of him into her womb. 'But it might just not be.'

'I see.' Getting up, he stood above her. 'I really wish you had not told me this. It is an added complication just now.'

'I'm sorry. I felt I ought at some point to let you know. Perhaps I should have waited until I could be more certain.'

'Perhaps,' he said, 'that would have been wiser.' Then he too was gone.

She'd been waiting for this moment for weeks. She bathed her daughter, fed and changed her, then laid her on her stomach in the gingham-frilled crib she had prepared two months ago. She cupped one hand over the round fragile skull, thinking: it would take no more than a squeeze to crush those bones ... thinking: she depends on me entirely.

Carefully she pulled the door to. Tiredness had attained a tangibility of its own. She went through the rooms still luminous with the high light of a late summer evening and felt herself trailing fatigue as though it were a shadow. *I must sleep*, she told herself, *I have to sleep*. In the small carved mirror on the wall which had once hung in the Richmond house, she saw her own reflection and was astonished at the darkness under her eyes, the hollow places in her cheeks. I should be rounded, buttery, she thought. Instead I am flesh-less, as though I were dying.

She walked through the French windows out into the unkempt garden. For a moment she stood among the deep grasses, under the sagging buddleia branches. Butterflies stood along the purple wedges of bloom, blotches of chestnut and red fanning with the slow rhythm of sighs; tiny golden insects whirred in a circle of spinning wings. Grass-hoppers leaped with a dry rustle among the grass-stems; the elder bush which hid most of the shed was heavy with flat white plates of bloom. She could feel the earth under her thin-soled sandals and wanted to take root there, stay fastened to the globe by a network of white roots, anything rather than go on; to smell the creosote smell of the treated wood, pull open the creaking door and go into that spider-webbed gloom where her work waited. With a clarity she had not experienced before, she knew that it *was* her work, not some in-between-times hobby but something she was good at and could become better, given time and hope.

In another house a telephone bleeped, travelling across brick walls from some academic drawing-room. She moved forward through the grass and reached for the door of her shed.

It was open. It swung away from the doorpost on an uneven hinge; already the spiders had trellised the gap with gossamer strings. She moved faster now, aware of something wrong, breaking through the spider-lines, stepping into the warm, musty gloom. It took a moment to adjust from the light outside; then she saw her canvases.

Some had been slashed with a sharp blade, or jabbed, the canvas pierced as though by bullets. Some were daubed with paint sprayed from a can, others simply ruined by turps being flung at them so that the colours had melted, paled, run diffused down the canvas to the floor.

She stood very still, feeling dizzy, nauseous. The small space hummed with destruction, with directed hate. Like indigestion her breath lurked in her throat, thick and painful. Her predominant feeling ought, she supposed, to have been fear. But what she experienced was rage. She revelled in it, letting it rush over her body like a shower of hot water. Afterwards, reliving the moment, she remembered how she had dropped into a half-crouch, her eyes had narrowed and her hands readied themselves to kill. At the time she was only aware that all her fatigue had vanished, like smoke from a distant bonfire.

No one ... no one has the right, she thought. To do this ... to do something like this: it was like killing someone's child, like hurting something defenceless.

And again: is this what she meant, that raging woman, when she said I would be sorry? Did she creep through the garden with her spray can and her knife, knowing what hurt this would do to me, paying me back for the hurt I have undoubtedly inflicted on her? For a moment Harriet sagged against the door-post, remembering the mutilated headless doll caught in the grass, and her feeling of helplessness. Was Mrs Pearse responsible for that, too? And what more was there to come?'

· 20 ·

The health-food shop lay somewhat away from the rest of the shopping precinct known as Summertown. It stood halfway down a cul-de-sac which ran at a right angle to one of the little streets connecting the two great arteries of the Banbury and the Woodstock Roads. Here the pavements of battered tarmac gave way to brick; there were flower-stuffed gardens and slanting door lintels, markedly in contrast to the more modern buildings in the main road and the big Victorian houses which were its immediate neighbours. It was surprisingly peaceful, considering that only a minute's walk away it was possible to be speeding west or north in the constant stream of traffic entering and leaving Oxford.

With some difficulty, Harriet manoeuvred the pram up on to the brick pavement and parked it on the only stretch wide enough to hold it, a couple of feet away from the shop's old-fashioned semi-glazed door. Next to it was a place called Cupid's Darts, selling dried flowers and beeswax candles; beyond that a tiny secondhand bookstore spilled its paperback wares out on to the pavement in a series of green-painted boxes and shelves. Opposite stood a row of pastel-washed two-up two-down cottages with minute front gardens.

She walked along and leafed through one of the boxes labelled *ART BOOKS* in a delicate italic hand. She bought a battered edition of Vasari's *Lives of the Artists* and a coverless copy of a book on the Romanesque cathedral at Vézelay, then went into the dark interior of the health-food shop. Above her head a bell on a spring tinkled itself into silence. Light showed at the back of the shop. As though at the end of a tunnel, she could see the owner, Mrs Macrae, sitting in her garden on the edge of a low-walled flowerbed full of pinks, sipping coffee from a mug. At the sound of the bell, she shouted, 'Coming,' but did not move.

While she waited, Harriet poked about. She wanted more muesli, some dried bananas, goat's milk yoghurt. Leaning forward to peer past the notices in the window, advertising recycled loo paper and phosphate-free washing powders, she could just see the edge of the pram.

'What sized muesli did you want?' Mrs Macrae, a well-sized woman in a flowing flowered skirt, appeared behind the counter, tucking her grey hair back behind her ears.

'A kilo, please.'

'Just a jiffy, then. We've only got half-kilos made up.'

'I can take two of those, if you like.'

'Nonsense, dear. It won't take a moment to weigh one out for you.'

Harriet picked up a cellophane-wrapped packet of dried figs. 'What're these like?'

'Normally they're rather good, both juicy and chewy if you know what I mean,' said Mrs Macrae, dipping a galvanised iron shovel into a large brown paper sack of muesli. 'But to be quite honest, this batch is rather a disappointment. A bit dry, and they've been very heavy-handed with the sulphur. I've had to mark them down.'

'I'll wait for the next batch, then.'

'I should.' Mrs Macrae paused, looking up. 'Had the baby then, have you?'

'Yes.'

'Girl or boy?'

'Girl.'

'And what've you called her?'

'Well,' Harriet hesitated. 'I know it sounds ridiculous but I haven't called her anything yet. I'm waiting for the right name to appear.'

Mrs Macrae did not seem to find this odd. 'Beautiful, is she?'

'Not very, actually. Except to me, of course.'

'I'll come and have a look at her soon as I've totted this lot up.'

It was perhaps a minute and a half later that Harriet, followed by Mrs Macrae, stepped out on to the warm pavement.

The pram had gone.

Mind and heart ceased to mesh. Intellectually, Harriet knew it was not where she had left it. She could see its very invisibility. But emotionally she could not take in the fact of its disappearance. Gazing at the space it had occupied, she knew it was there, it *had* to be there, if she only looked properly.

Except that it was not.

She stared up and down the short street, not yet frantic, simply curious. Outside the secondhand bookshop, a donnish figure fingered detective novels. In a house across the street a child clambered over a climbing-frame of red-and-blue metal which took up most of the tiny front garden that it occupied. At the end of the cul-de-sac a high wall shut off someone's back garden. There was no pram. No baby.

Harriet ran to the road end of the street, Mrs Macrae coming after her, aware that something was wrong but not quite sure what. Knowing that what appeared to have happened — that the pram had been wheeled away — could not possibly *have* happened, Harriet felt no panic, no worry, simply a desire to get the pram back again in the place where she had left it. The road itself was empty, though she could see the rush of traffic at both ends — and there, further along, outside one of the big red brick houses was, as she knew it must be, the pram.

Kids, she thought, running towards it. A stupid childish trick: thinking it would be a joke to move it.

She had done the same thing at university with friends' bicycles, once even with a car when a man she knew had left his keys in the ignition and the door unlocked.

Her heart started suddenly to pound. Her mouth was dry.

Kids ...

Running ...

Feet pounding, pounding ...

Time frozen ...

Stupid childish tricks ...

Running, running.

The pavement hot under the thin soles of her sandals.

And, as she ran, two absolutes jostling for prominence in her mind.

One, that the baby was, of course, in her pram asleep; how else could it be?

The other, that the baby was gone and she would never see her again.

She moved as though through oil, limbs weighed down, the daylight which surrounded her curiously refracted, very bright and slanting. She was conscious of nothing but the desire to be reunited with her daughter. At the same time she was acutely aware of details: the intense green of a car parked against the curb, the blood-red jets of fuchsia lying along a garden wall, lace curtains at an upstairs window.

She reached the pram at last as though breasting a giant wave; grasped the handle; looked down.

PART THREE

PART THREE

· 21 ·

'The way I see it,' Detective Inspector David Buchan said, 'we can go one of two ways. Either we call in the Press, give this full coverage, keep them whipped up with a bit of careful briefing, or we can put a blanket on it, say nothing, see how we go.'

'I don't care,' Harriet said dully. 'All I want is my baby back.'

'Well, there's advantages to both, but in the end I'd go for giving it to the Press. What do you think, Sally?'

Sally Rogers, the Woman Detective Sergeant who sat facing her superior across Harriet's dining table, nodded. 'It certainly worked with that case where the baby was taken right out of the hospital,' she said. She gazed at Harriet intently. Both of them maintained direct eye contact with her whenever they spoke. Harriet found it difficult not to slide her own gaze away from them. Perhaps that was the intention.

'The problem is, of course, that they'll be door-stepping you night and day if we give them the chance,' Buchan said. His eyes were hazel, almost square. 'Do you think you could cope with what might be virtually a siege?'

'Anything,' Harriet said. 'Absolutely anything.' She would have said more, might have launched into extravagances — my right arm, everything I have, my life's blood, my *life* — but felt her voice vibrating out of control. Speech had become an effort that took all her strength; she still had not encompassed the unbelievability of what had happened.

He leaned confidentially across the table. 'Look, could we get a couple of things straight first? If we're going to get your baby back safe and well, we've got to be in close cooperation on this one.' He looked to Sally again. 'How long was that other baby missing?' Harriet had the feeling he knew the answer perfectly well.

'Sixteen days,' the WDS said, nodding as though to confirm something he had said.

'Sixteen days?' Harriet whispered.

'That's right.'

Sixteen days: it was a lifetime, an eternity. As in childhood, Harriet saw each one of those sixteen days strung on a wire, marking off the future. Then they had gleamed red and green and blue; now they were grey, black, overcast, stretching into foreverness. 'But that's ... over two weeks,' she said.

'That was abnormal — in that particular case the woman responsible had planned it fairly well. Usually these things are done on the spur of the moment. Five days, maybe; that's the general sort of time. But what I was going to say was, can we dispense with surnames and titles? You call me David, right? This is Sally. And we'll call you Harriet.'

'Of course.' Still numb, Harriet nodded, then found she was unable to stop; her head wagged madly atop her shoulders as though she were one of the fuzz-coated dogs people keep in the backs of their cars.

The WDS — Sally — got up and put both hands firmly on Harriet's shoulders. 'It's all right, dear,' she said. 'We'll get her back,' and though both of them knew it was not all right — that it was very far from all right — the words acted as a clamp on Harriet and she stopped abruptly, her head snapping forward to hang over her lap.

'A cup of tea, Sal,' Buchan said. 'I think a cuppa all round would be a good thing at this stage.'

While Sally was in the kitchen, he said gently: 'Harriet, listen to me. This is the most dreadful thing that can happen to a woman, to lose a baby. But in ninety-nine per cent of abduction cases — and they're very rare indeed — the baby is returned unharmed to its parents in a very short space of time. Ninety-nine point *nine*.'

Was that really true? And if so, what about the point one per cent? Harriet dared not ask the question.

'I want you to remember,' Buchan continued, 'that the

likelihood is your baby's been taken by a woman desperately in need of something to love, a woman who has maybe lost her own child recently. There is absolutely no reason to think that she will harm your daughter; quite the opposite.'

'Mmm.' The sound forced itself past Harriet's stiff lips; she could not speak.

'So the other important point you have to cling on to is that the trauma of all this is happening to *you*, not to the baby. It may sound a heartless thing to say, but she's still far too young at this stage to want much else than regular feeds and changing, and someone to cuddle her.'

'She's nearly six weeks old,' Harriet said. 'She knows me. She'll miss me.'

'Maybe. But please believe me, the suffering is yours, not hers.'

WDS Rogers came in with a tea-tray. One cup did not match the others, and the jug holding the milk was one Harriet kept for serving cream. She had to clench her fists to stop herself screaming aloud at this rupture of normal orderliness.

'OK,' Buchan said. He stood up, hands holding the edges of his expensive grey suit. 'Harriet, would you mind if I took my jacket off?'

One half of her mind was numb; the other worked overtime, annotating, analysing, recording everything with microscopic clarity. Rationally, she appreciated that what he was doing was an attempt to create intimacy, smoothing the way into alliance, and that he had to do so if they were to work positively together. 'Please ...' she said.

'Now,' he said softly. 'I know how terrible all this is for you, but we have to get as much information as we can from you. The baby's name, for a start.'

He waited, pen poised above a notebook, while Sally Rogers poured tea for all three of them and carefully pushed the cups towards them across the table.

Harriet lifted her head. 'She hasn't got one ... not yet.' He seemed surprised. 'I was — I was waiting for the right name, the one which belonged to her, only she was so little, you see, and I hadn't ...' She played with the ring on her finger and said defensively: 'I was going to go down and register the birth as soon as ... I've still got a few days.'

He was patient, fingering his silk tie, capping and uncapping his pen. 'I understand,' he said, though she could see he clearly did not — a man for whom things worked out right, whose lawn was mowed and whose windows were washed, whose children's births had been registered at once, their names chosen in advance. 'But if we're going to the Press, we'll have to give her a name.'

'I see that.'

'Any ideas?'

Harriet shook her head. Names rang through her head, diapasons of them: Mary and Jane and Anne and Emma, Charlotte and Victoria, Henrietta and Clemency: peals of lovely names for a girl to carry through life: Olivia, Hannah, Sophia, Alexandra. 'It's so important, a name,' she said helplessly. *Jessica, Julia, Rosemary, Catherine*, the names chimed like soft bells, each one gathering to itself the possibility of a life, a future, as her daughter's, *Diana, Susannah, Anthea* ...

'Nothing?' Buchan said.

'No.'

'We'll leave that one for the moment.' He scanned the notepad again. 'What's the name of that shop where she was taken?'

'Harvest Health Foods,' Harriet said.

He exchanged the minutest of glances with the WDS and she knew he was labelling her as weird, eccentric, a woman who had not yet given a name to her five-week-old baby, a woman living off pulses and cracked wheat, a yoghurt freak, a nutter, a crank.

'And what was the baby wearing?'

She itemised for them the little Viyella dress threaded with yellow satin ribbon, which had been handmade by Maggie, the nappy pins with yellow heads, the white and yellow bootees, remembering how she had dressed the tiny body, covered the purple baby feet, checked the napkin, and folded back the blanket as they walked, since it was so mild.

'Nothing on her head?'

'No.' Did *that* make her a bad, a careless mother? 'It was so warm you see,' she said, desperate to justify herself, to prove she was fit to have the care of a child. 'Even just in the dress, she was sweating, so I couldn't see any need —'

The long windows into the garden were open. She could see uniformed men out there, pushing aside leaves, probing one of the flower-beds, searching her studio; she wondered what they could be looking for. The figure of Pan leered from under the lilac tree.

'It's all right, Harriet.' Sally Rogers stroked Harriet's wrist gently. 'Nobody's blaming you.'

Harriet banged both hands on the table, startling the other two. '*I'm* blaming me,' she said, aware that she was shouting. 'I shall never forgive myself as long as I live, I left her outside like that though everyone knows you should never do that. I could so easily have taken her in, but she was asleep and the street was empty and I was only going to be a minute.' Except that Mrs Macrae had not made up any kilo bags of muesli that morning and the dried figs were not up to standard and for a few precious seconds — ninety of them — she had taken her eye off the pram.

The academic man at the secondhand bookshop had turned out to be a bus-driver on his way home from night-shift, hoping to find a Dick Francis novel he had not yet read; he had noticed nothing. The child on the climbing-frame had not been aware of anyone else, though his mother remembered seeing the pram there, and had debated crossing the narrow street to have a look. 'Such a nice stage,' she had said, tightly holding her little boy's hand. 'Before they get whiny and into everything and drive you insane sometimes with all the questions . . .' and had then petered out, realising that these were things Harriet knew nothing of — and might never know, if things turned out badly.

On the street which ran between the Woodstock and the Banbury Roads, where the pram had been abandoned, an elderly man had seen something being put into the back seat of a car.

'But I didn't take any particular notice,' he said. Behind thick glasses his eyes were full of sympathy as they glanced at Harriet and away and then back again. 'I don't live around there, don't know any of the people in the houses. I just assumed, with the pram there on the pavement, that he was going to pick up his wife or something. There's a lot of graduate students live round this way, with working wives, that I do know, and that's what I thought it was, if I thought anything at all — which I really didn't — just took in a fleeting impression.'

'*He?*' Buchan had said. 'You thought it was a man?'

'I thought so.' The old man reached down to the plastic shopping bag at his feet as though trying to keep a hold on normality, a life reduced to eggs, a small granary loaf, chicken pieces.

'Why?'

'I don't really know.'

'Try and remember. It could be important.'

'Trousers, was it?' The old man shook his head. 'Maybe that was it. That's all I noticed, the lower half of someone. The rest of him — or her — was inside the back of the car. It could have been either, really.'

'Lots of women wear trousers these days,' WDS Rogers had said. 'Was there something else that made you think it was a man?'

'The — uh — bottom?' He looked apologetic, ashamed of prurience at a time like this. 'There's a difference between a male and a female — uh —' He displayed the embarrassment of his generation when confronted with words like bottom, knickers, breast.

'And this was a male one?' Buchan said.

'Like I said, it was only a glimpse I had,' said the old man. 'Just a glimpse. I was checking the traffic before I crossed the road. That's all. If you hadn't asked about it I wouldn't have given it a second's thought.' He had been making his tremulous way back again from the shops as Harriet, finding the empty pram, began screaming; and he had been pounced on by Mrs Macrae. 'I'm ever so sorry, my dear, I really am.'

'You've been very kind,' Harriet said. And it was true. Everyone had been kind, far kinder than she deserved, a mother who could leave her helpless child outside a shop and not even check it every couple of seconds, a mother whose still unnamed baby had been stolen and who must be held to blame. The last couple of hours had been a whirl of hot pavements, the cool stares of the gathering crowd, a blue light flashing on the roof of a car, someone coming with water in a glass, the strong red of the fuchsia bush beating against her eyes, not the colour of blood but nonetheless reminding her of it, spattered on the brick wall, brilliant, cruel.

'She wasn't on any kind of medication, was she?' Buchan asked.

'Sorry?' Harriet blinked. 'The baby? No. There was nothing wrong with her. She was perfect. A perfect baby.' The health visitor had been only a couple of days before, and said so, bouncing the baby up and down on the weighing machine, checking off notes of weight and height on a diagrammed sheet, her madonna-blue uniform filling the nursery with power and approval.

'What do you think, Sal?' Buchan looked at the WDS. 'We'll say she's got something — jaundice, do you think? Or a stomach disorder? Needs regular medication, something like that?'

'We'll have to be careful,' said Sally. 'We don't want to gild the lily.'

'If anyone comes on to us about it, I can always say I got the facts wrong,' Buchan said. 'Frankly, the means probably justify the end.'

'She's a bit old for jaundice,' said Sally. 'Say a slight digestive problem. Needs to see the doctor regularly.'

'What are you talking about?' demanded Harriet. 'There was nothing wrong with her. Nothing at all.' Except that she had the misfortune to be born to a mother so wickedly incompetent that she left her unattended outside a shop for long enough for her to be stolen away.

'Of course there isn't. But it just gives us an edge,' said Buchan soothingly. 'Whoever took your child is going to be reading the papers, trying to see what we know, whether we're on the track.'

'If she thinks the baby has something wrong with it, that she might endanger the child's life if she doesn't take it to the doctor, then she's going to be just that much more ready to give it back when the time comes,' explained Sally.

'Because that's always at the back of her mind,' said Buchan. 'She's going to find the whole thing a tremendous strain. She's already under pressure, to have taken the child from its rightful mother in the first place. And each day that passes, the guilt's getting greater and greater.'

'And,' added Sally, 'there's always the risk she'll be found out, the strain of knowing that any moment some friend will come up and say, "I didn't know you were pregnant, dear," or there'll be that knock at the door . . .'

Harriet sensed a hardness in them both, a shared and dispassionate loathing for those who broke the law. It was strangely comforting. 'You keep saying "she". But the old man thought it was a man who took her,' she said.

'The old boy did his best,' said Buchan, 'but he's not exactly a reliable witness. Poor eyesight, not really looking. He couldn't even remember the colour of the car, beyond the fact that he thought it was dark. And there's no guarantee that even if he did see a man putting something on the back seat of a car, it was your daughter he was putting there.' He stared at Harriet reflectively. 'Besides, it's usually a woman who pulls a stunt like this.'

A man put his head round the door. 'We've been through the place, Guv. Is there anything else?'

With a brief glance at Harriet, Buchan said: 'Find anything?'

'Not a dicky-bird.'

'Better start packing up then.'

'Right, Guv.' The man disappeared into the hall.

For the first time it struck Harriet that perhaps they thought she had manufactured the whole thing, that she had never had a baby or that, having it, she had dreamed up this whole elaborate plot to conceal the fact that she had killed it herself in a fit of post-natal depression. Women did such things; she had read about it. She remembered, as though through fog, Buchan's voice saying, as he arrived, 'I want her drum thoroughly spun,' and realised now what he had meant.

He took more details, writing them down in a swift hand, using a lot of dashes. Finally he stood up. 'I've got to get back to the factory, Sal,' he said, looking down at the Rolex on his wrist. 'I'll get an Incident Room set up, start the programme running. The lads are still talking to the neighbours and the woman from the shop, but someone'll be round shortly to get the taping gear on the telephone.'

'Right, boss.'

'You be OK, Sal?'

'Yes.'

To Harriet, he said: 'Sally Rogers will stay here with you tonight. Is there someone else who could come in to be with you — your mother, a close friend?' He nodded encouragingly, eyebrows raised, familiar with a world where everyone had parents, friends, someone able to come in; not a fraught, blighted world like Harriet's.

Numbly, she shook her head. Her father was in Brazil, Stephan had gone, Christina vanished to Spain, Maggie up in Scotland, Matthew on business in the States. She had no mother. Sharp as a sword came the sudden thought: how could she have left me? Did she feel this kind of pain?

There was no one else she could ask to come ... until she remembered Tom Seaton. Anxious to establish her credentials as a normal person living an ordered life, she told them his name and gave them the number.

Did she imagine it or did they exchange looks which said as clear as words: *no female friends, eh? All sorts of men on the side, but no female friends, just this male friend, nudge nudge, we all know what that means. Sounds a bit dodgy, if you ask me, sounds a bit like an unfit mum we've got here, leaves her kid outside the shop, natters away for hours, doesn't give a damn.*

She knew she was being unfair, that the police were sympathetic to her rather than hostile, but she could not help seeing herself as on one side of a barrier and them, the rest of the ordinary world, on the other.

She longed to say about Tom: 'I don't like him much; actually, he means nothing whatsoever to me except he happened to be around when the baby was born; he's reliable; he would cope.' But what point was there in such justifications?

Sally Rogers dialled Tom's number; there was no reply. She said: 'Could I ring Dick, my husband? Tell him I won't be home?'

Harriet nodded, heard her dialling, imagined Dick, stolid, dependable, rather good-looking with smooth brown hair and a striped short-sleeved shirt tucked into dark slacks.

She fiercely wanted to be on her own, but recognised the wisdom of another presence in the flat. The doctor had been called and left pills for her to take before she slept. Sally Rogers made more tea and told her to take a couple of them.

'I don't want to, I want to be awake if there's any news,' Harriet said, yet already the thought of sleep, of escape from the present drew her, and the desire to fall into oblivion, however short-lived, was suddenly overwhelming.

'I understand, dear,' Sally said. 'I'll wake you if —'

'Have you got any children?' Harriet asked roughly.

'Two, actually. A boy and a girl, six and eight.'

'Both well, going to school, doing the normal sort of things?'

Sally nodded, taken aback. 'Yes.'

'Then don't tell me you understand, you can't possibly understand the horror of what might be happening to her. You can't know how ... painful ...' The last word came out almost as a scream.

'Of course I can't.'

'Then shut up, shut up!' Harriet shrieked. Inside her chest her bones felt very brittle; she could feel her heart leaping like a hare. 'Don't say you know how I feel because you couldn't begin to.'

'I had a miscarriage between my first and second child,' Sally said levelly. 'I can appreciate something of what you're going through.' She put an arm around Harriet's shoulders and guided her into the bedroom.

The last thing Harriet heard was Sally saying: 'Tomorrow it'll all seem very different,' and herself thinking: no, it won't, it will all be the same only worse, because I won't be able to feel that it is all a nightmare, I will have to face up to it, face the fact that I've lost my baby.

Only as she drifted off into chemical sleep did she wonder where Tom might be.

Tom was in London. In front of him, the river flowed past, smooth and brown. He'd read somewhere that the Thames was now so clean you could practically dip a mug in and drink it without risking either typhoid, tetanus or a simple case of the runs. Maybe. It was not a risk he was prepared to take, preferring instead straight Scotch, straight *expensive* Scotch such as sat on the table in front of him, his third in the past half-hour. Picking it up, he winced as his fingers came into contact with the glass. The tips felt raw, as though they had been rubbed with sandpaper. Eight hours — less one hour off for a very necessary sandwich and an even more necessary pint of beer — of riffing through records can do that to a guy. He sucked them: he could feel their heat and wondered how many layers he had rubbed off, how many more he would take off tomorrow and the next day and the next, until he found what he was looking for. He tried to imagine what he would have done if he'd been searching without the head-start of knowing the names he was looking for.

'She married someone called Anthony Newgate,' Lydia had said, peering at him over the tops of the half-spectacles she had put on. They showed her in another light, made her seem grandmotherly, though her daughter had seen to it that a grandmother was one thing she could not be, for however fond she might be of Benny's children, they were not hers by blood — and that, Tom thought, reaching for his glass, probably should not but undoubtedly did make a hell of a lot of difference.

'They were married at Marylebone Registry Office. I've no idea where that is, but it shouldn't be too difficult to find.'

'Lydia, I really hope you're right. Otherwise I'm going to pay out a heck of a lot of dough on airline tickets just so I can spend my vacation doing exactly what I could do down at the office for free.'

'You're a dear, Tom.'

'I know,' Tom growled.

He had looked in the London telephone directory, of course. It was the first thing he did. But either Mr and Mrs Anthony Newgate had an unlisted number or they no longer lived in London. Which could prove to be an outsize pain in the ass.

Working through the Registry Office's records, it had not been too difficult to discover the exact date of the wedding between Helen Leuci Costello and Anthony Michael Newgate, or the whereabouts of the information filled in under PRESENT ADDRESS. He had even been down to the 'present address' — a small one-roomed apartment in a custom-built block in Camden Town — but none of the current occupants had lived there for longer than eight years. The place was no more than a roosting-perch for young couples, a staging-post along the long road from newly-weds to first parenthood to — eventually — death. So no one remembered — had even heard of — young Mr and Mrs Newgate.

Which was why he was currently searching for issue born to said Mr and Mrs Anthony Newgate, in the hope of finding a more recent address, through which he might be able to track down the former Nell Costello.

He was already coming to grips with her, not disposed to like her much, pretty but narrow-eyed, always seeking revenge for small slights. Lydia's thin harrowed face sometimes appeared to him, and he thought with contempt of the daughter who had left her to rot without more than an occasional telephone call, who had gloatingly informed her of her marriage without giving an address, had retailed the births of her children without giving their names.

On the other hand, Tom told himself, always fair-minded — a necessary attribute in his chosen profession — the woman had taken the trouble to keep in touch from time to time, so she must have understood something of what her mother was going through at the loss of her daughter. But not to tell her about the children ... He shook his head. What a bitch!

Not a bit like Harriet. Harriet ... for a moment there, he had hoped they could get a thing going. The night he had spent at her side as her labour advanced, he had seen her under conditions that no man except a husband should see a woman. It was a good enough start to a relationship.

He swallowed. The hot crowded hours had slid past under the bleak brightness of the overhead light, nurses coming and going in a rustle of starch. He had been enthralled by the blue-white skin of her huge belly, the veins spread like the deltas of some mysterious life-giving river. The extraordinary mystery of birth had both sickened and exhilarated him as Harriet had laboured to produce a child and at last he had seen, between her spread thighs, the bloodstreaked hairy scalp of new life. For the rest of his days he knew he would remember that amazing, that magical emergence.

Morosely he sipped his whisky. It was kind of a bitch that ever since then Harriet had seemed even more indifferent to him than before. Perfectly polite, of course; no one could fault the Brits when it came to courtesy, but she was distant in the same way that, after the initial gratitude, a man who has been rescued from certain death is said to shun, even resent, his rescuer.

Big Ben chimed the hour. He checked his watch against the sound. Soon he would drift across the Hungerford Bridge, up towards Covent Garden and on to Shaftesbury Avenue. He had a ticket for Alan Ayckbourn's latest play; while he did not mind being alone he could not help thinking how much nicer it would be if he had *two* tickets, one for himself and one for a female companion, one for — if he came right down to it — Harriet.

When the play finished, he would take the tube to Paddington and ride the train back to Oxford, then walk through the quiet high-walled streets, past carved college gateways, down the curve of the High, under the great tower of Magdalen and across Folly Bridge before cutting to the right and up the Iffley Road, where the streets grew gradually meaner, till he reached the house — triangular-gardened, dankly-looed — where Stephan's ground-floor flat was.

At eight o'clock the next morning the telephone began ringing. He was a slow waker: the woman on the other end made no sense, her level voice giving him news of importance that he could not at first take in.

'The police,' he heard. 'Woman Detective Sergeant Sally Rogers. Can you hear me, Mr Seaton?'

Covering the mouthpiece, he yawned hugely and shook his head to clear it. 'Hello?' he said briskly. 'Hello?' Maybe she'd think there was a fault on the line.

'I believe you are acquainted with Mrs Pearse,' the voice said.

'Pearse? I don't think so.'

'Mrs Harriet Pearse?' The voice was infinitely forbearing, a voice that had heard denials and prevarications from people in every walk of life and was not about to take no for an answer.

'Oh, *Harriet*. Yes, I know her.'

Rapidly the voice explained what had happened the day before. He listened, the pit of his stomach growing heavy. At the same time, he could not suppress a momentary jubilation at the thought that she had asked for him. 'So if you could perhaps arrange to spend a few nights keeping Mrs Pearse company,' the voice went on, 'it might be as well. I don't think she should be on her own at the moment, but there doesn't seem to be anyone else who could come in.'

Thanks a lot, lady, he thought bitterly. The jubilation drained rapidly away. *Nobody else ...* to be replaced with apprehension and horror. *Harriet ...*

'... and there's the Press. We'll be releasing a statement

later on this morning, so it would be helpful if you could be there to take some of the pressure off Mrs Pearse, where possible. As you can imagine, she's not really in a fit state ...'

'I can hardly believe this,' he said. There were a hundred questions he wanted to ask. 'Do the police have any ideas about what happened, any clues?'

'Not yet. But, as we told Mrs Pearse, if she can just stick it out for a few days, we have no doubt the baby will be returned safe and sound — as it is in the vast majority of these cases.'

It would be the tiny minority that would bother Harriet, he thought, packing a few things together. Her mind would not be able to avoid the black plastic bag on the corporation dump, the maltreated body found hidden under leaves in a wood, the frail skeleton discovered on a building site ... He shuddered, filled with compassion.

Three days passed ... four. Harriet could not weep. Her horizons, once so promising, had shrunk, dwindled, compressed themselves about her like some mediaeval form of torture — whereas the baby, once so small had expanded; now her absence swelled to fill the world, the universe. There was nothing else but that overwhelming non-presence.

She decided to call her daughter Laura; it was her grandmother's name. Sometimes she appeared on the doorstep and spoke, at D.I. Buchan's urgings, to the reporters gathered outside the door. 'Remember,' he said. 'They may seem like a load of vultures, but in fact at this stage they're your best friends. The more this is plastered over the front pages, the less chance that bitch has of getting away with it.'

'Bitch?' Harriet said.

'Sorry.' He made no attempt to look contrite. 'Shouldn't have said that. We're supposed to feel sorry for women who take someone else's baby, supposed to think they're not criminals but sufferers too.' He looked at Harriet out of his large square eyes and added: 'I know who *I* think does the suffering.'

Once she even appeared on the television, speaking to cameras set up in her sitting-room, the place suddenly very high and bright, full of trailing wires and serious muted voices. She had no idea what she said, only that she had broken down, her voice wavering into incoherence, that she had pleaded for Laura to be returned. Then the lights had been switched off, the equipment removed, and she was alone again, with Tom bringing brandy and waiting while she drank it down.

Buchan had privately told Tom that he was less hopeful than he made out. 'The person who did this obviously planned it ahead,' he said. 'It doesn't look like a random snatch to me. For a start, look at the scene of the crime. Much easier there than in the big shopping area where there'd be lots of people. And it's nice and close to the corner with the cross street, plus there's instant access to the main road leading directly out of the city.'

'But Harriet might not have gone to that particular shop for weeks.'

Buchan shook his head. 'She's there at least once a week: I've checked with the owner, and it's always at the same time when she goes. I've no doubt at all — though I haven't said so to Harriet — that she was watched for some while before the snatch. For the kidnapper it was just a question of waiting.'

To Harriet he said: 'I don't suppose the whole operation took more than forty seconds or so from start to finish: wheel the baby away to the car, pop her into the carry-cot or whatever, get behind the wheel, and away you go.'

'Forty seconds,' said Harriet. *Forty seconds in which I was gossiping with Mrs Macrae, talking of figs, thinking about something else, when all the time my daughter was being wheeled away into the unknown by a madwoman.* Or, possibly, a man; despite Buchan's scepticism, the elderly witness who had seen something being loaded into the back of a car might still have been right.

'It does open up a whole new ball-game, of course,' Buchan said. 'If this baby was a deliberate target, perhaps we should be directing our search at someone in particular. We've already been through the records of the women who've had still-births or lost new babies in the last few days, though so far it hasn't given us very much to go on. The local hospitals are always cooperative, but sometimes there's a delay in getting information from further afield. And there's the home-births and the private nursing homes still to collate.'

'But there must be something else you can do.'

'Look, love, we've got five teams of officers working round the clock. So far we've interviewed just about everyone who was within five miles of the place when your baby went missing. We've appealed for car drivers to come forward, in case they noticed something. We've put enquiries through to Scotland Yard for details on known child abductors. We give Press briefings every day. We all meet at least every two days, if not more often, in order to discuss what we've learned and the implications of the information. On a Serious Arrestable Offence like this, we don't sit about on our backsides and wait for things to happen: everything we can possibly do is being done, I promise you.'

His voice gave no hint of the busy Incident Room, the piles of action sheets, the files containing the results of interviews with neighbours, with local shopkeepers, with witnesses, plus the men and women detailed to the endless checking, the green blur of Honeywell computer screens, the constant updating of information as it blundered in from members of the public all over England convinced they had sighted the missing child, hundreds of leads to be followed up, even though most of them would prove to be dead-ends. Plus the inevitable nutters coming in to confess that they were responsible, each one dead keen to be accused of the crime; even when their stories were obviously a complete load of rubbish, they still had to be checked out, just in case. Plus the mediums and the psychics, the ones who had had a dream about the baby's whereabouts, or passed a car and felt dangerous vibes emanating ... The list was endless.

Time stretched blackly, punctuated by the scream of the telephone. Maggie called: she had broken her hip and could not move, otherwise she would have come immediately. Harriet's grandparents rang to ask if they should come to be with her. Harriet said no; they were too old for such distress.

But there were other calls, soft and vicious in the night, always the night, opening up glimpses of lives unimaginable.

'Hello, dear. I know where your baby is.'

'Where? Who's got —'

'She's safe and sound, dear, and ever so happy.'

'How do I get her back? Tell me, I'll do anything.'

'Just give your soul to Jesus, dear. Oh, yes, Jesus has taken your little girl to live with Him. Give your soul to Him and the two of you will be reunited when He calls you to His side.

'You fucking careless cow. I wouldn't leave you in charge of my rubber-plant, let alone a baby. Inside the shop chatting your useless fucking head off while that poor helpless kid's dragged off by some maniac who's going to stick his dick up her bum or down her throat — oh, yes: that's what they do, you know, that's why babies go missing, there's rings of them, all over the country, they've got contact magazines and everything, nothing they like more than a baby, especially a girl, you wouldn't believe the kind of things they can do when they really get roused ...'

'Whore! Bitch! Slut! Flaunting yourself, showing yourself off, letting them look up your skirt, letting them touch you, three or four at once, you don't deserve to have a baby, serves you right that she's gone, letting them see your knickers, letting them sleep with you, serves you right, slut, this is a judgement on you, bitch, a punishment ...'

'Look at it this way, there're too many damn kids in the world anyway, we don't seem to be able to feed the ones already on the planet so what's it bloody matter if one disappears, that's what my husband said when mine was taken, never even opened his eyes, poor little sod, still-birth they said, I wanted to sue them for negligence but my husband wouldn't let me, THEY KILLED HIM, MY BABY! Why shouldn't they kill yours too ...'

'Mrs Pearse?' A rich warm voice, this, full of understanding. 'I know how dreadful all this must be for you, how you must be suffering. I really do sympathise with this most appalling experience you're going through. I do feel that this is a story which could help others in the same position and my paper has empowered me to offer you a substantial sum for exclusive rights to your story. I wondered whether you would consider ...'

There were so many of them. And, under the horror, what made it so much worse was that the voices were all those of women.

Harriet had never been a particularly conscientious housewife; now she cleaned the flat compulsively, scouring, scrubbing, dusting, washing. Watching her buff up a silver tray she had meticulously polished only that morning, Tom said nothing, recognising that soap, beeswax, bleach served a dual purpose, not only occupying her but keeping unwholesome thoughts at bay.

Buchan was at the flat when she remembered something. 'Tracy Marling!'

'Who's she?'

'She had a baby about the same time as me,' Harriet said excitedly. 'Only she lost it — it died; it was ill or something.' She tried to recall what exactly Chris had said only a couple of weeks before. 'A respiratory problem, I think it was.'

'Tracy Marling, you said? Lost a baby?' Buchan frowned, recalling the lists already checked. 'Doesn't ring any bells.'

'I could call in, ask them to check the name,' Sally Rogers said. She had been sitting, as she often seemed to do, just behind her superior. At his nod, she left the room.

'Who exactly is this Tracy Marling?' asked Buchan when she had gone.

'She used to clean for my friend, Christina Crawford. I'm sure Chris said she lives somewhere round here. And when they moved out to the country, they still kept Tracy on. They paid her more, of course, because it was much longer for her to get out there, but then she bought a car — I think they helped her with the payments, actually.'

Sally Rogers came back. 'No one called Marling is on the infant death records,' she said. She frowned across at Harriet. 'Are you sure that was her name?'

'It's what Chris always called her.'

'Is it her married name?'

Buchan looked at Harriet enquiringly. She shook her head. 'I don't think so. I remember Chris talking about her once before, months ago. She'd bumped into her at the supermarket and discovered that she was pregnant. I distinctly remember her saying that Tracy wasn't married to the father.'

'Perhaps she changed her mind,' said Tom.

'It might be a good idea to get in touch with Mrs Crawford,' Buchan said. He balanced his pen against a fresh page in his notepad. The pen was an expensive one, a proper fountain-pen which used real ink, like the one Harriet was given when she first started at the grammar school — she could see it clearly, the name Conway Stewart on the gold nib, the pink-and-black mottle of the casing, the silver clip. No doubt his was a present from Mrs Buchan, Harriet thought. She could visualise her so clearly: small, neat, with a good complexion and hair done once a week at the local hairdressers, and a way of ... She pressed the palms of her hands against her temples to stop the irrelevant smokescreen thoughts which interposed themselves every time she tried to concentrate on the situation she was in; where Laura was, and who she was with.

'Christina's in Spain at the moment,' she said.

'Is there a number where we can call her?'

'There isn't a telephone, and I don't know the official address. We took a taxi from the airport and my — my husband just showed him the street and the number written down on an envelope. We didn't really know where we were going but — couldn't it be Tracy?'

Harriet knew she was gabbling; almost begging. 'I mean, she knows this area, she knows me and that I had a baby, because Chris met her in the shops just a few days ago, and she said she was looking awfully wild and weird because of losing her own child.'

Poor Tracy Marling — but Harriet rushed on, desperate to find what might be the solution to Laura's disappearance, stifling the pity she had felt, gladly condemning, happy to brand the almost unknown Tracy as a baby-snatcher, a thief, anything if it might bring Laura back.

'Yes,' she continued. 'Chris sacked her for stealing, about five months ago — maybe she took Laura as a way of getting back at her, because I'm her friend. That could be the explanation, couldn't it?' She looked at each one of them, eyes bright and desperate.

Tom thought: *this is too awful to watch. Such hopelessness. Such pathos.* He moved over and sat next to Harriet. He put an arm round her shoulders protectively. 'It sounds as if it might be worth looking into,' he said, in the deep authoritative voice he used for court appearances.

'It could be a lead,' agreed Buchan, 'except we don't seem too sure of the woman's name. You're certain it was Marling? Not Marley, or Manning, or Marland.'

'I don't know. Chris said Marling, I'm sure.'

'Perhaps she registered in the boyfriend's name even though they're not married,' Sally Rogers said.

'Trouble is, we don't know his name either. Nor where either of them is supposed to live.'

'But it must be around here if Chris met her shopping locally.'

'Not necessarily. She might have been visiting friends, or simply found it easier to come up here where the parking's more convenient. But we'll have a go at running it through the computer — see what we come up with. Also see if we can get through to your friend in Spain.' He took down a few more of Chris's details in Alicante. He made no comment when Harriet mentioned Denis's fatal fall, though she could imagine his unspoken thoughts: *Christ, what sort of women are these, with two dead husbands and a missing baby between them?* When he had finished, he shut the book. 'Why did your friend sack this Tracy Whatever, anyway?'

'She was stealing.'

'What — money? Silver? Jewellery.'

'I'm not sure what. I know she took some shoes,' Harriet said. 'Some red shoes.' The colour added authenticity to what now seemed an otherwise thin explanation.

'Seems a bit odd.' He turned to his colleague: 'If you were going to steal from your employer, would you take her shoes?'

Sally shook her head. 'Not even if they were the right size.'

'It wasn't just shoes,' Harriet said quickly. 'Chris mentioned some expensive underwear which had also gone missing. I think she said it was Janet Reger.'

'Sally?' Buchan had his eyebrows raised.

'Certainly not: Janet Reger or no Janet Reger. But, then, that's me. I like my own things, thank you very much, even if they aren't the world's most expensive.'

In her mind's eye, Harriet could see Sally's own things: a white bra, white pants with a thin lace trim, nothing fancy, except perhaps on special occasions when she and Dick could be alone or it was an anniversary or the kids were out for the afternoon and the two of them could go upstairs together, undress each other the way they used to when they were first ... Once more she pulled herself up short.

Buchan frowned again. 'Your friend must have thought a lot of this cleaning lady, to keep her on after she left here, and then even to help her buy a car.'

'Yes, she did. It was only because of this stealing ...' Buchan was right — yet, at the same time, she clearly remembered Chris saying Tracy was the worst cleaning lady she had ever had. Odd ...

'Did your friend ever suggest that Tracy was a bit odd in other ways?'

'Not that I remember. Perhaps it was being pregnant that made her act strangely,' said Harriet, remembering urges, desires, which had fastened themselves to her like limpets during the early months, quite exterior needs which seemed to bear little relationship to her normal self.

'We'll get on to it right away,' Buchan said. He stood. 'May I suggest, Tom, that you take Harriet out for a walk. She's not looking well ... maybe a pub lunch, or just the fresh air ...'

'I can't leave here,' said Harriet. 'Suppose you find her.'

'There's no suppose about it,' said Buchan. 'We'll find her. But it won't do any harm if she has to wait an hour to see you again. And if we don't, at least it'll do you good to get away from here for a bit.'

In ordinary circumstances, the chance to take Harriet out

would have delighted Tom. These circumstances were anything but ordinary. She sat hunched and miserable beside him in the car he had taken over from Stephan, her thin shoulders emphasising the big milk-filled breasts. He did not feel he could ask but imagined they must hurt, that in her bedroom Harriet would be involved in humiliating and hurtful routines of expelling milk which the baby was no longer there to consume. His heart literally ached for her; he longed to say so, to say anything at all that would be of comfort, but there was nothing which could possibly ease her troubles.

'You've been awfully kind,' she said now, staring intensely through the windscreen at the road ahead. 'I feel terrible that you've had to waste so much of your vacation on me.' Pain sat solidly behind the words.

'Harriet ...' Tom's voice cracked. He pulled the car up against a hedge of elder, the white saucers of florets beginning now to turn into clumps of hard green berries. She did not move, her eyes still fixed in front of her. 'Oh God, if you knew how sorry I feel, if you knew how desperately I wish I could help you.'

'I shouldn't have left her,' Harriet said softly.

'That's rubbish. No one keeps a twenty-four guard on a baby.'

'But if I had, she'd be here now.' He saw how her thighs dented with the pressure of her fists against her jeans.

'Harriet, you've got to stop blaming yourself.'

'It's been four days now,' she said in the same quiet voice. 'And no one has the faintest idea where she is or who took her. I can't see any reason why they ever will.' She turned her forlorn eyes on Tom. 'I feel as if I shall never see her again.'

'There's no reason to think that way,' Tom said roughly. 'You have to keep on hoping. That policeman said five days was about average.'

'Maybe.' She sounded as though she no longer cared. 'It'll be five days tomorrow.'

He took her to a pub where peacocks and undergraduates strutted and preened under ancient trees. Seated at a table beside the river, he tried to keep her interested in something outside her loss. He talked rapidly of himself, Amis, California. 'You'd love it out there,' he said.

She smiled oddly. 'I've been there. I met Conor — my husband — there.'

'Of course. You were working for the Costellos. Didn't Lydia Costello know your father?'

'Yes.'

'What was he doing in California?'

'I don't know.'

Nothing he said seemed to rouse her. In the end, from a mixture of nervousness and desperation, he told her of his search for Lydia's daughter. 'I'm sure I'll catch up with the woman eventually,' he said, 'but it's going to take a while; far more than the week Lydia asked for.' Then he wished he had chosen some other topic, remembering that Harriet, too, had lost her daughter.

But Harriet had thought of something else. 'Conor ...' she said. 'Could she possibly ... Surely not.' For a moment she sat, biting her lip.

'What?'

'Conor's mother.' Harriet's glance looked through him to someone else, in another place. 'Do you think she could possibly have taken Laura?' Rapidly she described the scene when the elder Mrs Pearse had shown up at the flat, her vague threats, the bitter antagonism.

'Don't count on it,' Tom cautioned, dismayed again by the bright flush on Harriet's haggard face. 'She'd have to be crazy to think she'd get away with such a course of action.'

'That's just it: I think she is.' Harriet picked up a beer-mat from the table and slowly tore it into strips. 'I mean, I think she always was, but since Conor died ... He was her only child.' Pity stirred in her chest, and shame; she thrust them both away. There was no place for either while Laura remained lost. 'And she definitely implied that she had been spying on me ... How else did she know about the baby? I certainly didn't tell her, though I probably would have done at some point. I *hope* I would, when ...' She was going to say: '*When I had decided which of them, Stephan or Conor, was*

Laura's father,' but it was a point too complicated to discuss with this comparative stranger.

'Perhaps she just wanted to see if something of her own child had been left behind,' Tom said gently.

He was right, of course — and unconvinced by what she had said. Gazing out over the river, she told him about the ruined paintings, her sense of desecration.

'Why would she do such a thing?' he said.

'Sheer nastiness? You haven't met her, but she hates me, simply for marrying her son. She truly does.' Leaning forward, Harriet stared directly at Tom; he could see bloodless white patches under her eyes, where the skin lay directly on the bone. 'Believe me, she does. It's the first time in my life I've ever encountered hate.' She got up. 'I'm sorry but I want to go home.'

Back at the flat, Harriet telephoned the police. When Buchan came to the phone, she told him about the scene with Conor's mother, exaggerating some of the details in order to emphasise the other woman's air of derangement.

He made no comment except to say, when he had finished taking down the telephone number and address of Conor's parents, 'Your friend is a difficult woman to get hold of.'

'How do you mean? Which friend?'

'Mrs Crawford. We've had a problem getting through to the Spanish police, for a start, and when we did, they seemed to be under the impression that the Crawford flat had been sold some time ago.'

'Are you sure?'

'No, I'm not. That's why we keep on trying. I don't speak Spanish and none of them speak much English, but they're supposed to call back later on today when they've rustled up an interpreter. I hope after all this that when we catch up with her, she knows something that'll give us a handle on this Tracy Marling of yours.'

She thought of the mutilated doll lying outside the French windows: should she tell him about that? She hesitated. The more such information she gave him, the stranger she herself must seem. How could a perfectly ordinary young woman have attracted so many bizarre events unless she herself was bizarre?

She decided to say nothing for the moment either about the damaged canvases or the doll, remembering the looks he had exchanged with Sally Rogers, reluctant to reinforce any impression he might have of her being in some way odd. If necessary, they could always be brought up later, if Laura continued missing.

Her previous despair gave way to euphoric hope. She had given the police two promising leads to investigate; besides which, tomorrow was the fifth day that Laura had been gone: the day they had held out to her as being the breakthrough time, when the baby-snatcher would have had a chance to realise that her own stress would not see her through, when the need to confess was strongest, when the guilt was catching up and the strain began to be overwhelming.

'If the baby cries a lot,' Sally Rogers had said, 'that often seems the final straw. Don't forget Laura needs feeding, and after being used to breast milk, she'll suddenly have been put on to a formula.' Looking at the tangle of Harriet's golden hair and the deep shadows round her eyes, she had added, perhaps unwisely: 'Really, my dear, there's every hope.'

That evening, stronger and more optimistic than she had been since the nightmare began, Harriet told Sally she was all right, that she would prefer to be on her own.

'I don't think that's a good idea,' the WDS said doubtfully.

'Tom will be here.'

'Well, if you're sure.'

'I am. Absolutely.'

But when Tom arrived that evening, she told him the same thing.

'What do the police feel?' he asked, unconvinced.

'I didn't discuss it with them.' She spoke haughtily, as she sometimes did when unsure of herself.

'I think I should stay —' he began, but she cut him off.

'They only wanted someone with me in case I took an

overdose. I'm not going to do that, you know perfectly well. And I've taken up far too much of your time as it is.'

He did not like to leave her, but in the end felt he had little choice. She was not a prisoner; he was not her keeper. 'I'll stay until bedtime,' he said, forcefully, hoping she would not argue.

After he had reluctantly left, Harriet undressed. She looked at herself in the long cheval glass in the bedroom — Matt's wedding present to her. The mirror was pitted with damp-stains in one corner; the glass had a greenish tinge which, in the light from her bedside lamp, gave her the air of a mermaid, a drowned Ophelia, floating just beneath the surface of a stream.

Her flesh seemed unfamiliar to her. Her legs were long and slender, beneath hips riper than formerly. Her breasts hung heavily from her shoulders, still swollen with the milk that she had to express each day, though no longer aching as they had when Laura disappeared. Since giving birth, her contours had subtly altered; they were not any more those of a girl. She looked, somehow, maternal, although she was not, for the moment, a mother; just as she had once been married but not a wife.

Without warning the dreadful possibilities invaded: paedo-philiac groups, satanic rites, sadists, all the horrors which accrued to present day parents, the extra dangers which comprised so much more than simple accident. Shaking, she saw that, as a mother, from now on she was doomed always to suffer doubly: on her child's as well as on her own behalf.

There was a pain in her heart; she felt her ribs constrict, her chest tighten until she could scarcely breathe. Her head was filled with light, with cloud; inside it her thoughts raged and boiled, and her skull ached, as though about to split open and scatter them seedlike across the carpet.

'Laura,' she said. In the mirror, her lips moved; she remem-bered the curve of her daughter's head, how it had fit into the palm of her hand, fragile as an egg. She wished passionately that Christina was there to help and comfort her. She thought, *tomorrow is the fifth day*, and dared think no further.

Switching off the light, she drew back the curtains so that the room was filled with swaying shadows of leaves. She lay naked on top of the covers; her body seemed insubstantial, possessed of no more solidity than a piece of paper, a length of silk. Falling eventually into uneasy sleep, she dreamed of herself unclothed, strutting through long grass in high-heeled red shoes, wanton, dangerous, while above her head branches from no living tree swayed in an icy wind. She opened her mouth to speak, but the voice which came out was not hers, and the face she wore, although she could not see it, belonged not to her but to Christina.

She woke to the telephone. She snatched it up. On the bedside table a clock glowed the time: 11:55.

'Is that Harriet?' The voice was tentative, female.

'Yes.'

'Harriet Pearse?'

'Yes.' Disappointment that it was not Buchan with news of Laura made her brusque. 'What do you want? You're tying up the line.'

'I just wished to say I'm sorry,' the voice said. The sibilants hissed through the night, strained, dejected. 'So terribly sorry.'

'Who are you?'

'It doesn't matter who I am. I wanted you to know that I understand what you're going through.'

'Is it you?' Harriet shouted. 'Are you the one who took . . .?' But the telephone had been put down.

Fingers clumsy with excitement, Harriet dialled the police station and gave the number of Buchan's extension. He answered immediately, his voice rough with exhaustion. 'Yeah?'

'It's Harriet. I think she just phoned me. The woman who took Laura, she was just on the telephone.'

'What?' Instantly the fatigue was gone. She could envisage him, watchful, alert, fountain-pen in hand, ready to take down information. 'When?'

'A minute ago. Two minutes. I called you at once.'

'How do you know it was her?'

'I don't. But she sounded so ... She said how terribly sorry she was. She said she knew what I was going through.'

'Bingo. We've got her.' There was satisfaction now in Buchan's tones. 'If it *was* her, she's cracking. First the conscience starts to prick, then comes the full-fledged guilt, then the realisation that she can't go through with it, and the next thing you know, the baby's been left on the steps of a police-station, or there's an anonymous call telling us where she can be found.'

'Oh, God. Do you really think so?'

Caution reasserted itself. 'Of course we can't be sure. But who else would it be?'

'I don't know.'

'Did it sound like Tracy Marling?'

Harriet considered. 'I don't think so. But I don't know if I ever heard her speak.' Hesitating, not wanting to sound snobbish, she added delicately: 'It didn't sound like the sort of voice I'd have expected her to have, though.'

There was a pause. Then Buchan said: 'We got through to the local Garda in Ireland. Seems that Mr and Mrs Pearse have gone away.'

'Where to?'

'Surprisingly enough, for a small Irish village, nobody seems to know. They were seen driving off a week ago, near as anyone can pin it down, and they haven't yet returned.'

'Do you think it could be ...?' Harriet could not complete the sentence.

'I don't know. Harriet, don't pin your hopes on anything at the moment. Just float; it's the only way. Sooner or later we'll get whoever took Laura, I promise you.'

Putting out the light again, she found she could not sleep. If it was Tracy who took the baby, then it could not be the Pearses; if it was the Pearses, then it could not be Tracy. Two suspects made it worse than merely one.

She would not consider that it might be neither.

In the morning she was woken by banging at the front door.

Before she could get there, the telephone rang. It was Buchan. 'I think we've got a line on the Marling woman,' he said. Satisfaction gave his voice a new vitality. 'If it's the right one, she registered at a hospital in Chipping Camden as Teresa Merlin. The local boys are checking it out now.'

Harriet felt weak. It meant nothing, she told herself, nothing at all. 'Do you ... do you think you'll find her?'

'I can't make any promises, Harriet. But we never give up where there's a child concerned.'

'Oh, David ...'

'I know. Mind you, there's nothing in the records about this particular woman losing her baby, but keep your fingers crossed. I promise I'll contact you again the very second I've anything to tell you.' He drew a deep breath. 'Float, Harriet. Keep floating. I've given some of this information to the Press — not names, of course. Sally's on her way round now. Is Tom with you?'

She called Tom: 'Sorry,' she said. 'Can you come?'

Sally arrived. The front-door knocker banged and banged again; someone from the local newspaper kept shouting through the letter-box. She heard Sally on the step, unaccustomedly severe:

'Look, you lot. You've already been told to leave it out. Any more and I'll do you for loitering — *with* intent. Now get away. We'll let you know as soon as there's anything more to tell you.'

Blood fizzed through her veins. It was the fifth day; had they really caught up with Laura's abductor?

As the telephone sounded again, she heard Tom calling and ran to let him in. Beyond him there was a waving newspaper. A headline flashed across her vision: BABY LAURA BREAKTHROUGH?

She picked up the shrilling phone as Tom got the door shut and leaned against it, smiling at her.

'Mrs Pearse: we understand there's been a breakthrough on the case. Do you have a statement ...?'

Waiting for Buchan and news of Tracy Marling, time passed with agonising slowness.

· 23 ·

Buchan's face was grey, all its lines drooping. Sitting opposite him at her dining-table, one part of Harriet recognised that he was on the edge of total exhaustion; the other wanted to whip him into action, force him to get out there at whatever cost to himself, make him find her child.

'Tracy,' he said wearily. 'Or, rather, Teresa — but Tracy's her pet-name. Right woman, wrong information. Yes, she used to work for Mrs Crawford. Yes, she did have a baby at around the same time you did. But her baby's alive and well, living with its mother and her boyfriend in a council house near Burford.'

The news confused Harriet, though the main message it conveyed was unequivocal: Tracy Marling had not stolen Laura — she would have had no need to do so. The subtext, though ... 'Are you sure she's telling the truth?' she demanded.

'My DS — Detective Sergeant Jones — and I saw the baby with our own eyes. Plus the hellish mess all round it: disposable nappies and feeding bottles and the like. Our Tracy's no housekeeper, whatever she may have done for Mrs Crawford.' Tiredness made Buchan brutal.

'How could Chris possibly have got everything so turned round?'

'I can't imagine, can you?' His square-eyed glance rested on her soberly, then moved away. 'Tracy says she did bump into Mrs Crawford about a month ago, but it wasn't here in Oxford; it was out at Burford, while Mrs Crawford was browsing round the antique shops.'

'That's ridiculous. There must be a mistake,' Harriet began, but even as she said it, she wondered whether Buchan suspected that the confusion came from herself and not from

Chris. Could he be right? In the days after Laura's birth, she had swum along on a tide of new sensation, more concerned with herself and the child than with the outer world. And there had been those phone-calls, night after night, until she could hardly see straight. Maybe she had simply been too tired to take in what Chris was saying. She felt herself grow hot. Was it her fault that the police had wasted all those man-hours on what had proved to be a false lead? Would they hold her accountable?

'Tracy told us she mentioned some girl who'd been in the hospital at the same time as her, who was having a bad attack of post-natal depression,' Buchan said, looking down at his notes. 'But she swears she never said anything about anyone losing a baby, least of all herself.'

'I see.'

'She also said that though she remembered you, she had no idea where you lived, and probably wouldn't recognise you if she passed you in the street.'

There was an unaccustomed roughness in his voice which made Harriet shrink in on herself like a retreating snail withdrawing into its shell. She was pretty sure he had already marked her down as weird; this latest information could only confirm his opinion. Thank God she had said nothing about the damaged paintings in her studio, or the headless doll.

'I'd still like to have got hold of Christina Crawford, if only to sort things out,' Buchan said. 'I suppose now we've cleared up this Tracy business, there's no real need.' He watched her through narrowed eyes. 'But it does seem strange that you should have misunderstood her. Doesn't it seem strange to you, Sally? I mean, according to Teresa Marling — Tracy — Mrs Crawford was a highly efficient lady who didn't often make mistakes.'

While I, thought Harriet, am clearly neither of these.

There was no sympathy in Buchan's expression as he told her about the cramped council house, Tracy in grubby pink slippers, the smell of unwashed nappies and sour milk.

'What about Mrs Crawford giving you the push?' he had said.

'You what?' Tracy's scarlet mouth had opened wide with indignation. 'Giving me the push?' She looked over at her boyfriend lounging on the green-covered sofa. 'I found out I'd fallen pregnant and she'd just lost her husband: there wasn't all that much work anyway, considering the long drive. It was a mutual decision we came to, thank you very much.'

'Wasn't there something about you pinching a pair of Mrs Crawford's shoes?' said Buchan. 'Red ones, so I heard.'

''Ere,' the boyfriend said, stirring himself. 'You calling Trace a liar or what?'

'Would we?'

'We're only repeating what we've been told,' DS Jones added.

Tracy looked uncomfortable. 'Matter of fact, there *was* a bit of bother with them shoes,' she said. 'She found me trying them on once, if that's what you're on about. Lovely shoes, they was. And just my size.' Defiantly she lit another cigarette, holding a Queen Anne-style lighter close to her face. 'She was furious. Didn't like people touching her things, Mrs C. didn't. But I've never took a thing didn't belong to me in my life, and anyone that says I did is a bleeding liar.'

'Right.' The boyfriend had pulled at the T-shirt stretched tight across an incipient beer-belly and looked aggressive.

'In my notes,' Buchan said, 'there's also mention of some underwear.'

'You *what*?'

'Some of Mrs Crawford's lingerie is said to have gone missing,' DS Jones said, with incongruous delicacy.

'I've got my own, thanks all the same.' Tracy indicated the messy room with a sweep of her cigarette. 'What do you think got me into this bleeding mess in the first place?' Her tone was overlaid with suggestions of crotchless panties, nipple-less bras and, above all, with contempt for the men who desired such things.

Listening to Buchan's account, embarrassment and shame coloured Harriet's pale face. She must have pulled some half-heard nonsense out of the air; quite gratuitously she had accused Tracy Marling — or Merlin — of something of which she was innocent. She had obviously got everything wrong. Dumbly she stared at Buchan.

'I'm sorry,' she said.

'Don't be. You're under a lot of strain.'

'I seem to have wasted everyone's —'

He interrupted brusquely: 'There's still your former parents-in-law to track down.'

Early the next morning he telephoned again, tugging her out of an uneasy doze. She wondered if he himself had slept at all during the night. 'We've traced them on to a ferry to Dun Laoghaire,' he said. 'We've alerted police forces all over the country. We'll find them if they're still in Ireland.'

'Where else could they have gone?'

'The Continent, for a start. Perhaps further afield — who knows?'

'Could they have taken Laura abroad, then?'

He said softly: 'Whoever's got her, that's always been a possibility, Harriet. And, if so, she'll be that much more difficult to trace. But let's cross that bridge later, if we ever come to it.'

Putting the telephone down, Harriet walked carefully into the kitchen. On the window-sill was the brown plastic container of tranquillisers which she had been prescribed the day Laura went missing. She read the label: TAKE ONE AS DIRECTED. She shook three of them into her palm and threw them to the back of her mouth, washing them down with orange-juice she drank straight from the carton in the refrigerator. Bent over the sink, she waited for peace, oblivion, a pause in the constant race and surge of the ugly thoughts inside her head: the pictures of Laura screaming, in need, bewildered and afraid.

It was noon when she woke again, long shadows slanting through a gap in the still-drawn bedroom curtains. Dust motes danced down the diagonals, thickening the air. For a moment she wondered where she was, what she was doing, before remembrance struck and she sat up suddenly. Laura. The sixth day. Nothing. Her breasts throbbed painfully. She got out of bed and walked across the hall to the sitting-room. There was a letter on the mat. She picked it up. Had it been there earlier? If so, she had not noticed it. The police were intercepting her mail, for reasons Buchan had had no need to elaborate on.

'Hate mail,' he had said succinctly. 'Nutters. You don't need to bother yourself with that. We'll sort through and pass on anything you ought to have.' After the telephone calls, she had no wish to protest.

She turned the letter over: manila envelope, unfranked, her name in a hand she did not recognise. Premonitory terror shook her. It was hand-delivered; it must therefore have been poked through the letterbox some time during the night.

Some instinct stopped her from ripping it open. Holding it by the edges, she went into the kitchen, found a knife, pulled a rubber washing-up glove over her right hand before carefully slitting the envelope. Almost before she had pulled the contents out, she knew what she would find.

The single sheet of paper had been folded once. The back was blotched with glue which had soaked through from the message pasted to it, in words made up of letters cut from newspapers and magazines. She read it once, and then again, hardly able to believe that the stuff of film and fiction should be materialising here in her hand.

if YOU want to see YoUr Baby again, get hoLD of £500,000 in small BiLLs & WaiT by the TeLEphone. DO NOT tell the POLICE or else.

Screams rose in her lungs, huge and overwhelming. The urge to give in to them was enormous but she was afraid that if she let them out, their force might tear her head off. She kept them banked at the back of her throat; they lay there like thunderheads, like storm-clouds, their colours those of hurricane or typhoon, grey, purple, violet. Violent. Her body shook as though she had a high fever. Her fingers trembled so badly she could scarcely dial Tom's number. She cleared her throat. *Be there. Be there* — her brain hammered out the message in time to the shrills of the telephone. *Be there. Be there* — And he was.

She cleared her throat. 'Tom.'

'What is it, Harriet?'

'Someone's got Laura. I've had a ransom note.' Her voice began to rise. 'Tom! What shall I do?'

'Hold on, honey,' he said calmly. 'Just keep holding on.'

'WHAT SHALL I DO?'

'The first thing you do is call David Buchan.'

'But the note says not to tell the police.'

'Harriet, you have no choice.'

'I know. Oh, God.' Harriet pressed her knuckles against her mouth.'

'Remember what Buchan said once: half your worries are on the baby's account — you're suffering far more than she is.'

'Yes. You're right. I'll ring him.'

Buchan picked up the receiver on the first ring; when she heard his voice, her own failed.

'Yes?'

'Dav ...' She tried for his name, but her mouth refused to form it.

'Buchan here.' He sounded impatient, busy.

'It's Har ...' She gulped, tried again. 'Harriet.'

The voice softened. 'Harriet. What's happened?'

'A ... letter. A ransom note was ...'

'I'll be there.' He cut off before the sentence was completed.

He arrived in fifteen minutes, WDC Rogers in tow. Seeing Harriet, he barked: 'Whisky, Sal. A double.' He pushed Harriet in front of him to the kitchen and sat her down. She could not look at the letter which lay poisonous where she had left it. Instead she watched the long line of his back as he bent, hands in pockets, to examine it from a couple of inches away, not touching, not even breathing on it.

'Hello,' he said. 'I see we've got a *Sun* reader here. What do you think, Sal?'

Sally Rogers pushed a glass into Harriet's hand and peered intently at the letter. 'Difficult to say, sir. A hoax, do you think?' She picked up the letter with a pair of tweezers and dropped it into a clear polythene bag.

'Almost certainly,' said Buchan.

'You can't possibly tell,' Harriet said hysterically. 'It could be some madman who's hurting her, who's ...' Imagination supplied pictures which she could not give voice to.

'Why would he wait almost a week before contacting you?' Buchan made a face, pushing the corners of his mouth down. 'Nobody's going to take care of a young baby for any longer than they need.' He turned. 'Sal?'

'A nutter, sir, if you ask me.'

'Right. But we'll have to treat it seriously. Anything strike you about it?' He still had not touched the letter.

'Not particularly, sir. Not straight off.'

'The word "bills". It's not really a British usage, is it? We'd say "notes", wouldn't we?'

'Yes, sir. Except that one's a lot easier to find in the maggies. The meaning's still perfectly clear.'

'You're right. But it's something to bear in mind, nonetheless.' He straightened. 'What do you think, Harriet? You've lived in the States, haven't you? What's your opinion?'

She was astonished at the tone of his voice. He sounded as if he ... 'You think it's me!' she said. 'You think I wrote that — that disgusting thing, and dropped it on my own doormat, don't you?'

'What makes you think that, Harriet?' He hurled the words at her as though they were stones.

'Is there something you'd like to tell us, Harriet?' In contrast, WDS Rogers sounded mild and friendly.

'No. No there bloody well isn't,' Harriet said furiously. 'I found the letter where I said, and that's all there is to it.'

'OK.' Buchan seemed inclined to drop the matter. 'At least we've already arranged for the telephone line to be bugged.' Harriet knew he would not let the authorship of the ransom note go until he was sure she had nothing to do with it.

'Whoever sent it must be someone who knows where I live,' she said. 'It must be the person who took Laura. It must be.'

'Not necessarily. It wouldn't take much effort to figure out where you live. For a start, you're in the phone-book — I checked myself,' said Buchan.

'Half a million,' Harriet said, looking desperately round the kitchen. 'How am I going to get hold of so much money?'

'Don't worry. We aren't going to pay this little sh —' His mouth hardened, '— this *dipstick* a single penny.'

Harriet went cold. She stood up. Her face felt small, as though all its features had shrunk in on themselves; sweat gleamed along her cheekbones. 'Listen. I don't care how much money it costs, or what I have to do to get it. If it means getting Laura back then I'll find it somehow.'

Buchan looked at Sally Rogers. 'Half a million. It's a heck of a sum,' he said thoughtfully. 'And if this dickhead's read his tabloid closely enough, he's going to know Harriet is on her own, doesn't have any money. So why so much? It's an unrealistic amount.'

'Perhaps he heard her appeal on the TV,' Sally said.

'So?'

'Well ...' Embarrassed, Sally glanced at Harriet. '... maybe he realises from the way she talks that she's not ... well, that she's middle-class and — uh — probably from the sort of background where, even if she hasn't got that kind of money herself, she could probably raise it. Through her family.'

'Come on, Sal. She's not an Arab princess, for Christ's sake.'

'No. But isn't your father a barrister or something, Harriet?'

Harriet stared at her, terrified. She could feel her bones weaken, a kind of fine tension at knee and elbow and wrist, a sense of sinew and muscle dissolving, falling from her, leaving her naked and skeletal. Her father: *promises of revenge*, he had written ... *death threats* ...

Was that what was behind this? Was it possible that the drug cartels her father was currently prosecuting were involved? Was it an attempt to pervert the course of justice in some distant Brazilian court which had led to Laura's abduction? And if so, how could she, powerless, pit herself against the kind of force such people had at their disposal?

She was aware that Tom had arrived as she found herself gasping out a torrent of words, telling Buchan at last about the wrecked canvases in the garden, the rag-doll suspended in the juicy grasses, the silent phone-calls, her father's letter. Dimly, she was aware of Buchan's cold eyes, of Tom's arms, of her own voice shouting, of a white pill lying large as a torpedo on Sally Roger's palm, the taste of whisky violent in her mouth, hands on her shoulders, terror before a final sweet oblivion.

They found a witness, a young woman doing a photographic course at the Polytechnic who had been kissing her boyfriend goodnight before driving back home. 'Yeah, I saw somebody,' she said. 'He drove up about one o'clock in the morning, and parked halfway along the road.'

'What kind of car?' demanded Buchan.

The girl started to shrug. 'I don't really —'

'Big? Little? Sports model? Estate? You must have noticed something.'

'Actually, I think it was a van,' said the girl. 'One of those small vans.'

'Anything painted on the side? A name? A telephone number? Think about it — you know what's at stake.'

'I didn't see anything.' Before Buchan could open his mouth again, she added hastily: 'I wasn't really taking much notice of anything outside the car.' Remembered passion brought a retrospective flush to her face.

'Call yourself a photographer? Remind me not to book you for my daughter's wedding picture,' Buchan said brutally. 'What about colour?'

'It's difficult to be sure — He didn't park under a street lamp. Red, I think. Kind of maroony-red.'

'And of course you didn't notice the numberplate.'

'Why should I?' The girl, conscious of a scoop lost, was defiant.

'What about the man himself?'

'I can't really — he just sort of slouched down the road. I assumed it was someone who lived round here.'

'Was he old, young, middle-aged?'

'Not old. Youngish, I suppose.'

'Black? White? Oriental?'

'White. With longish black hair.'

'How tall?'

'I don't know.'

'Clothes?'

'I can't remember. Dark. I think he was wearing one of those padded parka things. He came along the road and into the driveway here. He was out again and walking back to his car before I'd even registered what he was doing. I suppose, if I thought about it at all, I assumed he was something to do with your lot. He had the kind of stubble that isn't designer, if you know what I mean.'

Buchan gave a cold little chuckle. 'Oh, that's good, that is. You don't notice anything about the guy's car or his height or what he's wearing, but you can see he's got five o'clock shadow. That's really rich.'

'It was only an impression. You can't blame me for not taking notes.' The photographer looked at Harriet with frank curiosity and half lifted the camera slung round her neck. 'Any chance of a picture?'

'Not now,' said Buchan brusquely. 'Maybe later, when we've checked this man out. Need I say that if you don't keep shtum, you could be seriously endangering the baby's life. One single word leaked to the papers, and I'll have you, believe me.'

Harriet heard him on the telephone, calling the Yard. 'Room A Ten, please.' There was a pause. 'Yeah. Mike! David Buchan here. How are you, boy? ... Me, too ... Look, you know I'm on this kidnap case — the Pearse baby? Yeah, well there's a possible tie-up with a drug-case going on in Rio.' He gave details. 'Get your lads to check it out for me, will you, Mike? Give me a bell at the factory, OK? Thanks a lot.'

Two days later, the telephone rang. Harriet stared at it, feeling the tremble start in her fingers and behind her knees.

Sally Rogers, sitting on the sofa with a magazine on her lap, nodded encouragingly. 'Go on, Harriet. It might be him.'

The bell pealed on. 'What shall I say?' Harriet whispered.

'Just what we told you. Try to keep him talking, but don't worry if you can't. Ask for proof that he's really got Laura.'

She picked it up, knowing that somewhere the police were listening in, tracking the caller. A rough male voice said: 'Did you get my letter?'

'Who — who is this?'

'I've got Laura.'

'How do I know you're telling the truth?' Harriet strained for any signals the voice might give: anything which might help Buchan in his search.

'Lovely little yellow dress she's wearin'. Gettin' a bit grubby now, mind, know what I mean.'

Harriet swallowed, trying not to think of Laura unwashed, untended, at the mercy of the cruel stranger on the other end of the line. 'You could have got that from the newspapers,' she said, as instructed.

'They didn't mention the birthmark, though, did they?'

'Oh, God.' Blood rushed into Harriet's head; she could scarcely hear for the surge of it in her ears. She felt Sally Rogers move over to stand behind her. 'Is she all right? Is she all RIGHT?'

She heard him snicker — and hated him. 'Got a bit of a sniffle, but she's OK otherwise,' he said. She could tell he was smiling.

'What do you want?'

'What d'you fuckin' think I want, darlin'? Money, of course. You didn't talk to the filth, did you?'

'What do you mean? Who are —'

'The fuckin' police. The Old Bill.'

Harriet, hopeless at lies, said indignantly: 'Of *course* I didn't.'

'Got that money I asked for?'

'Yes,' she said, breathless.

'Right. I'm going to ring off now, just in case you're doing a bit of a doublecross on me — but I do so hope you aren't, because I'd hate to get blood on that nice little dress. I'll ring again later. If you want to see the baby again, be there.'

The line went dead.

'Well done.' Sally Rogers' warm voice cut through the turmoil in her brain. 'You sounded just right: terrified but hanging on.'

Harriet's laugh was shaky. 'How the hell else do you think I *feel*?'

She ran into the bathroom and threw up. Torturing pictures of blood, the yellow dress, the satin ribbons, the soft skin above Laura's temples, blood ... She would have given almost anything she possessed to talk to Chris. The newspapers in Spain would not have carried a story about a child gone missing in England; there was no way she could know what was going on. It was just a question of waiting, of hanging on. Any day now, Chris would be back, would telephone, would arrive and take charge. It was the first time Harriet realised just how much of a stand-in for her mother her friend Chris had become.

Buchan arrived, his grey suit crumpled, the rims of his eyes inflamed and red. 'We got a line on your in-laws,' he said.

For a moment his words made no sense at all. Harriet was caught up with the voice on the telephone; she could clearly see Laura lying on a sheet in some dingy room, a woman's rough red hands giving her a bottle, changing her, an unshaven villainous man in a dirty shirt, raising a bottle of beer to his lips. Anglo-Saxon attitudes, she told herself, a whole scenario based on a voice, a phraseology, an accent. Nonetheless the scene was momentarily more vivid to her than her own surroundings. 'In-laws?'

'The Pearses.'

'Oh, yes. Where were they?'

'We haven't found them, but there's been a fairly positive sighting of them in Limerick two days ago. Some dispute over a restaurant bill.'

Looking at the tortured face in front of him, Buchan did not add that Limerick was not far from Shannon International Airport, nor that flight lists were currently being checked for two seats booked in the name of Pearse — for any couple travelling with a baby.

Originally he had not taken seriously Harriet's fears about her husband's parents; now, however, transcripts of interviews between the local Gardai and the Pearses's neighbours had made it sufficiently clear that Mrs Pearse, always somewhat unbalanced, had become even more so since the loss of her son. As a policeman he could not afford to trust anyone, but he felt deeply sorry for Harriet; though divorced some years ago, he had two daughters himself and could easily imagine what she must be going through.

'I see.' Harriet nodded. There was no point in asking; it was obvious there had been no mention of a baby. Perhaps she had never really expected either Tracy Merlin or Mrs Pearse to be the ones who had taken Laura. The culprit had probably acted on the spur of the moment; it was no more than bad luck that it should have been Laura who was the victim, rather than some other unfortunate child. She thought: if it was me, if I was going to steal a baby, that's what I'd do: I'd go somewhere I'd never been before, with which I had no connection, and just hang about until the opportunity occurred.

And maybe Buchan was right; maybe the ransom demand *was* no more than a hoax. Hopelessness filled her. Head hanging, she said: 'She's gone, hasn't she? For good, I mean.'

Buchan grabbed her shoulders. His fingers dug hard into her flesh; the pain flamed down her arms and into her chest. 'Don't ever say that, Harriet,' he said. His teeth were clenched, his face distorted with anger. 'Don't even think it. We'll find her. Eventually we'll get her back.'

'No,' she said. 'You won't.'

'Look, love,' Sally Rogers said. 'We've just closed the files on a little lad's been missing for two months and turned up safely. You mustn't ever give up hope.'

Two months. Eight weeks ... Harriet's veins seemed to have been pumped full of ice water. She shivered. *Eight weeks* — could she survive this torment for that long?

'Even if you do find her,' she said dully, 'if it took too long, maybe it would be better if she stayed where she was.'

'What the hell do you mean?' Buchan said, unfriendly.

'Suppose it took months and months, even years. If you finally found her and she was happy, perhaps I wouldn't have the right to take her back. I mean, it could be worse for her to be uprooted at two or three years old than it was at five weeks.'

'So you'd bloody let the sod who took her get away with it?' he asked incredulously.

'Perhaps there's something stronger than justice,' she said, the words coming out thin and attenuated. 'Perhaps children deserve more than that. They're so vulnerable, so shaped by what we do to them.'

He turned abruptly away from her. 'I can't believe I'm hearing you say this. It's been what? A week?'

'You know as well as I do that it's nine days now.'

'And already you're giving up? It's ridiculous. It's cowardly. Think of Laura. Are you just tamely going to give her up without a fight?'

'I *am* fighting,' Harriet said. 'But I'm blindfolded, with my hands tied. It's an unequal contest.'

'That other newborn baby was gone for sixteen days,' said Buchan. 'And now there's the four-year-old Sally was talking about, just been found after all this time. You can't give up hoping.'

For the first time Harriet sensed uncertainty in him. The knowledge made her feel faint; under her feet the ground seemed to shift.

'Yes,' she said. 'So I get my hopes up, I pin everything on Laura being found by the sixteenth day. And then you come up with another child who was missing for two months before you found him; and when that deadline's gone you give me another, and then another.' She shook her head slowly. 'No, thank you. I'd rather face up to the fact that I may never see Laura again than live in an eternity of false hope.'

Contempt altered his face. 'You may give up, but I won't,' he said. Without looking at her again, he turned and left.

She stared at the telephone. The man who had asked for half a million pounds in exchange for Laura's safe return had not rung back. It seemed an absurdly small sum for such valuable goods; at the same time, were she to have to find it, it would be almost impossible for her to raise. Perhaps if Matthew, her grandparents, she herself, her father, all remortgaged their homes, raised bank-loans, they could do it: Laura would be returned to her, but she herself would then be responsible for the bankruptcy of the rest of the family.

She could hear Sally Rogers in the kitchen, talking to the Scene-of-Crimes officer who was monitoring the calls on the taped telephone. To them all this was no more than routine. It seemed suddenly extraordinary to her that, while she trudged through this nightmare, other people's lives carried on as normal.

The telephone rang.

She snatched it up. 'Yes.'

'Hello, darlin'.' She recognised the hateful voice at once; she did not think she would ever forget it. 'Got a pencil, have you?'

'Yes, yes.'

'Here's what you do, then. You take the A43 out of Oxford, then take the 421 for Bicester. Just beyond the third roundabout there's a turn-off to the left. Take that, and start countin' the laybys. The third one after you've turned is —' There was a distinct click on the line. The voice paused. 'What the fuck's that?'

'I don't know. I really have no idea.' Harriet fought to keep the panicky note from her voice.

'Oh, darlin'. You've been a naughty girl, haven't you? You've been talkin' to the pigs. I warned you what would —'

'I haven't,' Harriet shouted. 'I haven't contacted the police, I swear. The phone's always doing that. It's because ... there are trees right up close to the house, honestly. They interfere with the reception or something. I've had the telephone company round about it several times.'

There was a pause. If he had been to the house to deliver his letter, he would know she was telling the truth about the trees. Softly sinister, she heard him say: 'You know what'll happen if you're telling porkie-pies, don't you?'

She squeezed her eyes shut; her throat was dry. 'Yes, yes, I do.'

'I think you've set me up. I think you've been mouthin' off to the pigs. Well, darlin', you just signed your fuckin' kid's death warrant, that's what —'

'NO!' screamed Harriet. 'I haven't. I haven't said a word. Surely you can see I'm not going to risk my baby's life by going to the police.' She was hyperventilating, the breath panting from her throat in short bursts. 'I've got the money you wanted.'

He sucked air in sharply; she heard the hiss of it, could feel his imagination hover over gold coins, banknotes, wealth, riches. 'OK,' he said thickly. 'Third layby, got that?'

'Yes.'

'Drive off the road. There's a rubbish-bin halfway along. As you pass it, throw the money out of the car and carry straight on. Here: you do drive, don't you?'

'Yes. What about my baby?'

'Don't worry, darlin'. You'll get her back safe enough.'

'But when? I'm not going through all this unless you guarantee —'

'Shut up, bitch.' He was suddenly furious. 'I'll ring you again, tell you about the fuckin' kid.'

Before she could protest, the receiver had been slammed down.

She sank forward until her forehead rested on the table. How much more of this could she take? She did not even know for sure that he had Laura: at his mention of a birthmark, she had assumed he was talking about the mole under Laura's ear, forgetting that most babies had some blemish or other. It had been no more than a shot in the dark for him; had she been less agitated she would have recognised that. Now, she dare not take the risk of antagonising him further. If he did have Laura, he could so easily harm her, from rage or spite.

Sally Rogers came running in, followed by her colleague.

'Sorry about the blip, love,' he said. 'I was cleaning the tape.'

Sally hugged her. 'Well done, Harriet. That was a brilliant bit of improvisation about the trees.'

'Yes,' Harriet said drearily. 'If he believed me.'

'Even if he didn't, he certainly believed you about the money.'

'Why did he get so angry when I asked about Laura?'

'Could be because he's unstable anyway — on drugs, perhaps. Or drink. He probably had to psych himself up with something before he called you. Or maybe . . .' Sally stopped. She had been going to say that maybe he had not yet figured out how to get away from the layby with the money — the supposed money — before Harriet discovered that he did not have Laura after all.

The telephone rang again. Harriet snatched it up. 'Yes?'

It was Tom; he rang her each day, and each day they had the same stilted conversation: 'Are you all right?'

'Perfectly, thank you.' Even though they both knew she was not.

'Would you like me to come round?'

'That's quite unnecessary.'

'Are you sure?'

'Absolutely. The police are here most of the time.'

'Have you heard from that guy who sent the letter?'

'No.' Harriet had been warned to say nothing more to Tom. Privately Buchan was afraid that some instinct of gallantry would send Tom crashing around and frightening their hoax-ster off; or putting the baby at risk if he had her, though Buchan thought it highly unlikely.

'I expect it was just a hoax,' Tom said, trying to comfort.

'I expect so.'

Her cool little voice had somehow made him uneasy. Yet, aware of time passing, of a Europe waiting for him across the Channel as yet largely unvisited, of his commitment to Lydia, he had stifled his qualms and for the past few days had travelled daily up to the Records Office in London.

Sitting at a plastic-topped table in a hamburger joint, he told himself that it ought not to have been this difficult, it ought to have been no more than a question of turning the right page, running a finger — a finger by now so sensitive that it practically screamed — down the columns, and simply noting the name he was looking for.

The trouble with the damn Brits, he thought savagely, is that not only do they all get married, but they have too many goddamned babies. Hundreds of them. Thousands, even. Harriet still occupied his mind. Something was going down, he was sure of it; something she wasn't telling him about. The shithead who'd sent that letter: was she setting up some kind of meet with the guy? Were the police going to allow her to walk into danger, in order to trap him?

Once in his head, the thought of sad-eyed Harriet as Judas-goat, as sacrificial lamb, jolted his concentration. Back among the ledgers, his eyes began to rebel, refusing to take in what they saw, the names trundling past, the children born and registered, maiden names of mothers, present addresses, father's occupation, his brain slowing down so that when the names he wanted actually glided past, he missed them; he had turned over before they connected with his brain.

He had found what he was looking for at last. Nonetheless, the registration of birth which lay in front of him was nearly thirty years old; he felt his spirits sag at the thought of the clues still to follow, and sag even further when he saw that the address shown was the one he had already checked out.

There were various courses of action he could now take, all of them tedious. He could start to check up via medical records, once he worked out how. The child must have gone to school somewhere, maybe also to university — though in England that was not as much of a given as it would be back home. He could, of course, go on searching the birth regis-trations for the second child — Lydia had said there were two — in the hope that it showed a more current address ... but face it, he told himself, slamming the pages together: even when he found it, the child would still have been born some twenty-five, twenty-six years ago, and the chances of its parents still living in the same place would be small.

He found a pub, ordered beer, sat with it in front of him and tried to figure out where to go from here. The easiest way would be to try and trace Anthony Newgate. He was registered on his son's birth certificate as a law student; it ought to be possible to find him via one of the professional organisations to which he must surely belong. He recalled that, over here, studying law could have led him one of two ways: he could be either barrister or solicitor.

If that way didn't work out, he could always try locating the guy who'd come between Lydia and her daughter in the first place; it was more than likely that runaway Nell Costello might have turned to him for help. But Lydia had said he no longer lived in England. Drinking his pint, not liking it much, he decided that tomorrow, if Harriet didn't need him, he would contact the Law Society.

· 24 ·

The third layby ... Carefully Harriet signalled, although there was nothing on the road behind her, and drove slowly along the pitted tarmac. Her headlights caught the cylindrical black litter-bin, the logo on its side. On the passenger seat beside her was a royal-blue nylon hold-all containing the money for the man claiming to be Laura's abductor. Far away, behind her, she could see the lights of another car. Was that him? Or was it one of the four unmarked police vehicles which would be on constant patrol, driven by officers from a special unit of the Regional Crime Squad, whose aid David Buchan had enlisted in the hope of picking the man up?

He had telephoned again that morning, his voice choked with what sounded like both rage and fear. 'All right, bitch. Here's what you do. You drop the money, right? Chuck it out the window, right?'

'I'll have to stop the car,' Harriet said.

'No you fuckin' won't. Just chuck it out.'

She was beyond hysteria: in a state of unnatural calm. 'It's too big to get out of the car window.'

He was quiet for a moment. Behind him she could hear the pulsing beat of a heavy metal number. She guessed he was trying to imagine the bulk of half a million pounds in cash. 'OK. So you slow down, open the door, chuck out the bag. But you don't get out, right?'

'What about my baby?'

'Shut up and listen. You drive off. You come back in half an hour, and the kid'll be there — long as there's no fuckin' cops.'

'How —' She gulped, almost choked. 'How do I know you'll

keep your side of the bargain?'

'You don't, darlin', do you? But just ask yourself what I'd want with another kid. And I'm not exactly lookin' for a murder rap on top of everything else the pigs got against me.'

On the other side of the room, Harriet saw Buchan and Rogers raise eyebrows at each other. 'So I come back in half an hour — what then?'

'The kid'll be where the cash was, all right? I'll've had a chance to check it out, see you haven't been pulling a fast one on me. If you have — well, too bad for the baby, right?' He began to laugh wheezily — before the laughter turned in to a smoker's deep-throated cough. 'Here,' he said, gasping. 'Hope it's not rainin'. I wouldn't like little Laura to catch a cold.'

Harriet began to shake. *Laura* ... She wanted to tell him something of what she was going through; she wanted to say how unbelievably cruel, what a monster he must be. She clamped her jaws together, knowing that the slightest thing could set him off. 'Right,' she said softly.

The receiver was slammed down. The police had warned her he would be jumpy. 'After all, he could be an addict, and either way he's about to perpetrate an SAO — a serious arrestable offence,' Buchan had said. 'Either way, he's down for life — not that that means much these days. If he *has* got Laura he's guilty of abduction plus demanding money with menaces. If he hasn't, we still get him for serious fraud, plus wasting police time, plus obstruction in the course of their duty, plus ...' he smiled grimly '... he probably hasn't paid his poll tax.'

Putting down the receiver, Harriet closed her eyes. For the two police, this was a crime coming to some sort of successful conclusion. For her it was a life or a death.

'He's got form,' she heard Buchan say triumphantly. 'We'll have him.'

'And we already know he's probably a local man — knows the area,' said Sally Rogers. 'All that stuff about laybys and litter-bins.'

She opened the door on her own side, tugged the bag across her knees, threw it out towards the bin. There was a brooch-

sized microphone pinned to her sweater. She guessed —
although they had not said — that a similar device had been
planted in the blue hold-all. For a moment she listened, but
above the throb of the engine she could hear nothing. Now it
was up to the police. The lights of another car, coming in the
opposite direction, arced upwards into the darkness. More
police? She knew that somewhere in the cold fields beyond the
layby were watchers, that further along the road men on
motorcycles waited, that the chances of the man getting away
were almost non-existent. But what about Laura? For her, that
had always been the only thing which mattered. 'In half an
hour,' he said: those thirty minutes stretched endlessly away
from her. She felt herself to be beyond hope, beyond expecta-
tion, that all she was able to do was push forward into the
future, a minute, a second at a time.

She slammed the door shut, put her foot slowly down on
the accelerator and moved off, paused at the junction with the
road, pulled out, drove away from there into the black night.

'Steve Ripley,' Buchan said. He straightened his silk tie. 'I ought
to have recognised the toe-rag's voice.'

'DS Jones thought he'd heard it before somewhere,' Sally
Rogers said, pushing a cup of tea closer to Harriet across the
kitchen table. 'He said so after he listened to the tape.'

'Shit. And it was me who pulled him for that Chalfont House
job,' said Buchan. 'Do you remember? He'd got the gear right
there in the back of his van — the stuff was melted down
before he and his mate'd even got down the end of the drive.'

The police had waited half an hour before moving in to
arrest Ripley, on the off-chance he had Laura and would deliver
her as arranged. Following the homing device buried in among
the bundles of cash, they had trailed his red van back into
Oxford, round the one way systems to a little house in a street
off the Abingdon Road. He had scarcely been surprised.

'Knew I wouldn't get away with it,' he said, with the resignation of a man used to the inside of a prison cell. 'It was worth a
go, though, with Christmas coming up, and all. Thought I'd take
her and the kids to Torremolinos or somewhere. Ah well . . .'

It was now the sixteenth day since Laura had vanished. Tom drove round to Harriet's flat, despite her cool rebuff on the telephone. He knew that this day had a special significance, that it marked a kind of watershed for her. He remembered Sally Rogers telling him that there had been another case, a child snatched from a hospital, and recovered sixteen days later.

Seeing Harriet for the first time in several days, he was alarmed at the amount of weight she had lost. Even worse was the deadness of her eyes.

'Oh,' she said, staring as though she had never seen him before. 'Come in.' She turned back into the house and he followed.

'How are you?' he asked.

'Just fine.' Her smile was too bright in her white face; a vein throbbed bluely at her temple.

'Are you alone?'

'The police aren't here at the moment. But my grandmother may come.'

'But isn't she sick? Didn't you say she . . .'

'Or Maggie,' she said quickly, 'who used to look after us when we were children.'

'I thought you said she'd broken her hip.'

'Has she?' Harriet said vaguely. In spite of the chilly October morning and the fact that there was no heating on in the flat, she was wearing shorts and her feet were bare. As she walked restlessly about the room, he saw that two of the toenails on one foot and one on the other had been freshly painted pink; the rest were untouched, as though she had started to varnish them and then forgotten what she was supposed to be doing. He wondered whether she was eating; there was a faint sour smell to her which suggested she was forgetting to wash.

On the wall above the telephone she had pinned a card with numbers written on it: Matt, Daddy, Chris, Maggie. He resolved to try and track down the brother or the father: somebody should be here with her, somebody to whom she belonged. Even though both of them were on the move, difficult to get hold of, it ought not to be impossible. Her attitude towards himself was too ambivalent for him to feel capable of handling what he sensed was her closeness to nervous collapse.

'When did you last go outside the house?' he asked.

'I can't remember,' she said.

'What did you have for breakfast?'

'Breakfast?' She frowned as though the word was alien to her, a concept without meaning.

He took her arm; the bone lay just below the skin, unhampered by flesh. He took her into the bathroom, told her to strip and, when she simply stood looking at him, took her clothes off himself and made her stand under the shower. He found clean underwear, a sweater, jeans. When he returned to the bathroom, she was standing with her face to the wall, just as he had left her, the water running down over her hair and into her open eyes. He had the feeling she would have stayed there indefinitely. Her thin bones protruded; the knobs of her spine seemed infinitely sorrowful. He felt no stir of the libido at all as he pulled her into a towel, dressed her, dried and brushed her hair.

He took her quickly out to his car. A couple of diehard reporters still lounged against the bonnets of their cars, smoking, raising flasks to their mouths in an effort to dispel the cold. He fended off their questions, frowning to discourage further remarks. Harriet came easily, not holding back, seemingly content to go where he put her. She let him fix the seat-belt round her; she sat docile as he drove to an Italian restaurant, ordered pasta and a salad, a carafe of wine. When he tried to get her to eat, she shook her head, smiling at him. 'I'm not hungry, Stephan,' she said. 'Thank you all the same.'

Panic made him violent. 'Eat it,' he said. He piled lasagne on to a fork, pushed it close to her mouth, held it there until her lips parted and he was able to put it inside. Eventually she swallowed it, and he repeated the action, feeding her like a baby until half the dish had gone. He poured some wine; he waited with it pressed to her lower lip until she finally drank some. He felt bruised, terrified. Was she so far gone that she did not even recognise him, or had she merely used the wrong name because it was easier than searching for the right one? Only when some colour washed her cheekbones and her eyes seemed more alive did he eat himself.

'I'm going to Prague,' she said.

'What?' He almost choked. Had she really gone crazy? 'Why do you want to go there?'

'In case Stephan took Laura.'

'Harriet, for God's sake.'

'It sounds mad, I know,' she said, and somewhere behind her grief he saw the old sharp Harriet and knew she was aware of his concern about her state of mind. 'But there were things he said to me which make me wonder. And it was only a week after he was supposed to have left that Laura disappeared.'

'Do you have an address for him?'

'Yes. At least, of someone he used to know, someone he told me he would be contacting when he got there. I've had it for years and years. I always knew it would come in useful one day.'

He reached across the table and took both her hands in his. 'Harriet, just try to imagine what Stephan would do with a six-week-old baby. And then ask yourself if he, one of your closest friends, could ever dream of doing such a thing as take her from you.'

'It's his roots, you see,' she said. 'He wants to find them.' Tom saw doubt spread across her face. 'But I have to go. Just to be sure. I can't leave any stone ...' The sentence hung; he saw that she did not remember how to finish it.

'What about the police?' he asked. 'Does Buchan know what you're planning?'

'I can't say anything to them about it. I've already given them two false leads. I've wasted enough of their time.'

'Suppose they find Laura here while you're away?'

'It wouldn't make that much difference. After all this time, what does another day matter? I'll keep in touch with him. Or with you. I know your telephone number.'

'I won't be there. I'm coming with you,' he said.

It was another three days before he could organise hotels and tickets for the two of them. Prague — he had dreamed of going there, had even visualised a girl at his side, romantic dinners, walks across the statued bridges, a steep-pitched roofline of fairytale spires and gold-tipped pinnacles. The spires and statues would be waiting, and the girl would be at his side. He thought: nothing is as we expect it to be.

Before they left, he telephoned David Buchan and told him where they were going. 'Good thing,' Buchan said. 'Keep her occupied, give her something to do.'

'I suppose there's no further . . .'

'Nothing. The usual calls from the public, all of which have to be followed up, but even those are tailing off. Between ourselves, I suspect that the baby either died in the first couple of days after she was snatched, or else she's been taken out of the country and we'll never find her.'

'Any idea who might have done it?'

'None whatsoever, though we're still trying to check out those parents of her husband's. But if it's not them, I doubt if we'll ever catch up with whoever's responsible. This whole thing's been too carefully planned. Naturally I don't say any of this to Harriet.'

'Nor will I.'

'Stephan was in love with someone here,' Harriet said, as they took a taxi from Prague airport into the city.

'Elvira.'

'Did you know her?' Harriet was surprised.

'He told me about her once,' Tom said, remembering himself and Stephan talking across the candle stuck into the neck of a bottle, wine ruby-coloured and translucent, the rich smell of meat, Stephan's mouth lifting as he spoke of moons and forests and a girl who glowed silver in the darkness.

'He left me for her,' said Harriet. 'It hurt rather a lot at the time.'

'My wife left me,' Tom said, to his astonishment. 'That hurt rather a lot at the time, too.' And thought: it ought to still, but surprisingly does not. And thought further: when did that happen?

She was interested.'I didn't know you had been married.'

'There are many things about me that you don't know,' he said. He was overtaken by the wish to talk to her about those things, about the flat grey rocks of Maine, about sea-buried pearls and the way the wind stirred in the pine-trees, the verandah of the old house which his grandmother had left him in her will. Would he ever go back there? It held so many memories: above all, that last goodbye. Maybe, when this trip was over, he would return there. His parents moved some-where in a corner of his mind, turning to wave, forever young, younger than he was now, her fair hair blowing in the wind, his legs long and stocky, downed with dark hair.

'I think there are,' she said. 'When I've got Laura back, I should very much like to hear some of them.'

He squeezed her hand. 'I should like to tell you.' He felt her fingers relax against his palm.

He wanted to go straight to their hotel. Smiling dreamily at him, Harriet showed an address to the cab-driver and indicated that she wished him to take them there. They arrived at a house set in a garden near the top of a hill. Above it towered a huge block of offices. There was a gate set in a barred wall. They opened it and walked up a short path between white asters tied raggedly together with green string. At the top of some steps they rang the doorbell. Inside the house they could hear voices, a dog barking, someone shouting at it. After a while, a young woman opened the door.

'My name is Harriet Pearse,' said Harriet. 'Is Stephan here?'

'Stephan?' The girl was very plain, with the coldest eyes Tom had ever seen; her thin straight hair was pulled back from her face, emphasising the high cheekbones and severe mouth.

'Are you Elvira?'

'That is my name. But what —'

'Stephan was in love with you,' Harriet said.

'Which Stephan?' The girl's English was almost accentless. Harriet told her.

'Stephan from *England?*' The disbelief in Elvira's voice was convincing enough for Tom. He was about to mutter apologies and take Harriet back to the waiting taxi when inside the house a baby began to cry.

Harriet stiffened. The thought of this cold grey woman (how could Stephan possibly have loved her?) holding Laura close to her bony chest sent a chill through her. 'May I come .n?' she said, pressing forward so that the girl was forced to step back into the hallway.

'I don't think ...' Still holding the door, the girl called over her shoulder in her own language. Before anyone could answer, Harriet had pushed the restraining arm aside and was in the house. The baby cried again and Harriet ran in the direction of the noise. In a coffee-scented sitting-room, three people, an older couple and a young man, were sitting round a low table with cups in front of them. Harriet saw a piano, a music-stand, pictures of mice in bathing suits, a familiar tree full of helmeted fish, an owl in evening dress holding a pretzel. In a corner stood a collapsible bassinet. Ignoring the others, she ran over to it. A baby lay there, no more than a few weeks old; she was horrified to realise that she was not sure if it was Laura or not.

There were footsteps behind her, gasps. The cold girl brushed past her and snatched the child up, holding it tightly to her bosom.

'What do you want?' she shouted. 'What are you doing here?' Around her, the room was thick and blank with consternation.

'My daughter has been stolen,' Harriet said. 'I thought she might be here.'

Tom moved quickly to stand beside her. 'I think there's been some mistake,' he said, deep-voiced. 'Mrs Pearse understood she might find her baby here.'

'This is *my* child,' the girl — Elvira — said. She indicated the young man, who was staring at them all in astonishment. 'And my husband's, of course. We've called him Vaclav. After our new President.' Less threatened now with the baby in her arms, she said: 'Why have you come here?'

'I thought Stephan might have ...' said Harriet. Faintness was seeping through her; she longed to lie down somewhere.

'What does Stephan have to do with this?'

It was too complicated to explain. 'My baby is a girl,' Harriet said.

Elvira set her lips together. She unwrapped her child, pulled down rubber pants, a thick towelling napkin. 'This is a boy,' she said. 'You have made a mistake.'

'Yes.' Harriet looked round at the open mouths, the eyes full of both suspicion and pity. 'I'm really sorry. Only Stephan said he was coming back to see you —'

'I know where he is, if you wish to visit him,' Elvira said unexpectedly, ready to be kind.

'Where?'

'He is in the eastern part of the country, near our border with Germany. He is helping with the forests, where there is pollution, bad, from the lignite factories.' Emotion was loosening Elvira's grip on the English language.

Tom took Harriet's elbow. 'Thank you. I'm sorry to have disturbed you.'

As he bundled Harriet into the waiting taxi, Elvira appeared again and gave him a piece of paper. 'Stephan's telephone number,' she said. 'He called me when he arrived in Prague, but we did not meet.' Peering in at Harriet, lowering her voice, she added: 'I am very sorry about your friend.'

My friend ... He nodded.

The number she had given them did not answer. Tom took Harriet walking through the city; after the first five minutes he held her hand tightly in his to ensure that she did not stop dead in the middle of the traffic, or wander away from him. The city was ebullient in the aftermath of its victory against Communist rule; in Wenceslas Square there were hunger-strikers, a jazz band, skinheads in studded leather, punks with brilliant cockatoo hairstyles. They stepped inside a church whose candlelit interior seemed carved entirely from pink soap; they watched a clock strike the hour while the figure of Death, clutching an hourglass, moved jerkily beneath its face. The old town with its cobblestones, its air of life being lived somewhere around the next corner, enchanted Tom. He longed to share it with the silent woman at his side.

Returned to the hotel, he tried Stephan's number again. This time a woman answered, but he could not understand what she said, nor did she speak any English. 'Stephan,' he said, several times. In the end a man came onto the line. 'Stephan go,' he said. 'Stephan go back to United States.'

· 25 ·

'What you mean is that the police have given up.' Harriet said; she spoke with the calmness of despair. Something inside her had ripped like old silk at the shock of Buchan's words; the Harriet she once was had torn away to reveal a new Harriet, metal-cased, bullet-hard.

'I'm not saying that at all.' Buchan was, as always, patient. 'I've told you before, this is far too personal for us to give up on. Coppers have kids too, you know.'

Was it real, that patience? Harriet wondered, the other Harriet who soaked up detail like a sponge. Or did an intolerant, bad-tempered Buchan lurk beneath the surface, the serenity merely a mask assumed for his job and discarded when he returned to his self-possessed wife, his well-behaved sons?

'It sounds very like it to me,' she said.

'There are at least forty personnel still working all the hours God gives on this case.' His angular eyes were not friendly. 'The file remains open, and will do until the case is concluded, either with the discovery of Laura and the woman who took her —'

'You're still convinced it wasn't a man?'

'It's always a woman,' he said, impatient with biology, '— the woman who took her, or else —' He broke off.

'Or else what?'

'Or not, as the case may be,' he said. They both knew it was not what he had intended to say. His voice softened as he took her hand. 'Harriet, love, you're going to have to face the fact that Laura may well be ... dead.'

'I don't accept that.'

'You may have to.'

'The only fact I'm facing,' said Harriet loudly, 'is that basic-ally, you've given up on Laura.'

'No!' Exasperated, he slapped the table with the flat of his palms as he stood up. 'Because I've been assigned to another case does *not* mean I've abandoned this one. There's absolutely no way we'd give up on a case like this. But you have to understand that we handle a full work-load and our resources simply don't stretch to keeping a senior man exclusively on one case. Our budget allocations are too small to cover all the manpower and personnel that we would like to employ. The Government consistently rejects our demands for an in-creased ...' He moved into a speech he had obviously made more than once before.

Listening, Harriet reflected that if she had changed over the weeks since Laura's abduction, so had he. Once he had seemed strong, all-powerful. Now he appeared smaller, somehow, unsure of himself. Whereas she ... She watched the well-used words roll from his mouth and reflected that they had moved into a new phase, Buchan and she. Whatever he said, for him the search for Laura was no longer top priority. She must assume responsibility herself. Had she thought about it earlier, she might have found the prospect daunting, but the horror of the past weeks had altered her, had divested her of clutter and irrelevancy, reduced her to the essence of herself, hard and elemental.

She felt that for too long she had been standing on the edge of a vast abyss. The arrest of Steve Ripley, the mistake over Tracy Merlin, even the discovery of Conor's parents, idly motoring through Ireland: all of that had been part of a process of not facing up to the truth. Now she could put it off no longer; she must throw herself into that waiting space, let herself be engulfed by whatever horror waited below.

Buchan went on speaking. When he had finished, she said: 'I shan't give up.'

He lifted his shoulders and dropped them again in a rush of expelled breath. 'Nor have we. I keep saying. There are still three teams of people working on it night and day. We never give up, ever, on these cases. However long it takes . . .'

'I shall find her.'

'That's fine. But, Harriet . . .' He took her hand and held it between his, the hand that had doubtless comforted neat Mrs Buchan, held steady the shoulders of those imagined sons, perhaps even lingered on the body of a lover. 'If there's information you've not passed on, if you think you know something, anything, which could lead to Laura's abductor, you'd do much better to tell us.'

'There isn't. I've told you absolutely everything I can think of.'

'All right. I can't stop you looking for her in your own way — I wouldn't want to — but be prepared, won't you, for the worst?'

She looked into his square eyes and said: 'No.'

When he had gone, she walked restlessly about the flat. There was a dirty glass on the kitchen counter: she washed and dried it with unnecessary care, polishing it with the tea-towel for some time before replacing it in the cupboard. She plumped up the cushions on the sofa, straightened the hang of the curtains, picked a dead leaf from the fern in the hall. She switched on the television and flipped through the channels: a newsreader interviewing politicians, three manic oranges dancing with a lemon, a man smoking a cigar, two women wrestling in a mud-pit.

She turned it off and went into the bathroom. She felt immeasurably heavy — yet, at the same time, strong. She felt herself to be impregnable. Over the past weeks she had avoided facing a truth of which she hardly knew she was aware: somewhere inside her lay the knowledge she needed to regain her daughter.

She ran a deep bath and lay soaking in it. She washed herself carefully all over; she shampooed her hair, rubbed cream into her skin. In her bedroom she made up the bed with fresh sheets, drew the curtains closed, took the telephone off the hook. It was just after two o'clock in the afternoon. Getting into bed, she drew the covers up over herself, turned on her side, willed herself into unconsciousness. After all these weeks of delay, there was work to be done; if she was to recover Laura, she could not afford to waste any more time in grieving. Within seconds she was asleep.

At some point, she dreamed of herself running towards Laura through thick mud, hardly able to move, of wrestling with someone: Conor, Chris, her father? Somewhere there was an angel descending a ladder, but there was no shining presence, no rainbow wings; just a leaden immobility and the rustle of leathery, blackened feathers . . .

It was six o'clock the next morning when she woke, nearly fourteen hours later. Her body felt unaccustomed, unused. Lying in the cold dawn, she was aware that some kind of door had lifted in her mind: pictures clicked through her head with the stiff jerkiness of a slide show. Red shoes, Christina under the gazebo, Denis lifting a glass to his mouth, red shoes, photographs, herself lying across Christina's counterpane, saying: 'Have you got a lover?'

She remembered Christina carefully wrapping Laura in a blanket; she remembered crawling about on the floor of Christina's closet, picking up shoes, remarking that Christina had more pairs than Imelda Marcos, tossing them into a cardboard carton, black patent and brown leather, walking shoes, court shoes, evening shoes, shoes in burgundy suede and green alligator, Italian shoes and handmade shoes and, at the back, tucked away behind an empty box, a pair of red shoes, red shoes which should not have been there.

It was no Damascan burst of light. Simply a new look at old facts; a recognition of how they fitted together.

Hunger flared, the first for weeks. She got up. There was very little food in the kitchen; she broke five eggs into a basin, whipped them up, added the grated heel of some cheese, cooked them in butter. When she had eaten that, she opened a tin of beans and ate them cold from the tin and followed them with a tin of peach slices. Returning strength roared through her veins; she felt herself to be cloaked in invincibility.

She knew who had taken Laura.
Now she had to get her back.

Knowing brought peace and, behind it, determination. Cunning must be met with cunning. Grief had to be postponed while she found evidence, forged a chain of proof. After that ...

Looking back over the past few months, Harriet began to see how carefully it had all been planned. The one question she still found difficult to answer was: why Laura?

She put on a coat and scarf. Outside, the drive was empty, frozen. The reporters and journalists had long ago left for other assignments. It was still early, and very cold. While she had been lost, abyssed in her misery, the seasons had turned, summer had died, autumn had changed to winter. Walking briskly down the Banbury Road, details absorbed but not scrutinised during the past terrible weeks began to swim towards the surface of her mind: faces, headlines, snatches of conversation.

The University Parks, frost-bound, sparkled in the weak sunshine of early morning. The diamond grass spread, became playing-fields and games pitches, each separate grass-blade stiffly rimed. Frost edged the trees, the empty flower beds, the river moving coldly between frozen banks; her breath clouded the air.

Why Laura?

There had to be a reason; there had to be some proof of that reason. Watching the ducks squawk and squabble among the dead reeds of the pond, Harriet remembered words spoken, eyes which falsely smiled, evasions, above all, lies.

There had been so many of them: it was time now for truth. She saw it like a sword, shining and implacable, and herself breastplated, wielding it. 'Have you got a lover?' she had idly asked, and remembering, found at last she had a possible answer to her question.

The frosty park glittered; the clear bright air gleamed with cold. She opened her mouth and felt it invade her body, envelop her heart; she turned towards home.

*

On the dusty mantelpiece, among old letters and empty envelopes, Harriet found the card which Mike Potter had left when he had visited her before Laura's birth. She dialled the number and asked for him.

'Just a minute,' an adolescent voice said.

She waited, tapping her pencil against her teeth. Clearly, she could see where she was going and what she might have to do.

'Yes?'

'Mr Potter?'

'Speaking.'

'This is Harriet Pearse — Conor Pearse's wife. Widow, I should have said.'

There was a long pause. Then he said: 'I'm really sorry about your — about what's happened to your baby. I should have written — I'm so sorry — it must be dreadful for —'

'I need your help,' she said crisply.

'Oh?'

'When you came to see me in Oxford, you were obviously surprised when you realised who I was.'

'Was I?'

'Mr Potter, we both know you were. Tell me who you expected to see opening the door — I mean, describe what you expected Conor's wife to look like.'

There was an embarrassed laugh. 'Well, really, I don't know exactly what I —'

'You'd already met me. You said so on the phone when you rang to tell me Conor had been killed. At a conference on river pollution in Eastern Europe, you said. Where was that held, by the way?'

'Uh — in Paris.'

Harriet nodded. 'Of course.' The pieces were beginning to slot into place. 'So, we met in Paris.'

He hesitated. 'I don't want to get anyone into trouble.'

'Mr Potter, nobody could be in more trouble than I am. What you tell me might help me get my baby back. Conor's dead now; if you're worried about my feelings or his reputation, I think everything's gone beyond that.' Far, far beyond:

she could scarcely remember Conor now. 'I suspected he had affairs, anyway. That doesn't bother me.'

The pause lengthened.

Finally Harriet said: 'Did you expect me to be smaller than I was? Older? Dark-haired, perhaps?'

'Well, yes, as a matter of fact. All those things. Not that Conor brought you — or at least, the woman he said was you — to any of the meetings or anything, but I ran into him in a restaurant one evening during the Paris conference and he introduced you — at least, the other person — as his wife.'

'What did he call her? Harriet?'

'Maybe. I really don't remember,' Potter said. 'I think he just said: "This is my wife." I didn't have any reason to disbelieve him.'

It was not conclusive proof. Before she tried and condemned, she must be certain. Potter lived about an hour's drive from Oxford. 'Will you be home this morning?' she asked.

'Well, yes, but —'

'I'll be at your house before lunchtime.'

'Yes.' Potter was uncomfortable. 'That's her.' He looked down at the photograph which Harriet held out to him. 'Absolutely no question. She's a very striking woman.'

'Yes.' Harriet was amazed at her ability to be so dispassionate. 'Not pretty, but very attractive.'

'Exactly.'

'Thank you,' Harriet said. 'You've been very helpful.'

He cleared his throat. 'Uh . . .'

'Yes?'

'There's something else.' He went over to a filing cabinet and pulled out one of the metal drawers. 'I returned Conor's things to you, naturally, but these were recently brought back by one of our colleagues who was home on leave.' He handed her a large manila envelope. His face had gone red. 'He found them on top of Conor's wardrobe. I didn't like to send them on to you, but I didn't feel I had the right to destroy them.'

She drove away from his house before she opened the envelope. Photographs tumbled out on to her lap; she let them lie there. Bodies. One of them she knew intimately, had seen it many times; the other she had until now only guessed at. Bodies. A man's, a woman's. Conor's, Christina's. Naked, opened, flaunting.

She brushed them off her knees and on to the floor of the car. She felt nothing.

Later, she started to tell herself that somehow she must always have known but she knew it was not so. She had never known, could never have suspected in her wildest imaginings, that Christina and Conor ... They had seemed to be mutually incompatible, two of a kind yet forever alien to each other. She tried not to think of them in bed together, Conor and Christina, but failed to keep the images at bay; what surprised her was how little it seemed to matter.

Why Laura? she had wondered. Now, she kept hearing, like an elegy, like a sentence of death, her own voice saying: 'I don't want this baby.' In saying it, had she unwittingly begun the long train of events which had led to Laura's abduction? Would any of it have happened, the lies, the betrayals, if she had left those words, so much felt, unsaid?

Lies. So many of them. If Christina had taken Laura, it must mean that her protestations about having children were false. In that case, perhaps she had tried — and failed — to adopt. Harriet was aware of a spurt of compassion, but fiercely disregarded it. There was no room for pity, no time to feel sympathy for a woman who longed to bear children and found she could not, and had covered up the failure with falsehood.

Home again, Harriet telephoned the headquarters of the major adoption agencies, checked the infertility clinics; they all refused to give her any information. She was not deterred. Before applying to an agency, Christina would surely have had checks, tests, consultations. Probably many of them.

She knew who Christina's doctor was; so, using the name

of her own health visitor, she telephoned the hospital. 'Some confusion about dates,' she said when she was finally put through to the Records Department. 'She's not sure when she's supposed to come back in for another check-up, and Dr Meakins doesn't seem to have made a note.'

The woman on the other end was brusque. Harriet heard the click of computer keys. 'There doesn't seem to be any need for check-ups,' she said coldly.

'I took over from her last visitor,' Harriet said humbly. 'Perhaps I didn't get all the relevant facts from Dr Meakins, and the patient herself isn't quite ...'

'Dr Simpson couldn't find anything wrong when she was tested here at the clinic,' said the woman, disapproving. 'Chronic irregularities in the cycle, but nothing really major that could have prevented conception.'

'I see.'

'I hope she's not going to want to start the whole thing up again; they won't find anything different from last time. And frankly, given the patient's birth-date, you'd be better off dissuading her from it.'

'I'll talk to her about it,' Harriet said.

Lies. Christina under the gazebo one afternoon, patterned with leaf-shadow, shuddering at the thought of babies. Christina holding her slim body, her childish breasts, and saying that if Denis really *really* wanted, she would give up her job and have a baby. *I'd do it for you, darling* ... Except that she was not able to, she had not managed to conceive, though she wanted to badly enough to have the humiliating tests done. And she was too old for adoption: the agencies would not have wanted to give a newborn to a couple where the husband was over fifty.

Lies ...

Just as, at the age of fourteen, she had had to reassemble the past in the light of new information about her mother, so now Harriet had to re-examine her marriage, her friendship with Christina. She felt physically ill. Christina must have decided what she was going to do from the moment she heard that Harriet was pregnant.

Had Tracy Merlin's pregnancy just been fortuitous, an extra strand to be woven into the thick texture of falsehood and deception which she was knotting for Harriet? Or would Christina have set her up anyway, an innocent red-herring? The theft of shoes, of underwear, had been an excuse; she must have written Tracy's part before she had even got rid of her.

Harriet remembered Chris's lists. The four of them used to joke about the timetables she drew up, the plan of the supermarket she had made so she would not have to retrace her steps for an item forgotten. Christina had once shown her the meticulously measured diagrams she had drawn when she and Denis moved from Oxford, with the dimensions of each item of furniture carefully marked in to scale.

The new house: the *new* new house which Christina had bought up north, in the village of Whitemoor. Had that too been planned well in advance, one step moving logically on to the next? Had she drawn up one of her check-lists: sell the Cotswold house, find another well away from Oxford, prepare it for the baby she intended to steal?

Harriet's heart stamped unevenly between her ribs. *'Straight up the A1, turn left at Scotch Corner, keep on for twenty miles ...'* Christina had said. With dread, she found a road map on the bookshelves, followed the A1 northwards, looked for a village called Whitemoor.

Even as her finger moved across the pages, she knew it would not exist. For the first time it was borne in on her that she had no means at all of contacting Christina. All the telephone calls had come from Christina, from a callbox; Harriet had never been able to call her (*'Sorry, darling. Those wretched telephone engineers ...'*). She could have been ringing from anywhere in the country.

Harriet ignored the panic she felt. *Invincible*, she told herself; *I am invincible*. She packed a few things, got into her car and set off. Even if there was no village called Whitemoor, perhaps there was one called something else twenty miles left of Scotch Corner.

If not, how was she to track Christina down? What mark of recognition did she have? Did the barrister exist, the courtly barrister who was supposed to be Christina's neighbour, who had bought flowers to cheer her up? And the headmaster on the other side, with his three children: were they, too, creations of Christina's agile brain?

Harriet allowed herself some anger. Not too much or she would lose the clearheadedness which was essential if she was to outwit, out-think Christina. Just enough to get the adrenalin flowing, to give her the impetus to behave as coldly, as ruthlessly as her opponent.

She wondered what Denis would have made of this, had he still been alive. It was only then that she realised just how dangerous was the game she was playing, how lethal. She tried to skirt around the thought but it kept recurring: Denis's death — *no!* — must have been part of the planning, too, one of the careful calculations. She remembered how it was only after she had mentioned her pregnancy that Christina had appeared seriously worried about his drinking, how she had whispered that it was affecting their sex life.

And the sudden trip to Alicante, outside their normal routine, that too must have been deliberately organised, a spontaneous visit with death in mind.

Seeds, Harriet thought. Christina had been sowing seeds, just as she did in her garden. Seeds planted as soon as she learned of Harriet's pregnancy and, after that, carefully watered, so that Denis, pitching over the edge of a balcony while the harbour lights, tossing and swaying below, had suddenly come rushing up to meet him, would seem to be the victim of his own excesses. Had there been any suggestion of foul play, Harriet herself would have testified that, yes, his wife was increasingly worried about his drinking, had been for some time, and Denis had only himself to blame.

Which indeed he had, she thought grimly. With Denis around, it would have been impossible for Christina to pass someone else's baby off as her own. Nor could she have pretended it was adopted; she would have needed Denis's full cooperation for that. Since he would have been bound to ask all kinds of awkward questions, Denis had to go.

Harriet shuddered, gripping the steering-wheel. Tears came into her eyes and she dashed them angrily away. Poor Denis, dropping through the night sky, wondering as he fell to earth why his wife had come out on the balcony behind him, why she had pushed him. When the police came, she would have been back in bed, nightgowned, sleepy, wanting to know what had happened, raising a hand to lips gone pale, saying, 'I told him, I *told* him not to drink so much,' perhaps indicating an empty wine bottle on the table, another in the kitchen, and the police would never know how she had emptied one down the sink and run the tap water to flush it away before slipping back into bed to await their arrival, to practise her expressions of horror and surprise.

In one suitably located village, Harriet found a barrister. In two others, a headmaster and his family. None of them knew a Mrs Christina Crawford nor anyone of her description. Harriet wondered how Christina had chanced on the name Whitemoor, the barrister and the headmaster, whether indeed she had ever come up here at all.

Driving dispiritedly back to Oxford, she suddenly remembered the photograph Christina had shown her of the house she intended to buy, a house with wooden trim, a prolific pear-tree. Excitement hovered at the back of her mind then crept hesitatingly into view: was it possible that Christina had made a mistake, left a fingerprint at last? Harriet concentrated, clearing her mind of everything except the road and that distant afternoon. They had been at Harriet's flat, sitting on the sofa. Christina was wearing a black sweater over black slim-legged corduroy trousers; she had been depressed, the mourning colours emphasising her boyish figure. 'What do you think?' she had said, handing the photograph over. 'It's only about three hours' drive from here.'

And Harriet, still fogged by circumstance, by Conor's death and Denis's, by the baby inside her, had held the photograph, had noted the details — pear-tree, agent's board, the line of moors behind — had advised her to go for it.

What had she done then?

Tea. She had made some tea, had brought it back into the sitting-room, there had been biscuits on a plate, and Christina laughing, saying really she mustn't but taking one all the same.

The photograph. What had she done with the photograph? She could not remember. She had got up, walked across the room, gone into the kitchen: had she left it on the table for Christina to pick up and put back into her bag? Or had she taken it with her, left it on the counter-top, swept it into a drawer when she found it later? Vaguely, it came into focus like a negative in solution, the house, the tree taking shape, defining themselves within a thin white border, imprinting themselves on to the image of her kitchen counter. Changing gear as a lorry pulled out in front of her, she tried to decide if it had really happened like that or whether she was merely manipulating the past. Yet the more she thought about it, the more she was convinced she had taken the photograph into the kitchen with her and had not — this was the important thing — had not brought it back into the sitting-room when she carried in the tea-tray. Which meant . . .

She swallowed painfully, pressing her foot down on the accelerator. Fifty miles to Oxford . . . thirty, fifteen: she could hardly wait to get back, to search through her untidy drawers. If it was there — it *had* to be there — then perhaps she could identify the estate-agent from his board, could locate the house and maybe, just maybe, find Christina living in it with a child who was not hers, a child stolen from her best friend, a child she thought was also her lover's child and therefore, by some twisted logic, a child to which she had a right. Particularly after Harriet had so foolishly said she herself did not want it.

As the miles dragged by, Harriet thought about the logistics of it. Christina would have had to appear at the new house — wherever it was — from time to time. If she was eventually to settle there with a baby, she would have had to appear increasingly pregnant, she would have had to make up a story to cover the lack of husband, she would have had to register with a doctor, a hospital, she would need medical records. On the other hand, it was easy for the clever to dupe the trusting. All she had to do was invent long years abroad, perhaps a foreign husband, now dead. Having bought the house and established her new name and persona, her pregnancy, she could say to anyone interested that she was having the baby somewhere else, with parents who lived in another part of the country. Five weeks later she could arrive to start her new life as a respectable widow and mother.

Would she, speaking of it to new friends, give her husband's name as Conor? The possibility made Harriet clench her teeth with a dark anger; carefully she chased it away.

Four miles to Oxford, then two, one. She negotiated a tricky roundabout, got caught behind a bus, pulled out to pass two bicyclists and had to drop back again behind them. 'Come on,' she urged through her teeth. 'Come *on.*'

At last she was turning into the gravelled semicircle in front of her house, switching off the engine, running towards the front door. In the kitchen she grabbed the handle of the second drawer down and tugged it open. Clutter: candle-ends too long to throw away, spare batteries, one of Conor's shoe-laces, drinking straws, plastic bags, a roll of greaseproof paper. No photograph. She pulled out the next drawer, and the next: bin-liners, the instructions for the dishwasher (so *that's* where they went), more batteries, old bills, some clothespegs, corks from long-drunk wine bottles, a patent nutcracker which had never worked. She emptied the drawers on to the kitchen table, but there was no photograph. She refused to give up: it had to be there. She pulled out the drawer in the kitchen table where she kept place-mats, looked under the dishwater, the washing-machine, the microwave. She dragged the tall fridge-freezer away from the wall: perhaps the photo had slipped down behind it. But it had not. She pulled down her recipe books, flipped through them. Nothing. Standing on tiptoe to put them back on the shelf, she caught sight of the flat basket on top of the fridge which acted as a catch-all for recipes cut out of the paper, for letters, for bills. Clumsily she lifted it down and sifted through the papers it held. *Oh, God, let it be there.*

It was.

Stuck to the underside of a recipe for baked ricotta, the photograph was streaked with kitchen dust but nonetheless indisputably there. Christina grinned back at her; the pear-tree stood black against the sky and the smooth contours of the moors. The agent's board was to one side, so that less than half of it was visible. On the top line, ALE in large black letters; under them *ckell*. Beneath that was part of what must be a contact address and telephone number, far too small to be read.

ALE was obviously part of FOR SALE; what about *ckell*? A name, obviously. Something and — what? *Buckell*? *Tickell*? She thought: the police could find out, easily. Then she remembered Buchan's closed-up face, the coldness which had gradually crept into his eyes to blot out sympathy. No. Better if for the moment she went on searching herself. And surely, surely, if she took it to a local estate-agent, they could find the name. There must be directories, they all had to belong to associations these days, didn't they; some kind of official body to establish their bona-fides?

Not stopping to find a coat, she ran to the shopping precinct round the corner; in the first estate agency she came to she showed the picture, asked for help. They knew who she was: their local celebrity. Eyes not meeting hers, a young man took her into the back and produced a directory.

'It's obviously not one of the big chains,' he said kindly, looking again at the photograph. 'Any idea which part of the country? The names are divided into region.'

'None,' Harriet said. 'But look: those are moors behind, aren't they?'

'Could be moors. But they could also be in the south-west, or even bits of Kent or Sussex. Or Wales. Anywhere, almost.'

'I'll try the North Country first.'

'OK.' He found the page for her. 'Good luck.'

So many names: as she turned the pages, moving rapidly from name to name, she was struck by the unceasing business of the world. People everywhere, doing things: getting married, having babies, buying houses, mowing lawns. People catching butterflies, sailing boats, playing in orchestras, borrowing books. And for each activity a substructure to service it: ship's chandlers, public libraries, doctors, seedsmen, publishers of music, garden centres. And behind those, yet another edifice of suppliers, factories, secretaries, receptionists, experts, administrators.

Slowly, she covered the north-east, the Lake District, Cumbria. No name leapt at her from the pages. She turned to the south-west, to Cornwall, Devon, Somerset, Dorset: nothing there. Kent and Sussex, Wales: nothing. She went back to the north. Those gentle outlines, unbroken by walls or hedges, unpatterned by fields, were northern moors, she was sure of it. In her university days she had walked them too often to be mistaken. She stared at the photograph again: was it really *ckell* she was looking at, or had she mistaken the double curve of an *l* — was it a double *t* instead? She held it close to her eyes: it was possible.

Say it was a *t*: that would give her *ckett*. Reckett? Beckett? Buckett? Hackett? She started again at the beginning of the northern listings, more slowly now, her finger hesitating over names which in fact bore no resemblance at all to the group of letters she was looking for. From its placing under the words FOR SALE it had to be two names: Something and Something, and even as she thought this, she saw it. *Askrigg & Birckett, Hexham*, with branches in several other little towns, all of them listed.

She leaned back in the hard chair and closed her eyes. *Have I found her?* she wondered. *Have I tracked her down because she made a mistake; she left the photograph behind when she should have taken it?* Elation would not come; she sensed it could not be that easy. She closed the book. In the front office, one of the girls sitting at a desk set sideways to the room looked up and said determinedly: 'I'm ever so sorry about your baby, Mrs Pearse.'

Most people shied away from tragedy, even avoided those who suffered it. Recognising courage, Harriet smiled; her mouth felt strange as though the skin of her face had long since accommodated itself to not smiling. 'I'll find her,' she said.

'You think she's all right?'

'I know it,' Harriet said firmly. Out in the street again she realised that she did know it. Whatever other worries she had, the fact of Laura's safety seemed established. Christina would be taking good care of the prize on which she had expended so much effort, for which she had made so many plans. The prize for which she had almost certainly murdered.

The telephone was ringing as she let herself into the house. It was Buchan. 'How are you?' he asked.

'Fine, thank you.'

'Are you sure?'

'Yes.'

'I tried to ring you yesterday, but there was no answer.'

'I had to go somewhere.'

'I'm afraid there's still no news. We're following up all the leads we get, but even working flat out it takes a long time.'

'I'm sure it does.'

'Harriet.' His voice sharpened. 'You're not alone, are you. You sound . . .'

'Tom's here,' Harriet lied. She wished she had something concrete to show him, something that would set his huge and efficient machine searching for Christina. But after the Teresa Merlin business, and Conor's parents, she was reluctant to embroil him in something that was, after all, no more than suspicion. What did she have, beyond her knowledge of Christina, to make her so sure that her friend was the one who had taken her daughter? Nothing. Nothing beyond an expression, a pair of red shoes which should not have been where they were, a set of photographs which showed beyond any doubt that her husband and her best friend had been cheating on her. It was a long step from there to abduction. She would have to have something less circumstantial before she went back to the police.

'Oh,' Buchan said. 'That's all right then.' He cleared his

throat. 'We'll go on until we find her,' he said.

'I know you will.'

She picked up her bag, still unpacked from her trip up the A1, added clean underwear, a fresh blouse, clean jeans and a sweater. She stowed it in the back of the car and drove out of the gate and back into the stream of traffic heading north. *This time*, she thought, *maybe this time . . .*

· 26 ·

Rising from his seat as his uncle and aunt came towards him across the lobby, Tom embraced them affectionately. 'Aunt Elizabeth! Jack!' He was amazed at how they had aged since he saw them last; he wondered why he should be. His parents had had no choice but to remain forever young, trapped in a summer's day, with a sea breeze ruffling their hair and death waiting for them beyond the pine trees; Elizabeth and Jack had been free to walk on into middle-age and beyond.

'I'm just so glad we finally made it over here,' Elizabeth said. Her aristocratic bloodlines showed in the shape of her head and the almost aquiline nose with its high nostrils, the eyes set under a fine brow. He was unaccountably gladdened by the way her patrician profile softened as she turned her cheek into her nephew's kiss.

'Me, too.' Jack touched his wife's hand briefly. 'All these years we promised ourselves this trip. Guess we might not have made it even now if it hadn't have been for you, Tom.'

'That's absolutely right,' said Elizabeth. As always her clothes were beautifully cut, impeccably maintained, dull. Beside her, Jack seemed fashioned from different material, both stronger and coarser. They make a good pair, Tom thought, leading the way through Oxford's crowded streets to the restaurant he had chosen. He tried to remember what his father Ned, Jack's brother, had looked like, but could not. Just the dark hair blowing, the smile, the farewell wave. Would he eventually have looked as Jack did now? It was difficult to imagine; even more difficult to imagine Jack young. Yet once he had been, once he too was adolescent, had yearned for things he could not articulate, had grown up in the house in Maine, sailed with his brother off the rocky shores, got drunk, fallen in love, fathered a son.

'We bumped into Rebecca the other day,' Elizabeth said, when they were settled into their seats.

'Really? How's she doing?' Tom was not particularly interested; he was busy realising how much, after more than four months away, he missed the warm accents of home.

'Still trying to make it on Broadway,' Jack said heartily. 'Thank God you and Amis never had the acting bug, Tom. Of all the precarious professions to choose . . .'

'She sent her love,' Elizabeth said. She watched him carefully across the posy in the middle of the table.

'Did she now?' Tom ordered wine, asked what they wanted to eat, passed round bread rolls. He did not wish to talk about Rebecca.

'She asked if you were happy.'

'I hope you told her I was ecstatic.'

'As a matter of fact . . .'

'Tom didn't travel three thousand miles to listen to gossip about his ex-wife,' Jack said. 'You heard about Amis, I guess.'

'I sure did. Last time I called Margaret seemed a bit happier about his condition.'

'Still has that short-term memory loss, though. Doesn't remember a thing about it.'

'I still haven't figured out why anyone would break into an attorney's office,' said Tom.

'Nor me. Guess we'll just have to wait until he can talk to us about it.'

'Meanwhile, tell us about Europe, Tom.' Elizabeth said. 'Are you having a good time?'

'It's everything I hoped it would be,' said Tom. 'In one way. In another, it couldn't be more different. I've gotten involved in helping the friend of a friend, someone who's in a lot of trouble. And there was a commission I had to carry out for a client in California. It's all taken a lot longer than I expected.'

'What kind of trouble?' said Elizabeth.

As they ate, Tom explained about Harriet.

'Oh my goodness, how terrible,' Elizabeth said. 'That poor

girl: how on earth is she coping?' Her eyes asked other questions; chiefly they wanted to know how Tom felt about this girl and whether she was more than merely the friend of a friend.

Tom expressed none of his own feeling of desolation at the abduction of the baby. Having seen Laura born, a bond, however tenuous, had necessarily been forged between them; her loss had a personal quality. Passionately he wished he could restore her to her mother, not with any hope of thereby gaining favour in Harriet's eyes, but because that way order would have been restored, chaos conquered.

'Recently I've managed to take a couple of short trips abroad, see some of the places I always wanted to visit,' he said, not adding that this had been made possible only by Harriet's clear indication that she would prefer him to keep away. 'I'm hoping to get back to Paris for a longer stay than when I first got here. And Moscow — I'd really like to swing a visit there if I could.'

Jack started a predictable diatribe against the devious Russians and how they were not to be trusted. Six months, a year ago, Tom, irritated, would have taken him on, argued, grown impatient with his uncle's knee-jerk attitudes. Now, drinking wine, calling for a second bottle, he merely smiled. It was precisely the predictability, the attitudes, that made Jack dear and familiar.

'All the same,' he said. 'It would be an interesting place to visit. Trouble is, I don't like to leave Harriet for too long.'

'Harriet?' Elizabeth asked.

'The girl whose baby was abducted.'

'Doesn't she have family of her own?'

'Sure she does. But the father's on an extended vacation in the South American jungle, if I understood it correctly, and the brother's travelling round the States selling antiques, and difficult to pin down. As a matter of fact, I did try to locate them, but didn't have any luck at all.'

Later, Elizabeth, carefully slicing her spoon through a mound of mango sorbet, said: 'Rebecca would love to see you, Tom.'

'Would she?'

'I'm sure that the two of you could get together again.'

'We *what*?'

'Of course she didn't come right out and say so, but I got the distinct impression that if you were to call her when you get back, she would be very happy to meet up with you.'

Rebecca was a million miles away, lost in a past he had deliberately tried to shed. Even so, he could still remember the feeling she had roused in him, the look of her brown body against a white sheet, the sick sweetness of his constant need for her, the way she had sparkled through his life with the fierce, unwatchable brilliance of sunshine along the edge of a wave. 'Aunt Elizabeth,' he said quietly. 'I have no wish whatsoever to meet up with Rebecca.'

'But why not? You always seemed so suited to each other. I never really understood why you split up.'

He wanted to say: 'We split up because pretty Rebecca Seaton was the most selfish, the most self-absorbed person you could ever hope to meet, although it took me years to realise it.' Instead, he said: 'All that's over and done with. I've changed. I want other things.' I want Harriet, he thought; I shall probably never get her.

'What sort of things?' asked Jack.

'I'm still not sure.' But even as he said it, Tom understood that in among the things he wanted was kindness, involvement, friendship: concepts which Rebecca had apparently never understood.

'And how do you like working in California?'

'The work's fine. It's the place I have a problem with. Too much sun for me. Too much brightness.' He liked shadows, dimness, grey fog rolling in from the sea, the smell of rain on the air.

'Ever thought of moving back home to Maine?'

'Often. Why do you ask?'

'Well, I'll tell you, Tom. Ned and I were partners; we always planned it that way and that's exactly how it turned out. And after he — well, I carried on, expecting Amis to join me, and he didn't, or even you, Tom, but I guess both of you had better things to do than join a one-horse firm in a one-horse town.'

'Hey, listen,' Tom said. 'If you want one-horse, you should see Seaton & Seaton, out in Bellamonte.'

'OK. Amis is settled there now, him and his girls. I asked him but he doesn't want to come back. But since you seem kind of unsettled right now, I'd like to put it on record that I'd be happy, really happy, if you'd consider joining up with me, Tom, the way it ought to have been.'

Looking at him, Tom thought: in spite of everything, I've been lucky. I've had stability, Jack and Elizabeth, my grandmother.

It could have been so much worse; he could have been destroyed by the tragedy that had touched his life: the double drowning, arms waving above the cold seawater, clutching at the bright air, sinking, leaving desolation behind.

'I'll certainly think about it,' he said, and was surprised at how warm he felt at the possibility of returning to the old house set between freshwater lake and pounding sea. Briefly he saw white curtains blowing, a woman at the piano, children running towards the pines. 'Yes, I definitely will. I'd have to make arrangements with Amis, of course.'

'Of course.'

'He'll need time to find another partner. But as a matter of fact he's been half-expecting me to move on for a while now.' Suddenly Tom grinned. 'Yeah,' he said. 'Great.'

Elizabeth, having drunk her share of the wine, followed her sorbet with Irish coffee. There was an unaccustomed laxness about her; she laughed loosely, leaning against Jack's shoulder and opening her mouth wider than seemed necessary. Hitherto there had been a pleasing symmetry between her cool persona and the pared-down spareness of the furniture she collected. The Elizabeth he saw now was quite different. He thought, amused: am I witnessing the dissolution of a Yankee lady here, or what? He wondered how his mother might have been at the same age as Elizabeth.

'Tell me about my parents,' he said suddenly.

'Oh, Tom ...' Elizabeth looked quickly at her husband.

'I've never asked before. We've never discussed them. I know so little about them.'

'You're right,' said Jack. 'We should have talked to you, especially when you were younger. But the shock of it, the ...' He lifted his shoulders. '... the pain, really, of losing a younger brother.' From under bushy white eyebrows he looked at his nephew. 'Ned. I loved him, you know. I loved that guy. Losing him ... well, it's taken me years to recover.'

'And Ellen,' said Elizabeth. 'So vital, so pretty. We both loved her. It was impossible to take in the fact that we'd never see either of them again.'

'Unbearable,' Jack said. 'I suppose that's why we never discussed them with you.'

'I thought about it so often, you know,' said Elizabeth. 'I couldn't stop thinking about it, about Ellen out there, drowning, with the shore still in sight, wondering whether she saw you, Tom, imagining in her last moments that she saw you among the pine trees.'

'Elizabeth,' Jack said. 'I don't think —'

'No.' She put her hand over his. 'I've seen it in my mind's eye so many times, imagined it over and over again, especially on sunny days, the kind of day when they went out that last time. They say you see your past life flash before you when you drown, but I know Ellen would have only seen you, Tom, only your life and what it was going to be without her. She loved you so much.'

'Hell, both of them did,' said Jack gruffly. 'Doted on you.' Tears came suddenly into his eyes; into Tom's, too.

'We should have talked about it before,' Elizabeth repeated.

'That's OK,' Tom began. 'It doesn't matter.' And in a way, it did not. What would it have changed if he had known more? Perhaps it was best that he had waited until now, perhaps he had not needed until now to know. He touched Jack's sleeve; put a hand over Elizabeth's.

'We just couldn't do it.' Elizabeth nodded at him, her face serious. 'And you didn't ever ask'.

'I know. I couldn't face it.' No one had ever known how much the loss of his parents had wounded him, how the mere thought of them had been so painful that he had tried simply to forget they had ever existed.

For a moment the three of them sat in silence. Then Tom said: 'Where did she come from, my mother? I don't even know that. I don't know anything about her side of the family.'

'She didn't have any,' said Jack. 'I believe they'd all been wiped out in a car accident and she'd been reared by an aunt who'd died.'

'Is that right?'

His spine prickled. Parallels, echoes; they were everywhere. Had it been as easy as that for Nell Costello? Did she only have to say that she had no family, for the man she married — Anthony Newgate — to accept it? Could a disappearance be engineered that easily? Tom reflected, as he had so often before, how easy it is to put one over on Joe Public, simply because Joe Public, naive and trusting fool that he is, expects everyone to be as simple as he is. 'So when they got married, there was nobody there from her side?'

'Well, they got married secretly,' Elizabeth said. 'Ellen told me once she couldn't have borne the fuss of a big society wedding, so the two of them just found a judge and got married that way. There was a reception later, of course. A big one. They had lots of friends. There must have been a hundred and fifty people, weren't there, Jack?'

'I was too busy drinking champagne to count,' Jack said. 'But, yes, a big crowd.'

'But no family, on my mother's side?'

'That's right. At least, not as far as I remember.'

'Where did my parents meet?'

'At college,' Elizabeth said. 'Ned was at Harvard and she was at Radcliffe. I remember when he first brought her home, the summer Jack and I got engaged.'

'Where was she from.'

His aunt and uncle looked at each other. Jack frowned, skimming his memory. 'I know she'd spent time on the West Coast. She told me once she hated all that sunshine, much preferred the East to the West Coast.'

'I have a feeling she'd grown up in the South,' Elizabeth

said. 'Atlanta, or somewhere like that. Though she certainly didn't have a Southern accent.'

Again Tom was struck with the lack of curiosity that the average person displays. As though sensing what he groped for, Jack said: 'She was a wonderful person, Tom. And marvellous for Ned. We thought the world of her.'

His response was oblique. 'I'd love you to meet Harriet. I'll see what I can fix up.'

'This house,' Harriet said, handing over the photograph. 'Do you recognise it?'

'Certainly do,' sang the woman at the desk. She wore a red suit with a red and white striped blouse. Her head looked as if not long before it had been in the hands of a master plasterer, the orange hair sculpted into immobility. 'That's the Tarnbridge house, down at Holsham.'

'And you sold it recently?'

'Yes.'

'How long ago?'

The woman gave it some thought, smiling brightly as she did so. 'Must be four or five months ago now.' She peered more closely at the photograph. 'Oh, look! There's Mrs Crawford.' She patted her hair. 'She asked me to take a picture of her in front of the house so she could show it to her husband.'

Who was already dead by then ... The muscles of Harriet's stomach tightened. 'Mrs Crawford: is that the name of the person who bought it?'

'No. Not in the end. She was dead keen, even had a survey done, but then — I remember the poor soul coming in to tell us — her husband was killed in an accident and she had to withdraw from the sale.' She shook her head. 'It must have been a difficult time for her.'

'Yes.' Harriet remembered how Christina had rushed down to Oxford as soon as she heard that Laura was born. Christina had insisted that Harriet rest and let her take over everything, even the baby. Harriet's position as the child's mother was being usurped even then, and she had not noticed a thing.

She put a hand on the counter to steady herself. Wherever Christina had planned to take the baby, it was not to this house, not if she had not bothered to pretend to be pregnant, a piece of information the sharp-eyed agent would certainly have picked up and commented on. So this was a false trail. She could almost see the dance of Christina's dark eyes, hear her teasing voice and mocking laugh. It was as though she had known Harriet would eventually trace her this far and was saying: 'You can't catch me.'

But I can, Harriet thought; I can and I will. 'So is the house still empty?' she asked.

'No. There's a family in there, ever so nice, a headmaster of one of the local primary schools and his three children.' Was that where Christina had got the idea of the headmasterly neighbour? 'And his wife, too, of course. Ever so nice they are.' Belatedly, it occurred to her to ask: 'Why're you enquiring, anyway?'

Harriet's cover story, dreamed up in the car, was thin; she did not, however, expect to be cross-examined on it. On the whole, people accepted what you told them at face value. 'I met Mrs Crawford some months ago at a coffee morning,' she said. 'She was talking about this house. She showed me this photograph, actually. The thing was, she turned out to know a girl I used to go to school with and promised to give me her address, but she had to leave unexpectedly and I never got the address. It just occurred to me that you would know the house and I could call in and get it.'

'Oh.' The woman was frowning. 'But —'

'Of course, I had no idea then that Mrs Crawford's husband had died. What a terrible thing to happen.'

The woman was diverted. 'I know. Some people really do seem to attract bad luck, don't they?'

'I don't suppose you know where she went instead.'

'I don't, hen. She didn't really say, and of course I didn't like to ask, in the circumstances.'

'Of course.'

So, Harriet thought, driving away down the long miles which stretched between there and Oxford, where possibly, just possibly, Buchan was trying to telephone her in order to let her know he had found Laura ... so Christina, having laid another false trail, had simply climbed into her car and zoomed away into the unknown.

It was another thirty-five miles before the significance struck her. Christina's car: there weren't that many red MGs on the road; they could be traced, couldn't they? The police were always doing it, sitting in their radio cars, calling up the vehicle licencing place in Swansea; it would only take them a matter of minutes — seconds, — to track down a red MG.

Or would it? 'I'll have to get rid of it before the winter sets in,' Christina had said. Before the winter sets in, before you catch up with me. Another tease; Harriet almost heard the malicious laughter in the air. And she remembered again Christina hesitating, looking at her across the roof of her car, saying she was sorry. At the time, Harriet had assumed she meant about the fact that she had been left on her own with Laura, without Conor. Now, she wondered if it was an advance apology for what Christina was about to do.

She pressed the back of her hand against her mouth. She knew already it was useless. Christina would have sold the car by now; the trail would have been covered over. Was it nonetheless worth asking Buchan to put somebody on to it? Would it be a lot of work? Would he even do it, or simply see it as the further ravings of a woman driven half-demented by the loss of her child? And if all those questions proved surmountable, would he demand to know why she wanted that particular car traced?

She shrank from the idea of saying anything about Christina. She had to be sure, this time. She had to present him with so much evidence that he would be compelled to believe her. It was evidence she did not have — not yet.

Back in Oxford, she telephoned him.

'I've been trying to get you,' he said crossly.

'I went somewhere. Did you have anything special to tell me?'

'Only to say that we're still following any leads we can. In spite of what you think, we haven't given up.'

'How easy would it be for you to trace the owner of an MG?' she asked.

'If you've got the licence number, about three seconds. If not, considerably longer.' His voice sharpened. 'Why?'

'Something that occurred to me. It was —'

'If you have any information, anything at all that could help us find where your daughter is, I assume you'll tell me immediately.'

'It's my friend, Mrs Crawford,' Harriet said reluctantly.

'What about her? You think she's the one who stole Laura?'

Did she imagine it, or was there scepticism in his voice? If so, it only confirmed her decision to say nothing about Christina until it could be backed up with solid fact. 'No,' she said. 'But since she moved, I haven't been able to get in touch with her, and it occurred to me that I might be able to trace her through her car.'

'Except you don't have the number.'

'It's an old one, red, with one of those three-letter three-figure licence-plates,' Harriet said. 'I don't remember the letters, but the numbers are 543.'

There was a pause. 'I'll see what I can do,' said Buchan.

She rang Tom's flat. When he answered, she said: 'Come to dinner with me tonight.'

'That would be marvellous,' he said. 'Listen, my aunt and uncle are in town for a few days. I'd love for them to meet you.'

She said firmly: 'Another time.' Then, as if realising she sounded hard: 'We'll fix a day when you get here tonight.'

'Fine. I'll bring some wine.'

Harriet shopped for steak, vegetables, an exotic lettuce, double cream. She bought cheese from the specialists on the covered market. She cleaned and dusted the neglected flat, arranged some flowers, laid the table with care. They were actions performed often before; for the first time since Laura had gone, she was aware of the continuity of things. How many times in the future would she fill flower vases, polish silver, shake cream and brandy together into a sauce? And would Laura be with her when she did so, or not? It was a question she was not going to think about. The only way to survive was by skating along the surface of her thoughts, by — yes — making plans.

She could see from Tom's expression that he thought her recovered to a certain extent. 'You look ... wonderful,' he said, stepping into the hall behind her, not quite hiding his relief. She wore a full-skirted dress of sea-green wool which emphasised the shape of her breasts; her tumbling hair had been tied up with a scarf of the same colour.

She moved quickly away from him; she could see in his eyes the desire to touch her. She was not prepared for any of that, not from him, not from anyone.

'I feel better,' she said. Did he realise that behind the facade, inside her casing of streamlined steel, she still seethed with loss and anger? For the moment she would keep it contained; emotion could come later, when she had brought Laura home.

They had drinks before dinner: whisky for him, a martini for her. A fire burned in the grate, its reflection glimmering on the polish of the table in front of it, glowing at the sea-green heart of the glass egg.

'I love this room,' Tom said. *And you, Harriet, with your mermaid hair and your sad, sad eyes, I love you too.*

'It was the first time I've ever decorated anything,' she said. 'It worked out well.'

'You have an artist's eye.'

'Maybe.' She picked up the egg and cupped it between her hands, staring pensively into its depths. An artist: was that what she was? She could feel in her fingers the desire to hold a brush again; until now she had painted very little, but she knew that what she had produced so far had merit.

Tom put down his drink. 'Harriet,' he said. 'What is it you want me to do for you?'

She looked up, startled. 'Uh ...'

'I'd like to think that you invited me here simply for the pleasure of my company,' he said gently. 'However, I'm realistic enough to accept that you didn't, that you don't think of me in those terms. I can even understand that it embarrasses you to know that I was the one who took you to the hospital when you went into labour, and that you wish I would go away so that you wouldn't have to remember that a stranger held your hand while your first child was born.'

She flushed, started to protest, but he laid a finger across her lips. 'Harriet. Dear Harriet. It's all right. Now just tell me what you want me to do and then we can broil the steaks and have a nice evening together, and then I'll —' he hesitated, thinking of the alternatives '— I'll go home.'

'Tom,' she said. She was appalled at the nakedness she sensed behind his words. She took his hand and held it for a moment. 'Let's eat first,' she said. 'And you're quite right, I *do* want you to do something for me, but that's honestly not the only reason I asked you here tonight.'

'Isn't it?'

She looked away from him. 'No,' she said, and wondered for a moment if what she said was true.

Over dinner, she asked how his search for Lydia Costello's daughter was going. 'Not hugely well,' he said. 'Last time I rang the States they told me Lydia had had a stroke and was in the hospital.'

'She was so nice,' Harriet said. 'Will she recover?'

'They think so ... but only in the short-term. She hadn't got long to live anyway. I would so much like to straighten out this business with her daughter, and find the wretched woman before it's too late for Lydia.'

'Do you know the name of the man who seems to have been the cause of it all, the lover?'

'No. That's why I rang her. She said at the time that she would only give it to me if all else failed. Frankly, all else *has* failed, and now I can't get the answer from her.'

'I don't know if it's any help,' Harriet said slowly. 'But I know my father knew her years ago — he spent a year at Berkeley. It was through him that Matthew got a job at her nurseries — so did I, later.'

'She told me. Trouble is, we don't know where your father is, do we?'

'His office says he's due back at any time. I know he'll ring me the minute he shows up.'

'Great. I did ask my secretary — if that's the right word — to call at the hospital but Lydia's not allowed visitors at the moment.'

'How do you mean — if that's the right word?'

So Tom explained about Miss Roma Hogg and the cork wedgies and dirndl skirts which she favoured; not at all the sort of clothes that the average secretary went in for, not that the average secretary weighed close to three hundred pounds. Nor, as a general rule, Tom added, thrilled to see that Harriet's face was lifting with the anticipation of laughter, did the average secretary, as far as he knew, keep asking for time off to take part in quiz-show programmes down in LA, the way Miss Roma Hogg did.

'I wouldn't even mind that so much,' he said, smiling ruefully, 'if she didn't keep winning things.'

'What sort of thing?' Harriet held a glass of red wine in one hand; her curving mouth was soft, soft and desirable . . .

'Like refrigerators and self-assembly greenhouses and redwood loungers,' said Tom firmly. All of which meant someone had to drive down the freeway to collect them, since the quiz-show programme organisers made it very clear that under no circumstances did they deliver the goods won by participants in their shows. 'And guess who the someone who drives down the freeway usually turns out to be?'

'You?'

'Who else. Amis — that's my cousin and partner — has three daughters, you see, who're always off playing some-where in school concerts, so Amis and his wife Margaret have their work cut out just getting them *to* the concerts and picking them up *from* the concerts.'

The only illumination in the room came from the fire and from the candles she had lit; the indefinite flickering light had smoothed away the shadows from under her eyes and softened the new gauntness of her face.

Tom poured the last of the wine into their glasses and said: 'OK, Harriet. Let's have it.'

'Have what?'

'Whatever it is that you asked me here for.'

For a moment, she gazed beyond him at nothing, marshalling her thoughts. Then she said: 'I need an analytical brain like yours to look at something and tell me whether I've simply gone crazy or whether there's actually some possible foundation in what I'm going to tell you. So please don't say anything until I've finished, all right?'

He nodded.

She made coffee while he poured brandy into glasses for them both. Then, sitting next to him on the sofa, she carefully laid before him her suspicions, her conclusions, her certainties about Christina, trying to make him appreciate the logical piling up of facts, the plan made long before, each objective doubtless ticked off once it had been achieved.

When she had finished, Tom said nothing for a few moments, going over it again in his mind.

'It certainly hangs together,' he said finally. 'The point at issue is whether you're simply clutching at straws, or whether you're right when you say this so-called friend of yours could really have planned all this so much in advance without giving you the slightest indication of what she was thinking.'

'The more I think about it, the more I know I'm right,' said Harriet. 'I have an impression that she feels she's entitled to this baby, because it's Conor's child. I'm sure that's what's behind it. And I've already been proven right on a couple of things, like there not being a village called Whitemoor where she said there was . . .'

'That could have been a misunderstanding on your part.'

'No. She was very definite about it. She mentioned it many times, she even gave me directions to it.'

'OK.'

'And there're those infertility tests she took. Surely that proves she's capable of long-term deceit: all those years of shuddering at the thought of having a baby when all the time she was trying to get pregnant herself.'

'That's curious, I agree. But it doesn't really prove that she pushed her husband over a balcony.'

'I know that. But there's just too many other details. The red shoes, for instance, which she told me Tracy Merlin — and I *know* she called her Marling — had stolen.'

'Doesn't necessarily mean a thing,' Tom said, shaking his head. 'She could have made Tracy give them back. Anyway, according to Tracy, she didn't steal them, just tried them on.'

'Even so, Christina was lying one way or another,' persisted Harriet. 'Particularly about this village which doesn't exist, and the neighbours, and the house which it turns out she never bought. If I hadn't found that photograph I'd never have been able to prove it, which is what she was presumably counting on.'

'What do you want me to do?' Though still sceptical, Tom tried to keep it from showing.

'You don't believe me. You think that losing Laura has made me unbalanced, don't you?'

'Of course I don't think —'

'I saw you, that day you took me out to lunch and made me eat something. I saw it in your eyes, and yes, I'll admit I was pretty close to a nervous breakdown at that point. But I'm not any more. I'm going to find Christina somehow, even if it takes me years, even if no one else believes me.'

Tom leaned across the table and tried to take her hand; she moved it out of his reach. He noticed that the wedding ring she used to wear had gone. 'Even though there could be logical reasons behind a lot of the things you've told me, I have to agree that there's still too much unexplained sh— stuff flying around here for this lady to be on the up and up. Like the fact that all these months after she moved away, you still don't have an address for her, or a telephone number where you can get her, even though you're supposed to be her best friend. That's pretty fishy.'

'And Denis's drinking, too. I mean, I never saw the poor man drunk, not even mildly. But she played it up for all she was worth.'

'The trouble is,' Tom said, 'she could be anywhere in the entire country.'

'If not the entire world.'

'That's unlikely. She wouldn't move outside England, I'm sure. She's almost certainly operating under a different name, because she guessed you might eventually realise who was behind Laura's kidnap. That means she'll have had to set up bank accounts under the new name.'

'She'd also have had to establish a second identity in wherever it is she's moved to, plus the fact of her pregnancy.'

'Right. I'd say it'd be a lot easier for her to do all that right here in England. Besides, the police would have been watching for a single woman travelling with a baby at that time. Everyone in the whole country would have been on the look out. Having taken Laura from the pram, she needed to appear back in her new place fast, and without causing any suspicion.'

'The new place where she'd already established herself as an expectant mother.'

'Right.'

'How would she have done that?'

'Padding?' He shrugged. 'It's probably not all that difficult. And after Laura was born, she'd have to establish herself with an actual baby.' He thought about it. 'Not difficult, either. She could easily have had some kind of doll or something for a day or two beforehand. Perhaps she hung out a few nappies, bought baby-food at the local store. Then, on the day of the snatch, she would have stuck the carry-cot on the back seat of the car in full view of the neighbours, giving herself an alibi for when the hue and cry was raised.'

'It's easy, when you plan it,' Harriet said. She saw a garden, old apple trees with a line strung between them, nappies blowing in the sunshine, a woman at an upstairs window rocking a bundle in her arms. So easy. 'The neighbours would never suspect for a moment that it was a fake; they'd probably be prepared to swear there'd been a baby in the house for days.'

'So when she showed up in her car —'

'Her new car.'

'— immediately after the kidnap and carried the baby

basket back to the house,' Tom said, working it all out, 'it'd never occur to them that it didn't hold what it had held earlier, that it now contained missing Baby Laura,' Tom said.

Harriet turned to look at him. 'Oh God, Tom,' she said quietly. 'You really do believe me, don't you?'

Tom thought he had never seen anything so lovely as Harriet by firelight, her warm mouth, the highlights in her multi-coloured hair, her whole body leaning towards him, ready, ripe, waiting. But although he longed to pull her close, to feel the softness of her lips under his, he moved away from her, nodding. 'Yes,' he said. 'I really do.'

'You don't think I'm mad?'

'Not in the least.' *Lovely, yes. Vulnerable. The woman I want. All those thing. But definitely not mad.*

'OK. So I'm not mad. So how do we find her?'

'What about the police?'

She shook her head so hard that her hair flew out on either side of her face. 'No. Not yet. I can't bear to see David Buchan's eyes glaze over while he tries to stay polite. Can you understand?'

'Not really. But I guess I can go along with it.'

'Besides, the police've got no more than we have to go on, so even if we told them and they believed us, they'd still have to work out where to look next. We can do that just as well as they can, can't we? Once we've got something definite to follow up, we can tell them then.'

'All right.' Tom became brisk, lawyerly. He began to make notes. 'Let's begin with what we know about Christina.'

'Nothing very much. I know she was brought up by the sea somewhere, that her mother was French, and that she collected antique dolls.'

'And that's it?'

'Just about.'

'For best friends, you don't seem to have exchanged much information.'

'She knows about me. I'm only just realising how she somehow slid around answering any personal questions.' Harriet's expression changed. 'There is something else, though,' she said slowly. 'Someone left her and Denis a house somewhere: Denis's aunt, I think. Do you think she could have taken Laura there?' Except she also remembered Christina's quick light voice saying once that she had sold the house: was that the truth or a lie, intended to put Harriet off the scent?

'Anything's possible. Any idea where this house was?'

'None at all. She did say she'd sold it, but maybe she was lying.'

'When was that?'

'After Denis died.'

'Sounds more as if she was telling the truth, otherwise why was she looking for another house?'

'I don't know what, if anything, we can believe of what Christina told me.' The answer rang loud and clear in her head: *nothing*. 'She seems to have been an extraordinarily accomplished liar.' She saw again the baby lying in her pram; the picture made her want to weep. Sometimes it seemed as if the pain of her loss grew hourly, flourishing like a cancer; sometimes she felt as Antonio would have done, had Shylock succeeded in cutting off his pound of flesh.

'Something else we know about her,' said Tom. 'She doesn't make many mistakes.'

Harriet gripped the edge of the table. 'What about the photograph of the house which she left here?' she asked, hoping her voice did not sound as out of control as it felt.

'Since it led to a dead-end, it could have been deliberate,' said Tom. 'Kind of a nose-thumb, if and when you caught up with her.' He paused. 'You know, she doesn't sound like a terribly nice person.'

'But she was,' Harriet said. 'Or I thought she was. Kind, generous. She was my friend; I loved her.' Did I rely on her too much? she wondered now. Did I impose? Expect from her more than she could give?

'All that's beside the point. We have to work out where she could possibly have gone.'

'How?'

He grinned at her. 'That's why I'm here, isn't it?'

But though they went over and over it, neither of them could come up with any ideas apart from the possibility that Christina had not, as she said, sold the aunt's house but had holed up there.

'That's something we could give to the police,' Tom said. 'They'd have much easier access to records than we would.'

'But we haven't any proof at all that Christina's involved. They might do it if we can come up with that, but not otherwise, I'm sure.'

'I think you're wrong,' Tom began, but Harriet's face was so distraught that he stopped. He could imagine how she felt, discovering how her closest friend had betrayed her not once but twice.

'What we've got to do,' he said slowly, 'is check out this aunt's house. Do you have any clues as to where it might be located.'

She shook her head. 'None. I don't believe she ever said.'

'But she told you about it: didn't she say something like: we've been left this cottage in Wales, or this croft in Scotland?'

Harriet shut her eyes. The past remained obstinately distant. 'I'm trying to think,' she said. 'There must have been something, but I don't know what.'

'So you don't have any mental image of the place at all? Where it might be in relation to the rest of the country, for instance?'

'Nothing. Just a feeling that there were trees around it — she must have mentioned that.'

'Keep thinking.'

As he left, opening the front door on to a moonlit night of frost and cold clear sky, Tom said: 'Maybe once we've slept on it we'll come up with something. I'll call you tomorrow.'

'Yes. And thank you, Tom.' Harriet leaned forward, huge-eyed in the silver light. Behind him, the black winter branches of chestnut and plane trellised the moon. Her warm lips caught the side of his mouth as she kissed his cheek: it was the first time she had done so. He put a hand lightly on her back, hoping she did not sense how much he longed for something more, for the feel of her warm body against his, the brush of her breasts against his hands; the sweetness of her mouth.

Harriet had thought sleep would be impossible, but it came suddenly, blotting out the always-lurking images of Laura which swarmed like wasps inside her head. That night she dreamed of Christina again, her narrow feet thrust into sandals red as blood as she strutted knee-deep in ripe grasses, the alien tree sighing and waving above her head, and caught in its branches, an empty cradle made of swirling sea-green glass.

· 27 ·

Early the next morning, Stephan rang: 'I just got back,' he said.

'Oh?'

'From the States,' he said. 'I had to go over.'

In spite of her certainty about Christina, pictures flocked into Harriet's head: a white-frame house, a lawn somewhere in the core of Middle America, a woman bringing home groceries in brownpaper sacks, stooping inside a car to untie a baby not hers from its car-seat. Harriet could not help asking: 'Are you alone?'

'Of course.' He laughed. 'Who did you think would be with me?'

'I don't know.'

'Can I come and see you? I brought you a present.'

'Uh —'

He cut in quickly, not wanting to be refused. 'How's the baby? Did you find a name for her yet?'

The answer was so slow in coming that he started to say: 'Are you still there?'

'Didn't you know?' Harriet cut in, although it was clear from his voice that he did not. 'Laura's disappeared.'

'Laura?'

'That's what I called her in the end. She's gone.'

'Gone where?'

'Someone took her. Stole her.'

There was a long silence. 'Oh, my God,' Stephan said. He sounded ill.

He arrived at lunchtime. 'Harriet, my poor love,' he said,

crushing her against him. His chest was wide; the heart inside it beat with the strength of a hammer, drumming against her ears as he held her tight. 'What happened?'

She told him what there was to tell. Halfway through her account, he dropped his head into hands. He said: 'If only I'd known sooner.'

'What could you have done?' Harriet held the glass egg in both hands; its cold surface was no harder than the shell which encased her heart. 'What can anyone do?'

He side-stepped. 'And you think Christina's responsible?'

'Yes.' She did not add that she drew a certain amount of strength from the thought that at least the baby was cared for.

'Christ, I hope you're right,' he said, then added abruptly: 'Remember that doll we found outside in the garden?'

'I'm not likely to forget.'

'I think I know who did that.'

'Who, for God's sake?'

Again he dodged answering. 'This is so difficult . . .' He took her hand. The skin of his face was pulled tight across his skull; he seemed frightened. 'Harriet. Will you come home with me? To my home, I mean?'

'Now?'

'Yes.'

'But why?'

'It could be terribly important.'

'I can't. I've too many things to do.' She had been looking forward to meeting Tom's relations the following evening. It was the first occasion for weeks that she had anticipated with any kind of pleasure.

'Please,' Stephan said desperately.

England, the long road north to Stephan's home, spread away from her. She had no wish to go with him, yet at some instinctual level, as soon as he suggested it, Harriet had known she must.

'All right.' Although she ought to stay here, directing all her energies towards the search for Christina, just beneath the surface of conscious thought, elusive as an eel, floated the memory of something else, something she could not quite grasp but which echoed his insistence that this visit could be vital to her search.

It began to rain as the car reached the motorway. For a long while neither of them spoke; the only sound was the tap of rain on the car roof and the swish of the windscreen-wipers. Harriet was apprehensive; in retrospect, the inimical stare of Stephan's father lost none of its chill intensity. As they drew closer, she felt that Stephan, too, increasingly dreaded whatever lay ahead. 'What is it?' she asked. 'What's wrong?'

He only shook his head. 'I can't talk about it.'

'Is it something to do with Laura?'

His mouth tightened. 'Wait until we get there.'

But as the land began to steepen under the heavy skies, as hills appeared in the distance, insubstantial behind slanting lines of rain, he suddenly said: 'Have you ever met anyone who was insane?'

She met the question seriously. 'Not as far as I know.'

'I think my father may be. If paranoia is insanity.' He sighed heavily. 'I should have seen it years ago.'

Harriet remembered Josef's big red hands closing round a knife, the way he sidled into a room with his back to the wall, the mistrust which drew his brows together. Would she become like that if Laura did not return? If she were wrong about Christina, would she forever stare at people and wonder if they were the one who had stolen her baby? Would the world from now on be filled for her with potential suspects — with evil?

'When I was little ... Stephan said. 'When we lived in Prague, the police were always coming for my father, always beating him up.' He heard again the blows, the dull thump of wood on flesh, the chilling absence of voices. 'Maybe whatever's wrong with him stems from those times, from the mental stress as much as the physical assaults. I don't know.'

The dank smell of the apartment block's stairwell rose in his nostrils as though he were a small boy once more, hands clasped round the cold green metal of the top-floor banister rails, his mother's breath warm against his shoulder, while

Josef and his captors descended into the spiralled darkness. He turned in the rainy gloom of the car and glanced at Harriet. 'You can't imagine what it's like to hear your father being beaten, the noise of boots making contact.'

Harriet tried to conjure up a world where such things were commonplace, tried to imagine an unshaven shirt-sleeved Noel Arden-Smith being hustled out of his comfortable middle-class milieu in the care of guards without respect for human rights and protective laws. 'No, I can't,' she agreed.

'He never made a sound, you know.' There was desolation in Stephan's voice.

For reassurance, Harriet said: 'Perhaps he didn't want you to hear him screaming. Perhaps he wanted you to be spared that.'

'Perhaps,' Stephan said. Was that the way it had been? 'Maybe that's why he hates me now, because of the pain he suffered on my behalf. Maybe it's as simple as that.'

'Hates you? Your own father?' Harriet had been unnerved by the blankness behind Josef's pale blue gaze when it rested on her; she had hoped she was imagining the way that blankness had turned to something far more brutal whenever Stephan appeared.

'Yes. That's why we have to get up there.'

They had left the motorway now and were on the lower moors. The wet road merged imperceptibly with the flat turf which spread away from them towards bluffs of stone. To one side a shallow stream ran over a rocky bed; on the other, blackfaced sheep moved slowly between clumps of heather.

'I don't understand what your father has to do with me,' Harriet said uneasily. 'Why exactly are we going to your parents' house?' Apprehension bloomed. 'Is it — do you think he's connected with Laura?'

His silence was suddenly terrifying.

'You do,' she said loudly. 'Otherwise, you wouldn't have made me come with you.' Her simmering fear began to solidify; she could feel it growing larger, squatting, dark and ugly, alongside her cold bruised heart. There had been pine woods near the guest-house: vividly now, she saw herself running, water glinting between the narrow tree-trunks, pine needles slippery underfoot, and dogs, dogs sniffing and scratching at the earth, a shallow grave, a tiny arm, dirt-covered, and Josef's terrible blank face smiling ...

'No!' she said. She raised both hands to her face. 'You think he could have taken her — killed her — don't you?'

Again he said nothing.

She remembered the witness who had been certain that the person loading up the back seat of a still-untraced car had been male. She remembered David Buchan saying that it was always a woman who stole a child and Tom's calm voice pointing out that the whole country would have been on the lookout for a woman travelling with an infant. True. No one, she thought, would have been watching for a white-haired respectable grandfather.

'Is that what you think?' Without warning, she had grabbed at his arm and the car swerved on to the grass; sheep scattered, their sodden fleeces spraying raindrops.

'I don't know. How can I know?' Stephan said helplessly. 'I only know that after we visited them that weekend, my parents seemed to think the baby was mine, even though I kept saying it wasn't. And whatever's mine, my father tries to —'

He stopped. They were still many miles from the guesthouse; he could not let Harriet travel those miles knowing how often his father had destroyed the things he was certain that Stephan loved. Did he himself really think Josef could have had something to do with Laura's disappearance? He was too confused to be sure. But if so, then he himself was as much to blame as his father. Though he had recognised the mutilated doll at once, he had said nothing when he ought to have spoken. Now, for Harriet's sake, he had no right to remain silent, yet he could not speak.

Beside him, Harriet began to sob. It was the first time she had really wept since Laura's loss; her tears felt as though they were her life's blood, each drop squeezed with agony from her raw flesh. 'Laura,' she moaned over and over again. 'Oh Laura.' The grief she had tried so hard to keep at bay was all round her suddenly, unstoppable, flooding her with successive waves of pain so strong she thought it might kill her. The images, the hideous pictures of Laura mistreated, mutilated, crushed, rolled down over her, suffocating her. Claustrophobic, she began to beat on the window with her fists. 'Let me out,' she shrieked. 'Let me out.'

Stephan slowed down. Before he could bring the car to a halt she had jumped out and was running blindly into the rain towards the rocks and heather which sprawled across the short uneven turf. He ran after her, splashing through drainage ditches and patches of boggy peat; the ground was saturated. Ahead, he could hear her voice carried back by a cold wind as she howled her daughter's name.

He knew her eyes were full of tears; if she came to one of the sudden cliffs or little ravines which bisected this part of the moors, she would see nothing until it was too late. He ran on, struggling through the thick roots of heather, falling to his knees where the ground gave way, the air stumbling through his lungs. He caught up with her at the bottom of an outcrop of grey rock footed by loose scree. There was blood on her legs; the palms of her hands were raw and bleeding. She pounded at the rough stone as though trying to split it apart, shouting Laura's name into the wet grey air; her despair, her loneliness, wrenched his heart. He grabbed her wrists; she twisted in his grip, her hair whipping about her face. He slapped her hard across the cheek and saw the shock bring her back to reality.

She stared around at the empty hills and, below them, the road and his car with the doors still hanging open. 'It hurts,' she said quietly. 'You can't imagine how much it all hurts.'

Her eyelids drooped as though she were about to sleep; she fell against him and he stumbled backwards. They lay together among the coarse growths of heather and dead dripping bracken; even through the thickness of her sweater he could hear the wild beat of her heart lying above his own. His hands smoothed her. Through her wet skirt he felt the thin hip-bones, the curve of her belly. He held her close until the jagged sobs had quieted, soothing her with soft meaningless words, with apologies.

'I'm sorry,' she said eventually. Her throat was hoarse.

'*I'm* the one who should be sorry, not you.'

'I'm so tired of trying not to think about it all,' she said. 'So utterly, unbelievably exhausted. When this is all over I shall sleep for weeks.'

'Of course you will.' When this is over? He thought grimly: if it ever is.

'I haven't cried about Laura before. I haven't been able to.'

'Much better that you should.'

'I want her back, Stephan. Oh, God, if you only knew how much.'

'Yes.'

Her wet face briefly touched his as she shifted her weight. 'I ought to have given way before, not held it all in, not been so brave. I was afraid people would be embarrassed if I broke down.'

'So British,' he murmured. It was an old joke, from their shared past.

For a moment she nodded. She had thought herself impregnable, armoured for her righteous fight against Christina. It was a shock to realise how vulnerable she was, and would remain.

She moved in his embrace, and obliquely her mouth touched his. Unreasonably, desire, acid-sharp, heated his veins; he fought it, twisting away from under her until they lay side by side on the wet sheep-nibbled grass. Once before they had lain together like this on moors similar to these; the sun had been shining, a streamlet trickled close at hand between curving ferns. They had not anticipated then that life might mistreat them.

Because, although he spoke to his mother often on the telephone, he seldom visited home, Stephan's mental picture of Helena had remained unchanged from his youth. Coming across her now, unexpectedly, he was astonished to realise that she must be close to sixty. The coiled hair was mostly grey; there were new lines cutting deeply across her still-placid face. She was in the big warm kitchen when they came in, pinching pieces of dough and shaping them into clover-leaf rolls. Seeing Harriet, she spread floury arms. 'You poor, poor girl,' she said. 'My Stephan has told me this morning of your worries.'

'Where's my father?' Stephan said.

Helena continued to fill the greased black baking tins; her head tremored slightly.

'Mother, where is he?' Stephan asked again.

Helena raised her head and looked at her son. 'In our room,' she said.

'I'll go up and talk to him.'

She gave a faint smile. Reaching into the pocket of her apron, she said: 'You will need this.' A long-ago accent gave the syllables dimension beyond their sounds, edging them for Harriet with a memory of verdigrised domes, baroque castles, cobblestones, a grinning skeleton who marked the passing of the hours. And a tree glimpsed somewhere, recognised.

Stephan frowned. 'Why?'

'You will see, Steffi. Most of the time he is fine. He is writing a book now. He travels often to the south, to museums, for research and so on. But sometimes — not always — it is better to keep him safe. You will see.'

Harriet followed Stephan up the wooden stairs covered in floral carpet. 'Wait here,' he said, as they reached the second floor. She watched him walk towards the door of his parents' bedroom, stiff with tension. As he pushed the key into the lock, he looked back at her, his bright hair lit by the watery light from a window at the far end of the passage.

How like an angel, she thought, then thought again: but I no longer dream of angels.

She walked down the strip of carpet which lay along the polished boards and paused at the door of the bedroom. Stephan had already gone in. She saw an old man seated in a rocking-chair, gazing out of the window. Stephan's father was hardly recognisable; in the months since she last met him, he seemed to have aged twenty years. His features warped by habitual malevolence, he looked up as his son approached and his face twisted with dislike. Beside him on a table lay an assortment of tools: hammers, screwdrivers, scissors, a nail-file. He picked up a vicious-looking carpet knife, holding it lightly in his lap.

Stephan stopped beside the chair. 'How are you, Pappi?'

Josef ignored him.

'Are you well?'

Again there was no answer.

Stephan glanced unhappily at Harriet. 'Pappi ...' Suddenly he clamped a hand down on his father's shoulder. 'How long have you been spying on Harriet?' he demanded harshly.

Josef smiled but said nothing. His heavy body leaned forward, then back, as he tilted the rocking-chair into move-ment. Harriet could see that Stephan's distress gave him plea-sure.

'You've been down to Oxford, haven't you?' Stephan said fiercely. When there was no reply, he continued: 'I know it was you who put that doll outside Harriet's windows.'

How could he know any such thing? Harriet wondered. Nor could Josef be the person who had been shadowing her; she would surely have noticed that massively domed head, that abundant white hair, that furious mask.

The room was crowded with objects. On the wall above a boat-shaped mahogany bed was a carved crucifix; on the bureau stood an icon set in a frame of faded blue velvet. Two rosaries hung from a hook; pictures, photographs, gilt mirrors, crystal boxes made of red Bohemian glass, painted porcelain candlesticks crammed the surfaces of the room. A whole middle-European culture was gathered here to assuage a hunger for home which she guessed Josef and Helena had never allowed themselves to admit.

A picture hung by the door, reminding her of something glimpsed briefly not long ago. On a hill, above a city she recognised as Prague, stood a tree, its wide branches spread, the rainbow-coloured leaves evolving surreally into cigars or flagpoles or the big-bosomed figureheads of ships. She frowned. It meant something, but what?

The bed was covered with a white eyelet counterpane; on

it lay a tumble of little cushions: satin and patchwork, plaited ribbon, embroidered velvet. In among them was a doll. Harriet drew a sharp breath. The doll was flaxen-haired, sailor-suited, its blue eyes wide and vacant. Round its cap was a ribbon printed with some unpronounceable name. It was all too easy to imagine that it had not always lain here alone; that once it had had a partner, a lover, in a gingham dress, with yellow plaits of wool.

'You wanted to scare her, didn't you? You hoped it might even harm the child she was carrying, the baby you thought was mine, didn't you?' Stephan was shaking his father's shoulder.

There was still no reply.

'I don't know why you hate me so much,' Stephan said softly. 'All my life I've tried to do what I thought you wanted: to be English, be successful, make up for the life that was taken away from you.'

Josef continued to rock. Stephan knelt in front of him. 'Pappi, tell me: did you take Harriet's baby?'

Josef said nothing, though his mouth split into an ugly smile.

'Please, Pappi. The baby isn't mine; it's nothing to do with me. For Harriet's sake, tell me if you had anything to do with it. Can't you understand how terrible it is for her not to know? To imagine every minute of every hour that her baby is being hurt? If she's dead, if you did it, then tell us so that we know. Please, Pappi.'

'It's not him, it's Christina,' Harriet said. For an unguarded moment she had let herself hope that this mad old man might hold the solution to Laura's disappearance in his hands. But, looking at him, she saw how foolish it had been either to fear him or to hope. His capacity for evil extended to no more than a broken doll, spoiled canvases, some kind of twisted revenge for all that had been denied him.

Stephan looked at her over his shoulder. 'How can you be sure?'

'Whoever took Laura spent a long time organising it. If it had been for murder's sake, Laura would have been found by now. So it was for something else; it was a long-term abduction. Look at your father: is he really capable of planning something so complicated? And would he still be here, if he was?'

She saw the thin relief which spread over Stephan's features. Compassion for him filled her; she remembered how once they had meant the world to each other.

Josef's baleful stare turned on Harriet. As his hand tightened on the knife, she clearly recognised behind the pale eyes the desire for destruction. 'Be careful,' she said.

She turned away, thinking that even if Josef *had* taken Laura, he would die before he told her. In a man himself so full of anguish, there could be no desire to ease another's pain.

Stephan joined her in the passage, carefully turning the key in the lock. 'He ought to be in an institution,' he said. 'He's going to do something dangerous one day — if he hasn't already.'

'Is that why your mother keeps him locked up?'

'I imagine so. But it's not enough. He's as strong as an oxen.'

'An ox,' Harriet said. Affectionately she touched his face. Just occasionally Stephan reminded her that he was born in a foreign country. She thought: perhaps we all are.

They walked out into the garden. It was soaked with winter rain, the grass yellowed, the flowering bushes brown and dead. Stephan said: 'I really have to come to terms with my father.'

'In what way?'

'I don't like him.' On the high moors behind him there lay already a thin line of snow; winter had come early this year. 'It's as simple as that. You think that because someone is bound to you by blood, you have to like them, have to love them. It's not true.'

'I know.' My mother ... thought Harriet. She didn't like us, Matt and me, or she would never have left us. Whereas I ...

'It's very liberating to come right out and say it,' continued Stephan. He pointed to the stump where years ago the willow-tree had cascaded in summer. 'I used to spend most of the summer holidays under that tree, reading poetry to myself. It was like my own private house, a sort of extra room — so he cut it down.' He remembered again the torn and wounded tree, the bitter smell of sap, his own disbelief. 'Why should I like him?'

Harriet looked at the remains of the tree. A few yellow-stemmed shoots had established themselves, sprouting from the severed stump, though they were leafless now. She shivered. 'It's cold out here,' she said, though it was not the icy air which chilled her. 'Let's go back inside.'

As they walked towards the back door, between desolate flowerbeds and rosebeds of sharp-thorned twigs waiting for the spring, she looked up. Josef was watching them from his window on the second floor.

She thought: one by one the roads I walk down close in front of me. Soon there will be no hope left, nor any path for me to tread. For others there will be another spring but for me, without Laura, there waits only an endless winter.

'Also I made these last time you were here,' Helena said, watching as Harriet split one of the freshly-baked rolls and spread it with butter.

'Yes.' Harriet smiled, remembering last time. 'You brought me breakfast in bed.'

'In your condition, it is good to be lazy,' said Helena. 'When I was expecting Stephan I did nothing all day but read.'

Read. Last time. Harriet dropped her knife. *Last time* ... 'That's it,' she said. 'I've got it.'

'What is it you have got?'

'There's a picture on the wall in your bedroom.'

'Yes.'

'Last time I was here it was in the room where I slept.'

'That is right. It is painted by an artist from Prague, a friend of ours. It is a nice picture. I moved it where we could see it more often.'

'It hung above a bookcase,' Harriet said. 'I remember looking at the books.' She turned to Stephan. 'One of them was about rare trees.'

'Was it? We had such a book, certainly.'

'Please get it,' Harriet said urgently.

He pushed back his chair and went. Harriet waited; this was why she had come, for the faint memory of a tree, an alien tree which stood rooted in her subconscious and reached her only in dreams. It was a tree which grew in the garden of the cottage which Denis's aunt had left him. She could not recall the name, but she could see the picture; idly turning pages in the guest-house's spare bedroom, she had noticed it only because Christina had once mentioned the name.

'Here we are,' Stephan said. He put a square paperback book on the table and she flipped quickly through until she found what she was looking for.

'*Ginkgo biloba*,' she said. 'The maidenhair tree.' She sat back. For a moment she allowed herself to relax, to believe that this time she would catch up with Christina, that her nightmare would be over. But it would not be over until Laura was back in her arms.

'What are you talking about?' Stephan said.

'An ancient primitive tree,' read Harriet. 'Fertilisation by free-swimming male sperm ... fan-shaped leaves ... Chinese temples ... "silver fruit" ... leaves turn to a bright amber in the fall ...'

'I know about the maidenhair tree,' Stephan said, reaching forward to take the book away from her. 'What's your interest in it?'

'Christina and Denis were left a cottage by an aunt who died a year or two ago,' Harriet said. 'It had a ginkgo tree in the garden. I distinctly remember Christina saying that the aunt who had owned it had written to Kew Gardens about it.'

'Why would she do that?'

'It was after those big storms a few years ago. Didn't they ask for people to write in so they could keep a register of rare trees which had survived?'

'That's right. But the maidenhair isn't a particularly rare tree.'

'Even so, this aunt wrote in about it, according to Christina.

So couldn't we check with Kew, see what addresses they had for people who might have registered ginkgo trees? There's probably not more than a dozen.'

'If that.' Stephan got up. 'As it happens, I know someone who works there: we were at the same seminar recently. I'll see if I can get hold of him.'

'Fifteen people.' Stephan said. He put a piece of paper torn from a yellow legal pad in front of Harriet. 'Here are the names and addresses. Any of them ring any bells?'

Waiting while Stephan got hold of the necessary information had been hard for Harriet. Eventually she had gone out. Striding across the moors in the rain, she had felt weighed down by impatience, polluted by inactivity. Ahead of her stretched the blank sky, the green roll of the moors, durable, unchanging. She had come back a couple of hours later, comforted in some measure by the permanence of the landscape.

Now, she ran her eye rapidly down the list. 'None. But look — there's only one Miss. The rest are either Mr & Mrs, or plain Mr. So it more or less has to be this one: I know Denis's aunt wasn't married.' She indicated a Miss Adela Lewis, the address given simply as Plum Cottage, Nr. Welshpool, Powys, Wales.

'I thought you said Christina had sold the cottage,' Stephan said.

'That's what she *told* me. But I have to check it out, just to make sure she really did so.' She put a hand on his arm, her eyes wide in appeal. 'Stephan, will you drive me down there?'

'Now? Tonight?'

'Yes.'

'It's a long way.'

'I know. But you do see, don't you? I have to know.'

He thought: women are so easily damaged. He said: 'As it happens I have also a friend who's working for the National Trust Gardens at Powys Castle right now. That's very near Welshpool. Before we go chasing down there, why don't we see if he could check out this Plum Cottage and find out who's living there? If it's a woman with a new baby, we'll drive down immediately, I promise you.'

'How long will it take?'

'I'll get him on to it right away. He might even have known this Miss Adela Lewis. If she's interested enough in horticulture to write to Kew Gardens, she probably goes and swops gardening tips with anyone she can find — you know how gardeners are.'

'Not really.' Harriet tried to keep the impatience out of her voice. 'Anyway, Miss Lewis herself is irrelevant.' She walked rapidly to the door and then came back to him. 'Look, how long do we have to wait for this friend of yours? Suppose he's away on holiday, or attending a meeting.'

'I'm sure he'll be —'

'If he hasn't come up with anything by tomorrow morning, I'm going down there myself. If you don't want to come, you can put me on a train or something and I'll hire a car the other end.'

Her need for action was palpable. Stephan said soothingly: 'I'll drive you, you know that. Let's wait and see what Mark comes up with before we start making contingency plans.'

Mark was at home. 'I didn't know the old girl,' his voice said, booming and confident. 'But several of the other guys here did — she was quite a character, always chatting to them about this and that, and trying to take cuttings from the flowerbeds. Completely amoral, like most gardeners.' There was a huge laugh. 'Apparently her own garden was absolutely spectacular; she used to open it to the public a couple of times per summer, and give the proceeds to the National Trust. Trouble is, she died about three years ago.'

'I know.' Stephan held the phone away from his ear so Harriet could hear the conversation too. 'What we want to find out is who's living in her cottage now.'

'Oh, yes?'

'It's terribly important, Mark.'

'How're you expecting to find out?' There was a quizzical pause. 'I suppose Muggins gets to go and look, is that right?'

'Absolutely correct.' Stephan said. 'After which Muggins reports back to this number immediately.'

'Have a heart, Steph,' grumbled his friend. 'I'm supposed to be meeting someone for a drink this evening, a really good prospect, and I'm not talking business here either ...'

'It's a matter of life and death, Mark,' Stephan said. 'Literally.'

'Are you serious?'

'Very.'

'In that case ...'

They could not have reached the end of the trail; it could not be that simple. Waiting for Mark to ring back, Harriet was unable to feel Laura coming any closer. Nonetheless, she sat with Stephan and his mother in the kitchen, peeling apples and, like a drug addict contemplating the next fix, allowed herself to hope, to imagine that Christina was indeed living at Plum Cottage with the baby, and that all that remained for her now was to collect Laura and take her home. She ran the knife over the surface of the big green fruits, remembering childhood, the long scalloped curls of apple-peel falling from Maggie's knife, the small sharp one Harriet was not allowed to touch, and she herself darting out a hand to grab at the freckled fragrant skin. Would Laura ever do the same? Or was it already too — She stopped herself: she must not think like that.

When the telephone rang at just after nine, she jumped. *Oh God, let Christina be living there*, she prayed silently. *Please — so all this can stop and I can go back to my life.*

'What're you looking for,' Stephan's friend asked.

'Why? What did you find?' said Stephan.

'There's a woman living there, with a small baby.'

Harriet snatched the telephone away from Stephan. 'Did you see her?' she demanded.

'Who is this? What happened to Stephan?'

'Tell her, Mark,' Stephan shouted. 'It's OK.'

'Yeah, I saw her,' said Mark's laconic voice.

'What did she look like?'

'Dark-haired, slim, young. Pretty.'

'How young?'

'Difficult to say. The cottage is on a bend in the road in the middle of nowhere. I was having enough to do avoiding head-on collisions with anything coming in the opposite direction, let alone keeping my paint-job safe from the ravages of sheep and brambles, thanks. It didn't leave much time for assessing the exact age of strange females, if you want the truth.'

'But young young?' Harriet said. 'Or just not old.'

'Thirtyish, I'd say,' said Mark. 'Nice figure. Nice hair, too. Definitely beddable.'

At any other time, Harriet would have objected to his attitude. All she said was: 'Does she have a man around?' If there was a husband, it almost certainly could not be Christina.

'Not according to the locals. I asked in the pub,' Mark said. 'Real Sherlock Holmes stuff, eh?'

Stephan took the phone back. 'Did they say how long she'd been there?'

'Not long. A couple of months. Lots of curiosity flying around about why a woman would want to bury herself in an isolated cottage with just a baby for company, but nobody really knew much about her.'

'Thanks, Mark. I owe you one.' Stephan put the telephone down and turned to Harriet. 'It's her,' he said. 'It has to be.'

'I think it might be.' Excitement welled and spilled in Harriet, like sunlit water gushing up from a deep spring. 'It really might.' She brushed at her eyes. 'Let's go and say thank-you to your mother and get going.'

'You really want to go tonight?'

'Of course.' Harriet took his face between her hands and kissed him lightly on the mouth. 'I want to be there first thing in the morning, when … when Laura wakes up.' It was the first time she had applied the name directly to her daughter; she felt unaccountably shy.

He took her arm. 'Let's do it.'

They made it past Chester before Stephan said he absolutely

had to stop and have something to eat.

'But we'll go on after that?' Harriet asked.

'No. We'll find a hotel.'

She started to protest but Stephan caught her elbow. 'Don't worry, my love. We're halfway there already. We'll get up early in the morning — I'll have the hotel call us.'

Two miles further on they came across a small country hotel set back from the road in its own grounds. It seemed pointless to book two separate rooms; they were shown to a double bedroom with a balcony which overlooked the back of the hotel. Harriet stepped out on to it. There were no lights out in the blackness, no distant neon to copperplate the night sky. She could hear the murmur of trees stirring, and under them the liquid sound of water falling darkly over stones. There was the scent of pine on the chill air which blew down from the mountains of Wales. Somewhere an owl called.

Melancholy touched her; it was an emotion quite different from the searing pain she felt when she thought of her lost daughter. Laura must not be denied this, she thought fiercely: this lovely coalescence of darkness and wind, past love and running water, the hoot of a hunting owl, hope, these small distillations of happiness uniting past and present and future.

She thought: I shall remember this moment always.

She turned back into the bedroom. Undressing, she felt no embarrassment: Stephan already knew her body intimately. Besides, he no longer seemed to have much to do with her; she had journeyed to a different place. The darkness which had enveloped her for the past weeks was lit now with fragments of memory like sparks of light: the fragile baby skull, Christina's hair falling across her cheek, fuchsias brilliant against old brick, a cobbled winter city full of golden spires, Tom Seaton's strong mouth, the sea-swirling colours of her glass egg.

Lying under the covers, the muffled thud of her heart sounded like a drum, like footsteps on a lonely road. It was possible that no more than a few miles separated her from

Laura. Nor were they unknown, leading to a place not seen before and therefore unimaginable; they were miles which would end at the door of a cottage on a bend in a brambled country lane.

Her brain insisted that she should not place too much reliance on the chances that the woman living in Plum Cottage was Christina. Her heart told that it was, that it had to be, that in the morning, she would be reunited at last with her precious child.

It was still dark when they set out the next day. Gradually the tops of the trees on either side of the road began to lighten; as the sun rose, a luminous green edged their leaves and the close hills were silhouetted in fire. They passed a small lake; mist hung in a thin smoky veil above flat water gilded by the rising sun. Bulrushes stood black against the hills beyond; a flock of white birds rose as they passed, and wheeled, and returned to sit on the flaming water. Harriet was pierced by beauty, by the realisation that sometimes it was enough to live for the moment. That did not prevent her from straining to see around the next corner, and the next.

· 28 ·

The restaurant was tiny, not much larger than the average washroom. As though to compensate, its prices were through the roof; Tom studied the menu, trying not to wince. Benny had said it was one of the *in* places to eat: just how the hell did he know, Tom thought sourly, since he'd never, to Tom's knowledge, been in London before.

When it came, the food was good, he had to admit, though not *that* good. And the portions were designed to leave the average man still hungry when he got up to go. But there were candles on the table, and fresh flowers, and the wine-list was not at all bad. Across the table from him Benny, in a dark suit and striped silk tie, seemed diminished, his exuberance battened down by the weighty fact of being six thousand miles from home. They had talked of Bellamonte, of the current grape harvest, of Benny's wife Dale, of Lydia. Now Benny said: 'How's the search going, Tom?'

How did he know about that? 'Search?' Tom said.

'For Nell, my long-lost half-sister.' Benny raised an eyebrow. Above the collar of the formal shirt, his big red face was sweaty. 'Did you think I didn't know about it?'

'Yeah. As a matter of fact that's exactly what I thought.'

'Lydia told me, last time I visited her in the hospital.'

'I see,' Tom said. Lydia had seemed fairly set on not telling Benny when he had last seen her: it seemed unlikely to Tom that she would have changed her mind.

'So, did you catch up with her yet?'

'Uh — not entirely.'

'I don't suppose you will, either.' said Benny.

'Why not?'

'Come on, Tom. Don't you think she's dead?'

'Why do you say that?'

'My Dad certainly thought so. Lydia just couldn't come to terms with it, had to go on hoping, even after all these years.' He poured more wine. 'I guess Dale would probably do the same if something happened to one of our girls.'

'Lydia had more than hope to go on,' Tom said.

'Did she? Like what?'

'Like, for instance, a number of telephone calls from your sister long after her body was supposedly discovered in that canyon.'

'Why the hell didn't she ever say anything.'

'Uh — I don't know.'

Benny stared with exaggerated disbelief at the artistically decorated morsels of food on his plate, and glanced over at the waiter. 'Jeez, are they worried about my weight problem here, or what?' he said. Then, lifting a fork, he began chewing, added casually: 'So did she tie the knot with Mr Wonderful in the end?'

Tom knew he was being indiscreet. On the other hand, Benny might be able to give him some of the information he was temporarily unable to get from Lydia. Surely she would understand. 'Mr Who?' he said.

'That's what my Dad used to call the limey jerk who was screwing Nell's brains out,' said Benny. 'And Lydia's, too, though I don't think Dad knew about that little item. The guy was making it with mother *and* daughter: boy, I never got that lucky. Not that I'd have wanted to screw most of my girlfriends' moms.'

Embarrassed, Tom wished Benny would keep his voice down. Already the people at the next table were raising English eyebrows. 'I can tell you,' he said stiffly, 'that, according to Lydia, the man your sister married was not the man she — uh — had an affair with.'

'I see. So poor old Neil lost out.'

Did he mean *Nell*? Tom was torn between giving away the fact that he did not know the name of the Englishman concerned, and so handing Benny an advantage he did not want the big man to have, and the need to drag the guy's name out of Benny at any cost. 'Neil?' he said.

'Some damn name like that.'

'Lydia didn't tell me what he did.' Tom abandoned any pretence of superior knowledge. 'The — uh — the limey, I mean.'

'Some kind of student,' said Benny carelessly. 'He was spending a year at Berkeley, if I remember right, boning up on corporate law or something like that.'

'So he was a law student?'

'Guess he must have been.'

Tom tried not to let his satisfaction show. So far he had not been able to track Anthony Newgate down. The lists at the Law Society had proved useless; so had all the other lines of enquiry he had followed. What was supposed to take a week was turning into a full-time occupation. But the fact that Nell Costello's two-timing lover had been a lawyer might mean — might it not? — that there was a chance she *had* indeed gone to him for help when she reached London, and even that it was through him she had met her husband.

'Are you sure?' Tom used one of the oldest lawyer's tricks in the business, arching his eyebrows with well-judged incredulity.

'Sure I'm sure. Think I'd forget? The guy was directly responsible for my half-sister running away from home and, on top of that, damn near broke up my father's marriage. Which is why I thought Lydia was crazy to have his kid working at the nurseries one year, even though Dad was long dead by then.'

His *kid*? Tom wrinkled his forehead. With a name he would surely be able to trace the limey, and so — with any luck — get a handle on the Newgates. 'Did I meet this kid?' he said. 'I can't remember.' Under the table he squeezed his hands together: would Benny — garrulous Benny made more so by wine plus the two dry martinis before they sat down to eat — come across with the name he wanted so badly?

'It was before you and Amis set up shop in Bellamonte.'

'Ah, yes, I think Lydia mentioned him to me,' Tom said. He was getting pretty desperate. 'What the hell was his name?' He

looked vaguely around the crowded room as if he did not
really care one way or the other. He wondered whether to snap
his fingers as though the name was on the tip of his tongue,
but decided against it.

'The kid's name?'

'Yes.'

'Matt Arden,' said Benny. 'Nice kid, I have to say. Not a bit
like his old man.'

Matt Arden: why did that have a vaguely familiar ring? Tom
frowned. 'And you think that the boy's father had originally
hoped to marry Nell for her money?'

'That's certainly what my Dad thought. We're talking way
back when. I didn't personally have too much of an opinion
one way or another.'

If he could now track down this Neil Arden, which should not
be too difficult, Tom thought he might be home and dry at last.
Unless, like Anthony Newgate, *he* didn't figure on the professional lists either. Except, darn it, hadn't Lydia said the guy
lived abroad?

Trying to recapture some of the ground he felt he had lost,
he said: 'As a matter of fact, I'm pretty close to finding your
sister.'

'You are?'

'Yes. It's only a question of solid identification now. Obviously I don't want to burst in on some woman and accuse her
of being the former Helen-Known-As-Nell Costello unless I'm
pretty damn sure of myself.' With his knife he scraped bread-
crumbs into a heap by his plate. 'Which, I may say, I am,' he
added modestly.

'That's great. Lydia will be really pleased.'

*And you, Benny, how pleased would you be if what I told
you was true? After all, you stand to lose a couple of million
bucks if I catch up with this lady and her two kids.*

'Right,' Tom said. 'I can't wait to let her know.' Matt Arden.
He thought: I've seen that name somewhere; it was at eye-
level; I can see it; where was it?

Benny called for brandies; he lifted the big balloon to his
mouth. 'Here's to Nell,' he said. 'Little Nell who's going to come

into a fortune, soon as her mom dies.'

'Not her — her children. And not all of it, either,' Tom said.

'Enough to louse up my deals,' said Benny. He drew brandy into his mouth, giving Tom a surreal view of his lips caught within the rim of the glass, predatory, hungry. 'If I'm not mistaken, Tom, the money reverts back to me if the kids die first, doesn't it?'

'Most of it,' Tom said unwillingly.

'Quite right, too.'

There was savagery in Benny's voice. Uncomfortable, Tom tried to change the subject but Benny stopped him. 'Say, Tom, I've been meaning to tell you I thought it was pretty damn mean of you and Amis keeping that stuff about Lydia's will to yourselves.'

'We wouldn't last very long as lawyers if we couldn't respect our clients' confidence,' Tom said. The hell with it if he sounded pompous: it was true.

'I know that. But given the circumstances: I mean, that big deal I put together six months ago. You must have known that was going to land me up the creek if anything went wrong, if Lydia were to die before I could start the repayments.'

'Amis warned you that you were getting in over your head, if I remember rightly.'

'But not how far.' Benny's neck was getting redder; in the small folds under his chin Tom could see drops of perspiration glinting in the light cast by the candle flame.

'We weren't at liberty to say anything more.' Tom remembered that hot California afternoon: Benny on the sidewalk lighting his cigar; Amis nervously rubbing his high forehead at the narrow escape he had just had.

'Well, I don't think it would have done any harm to slip me just a hint,' said Benny. He caught the eye of the woman at the next table and winked; she stared haughtily, as though wondering why the management had allowed him in through the door. 'Why should Nell's kids get it when neither she nor they has put one damn stroke of work into Costello Nurseries, or ever will?'

'Lydia can leave her money where she pleases,' said Tom. To

change the subject, he began talking about the first thing which came to mind: Harriet. Watching Benny's predictable responses — 'the poor kid ... do the cops have any ... how long's it been? ... terrible ... terrible ...' he thought: I never noticed it before but he *is* predatory, like a shark, the way he smiles, showing all his teeth, those little eyes.

'And they still haven't an idea where the baby might be?' Benny said.

'None at all.'

'That's too bad.' Benny leaned on his elbows and pushed his head forwards. 'I'll tell you something, Tom.'

'What's that?'

'Life can really be a bitch.'

'I guess you could say that, Benny.'

'What's this girl's name, anyway?'

'Harriet.' Tom was annoyed with the way his heart flipped as he said the name. Dammit. He would be back in the States by Christmas, and Harriet would never even know what he felt about her, let alone return it. He opened his mouth to say: 'Harriet Pearse.'

At the same time, Benny said: 'Harriet? There was a girl who came to work for Lydia called that.'

'It must be the same one,' Tom said. 'It was Lydia who told me to get in touch.'

'She was the English kid's sister, now I think about it,' Tom said. 'Yeah, that's right. Harriet Arden, Matt Arden's sister.'

'What? Are you sure?' But even as he asked the question, Tom remembered the square of pasteboard stuck to the board alongside Harriet's telephone number:

MATT ARDEN

Antiques

Tel: (0370) 628793

Was it possible that Harriet was the daughter of the man with whom Lydia had had an affair? That Harriet's father had been the indirect cause of Lydia losing her daughter? That if he'd asked Harriet a simple question, he might have by-passed all those long hours in the Records Office?

Surely not. Yet, although at first sight it seemed too much of a coincidence, it was not necessarily so. After all, it was Lydia who had told him to look Harriet up; Lydia who had said that she used to know Harriet's father. And even as he thought this, another thought came to him, so fantastic that he almost laughed aloud. Could Nell Costello possibly be the mother who had left Harriet and her brother, had run off with another man by whom she had eventually had two more children? Surely, surely that could not be right.

'Hey, what is it, Tom?' said Benny. 'You look like you just got hit on the head with a hammer.'

'Close,' Tom said.

'Don't tell me you just figured out where Nell is.' Benny gave a great belly-laugh to indicate his derision, and he winked again at the woman on the next table.

'As a matter of fact ...' began Tom. He shook his head. 'No. It can't be.'

'What can't?'

Tom knew he should be circumspect, with Benny of all people, but excitement made him unaccustomedly indiscreet. 'It would be just too fantastic to be true if Harriet Pearse — the girl I was just talking about — turned out to be Lydia's granddaughter — and your niece, I may say.'

'Why?' Benny caught the waiter's eye and lifted the wine bottle to indicate that he wanted another. 'Maybe that's why Lydia put you on to her in the first place. Maybe she kinda suspected she was Nell's kid and wanted to check it out.'

'No. It's too slick to be true.' Even so, and despite his lawyer's training, Tom could not entirely dismiss the theory. After all, there was some mystery attached to Harriet's mother. And there seemed to be no question that her father was the man so involved with both Lydia and Nell Costello, all those years before.

Suddenly he could hardly wait to be shot of Benny. He wanted to be on the Oxford train, he wanted to be standing on Harriet's doorstep, ringing her bell, knowing that in a matter of seconds he would be with her again, would be taking her into his arms when she opened the door to him, turning her face up to his and feeling that warm sweet mouth under — *Hey*! he warned himself, *slow down, hold your water, it's not like that between Harriet and me*. Not yet. Maybe — probably — not ever.

'. . . Oxford, you say?' Benny was asking.

'Yeah.' He would be seeing her tomorrow, anyway. She had already accepted his invitation to dine with him and his aunt and uncle. He would have to wait until then. Lines read to him years ago by Stephan kept recurring: *Gather ye rosebuds while ye may / Had we but world enough and time / My hasting days fly on with full career.* He told himself he must tell Harriet how he felt. The very worst she could do was to reject him and, hell, he'd been rejected before; he wouldn't like it but he could survive it. Whereas if he returned to the States without saying anything, she might think he didn't give a damn about her, might never know how absolutely she had taken hold of his heart.

On the other hand, only a jerk would start pressing his suit — if that was indeed what he was contemplating — to a woman suffering as Harriet was.

'Thought I might get down there myself,' Benny said. 'It's supposed to be a real historical town, according to my travel agent.'

'You have my number. I'll be glad to show you around.'

'I'd sure like to meet up with my little niece, if Oxford's where she's at,' Benny said. He tried to make it sound casual; Tom, analysing precisely why it did not, felt his fingers tighten round the stem of his glass.

Was Benny up to mischief in some weird way? And if so, exactly what kind? All the way back on the train he put two and two together and found they consistently made five. Footsteps outside Lydia's house; a snapping twig in the dark, Benny taking a trip to England at the nursery's busiest time.

He wondered why Nell had come back to the house the day she ran away. He wished he had thought to ask more about Lydia's stroke.

Back at the flat, Tom put a call through to California and got Roma.

'How's Amis?' he said.

'Still cain't remember a durn thing,' said Roma.

'I want you to check the Costello file.'

'Check it for what? Woodworm?'

'Cut it out, Roma. See if Lydia's will is still in there, will you?'

He heard the cork heels of her shoes slap across the floor, the sound of a filing drawer being pulled open, the rustle of papers, her feet slap-slapping back to the phone. 'Hello?'

'Yes?' he said.

'Now how in hell you know that, Counsellor,' she said. 'How in hell you know that will gone missing?'

Waiting for Tom and his family to arrive, Harriet sat absolutely still in a corner of the sofa. She was filled with the certainty that if she moved, she would shatter — blown apart by inner turmoil. Laura was slipping away from her. With each new setback in the search, she grew more insubstantial, no more now than a ghost-child, a twist of fog glimpsed from the corner of an eye, a stir of wind on grass or the ruffle of a wave, gone before fully comprehended. By now she would be unrecognisable, metamorphosed; how could it be otherwise? Whenever Harriet contemplated the moments missed: the first tooth breaking through, the first grab at a toe, the first smile, a kind of shell seemed to enclose her. However hard she called from within the prison of its solid walls, or beat against them, she was trapped inside, cut off, and would be until Laura was found. She knew it was perfectly possible that Laura was dead; the knowledge would in no way prevent her from hunting Christina down. And even if she was not ...

Murder no longer seemed an alien, unimaginable word.

That the abductor was Christina she still had no doubt whatever. That Christina had anticipated, even arranged for pursuit was certain. Christina was clever; Harriet told herself she must be even more so and tried not to wonder how. Wherever she turned, whatever destination she reached, Christina had already left. Yet her skin was thickening; each dead end only increased her determination to find another road to travel.

The latest had proved less traumatic than she expected, perhaps because by now she possessed so little hope. Plum Cottage was isolated, more than a mile away from its nearest neighbour, a good two miles from the village. It might have been built from her own imaginings: there was the uncut grass, the apple tree, the cot-sheets left out overnight, snapping in a cold wind, the winter skeleton of a garden that in summer would be beautiful. On either side of the porch, tubbed bay-trees stood like bodyguards; desultory smoke seeped from the chimneys.

She and Stephan had driven slowly past the garden gate and parked the car just beyond the dangerous bend. Rolling down a window, she could smell wet fields, sheep, mist.

'How do you want to play this?' Stephan said.

'I don't know.' So near to what might be Laura, Harriet felt boneless, her limbs turned to liquid. Suppose Christina answered the door. Suppose she did not. 'I just don't . . .'

'I could go alone. Or we could both go.'

'I can't.' This close, disappointment already swamped her. Intellectually she realised that the woman living in the cottage would not be Christina; nonetheless the possibility that it might be filled her with dread. 'Couldn't we just wait, see if she comes out?'

'We could. But it's not a particularly nice day.' The early morning sun had given way to cloud and spitting rain. 'She might decide to stay in.'

'Oh, God, Stephan. *I* don't know what we should do. I feel as if I'll never be able to make a decision in my life again.'

He held her tightly. 'It will all come right in the end.' He kissed her; she turned into his embrace and leaned against his chest. She wanted to feel safe; she wondered if she ever would, or if the events of the past weeks had made that a perpetual impossibility.

'I'll go,' Stephan said. 'I know her. Besides, if she tried anything, I'm bigger than she is.'

'Tries anything? What would she try?'

'Like slamming the door in my face. Or running away.'

'The baby's the most important thing,' Harriet said. 'I don't mind if she gets away, as long as Laura's all right.'

She watched him walk away from her and wondered if what she said was true or if, after it was over, she would not want recompense, revenge, for the pain she had suffered. After he had disappeared round the bend she could still hear the grind of his shoes on the loose grit of the road. Slumping down in her seat, she closed her eyes. How much longer could she live with this constant leakage of hope? Sooner or later the last drop of emotional juice would finally have drained away and there would be nothing left of her but a husk.

Listening, she heard the sharp rap of a knocker, the subsequent drawing of a bolt, voices. Already she knew it could not be Christina: the voices in that case would have been loud, sharp. Drama would have surged towards her through the morning air.

She heard the crunch of feet again, then Stephan appeared at the bend in the lane. 'Harriet,' he called softly. 'You'd better come.'

What did that mean? She squeezed her eyes shut, unable to bear the tension. Was it? Wasn't it? Slowly she got out of the car and walked towards him through the slippery rain; his face told her nothing. But if he had indeed found Laura he would — surely — be smiling, would have run towards her, embraced her, been exuberant.

At the door of the cottage a young dark woman waited, her face dismayed.

'I'm so sorry,' she said. 'I read about you in the papers, of course. I'm so sorry. I know how you feel, I really do. I couldn't help thinking how terrible it would be if someone had taken Philip, that's my baby, away like that. He's the same age as yours was — *is*, I mean, of course ...' Confused, embarrassed, she said simply: 'I'm Sarah Leggatt.'

Harriet stumbled. No Laura. Disappointment, stale grief welled; she wanted to be sick, to scream, to fall dead. Stephan, solid beside her, reached for her hand and held it tightly to his chest. 'Come inside,' he said. 'Mrs Leggatt told me something which may help you — us.'

The place was consciously charming, with chintz, dried flower arrangements, round tables draped with lace, pieces of pretty china. Harriet sat down on a hard chair against the wall while Sarah Leggatt explained that her husband was an officer in the Merchant Navy and thus often away for long stretches at a time. 'We bought the cottage six months ago, and I've been decorating it myself — gives me something to do, actually. Not that it was in bad nick or anything, but you like your own things your own way, don't you?'

She stood in front of Harriet, engaged by her distress, involved in something she thankfully did not have to share.

'Tell us about the woman who sold it to you,' Stephan said.

'Yes. Well, she kept saying that she didn't want to sell, it would have been ideal, except for that blasted tree.'

'Which tree?' Harriet's head felt immensely heavy as she raised it to stare at Sarah.

'We weren't really sure what she meant, but my husband rang up the people at the National Trust garden not far from here. Apparently the old lady who had it before Mrs Crawford was very proud of it — it's a maidenhair tree, out there at the end of the lawn.' She gestured at the small-paned windows.

'And what did Mrs ... Mrs Crawford say? She was selling the cottage because of the tree?'

'Yes. I couldn't see why exactly. I mean I wondered if it was poisonous, if it might do the baby some harm — but it isn't. Or so she said. It was funny really, the two of us standing out there under the tree with our big stomachs, talking about —'

'She was pregnant?' Harriet said sharply.

'Yes. She was due a few weeks before I was.'

'I see.'

Christina must have planned, then, to come here with

Laura, had organised her own false pregnancy so that the villagers she came into contact with should have no suspicion of her. It was easy to see how ideal the cottage was for her purposes: isolated enough but with people near at hand, people with whom she could be friendly without them asking too many questions about husbands and hospitals, or who would accept her explanations if they did.

Bleakly, Harriet wondered how it had been: had Christina gone to sleep one night and woken in the darkness, remembering that idle conversation with Harriet three years earlier, the gardening aunt in her wide straw hat, the devastating autumn storms, the letter to Kew about the ginkgo? And because of a single casual remark to Harriet herself, the cottage had suddenly ceased to be the refuge Christina sought and, being a potential lead to her whereabouts, had to be sold in a hurry, and a new harbour found.

'Don't you think it's enough to go to the police with?' Stephan asked. 'You *know* she couldn't have been pregnant — they can check that for themselves — yet here's a witness to say that she was pretending to be, but for what purpose? On top of that, she actually said she would have stayed there except for the tree: what else could she mean except that she knew she'd told you about it once, and was afraid you'd eventually remember and track her down if she stayed here?'

'Just a minute.' Sarah Leggatt, tidy, efficient, sat down on the arm of one of the flower-patterned chairs, slammed by consternation. 'Are you saying that Mrs Crawford stole your baby — Laura, isn't it?'

Even my tragedy is not my own; it has become part of the public's possessions, Harriet thought. She said: 'I'm pretty certain.'

'But that's terrible.' Sarah looked round at her pretty room as though it had suddenly been polluted by some foul-smelling stain.

'Did she say anything about where she might go from here?' asked Stephan. 'Can you remember anything which might give us a clue, anything at all?'

Concerned, the young woman shook her head. 'I can't

think — we only spoke that once, when I came to look round. I had to handle most of the negotiations myself, because of my husband being away at sea. That was the only time that Mrs Crawford and I met. Oh dear, I wish I could be more helpful.' She blinked. 'And she seemed so ... well, nice.'

'I believe she was,' Harriet said, her voice low. 'Yes. She was.' Until madness overtook her, or possibly despair.

'She left us a little present for Philip — it was so sweet of her,' Sarah Leggatt said. 'We found it when we moved in, lying on the fireplace, beautifully wrapped and everything, with a nice note. I'll show you.'

'She was good at presents,' Harriet said. Birthdays, Christmases, anniversaries, Christina had always remembered them, had always presented a package dressed in multi-coloured ribbons, unusual paper, artificial flowers, neatly folded corners, labels. Again the grief rose in her: Oh, Chris, she thought sadly, wearily, how could you have done this to me?

'Here.' Mrs Leggatt was back. She handed Harriet a Victorian rattle — and with it a crowd of memories. Harriet had seen it so many times before: coral and silver, tiny tinkling bells to attract a baby's wondering attention. And now that Christina had the baby, she had no need of the bauble.

She shut her eyes, leaning her head back against cushions. It would be easier in some ways to give up, to let Laura go. Maintaining hope was exhausting her.

Returned to Oxford, she forced herself to ring Buchan. It took a certain amount of willpower; hearing his hard-edged voice she found herself back in the midst of the shell-shocked feelings of those first early days after Laura disappeared.

'No news,' he said. 'We're still checking things out. I'm confident we'll get there in the end.'

'You don't sound it.' Even to himself, his words must have begun to appear a little hollow.

'I'm tired,' he said quickly. 'We're working overtime at the moment. I told you about that car of your friend's, didn't I?'

'You did.' Nothing, of course. The sale had gone through,

the new owner remembered nothing about Christina, nor was there anything further in the paperwork to indicate where she might have gone. 'It was obviously a red herring.'

'I thought it was a red MG,' he said. She could not tell if he intended that as a joke or not.

She thought: I can't tell him about Christina; not yet. He will ask questions again; he will bang and hammer them at me; he will desolate me again when I have somehow achieved, however precarious it may be, a certain stability. She did not mention Plum Cottage, the ginkgo tree, Sarah Leggatt.

She had told Tom to bring his aunt and uncle to the flat for a drink before dinner. As though to deny the damage Christina had done to her, she put on a jacket of patterned green silk with a very short matching skirt; it was a flattering outfit she had only worn once before. The anonymous emerald earrings hung from her ears; making up her face, she was alarmed by the rigidity of her own expression in the looking-glass. Christina had turned her into a person she hardly recognised.

Opening the door to Tom, she tried to analyse the feelings which the sight of him always roused in her. Although he possessed neither Stephan's brand of dynamic good looks nor Conor's immediate arrogant sexual appeal, he was nonetheless both attractive and sexy. Stepping back from the frank admiration on his face as he bent to kiss her cheek, she thought with surprise: What it is is that I'm afraid of him. *But why?*

The aunt and the uncle — Jack and Elizabeth — were the kind of Americans she particularly liked, low-voiced, cultured, enthusiastic. She asked Tom to pour drinks for them all, and saw with a spurt of amusement how Elizabeth noted his familiarity with the flat.

'Do forgive me,' Elizabeth said, when they were all seated. 'But your earrings are so pretty.'

'They were a present.'

Elizabeth turned to her husband. 'They're very similar to

that necklace of your mother's — the emerald one. Do you remember?'

'Uh — not really, hon.'

'The one Ellen borrowed when she and Ned got married.'

'Oh, sure.'

'Your mother was going to leave it to Ellen.'

'Right.' Jack nodded vigorously.

Harriet could see he did not recall it. She smiled. Film-going and novel-reading had led her to believe that American lawyers were lizard-slick creatures in expensive suits with careful hair and no morals at all. This bluff, crumpled man could have been a family doctor, even a gardener. She wondered what kind of a lawyer he made — then, marching on the heels of the thought, what kind of a lawyer Tom would be.

'The settings are different,' Elizabeth said, 'but the stones are very similar. Don't you agree, Tom?'

Glad of the excuse, Tom put his hand up to Harriet's face and let one of the earrings lie along his palm, remembering how he had pulled out the top drawer of the chest in his grandmother's bedroom, smelled the dry sweet odour of sandalwood which he always associated with her, seen the green leather box and opened it to find the note lying on top of the emerald necklace it contained. In her elegant hand she had written: *Tom, my dear, I believe you will choose more wisely next time. And when you have made your choice, give her these. They were intended for your mother.*

What would Harriet make of that house set between lake and sea? Would she love it as much as he did, were he ever to take her there; or would she remain always rooted in England and the life she had been bred up to expect? It was possible. Except that even he, in the short time he had been around, could see how she had changed, how she had been forced to evolve into something she might never otherwise have been. If she could change in one aspect, might she not be capable of changing in others?

He told himself again, despairingly: *I must speak to her.*

Harriet, shivering faintly as his finger brushed her cheek,

thought: Yes, it's fear I feel when he is around. I'm afraid of liking him too much. Of loving him, even. He is only temporarily here. Soon, like everyone else I've loved, he'll leave me. It's a risk I am too fragile now to take.

· 29 ·

Two days later, Tom stood in the middle of Harriet's sitting-room, listening for the telephone and waiting for her to return from posting a letter. He picked up the thing she often held when she was talking to him: an egg-shaped piece of greeny-blue glass. Its weight lay heavily within his palms. Absent, Harriet nonetheless remained a presence for him, detailed. At the open door of her bedroom he lingered, absorbing the particularities of white linen, fresh flowers, a silver box trailing beads, piled books, the cheval glass in one corner. Faintly her perfume hovered, breathing from the dress flung over a rocking-chair, the lace shawl which draped a pine blanket chest. Dust lay on the surface of a mahogany table; he smiled, knowing Harriet well enough to realise how seldom she noticed it.

When the bell rang, he assumed she had forgotten her keys, but the person standing on the doorstep was a stranger. He wore a stylish overcoat which reached his ankles; his straight, almost white hair flopped modishly over one eye.

'Yes?' Tom had never mastered that British ability to make the syllable sound like a raised eyebrow, both guarded and superior.

'Is Harriet home?' the man said.

'She will be. Who wants her?'

'I do. I'm her brother, Matthew.'

'Well.' Tom held out his hand. 'Hello, there.' He stepped aside so that Matthew could come in. 'I'm Tom Seaton. I'm a friend of Harriet's.'

Matthew was carrying a bulky parcel crowned with a fancy

pink and silver bow; a champagne bottle stuck out of one of the deep pockets of his coat. Following Tom into the kitchen, he looked about him. 'I just got in from the States this morning,' he said. 'Where shall I put this?'

'What is it?'

'A present for my new niece. I had it on my lap for the entire flight — that's real avuncular devotion.' He set it on the table.

'Lord.' Reaching for the kettle, Tom stopped dead.

'What's the matter?'

'We've been trying to get in touch with you for weeks.' He turned to look at Matthew, his expression resigned. 'You still don't know, do you?'

'Know what?' Alarm widened Matthew's eyes; he pushed the hair back from his forehead. 'It's not my father, is it? He's not ill?'

'Not him. Laura.'

'Laura?' He frowned. 'Who's that?'

'Harriet's little girl.'

'What about her?'

'Someone's — she's been kidnapped.'

'What?' Matthew paled, his face suddenly gaunt. 'Kidnapped?'

Tom nodded.

'*Kidnapped?* I can't believe this. Why?'

'We don't know,' said Tom. He ran water, found mugs. 'The police haven't been able to come up with anything, so far. There's a Detective Inspector Buchan dealing with the case: he's already told me that, after so much time, he thinks the baby is probably dead. It's not a piece of information I've passed on to your sister.'

'Naturally.' Pulling a chair out from the kitchen table, Matthew sat down. 'Could you bear to tell me about it?'

Tom poured boiling water on to coffee granules, avoiding Matthew's eye, and described the blind alleys, the false leads, the rise and fall of hope.

When he had finished, Matthew said: 'So where do we go from here?'

'Harriet herself had this idea that Christina was involved.'

'You mean that friend of hers?'

'Yes.'

'But why? What happened? How did —' He took a deep breath and said quietly: 'How long ago was this, anyway?'

'Weeks.'

Matthew stared down at his hands for a while then pushed out a sigh. 'My God. Poor Harriet. First Conor, now this. How has she coped with it all?'

'It was pretty di_ey in there for a while. But since she decided that Chris_ 'a was behind the whole thing, she's seemed to handle it a lot better.'

'What do the police think about that?'

'She hasn't told them. She's terrified of Buchan's reaction — that he'll give her a hard time, or maybe just laugh. He's a tough kind of guy and she wants to be able to give him some proof so that he can't ignore it.'

'Where do we get that?'

'You tell me. Unless we can come up with a lead to Christina's whereabouts, we're stuck.'

'And, meanwhile, every day that passes means Laura grows further and further away from her mother.'

'Exactly.' Tom nodded. Matthew had expressed the fear which Harriet herself dared not: that if — when — she finally found Laura, it would be too late and her child would belong, emotionally at least, to another woman. 'Frankly, at this stage, it'll probably be sheer luck if we ever catch up with the charming Ms Crawford.'

'Do you think Harriet's right — that it really was Christina who took the baby?'

'Yes, I really do.'

The shops were full of early Christmas decorations; already silver tinsel edged the greengrocer's shelves and paper Santas edged the windows of the newsagent. Irrationally, Harriet brimmed with hope. There was no basis for it, especially after the disappointment in Wales; nonetheless she was somehow convinced that the dark road was lightening, that if she looked hard enough she would at last be able to see around the next corner into a blaze of sunshine.

Opening her front door, she heard voices and again was besieged by a feeling of certainty that something was about to happen. She had occasionally experienced such moments in childhood, moments when for no apparent reason the world had seemed arc-lit, its colours purer, its outlines sharper, and she herself all-knowing, all-wise; there had been, too, a sense of being able to see through grass and earth and plant root, vision extending to the living rock beneath and on through that to the hard burning core at the very heart of the planet. They had lasted for no more than a microsecond of time, yet she remembered those moments still.

It was almost without surprise, as though no more than she expected, that she recognised her brother. He looked overtly different; his hair, bleached, was a statement, as were his clothes. Embracing him, she thought: of course — he's gay.

'Matt,' she said. 'Matt.' As in childhood, there was a security about his presence which her father had never been able to provide. Matthew and Maggie had been the twin rocks in her life; her father, aloof, had mislaid something infinitely precious.

'If only I'd known,' Matthew said, 'I'd have come back weeks ago.'

'You're here now.' She looked over his shoulder at the package on the table. 'What's that?'

'Something I bought for ... for Laura,' Matthew said. He touched the pink bows, awkwardly. 'It seems somewhat inappropriate now but it's a ... a cradle for the baby. As soon as I saw it, it seemed exactly right.'

'Open it, Matt.' Harriet turned away, feeling the heavy mass of her heart behind her breast.

'If I'd known, I wouldn't have ...'

As Matt hesitated, Harriet said again: 'Open it.'

'I got it in a crummy little shop in Virginia.' Matt pulled off the bow, tore apart the paper. 'It's an old Shaker piece. Very rare. And don't think the guy selling it didn't know it. I paid an arm and a leg —' His voice broke, died away, as he wrapped his arms around his sister. 'Harriet, love, I just can't believe what's happened.'

She did not respond. Gazing at the wooden cradle standing on the table, doll-sized, baby-sized, she said: 'I've seen one just like it before.'

'There aren't many of these around —'

'Exactly,' said Tom. 'Because the Shakers were celibate.'

'Yes, but they often took in children who'd been orphaned or abandoned,' Matt said. 'Sometimes a new member — a widow or widower — might join the sect with a child in tow.'

Harriet stroked the polished wood, running her fingers over the cleanly simple lines of the construction. 'Christina had one almost the same.' The ache of lost love, of friendship betrayed, shook her. Like a ghost the physical presence of Christina returned: the short dark hair, the thick rugs, the shining silver and heavy cut glass, the brilliant smile. She could feel the contours of her face begin to slacken as her mouth trembled.

'Listen,' Matthew said quickly. 'Sorry to be a party-pooper but I could really do with a nap — I came straight here from the airport and I'm whacked.'

'I'll make up a bed for you.' Tom saw how Harriet pushed the shape back into her features. 'In the nurs — the spare bedroom.'

'Only a couple of hours. And after that I'll take the three of us out for something to eat — OK?'

Harriet reached out a hand and set the cradle swaying gently on its carved rockers. 'OK.'

She dreamed. It was dark; above her head the tree shivered, moonlit, its silvered branches hung with stars, with glass-green eggs, with red shoes. The wind which set the cradle rocking high up among its frosted leaves sounded like the sea. She looked up; three tiny hearts swung there among the strings of crystal tears which decorated the tree. 'Yes,' she said, hugely happy. 'Yes ...' and then she was awake, running into the sitting-room, dragging at the drapes to let in the white light of early dawn, grabbing at the cradle and turning it upside-down. 'Yes,' she said again. 'Oh, yes.'

Tom had been persuaded to spend the night in the flat, after the three of them had returned from an evening during which the matter concerning them all most nearly had resolutely been left undiscussed. He struggled into wakefulness from the sofa, where he had been sleeping under a duvet. 'What?' he said. 'What's the —'

'Look.' Harriet switched on a lamp, pulled at his arm, showed him the underside of the cradle.

'What am I supp —'

'There. Where the rocker joins the base.' She jabbed at the place with an impatient finger.

'Yes.'

'Can you see a tiny little mark — three hearts, one inside the other; the smallest one solid, the other two just outlines?'

He peered closer. 'Yes.' He looked up at her. He could see the curve of her breast beneath her nightdress, and the way her hips swelled. It would have been so easy to reach up, to put his hands on her, pull her down into his warmth. So easy; so impossible. 'How did you know?'

'Because Christina owned it once. This very piece. She showed it to me. She said it was probably made by a man for his first child. Or a man whose name was Hertz.'

She leaned triumphantly away from him, nodding, almost laughing. At last, she thought. At last it's beginning to unravel.

'Are you sure?'

'Completely. That crack in the wood, the chisel marks, the maker's signature; it's exactly the same.' Her hair glowed. 'Don't you see? It all fits in. Christina used to have a collection of antique dolls and things, but now she's got a real child to play with, she doesn't need it any more. She's offloading — she left a rattle for the people who bought her cottage in Wales; she obviously sold this somewhere and it ended up in Virginia.'

'OK.' Tom was incisive, instantly grasping the point. 'Presumably this guy in Virginia keeps records of what he bought where.'

'Matt'll know. I'll wake him up.' She hurried off to the spare room.

While she was gone, Tom ran his hands through his hair,

stretched, opened his eyes widely several times. He would have to be ready for almost anything. He could not remember seeing Harriet so animated before.

'Yeah,' Matt said, groggy and jet-lagged, following Harriet into the sitting-room. 'I've got the guy's card somewhere.' He stared vaguely round. 'In my briefcase, maybe.'

'Here.' Harriet found it, undid the clasp, held it out. 'Find it.'

'Why?'

'So you can get him on the phone.'

'Now?'

'Right now.'

'Do you realise what time it is over there?'

'The hell with that,' said Tom.

'I don't even know if I have his private address.'

'Do you have his name?'

'Yes.'

'The telephone company'll find him,' Tom said.

It seemed perfectly natural, while Matthew talked at length into the receiver, for Tom to put his arms around Harriet. She did not pull away. He thought of the summer, her bare legs among the rich crushed grass, and the taste of strawberries. 'This could be what we were looking for,' he told her softly.

She nodded, her hair soft against his chin. 'Yes. This time. At last. Christina must have realised I'd eventually catch up with the house up north, and with the Welsh cottage. She can't ever have imagined that something she sold to an American from Virginia would find its way back here.' She put her own arms around his chest and squeezed tightly. 'Oh, Tom ... for the first time I feel as if everything's about to work for us, instead of against.'

They stood in silence. She trembled slightly; hope fermented, its rich yeasty bubbles rising through her to explode against her skull. What would she do if — when she caught up with Christina? How would she deal with the friend turned bitterest of enemies?

Matthew came back. 'Well, he wasn't too thrilled about

being woken up, but here's the score,' he said. 'He bought it from a dealer in Paris.'

'Did you get the name?' asked Tom.

'Of course.' He handed Harriet a piece of paper. 'That's the Paris number. Why don't you go and ring him?'

When she had gone into the sitting-room, he slumped into a chair. 'Better her than me. She speaks French like a native.' He tapped the table lightly with the tips of his fingers. There was a pause. Then he burst out: 'She looks so *ill*. Beautiful, but ill. As if she might … *die*.'

'Stress'll do that.'

'That bitch Christina. That utter bitch. I only met her two or three times — I always thought there was something phoney about her, as if she was pretending to be something she wasn't at all, and didn't really know how to be.'

There was another silence. Tom, leaning cross-ankled against the back of the sofa, cleared his throat. 'Could I ask you something quite different?' he said.

'What?'

'Have you ever come across some people called Newgate? Mr and Mrs Anthony Newgate?'

Matthew stared at him. 'Yes. They're — or they used to be — friends of my father's. Colleagues, actually, until Mr Newgate chucked up the law and went into the Church. They moved away after that, to somewhere very rural — I can't remember where.'

'Could you remember if you put your mind to it?'

'Probably not. But you should be able to get hold of him through *Crockford's* or something.' At Tom's uncomprehending look, he added: 'It's the clerical Who's Who. Most public libraries have a copy.'

'What was Mrs Newgate like?'

Matthew considered. 'Not terribly nice, as I remember. Not a warm person. They had a girl and a weirdo son called Clive.' He began laughing. 'Harriet got frightfully indignant because my father used to invite them to dinner from time to time, along with Clive. She was terrified people would think he was her boyfriend.'

'Was Mrs Newgate English?'

'I never really thought about it, but now you mention it she did have a faint accent of some kind. Irish, I think.'

'Could it have been American?'

'Yes, I suppose it could. Why do you want to know all this?'

'It's to do with Lydia Costello: do you remember her? You worked there one summer, I believe.'

'Of course. But what —'

Harriet came fast through the door. She leaned against the wall for a moment, breathing rapidly. 'Oh, God ...' Her face was blotched with red. 'This time ...' The words would not come. 'This time ...' She pressed a hand to her chest. 'We've got her. I really think we have.' She brushed at the tears which hung on her lashes.

'Tell us,' Matthew said.

'The man in Paris said he picked up the *berceau* — the cradle — in a flea-market near Boulogne,' said Harriet. 'And as soon as he said that I remembered something else I knew about Christina. She has a French grandmother who runs — or ran — a hotel in a little seaside resort just a few miles from Boulogne.' She turned her huge gaze on her brother. 'I know the place vaguely. Do you remember that summer I spent near there as a foreign exchange? The family lived in Paris but they had a holiday home there?'

Without waiting for an answer, she went on: '... not that any of that's important. But it's obvious, isn't it? She's taken Laura to France. It'd still be easy for her to get back to England if she needed to, if she wanted to draw money out of the bank or something — she could easily have opened an account in Dover or Folkestone. And there'd be a much smaller chance of anyone in France wondering about Laura, because they wouldn't have seen the English newspapers. If anyone did, she'd have a grandmother who's lived there for years to vouch for her respectability ...' Harriet spread her hands. The gesture was so Gallic that Tom knew immediately what she was going to say next, saw her already seated at a café table with a Pernod in front of her, the Eiffel Tower leaning crazily to one side, an accordion playing in the background — except that they were not going to run Christina to earth in Paris, but in some little town on the northern coast of France.

'So let's go. Now.' Harriet looked at her watch. 'If we left immediately we could be there by this afternoon.'

'I can't.' Matthew shook his head. 'Not till I've had some sleep.'

'Why not?'

'I'm sorry but I'm dead beat, love. Jet-lagged from the plane trip, plus three nights on the trot before that when I didn't get to bed before dawn. I'm all zonked out.'

'I'll go with you,' Tom said.

'All right.'

'But not today.' As Harriet started to protest, he raised a hand. 'No. I know your instinct is to get there five minutes ago, but you'll have to notify the police here, and buy tickets: for all you know the ferries might be full. Besides. I have some urgent business to attend to.' *Crockfords* waited for him in the public library. He would consult it and follow where it led. He was convinced that his quest — Lydia's quest — was nearing its end.

'But I don't want to wait,' Harriet said. She glanced from one man to the other. 'It's her. This time I know it's her.'

'You can't be certain. And Tom's right. Waiting another twenty-four hours or so won't hurt either you or Laura.'

'I could go without either of you,' Harriet said mulishly.

'No.' Tom put an arm round her shoulders. 'You need one of us. Please wait. I'll be back soon.'

He prayed, as he ran to his car, that Anthony Newgate had not been called to do God's work in one of the further reaches of the British Empire.

· 30 ·

At Dover, the sea loomed, restless, hostile; France bulked palely on the horizon. Through the interior throb of the ship's engines and the thickening smoke in the saloon, details swam in and out of Harriet's focus: a fire-scarred plastic ashtray, the frayed cuff of the barman's shirt, a woman in a dark sweater; mostly she stared out of the salt-streaked windows towards France while Tom, too much on edge to sit still, prowled the ship instead.

Yesterday morning, he had finally traced Mrs Anthony Newgate to a small living in a bleak Cumbrian village. She and her clergyman husband lived in a modern bungalow at the top of a hilly street of dark stone. Its design was ugly; nearer the small bleak church stood the handsome stone house which had formerly been the old Vicarage, and was now — having been improved by the addition of jacuzzis and a swimming pool — occupied by the owner of a string of garages and his family.

Mrs Newgate's face was set in the kind of frown which seemed permanently in place. The beautiful girl in Lydia Castello's photograph had grown into a pinched, gaunt woman with a turned-down mouth. 'Yes?' she said, opening the door to Tom.

He hoped her husband's parishioners did not often have to seek succour from her. 'I'm a friend of your brother's,' he said. He had thought long and hard about the best approach if he should ever find the former Nell Costello; the names of either Lydia or Neil Arden-Smith did not seem calculated to bring a smile to her face; Benny, on the other hand, seemed not to have aroused her opposition in quite the same way, all those years ago.

'A friend of Benny's?' Her mouth dropped open for a moment. '*Benny's?*'

'Yes.' He nodded encouragingly.

'But —' She stared beyond him at the dismal landscape, the overcast sky, the black little houses trailing down the side of the hill. 'How on earth did you find me?'

'May I come in?'

She led the way through a bare hall floored with worn linoleum to a comfortless sitting-room. Blue nylon slip-covers had been added to a board-hard three-piece suite. There was a cheap table at one end of the room, surrounded by ugly chairs, and a flimsy bookcase containing hymn books and back copies of the parish magazine. The difference in effect between this room and Lydia's home could not have been more marked. Settling himself with difficulty in one of the armchairs, Tom suspected that this was deliberate; that the erstwhile Nell Costello wallowed in discomfort.

'How is Benny?' she said. For a moment, a gleam of the girl she must once have been showed behind her eyes. 'It's been so long ...'

'He's absolutely fine,' Tom said. 'As a matter of fact, he's in England right this minute.'

'I wonder ...' She stared out of the windows behind him.

'I'm his lawyer. But I've really come as an emissary from your mother,' Tom said firmly.

As he expected, her expression changed. Even after all these years, he could see that her hatred still flourished. She stood up. 'In that case, it would be better if you left.'

'Lydia's dying,' Tom said.

She did not have the gall to say 'Good'; nonetheless he saw the word form itself in her brain. When she left the silence to expand, he said: 'Surely, after all this time, you can forgive her, can't you?'

'Never.' The word had a much-used sound. She repeated it, as though trying to remind herself of past conviction: 'Never.'

'She has asked me,' Tom said, 'to tell you that she would like to see that your children are represented in her will. She would —'

'We want nothing from her,' Nell Newgate said harshly.

'Can you speak on your children's behalf? They are surely, after all, adults themselves. Perhaps they would like to —'

'They have both been raised to despise material possessions. Besides, Melissa is married to a man who earns a more than adequate salary. She certainly has no need of handouts from someone she's never even met.'

'That isn't Lydia's fault.'

'In the long run, it is,'

'What about your son — Clive, isn't it?'

For the first time, she hesitated. 'Clive? I — I don't know. As you say, I can't speak for him.'

'Where is he?'

'He's ...' Mrs Newgate bit her lip and flushed. '... abroad.'

'Where?'

'Last time we heard, he was in New Zealand. Working with an electronic company.'

'How long ago was that?' Tom asked. She was clearly reluctant to discuss her son.

'You know how boys — how young men are about writing letters,' she said evasively. Her hostile glance slid away from him.

He suspected that history was repeating itself: that just as she had once left behind home and country, so now had her son. 'I think,' he said, 'I shall advise Lydia to do as she thinks fit.' As she began to expostulate, he held up a hand. 'After all, if your children don't want the money your mother leaves them, they can always give it away.'

'We don't want anything to do with any of that,' she exclaimed. Her voice was vehement. 'It's nothing to do with them — and very little to do with me, now. It was a long time ago.'

'Long enough for you to forgive your mother, surely.'

Her mouth tightened. He wondered whether her children loved her. 'I shall never forgive her.'

'Doesn't the Bible teach us to turn the other cheek, to forgive not just seven times but seventy times seven?'

She said nothing.

Tom stood up. He knew he would not enjoy repeating the details of this encounter to Lydia — that he would, indeed, try not to. It was best to leave the woman to her devouring hatred, her joyless implacability. He reached into his briefcase. 'I have a letter here from your mother,' he said. 'Please read it. There is no need for you to reply.' When she did not answer, he added: 'You know what it must feel like, having lost a child yourself.'

Again the flush moved across her jutting cheekbones. For a moment he was afraid she would pick the letter up and tear it into shreds in front of him, but she left it lying where he had put it.

Driving southwards, away from her, he was conscious of relief that a task had been finally completed, a duty done. It seemed that Benny would, after all, receive the inheritance which had at one time seemed about to elude him. He wondered whether Amis had recovered enough to identify his assailant; whether, indeed, that assailant would prove to be Benny himself, or merely someone hired by him.

As he and Harriet drove along the coast road from Boulogne, autumnal darkness was beginning to fall. In the little town a salty wind beat against shuttered houses and scoured the grass-topped cliffs which rose at the far end of the promenade. Gulls wheeled and shrieked coldly above their heads.

They had moved slowly eastwards through such little towns, making enquires at hotels, keeping their questions as discreet as they could. Harriet was terrified that Christina would somehow find out that they were looking for her before they could actually pin her down to a location. Now, running into the hamlet of St Luc-sur-Mer, she recognised it as a place visited long ago. It seemed scarcely to have changed in the twelve years since Harriet had last seen it. The same out-of-season melancholy still permeated the shabby streets running inland from the beach; the same polythene coverings flapped dismally over deserted stalls in the market-square; the rust-streaked concrete of the front was still potholed by the violence of last winter's seas.

'This is it,' she said.

'You said that about the other place we passed through ten miles back.'

'I said it *might* be. But I just feel sure ...' Harriet peered through the growing darkness. 'I don't know why — perhaps she said something that I subconsciously recognise.'

'Wouldn't she remember, and have moved elsewhere? Like she did with that tree you told me about in Wales.'

'Maybe. But it was such a brief conversation, no more than a mention in passing. The tree thing, and Denis's aunt and the Welsh cottage were much more recent, and they came up several times.'

Tom looked at his watch. 'We ought to start looking for somewhere to spend the night,' he said. 'Any ideas?'

'No. If we only knew which hotel Christina's grandparents run we could go there.'

'Harriet, you don't even know for sure that we're in the right place.'

'Ssh.' Harriet put her fingers in her ears.

He shrugged. 'OK. But do you think they'd still be running it? Wouldn't they be too old?'

'I don't see why.'

They drove slowly down the main street, which was separated from the sea by a double row of houses. Hotels proliferated but most of them seemed closed, the holiday season long since over. At the end of side streets the sea lurked, grey and uncaring. They could see lights blazing from a big hotel on the front, its ponderous façade patterned with red and cream brickwork. A sign announced that this was the Hôtel Splendide. 'There?' Tom said hopefully.

'No.'

They passed a cobbled courtyard, enclosed on three sides by pale rough-cast walls and separated from the street by iron railings set on either side of an arch. Weeds sprouted; a shutter hung crookedly at the side of a darkened window. Around the curve of the arch, faded letters read: Auberge Albertine.

'How about there?' said Tom.

'It's closed.'

'I'm sure I saw a light.'

'It's too late now: we've gone past. Let's take the next one where there's any sign of life.' She pointed. 'Look, over there.'

The Hôtel Meurice was small, efficient and open. It advertised vacant rooms, a restaurant, *tout confort*. Harriet negotiated for rooms while Tom parked the car.

'*Alors*,' said the man at the desk, pen hovering over a registration ledger. '*Une chambre pour monsieur et madame...*'

'*Non, deux chambres ...*' Harriet paused. She did not want two separate rooms — would, yes, very much, like to share *une chambre* with Tom. She knew, that if she did, it would be far more than sharing one with Stephan — friendly, familiar — had been. *Tout confort*: dangerous though it might be, she would have liked comfort from Tom at this moment, would have welcomed his arms around her in the dark. The thought caused a looseness at the base of her stomach, a sparking of anticipation under the skin of her wrists; it was a feeling she remembered well, so well, that when Tom spoke behind her, she turned with a start, blood rushing into her face. 'I'm just ordering a couple of rooms,' she said, and saw how his face dropped before he managed to control his expression. 'I think it's best for the moment, don't you?'

He nodded, plainly disagreeing. She watched him take in the implications behind what she had said, then smile.

The next morning she was up early. The day was overcast; on the beach, flat little waves rolled up onto the coarse sand, one after another, endlessly. She walked towards the cliffs, her feet sinking with each step into a mix of broken shell and fine-ground shingle, which eventually gave way to seaweed-draped rocks before degenerating into an untidy fall of chalk and outcrops of stone. From the cliff-face hung a steep railed path where steps had been cut into the chalk and reinforced at stages by fenced wooden platforms.

Climbing it, she found at the top a small enclave of substantial houses, set round a rough-mown area of grass. It was separated from the lower town by half a mile of scrub scattered with elder-trees and tumbles of hawthorn. It reminded her of her grandmother's house: there were benches set at intervals round the green, and railings. She could see a church clock behind some trees, and one of the houses, made of stone, had rosemary bushes on either side of the brick path leading to its door. Below the cliffs the sea lay calm and dull; a white road led back down towards the lower town; lavender clumped beside garden gates.

Although she had never been up here before, it all seemed very familiar, like a place she had once known and loved. She sat down and set her shoulder-bag beside her on the bench. Far out to sea, a rift in the cloud layer let a crack of golden light through; perhaps the day would be fine later. Sounds travelled to her; the slam of a car door, a dog barking on the beach below, the thin wail of a baby, gull screams.

Some impulse had made her slip the glass egg into her bag as they were leaving Oxford. She took it out now and held it, the solid weight comforting between her palms. The swirling colours hung suspended in solidity; they were the colours of sea and sky, of grass and water. Where had it come from? She wondered about the person who had made it, imagining the blob of molten glass turning at the end of the rod, the careful adding of the oxides and nitrates, the blob twirling slowly, the red-hot glare dying as the colours deepened, darkened, took on shape and force. Over these past weeks, she too had changed and strengthened, assumed a new existence.

In the distance, a bell struck the hour. Eight o'clock.

Almost immediately, the shutters across one of the windows on the upper floor of the stone house were pushed open. A grey-haired woman, wearing a wrapper pulled loosely around a comfortable figure, leaned out to anchor them against the wall. For a moment, narrowing her eyes, she gazed out to sea, then turned back into the room.

Harriet got up and walked to the cliff edge. Far below on the sand, a dark-clad figure was standing, staring up at her. Man or woman? She could not be sure. Behind it, the sea moved, solidly. She waved, and after a hesitating second the figure waved back.

Tom would be up by now, waiting for her. From the cliff road which led back into the centre of the town, she could see the small harbour at the other end of the esplanade, perhaps a mile and a half away.

The hotel dining-room smelled of fresh coffee. Tom was sitting at one of the small tables; he looked up and she felt a leap of the heart, instantly repressed, as he smiled at her.

'You ought to ask the people here about Christina's grand-parents,' he said. 'If it's anything like the town where I live, in a place this small everyone's bound to know everyone else.'

As he spoke, he realised how far Bellamonte had already faded into the past. Almost without conscious thought on his part, decisions had been taken. *A fresh start*, he told himself, handing the basket of croissants to Harriet; *I shall make a fresh start, go back to Maine, back to my grandmother's house. I shall stop running away from the memories of my parents; I shall confront them.*

'We could go to the flea-market, too, if it's open,' Harriet said. 'Ask if anyone knows about the woman who sold a wooden cradle.'

'Harriet ...' He reached forward and took her hand. He wanted to tell her not to hope for too much, to be prepared once again for disappointment. The golden ends of her hair had been blown about by the wind; there was a flush on her face which made her entirely lovely. 'You do realise, don't you, that this may be another false lead?'

'No.' She shook her head. 'I've always held back before, not allowed myself to be one hundred per cent convinced that I would find Laura. But this time ...' She opened her eyes wide. 'This time I know she's here somewhere. I can feel it.'

'I couldn't bear to see you disappointed again.'

'You're so kind, Tom. You've been wonderful, right from the very beginning.' Looking down at her plate, she said slowly: 'I suppose you'll be going back to the States soon, won't you?'

'I shall have to. I've been away long enough.' *A fresh start*, he thought, and added boldly, lightly, as though he had just thought of it: 'You'll have to bring Laura over to visit me some time. She'd love the place where I live — where I'm going to live, I mean.'

'The house you told me about? The one with the sea on one side and a lake on the other?'

'That's right.' He was still holding her hand; although she did not seem to mind, he pulled his away.

'So you've decided to go into partnership with your uncle?'

'Definitely.'

'Good.' She nodded. 'Good.' I am not involved, she thought fiercely. This man does not concern me. A memory returned: Tom wiping her forehead with something cool while she strained to give birth, and the fresh scent of his yellow shirt in that hot bright room full of effort, as he leaned across her, one collar buttoned down, one not. He had been there with her; that night they had shared an experience which would always belong to them alone, the two of them. She thought bleakly: I don't want you to go.

'We must make a plan of action,' Tom said. 'If we catch up with the grandmother, we have to decide how to proceed. We don't want her suspecting anything. If we're going to get Laura back, it's vital that nobody tells Christina that we're here since it's more than likely that your clever forward-planning friend will have warned her grandparents not to answer any questions about the baby, particularly from foreigners.'

'What should our cover be?'

'Uh —' Tom cleared his throat. 'Well, once we've found which hotel it is, and whether the old folk still run it, we could go in for a drink at the bar and then I'll . . .' He outlined his plan.

The man behind the desk of their own hotel shook his head when they asked him about the proprietors of other hotels in the town, explaining that he had not lived in the area for long, that he had come originally from Paris. With a shrug of his shoulders he managed to indicate that only the most adverse of circumstances could have brought a man of his urbanity and experience to a backwater such as this. He suggested they try another hotel nearer the harbour, whose owners had been there for longer.

At the second hotel they were given a name. 'Madame Lasalle,' Harriet said, as they walked away. Suddenly she was nervous. 'Auberge Albertine; we passed it last night. I wonder if it's the right one.'

'It must be. My French isn't very good, but even I understood that he was telling you they had a daughter who married and went to live in England.'

He had said more than that. Harriet had listened with mixed feelings to the tale of Madame Lasalle's hard life: the recent loss of her old husband, the handsome grandsons who had drowned in a sailing accident, the daughter who had killed herself, a pretty granddaughter who grew so thin, so sad, the shock of it keeping her a child for so long that her grandmother had despaired of her ever becoming a woman ... then widowhood. But all was well now, *madame*, the garrulous old man behind the desk had told her, for even though the poor granddaughter had recently been widowed in the middle of the pregnancy, she had come back with her child to be with what was left of her family, and this would make Madame Lasalle happy for her final days.

She had told him about her stay in a neighbouring resort years before, had invented an often-recalled meal taken in his own dining-room, had mentioned the name of the family from Paris.

'Ah, yes,' he had said. 'I know them well. Every summer, *madame*, they come to eat here with the grandchildren ...'

'And poor Madame Lasalle: does her granddaughter live with her?'

'No, no. She has a house somewhere up on the cliff,' he told her. He walked with her to the entrance and pointed. 'Up there, *madame*. A nice house.' He rubbed thumb and fingers together. 'It is sad to be a widow, but less sad to be a rich widow, is it not?'

Harriet could think of no way to ask what the grand-daughter was calling herself that would not sound unconvincing; to say that she was a friend would, in retrospect, make her questions seem redundant, might cause someone to lift a telephone, give a warning.

By daylight, Auberge Albertine proved to be even more down-at-heel than it had seemed the previous evening. The withered remains of geraniums slouched in neglected window-boxes, an empty birdcage swung from a hook inside a window. The place appeared to be shut but Harriet, marching across the cobbles to peer through the window, saw movement inside. Pushing at the door, she found that it opened into an empty shadowed room full of small tables, with a bar of brass-edged mahogany taking up one wall.

She and Tom perched on high stools set against the counter. The room was windowed only on one side, and dimmed by tangles of overgrown plants which stood in pots on each windowsill. A thick dusty quiet settled over them as if breath had been suspended, though they could still hear the dim roar of traffic passing in the street outside, and the sound of desultory hammering somewhere in the near distance. The ghosts of long-ago bucket-and-spade holidays padded barefoot around them; for a while nothing happened as they sat in the semi-darkness, waiting.

A curtain to the right of the bar was abruptly rattled aside and an old woman peered at them. Behind her was a bright-lit living-room full of the jumble of family life: they could see a hard table surrounded by metal-legged chairs, a big television screen, a plastic basket of folded washing, a sofa littered with cushions against which leaned an orange teddy-bear. For a moment she watched them, not blinking; she seemed surprised to see them there. Then she let the curtain drop behind her and walked around to stand behind the bar.

They ordered coffee. When she pushed it across the bar at them, Tom said solicitously to Harriet: 'Would you like to sit somewhere more comfortable, darling?'

Pushing out her stomach, kneading both fists into the small of her back, Harriet nodded wearily. 'Yes please.' Catching the old woman's eye she gave a complicit female smile as she followed Tom to the padded banquettes ranged along the window side of the room.

As they had hoped, the woman brought the coffees to

them, while Tom settled Harriet into her seat. 'My wife is pregnant,' he said, in French, smiling broadly, foolishly, the very picture of the first-time father-to-be.

'*C'est vrai?*' She seemed uninterested as she placed the small white cups in front of them.

'Yes. It will be our first one.'

'*Eh bien.*' Placing the bill under the edge of an aluminium saucer holding wrapped lumps of sugar, she turned to leave again.

'Do you have children, *madame*?' Tom asked.

She shook her head, '*j'ai une fille.*'

'And grandchildren, perhaps?' Harriet said, gazing fondly at Tom, hoping the old woman saw nothing more than a young couple on the verge of parenthood envisaging all the long years together before they too had grandchildren.

The old woman's face grew tight as she stared from one to the other. She shook her head and moved away, flicking with her cloth at the tops of the tables as she passed. Harriet and Tom looked at each other; Tom gave the tiniest shrug. Before he could speak, Harriet said, smiling broadly and keeping her tone conversational, 'Laura's been here.'

'How do you know?'

'Didn't you see that teddy-bear thing? On the sofa? Why would she have something like that, except to amuse a baby? And there were nappies folded up in the washing.'

'Do you think she was suspicious of us?'

'I don't know. She certainly looked it. Suppose she calls Christina and says that we've been here. She's only got to describe me and Christina will know at once who it is.' Harriet banged the table gently with a closed fist.

Christina would certainly have made contingency plans: even if she felt completely safe here, she was too careful not to have left herself a bolt-hole. Time was running out: one phone-call saying there were English people in town asking questions and Christina would take off. She stood suddenly. 'Tom. I'm going to walk up to the top of the cliff. I was there this morning. That's where the man in the other hotel said Madame Lasalle's granddaughter was living. Maybe I'll see her.'

'Right. Just let me pay the bill and I'll —'

'I'd prefer to go on my own.'

'Is that wise? Much better if I'm —'

'No.'

He caught a glimpse of the shiny hardness which had kept her going for all these weeks and, instead of protesting further, he said: 'What shall I do?'

'Walk about as though you were just someone here for a weekend by the sea. Watch out for her. We may not have aroused anyone's suspicions; she may be going about her normal routines, and this isn't a big place.' She knew how important routine was to Chris, how it anchored her in what must have been an otherwise unstable world. 'You never met her, did you?'

'No.'

Harriet took the photograph of Christina posed in front of the spurious house up north. 'This is her. Thin, elegant, with black hair. Very well-dressed.'

'Are you sure you don't want me with you?'

'Not at this stage. You understand, don't you?'

He said yes; she was not sure he did. But she felt she was on the verge of something deep and frightening, toes hooked at the edge of an abyss into which either she or Christina must fall. She could not deal with the distraction of another person if she was to get out of this with Laura intact.

There were few people about in the town, and none at all as she started walking along the esplanade back towards the white rise of the cliffs. A strong wind was blowing in off the sea, tossing the gulls about, and whipping the white tops off the waves in the water beyond the harbour wall. It was high tide, the sea leaping against the sea-wall. Away from the houses, the air grew chillier; spray blew against her face and she could taste salt in her mouth. She passed a woman in dark blue trousers and navy sweater who seemed familiar in a peripheral sort of way; the wind had lodged in her hair and thrown it around her head like a halo. She was hunched over against the cold, but on seeing Harriet she straightened and smiled. There was something very tentative in her expression, something moving which made Harriet stare back over her shoulder after she had passed. The woman was standing still, both ungloved hands on the cold iron railing; she was also looking back. There was something memorable about the face, something unusual: it took Harriet a moment to realise that the strangeness lay in the brilliance of the woman's gaze, and the thickness of her black eyelashes under the thick fair hair.

I've seen her before, Harriet thought, as she walked on. Where could it have been? And why does she stare at me as though she, too, remembers our meeting? She looked back again, but the esplanade was empty now, the only movement the blowing sea-spume and the crash of shingle flung up on to the concrete walk.

At the top of the cliff she heard again the church bell sounding the hour. Eleven o'clock. At the same time, rain began to sputter; she pulled a scarf from her pocket and tied it over her hair, wondering what the best way was to handle the situation now. Above the wind's roar, much louder up here on the exposed grass than down in the town, she heard a car being started up. Her heart clamped inside her chest; was that Christina? Had someone mentioned the young couple asking questions? Was she getting away? Hidden by the parked cars which lined the edge of the green, Harriet stared wildly round but could see no one, only the rough grass and the heaving sea and, above, the inhospitable sky.

The front door of the stone house opened and the woman she had seen earlier appeared, manoeuvring a pram out on to the path. She looked up at the sky and held a hand out to see if there was rain on the air. Her gaze swept the green, and Harriet instinctively ducked.

The woman reminded her of Maggie: there was the same plump security about her as she went back into the house and reappeared carrying her child. What sort of life did she live, Harriet wondered? Were there other children? Was the baby the last, a surprise perhaps, the other ones grown and gone? Harriet thought not: despite the woman's greying hair, she did not have the look of a woman that old. She debated whether to walk over and ask about the granddaughter of Madame Lasalle: living up here, this woman must surely know Christina; she might even be a friend. But in that case, she would have been warned by Christina not to talk about her. It would not have been difficult for Christina to dream up some reason: a jealous ex-husband, perhaps, or even a friend — Harriet smiled grimly to herself — who had lost her own child and seemed fixated on Christina's.

She pulled herself closer in to the parked cars as the woman began briskly wheeling the pram down the road which led into the town. If only she dared ask her; if only she dared go up to one of the closed doors and knock, to enquire whether they could tell her in which house Christina lived. It would be so easy; but since it contained the possibility of losing Laura again, it was a risk she could not take. Indecision perforated her; she hesitated, unable to decide on a course of action. Out to sea, the cloud cover broke again as it had done earlier, leaking citrus and saffron light which lay across the sullen surface of the water like a stain. Behind it shone blue sky. The woman with the pram was almost at a turn in the road; just as she reached it, the woman who had been down on the esplanade appeared suddenly from between the arching clumps of blackberry and bramble which hedged the road where the houses ended. She stood for a moment in the middle of the road, looking in Harriet's direction.

As before, the feeling of familiarity was strong. Where had she seen this woman before? And, as she asked the question, Harriet remembered. She had been on the same boat coming over: the woman at the edge of her vision in the ferry saloon. She frowned. Surely that was not the first time she had noticed the fine-boned face, that strange wild hair.

Irresolute, she considered once again the problem to hand. Hovering there might cause people to start wondering who she was, why she was lingering there on this cold day. She would have to go back to the town, or else continue out into the countryside, as though going for a walk. There was nothing else she could do, except to hope that, so far, she and Tom had not aroused suspicion. They would have to keep a close eye on the Auberge Albertine; they would have to carefully watch the houses up here. They dared not make further enquiries; even if the grandmother at the Auberge had been taken in by their charade, the word was bound to spread that they had been asking questions of the old man at the other hotel.

Below her, on the road, the woman with the wild hair turned and began to follow the pram back into town.

By noon, the day had lightened into cold sunshine. Once again Harriet sat on one of the benches at the top of the cliff. Earlier, she had walked into the countryside which lay behind the town, glad of the threshing wind, the desolate fields, the sense of things dying, melting back into the earth to wait for the resurrections of a future spring. Deliberately she kept her thoughts shallow; panic clung to the edge of her mind like a sea-anemone, tendrils of terror opening and closing, feeding on the fear which she could not disperse. Instinctively she knew that Laura was close; yet she might still be irrevocably lost if Harriet made a wrong move. The burden of that realisation was heavy.

At the same time, being this close — she was sure of it — to the end of her pursuit, she felt a curious reluctance to disturb a status quo to which she had however painfully, become accustomed. What lay on the other side of holding Laura again in her arms? The doubts which she had felt at the beginning of pregnancy resurged: could she be the mother Laura needed? Was she an adequate person to take on the responsibility of another person's life? And, most insidious of all, would she be doing the right thing by taking Laura back, snatching her away from what must, by now, be stability; or could she be causing irreparable harm by removing her from Christina's care?

She stood on the edge of a ploughed field, hands thrust deep into the pockets of her jacket, and watched the toss of leafless poplar trees against the lowering sky. Will I ever share this with my daughter, she thought? This bereavement, this isolation, this . . . desperate love I feel for her, for that other part of me I may, if I am not careful, never have again?

Tears began to form somewhere deep inside; she thrust them fiercely back down into the well of those still unwept. One day she would be able to cry freely again, but for the moment she had to remain strong. Easy to say. Nonetheless, Christina intruded; a woman desperate, unloved, alone. What must it be like to know that your body was unable to fulfil one of a woman's most basic functions?

The possibility of other children sits within my body, she told herself, walking back along narrow deserted lanes edged with grassy banks of chalk. They clamour, whereas for Christina this is her last, her only chance.

The wind threw dark birds at the field-edging trees and drove grey clouds into drifts. At the rim of the sky the clouds were beginning to bank; the thin sunshine seemed fragile. Was such a sacrifice possible; could she really contemplate leaving Laura where she was, with a woman who could take another woman's child, a woman who might well — though Harriet still had no real proof — have murdered her own husband? For a moment the world tilted crazily as she looked across the fields to the sea where whitecaps rolled and tossed — then it righted itself. Of course not. To contemplate such a notion even for a second was compassion gone mad.

She increased her speed. This was not subtle countryside; the nearness of the sea, the constant salt winds, seemed to coarsen, to encourage the growth of plants with thicker leaves, rougher stems, sharper thorns, than further inland. On the outskirts of the town, where concrete villas fenced with green mesh stood behind thick hedges of *leylandii* cypress, the sun began to appear again. She passed a church, gothic, purposeful. She paused at the entrance, catching in the air the odour of incense.

'*A serious house on serious earth it is.*' Stephan's voice sprang into her mind, reading Philip Larkin to her on a rainy afternoon. She would have liked to go in, maybe even cast a few silent words of appeal into the uncertain vastness which, although she did not give it a name, she knew others called God. *A serious house* ... but perhaps she had no right to petition where she had no belief.

Nonetheless, she felt less uncertain as she came down into a narrow street and past the redolent delicatessen doorway of a *charcuterie*. The window held vol-au-vents stuffed with chicken in béchamel sauce, tarts of glazed ham and veal, dishes piled with cooked beef, roast pork, variegated sausages thinly sliced and arranged in elaborate patterns. Suddenly empty, she went in and chose from the items displayed, stopped in at the baker's shop next-door for a thin length of bread, then, coming down between the houses to the green, she sat on a bench and picnicked.

The afternoon advanced slowly. The wind dropped slightly and the sun glittered on waves far out to sea. Shipping moved between France and England: a hovercraft spumed diagonally across the horizon. Mothers appeared with children in push-chairs; old ladies walked on flat feet, arms hung with grey cotton shopping-bags. A couple of ancient men in berets sat reading newspapers. Harriet, keeping a look out for Christina, spread a magazine on her lap. Surely, surely if Christina lived up here, if she had not flown away into an unfollowable future, she would appear. She *had* to appear. Turning a page, scanning the cliff-top, Harriet remembered her voice, the way she had stressed the importance of routine.

The church clock struck the hour. The strokes came and went, blown first towards and then away from her. One. Two. Three. At her grandmother's house, that had been the signal for a walk along a road much the same as this one, towards a similar bench. And like the shadow of an echo, Harriet remembered a woman who used to sit on summer afternoons outside the house in Cornwall, gazing from under her sheltering hat, a sprig of rosemary in her hand, her eyes hungry, desperate. She frowned. Who was it? Why, looking back, did the woman's face have present familiarity? And why should she remember so vividly how one afternoon of heat and blundering bees, she had seen tears on the woman's face?

Before she could pursue memory, the door of the stone house opened and the woman she had already seen twice earlier came out. She carried her baby in her arms and now laid it tenderly in the pram which waited outside the door. She wheeled it down the path; at the gate, she stopped and plucked a sprig of rosemary, crushing it between her fingers, then laying it under the nose of the child. There was such a passion of love in her face, in the way she leaned over the pram, that Harriet dropped her eyes to her magazine, not wanting to intrude, envious, deprived.

When she looked up again, the woman was on her way down the white road. Her feet scuffed dust up over her shoes and on to the hem of her long skirt; the bright fierce light of the sun, enhanced by reflection off the sea, emphasised the grey in her hair. When she had disappeared round the bend, Harriet got up and walked over to the house. Did she imagine that the smell of rosemary still clung to the air? She picked a sprig herself from the spiked branches leaning across the stone wall, and held it to her face. Rosemary. *Here's rosemary; that's for remembrance.* She had played Ophelia once, at university — *and there is pansies, that's for thoughts* ...

She ought to go back to the hotel and find Tom. Perhaps he had managed to discover something further, something that would lead to the end of her quest. Instead, she walked towards the very edge of the cliff, where the vertiginous path led down to the sea's edge. The smell of the herb was pungent on her fingers. She smelled them again. Rosemary — *rosmarinus*, rose of the sea, as her grandmother had liked to think of it. The Romans believed it to be sacred; the Christians associated it with the Madonna. What had Ophelia said again? *'Here's rosemary; that's for remembrance. I pray you, love, remember —'*

Harriet stopped dead.

I pray you, love, remember ... and, abruptly, she had. She remembered, yes, so many things, pulling at the blue flowers of the rosemary bush beside her grandmother's gate, a woman in a straw hat, Denis, voices falling in another room, three hearts entwined, Laura newly born, swinging to the ceiling in the doctor's triumphant hands, Christina bending over Laura's crib in Oxford.

Christina bending ... For a moment she felt as though every drop of blood in her body had drained away and was seeping into the earth beneath her feet, that she stood there moth-like, white and drained, no more than empty skin. The sensation lasted infinitesimally, then, as she turned away from the sea, anger sparked, propelling her into action.

She ran across the grass, past the old men with their newspapers, the young mothers talking over push-chairs, the leaning shrubs beside garden gates. Down the white road she went, past the blackberry bushes still bearing the last hard red fruits of autumn, down towards the town, the harbour. Chalk dust flew behind her; she felt it settle on her face, inside her panting mouth. *I pray you, love: remember.* And she had taken far too long to do so — to remember, to realise that, despite the added weight and the greying hair, the woman who had bent so tenderly over the crib in Oxford and the woman who had leaned over the pram just now were one and the same.

The road gave way to pot-holed hard surface and then to newly-laid tarmac. The houses began to grow up around her, to form streets, throw stockades of shadows in the afternoon brilliance. She was hemmed in, fenced, corralled. The town seemed deserted; between the houses lay the sea, blue now, gentle. Even the shops were closed. She came running down the street, her feet loud in the somnolence. Ahead, she saw a baby-carriage set outside a door, green and white against the faded paint of the house. She slowed, pressing a hand to her breast, reacting to it even though she knew it was not the one she looked for.

Had she remembered too late?

She wanted to shout for Tom, fling his name wide and send it echoing down the empty streets, summon him to her side. He would come, knight-like, she knew that; but the task was one she must finish alone. Again the rage foamed through her, surging through her limbs. She began once more to run.

I have been here before, she thought. I have run like this towards my daughter and lost her. But this time, this time I shall find her. And if I do not, if she is kept from me a second time ... She had no need to end the thought: images slammed through her brain, of blood, of violence, torn flesh, ripped skin, bones broken.

She came out beyond the houses to where the town became a port, and saw what she was looking for. The woman with the pram was walking towards the nearer arm of the sea-wall. On the near side was the edge of the beach, sand piled up against the parapet making a soft place to sit, sheltered from the wind; on the other lay the harbour and moored fishing-boats, a wherry, two or three sailing dinghies.

Once again Harriet slowed. She was almost there, almost home. The other woman, perhaps sensing the troubled anger which filled the space between the two of them, glanced over her shoulder. Her hands rested lightly on the handle; for a moment she stared at Harriet. Her mouth opened. Then she swung the pram around, back in the direction from which she had come.

'It's too late,' Harriet called. She blocked the way like a colossus. She felt huge and powerful.

'No.' The woman's voice trembled. 'No.'

'You can't get away.' said Harriet.

'No. No.' The other woman's tone was agonised. She pulled the pram round once more, so that it faced along the harbour wall towards the sea. 'Oh, no.' She pressed one hand flat against her chest, her face twisted with pain.

Harriet felt her heart stop, then start up again, beating with the force of a piston against her ribs. She could see the tide was going out; inside the harbour the water sucked and swung, knocking against the little boats. Overhead swooped the gulls, hysterical, ruthless, diving to the flotsam which rode the surface, and back up into the sky, graceful as fish.

Harriet could see no one at hand. It was as though the two of them faced each other alone, contestants in a tournament, armed with nothing but their equal desperation, their empty longing hands. Out of the corner of her eye she registered dark movement, a white face; she dared not break concentration for long enough to look.

The grey-haired woman set off at a fast run along the wall, pushing the pram in front of her, but there was nowhere she could go, no escape that way. Not unless she was going to —

Despair made Harriet weak. 'Come back,' she screamed,

her legs suddenly heavier than concrete as she tried to run after them.

The other woman turned her head. Words came tumbling past Harriet: '... mine now ... can't take her ... I won't let anyone ... rather die ...'

'Stop! Come back, for God's sake,' Harriet shouted, and wondered where God might be as under her feet the ground twisted, disappeared, slapped hard against cheek and elbow as she stumbled in one of the pot-holes and fell.

Breathless, she raised herself on hands and knees. There was nowhere the other woman could go once she reached the end of the wall: no boat, no jetty, only the sea itself. Vividly, Harriet imagined the cold shock of the water, the ease with which a child could drown; and, grabbing the rails which lined the wall, she dragged herself upright again.

The passage of time was unquantifiable. Days? Years? Or only the few seconds that afterwards she was to realise it must have been? However long, the fall had given the other woman time to snatch the baby from the pram and slither down one of the sets of green-slimed steps which led to a narrow runway along the wall on the harbour side, just above the water-level. For a moment she hesitated, looking back at the clustered houses, then she carried on, feet sliding over the slippery surface to where the open sea pawed at the gap between the two arms of the harbour.

Harriet, too, looked back. Behind her, small and faraway, she saw figures running: she recognised Tom and, behind him, someone in uniform, a harbour official, perhaps even the police. Beside her, little boats rocked on the tide, masts clanging as the water was pulled away from under them.

Turning to follow, Harriet turned her ankle sharply in one of the pot-holes and felt it give under her. The pain was huge and immobilising. She tried to stand, to run, and could do neither. Helpless, desperate, she watched as the woman with the baby raced on to the end of jetty. She had been so near, so close. She opened her mouth and felt it fill with wind. 'Laura,' she screamed.

The woman who had been on the ferry, and on the

esplanade that morning, came running past her along the top half of the harbour wall. Her fair hair was loose around her face. As she passed Harriet she nodded reassuringly and said something. Her words floated after her: 'Don't worry, Harriet.'

'Give her back,' Harriet cried despairingly. Doing so, she found herself wondering how, in so short a time, the Christina of last year, of a few weeks ago, had transformed herself from a slim boyish woman into this grey-haired earth-mother.

Disbelievingly, she saw the woman from the ferry slither down on to the same level as Christina. The two women reached the open end of the wall together. There were large boulders round the two ends. With the tide going out, the water moved rapidly out of the harbour into the wider sea which glittered beyond the gap. Small whirlpools spun; the sucking current was clearly visible as it dragged the harbour water out to sea. And then, in a single movement which flowed with the motion of the sea, the woman from the ferry had reached Christina, had snatched the screaming baby from her arms, and was backing quickly away, feet precarious on the slippery seaweed.

Christina stiffened, as though her spine had locked. She advanced, on the other woman, arms curled like claws. Too far away to hear, Harriet saw her mouth open as she spoke, a stream of words. The other woman was stepping backwards, towards the big rocks which protected the base of the arm. Her face was fearful as she tried to look over her shoulder, hoping for a foothold, somewhere safe to stand. Then, as Christina raised one arm, she reached out and pushed her, hard.

Harriet saw Christina fall, her body curving, into the harbour. As though in a dream, she watched as Christina's grey hair spread on the surface of the water like a fan; then it contracted around her head as she was pulled by the streaming current out into the open sea. Her mouth was open; her face was blank with terror.

· 32 ·

So this is what it had been like for the two of them, this cold gasping shock? She plunges under the surface of the water for five, ten, twenty bursting seconds before exploding back up into the blue daylight. There is salt at the back of her throat, salt in her lungs and stabbing her eyes. *Peter,* she thinks, *and Paul: are you somewhere close, are you here?*

Turning on the tide, she can see the harbour wall and Harriet clinging to the iron railings. She wants to explain what it had been like, that sense of never being good enough, of never matching up, not being male, unable to be female.

'I didn't mean to . . .' she cries but the words are stopped as the sea rushes to claim them. And she knows she *had* meant, had planned and schemed from the moment she knew about Conor's child, had done everything in her power to overcome the damage this very same sea had done her so long ago. She wants to say she had loved him, loved him, that she is not going to apologise for what was the best, the happiest time of her life, that Laura is all that is left of him now and that she can never, anyway, have a baby — while Harriet can and will.

The undertow sucks at her legs as though hands are reaching up to pull her down; she can feel the temperature layers, warmth where the sun has shone dropping to unimaginable cold. Her lungs feel as though they are filled with fire, her face seems about to explode.

'I'm sorry . . .' she calls, over the bitter glittering waves. 'I know the pain I'm causing you, forgive me, but you can take it, and Laura will be happy with me, safe with me.'

But even as she lifted Laura from her pram, she had known

it could not work. Perhaps that is why she has stayed here in St Luc, despite the danger that Harriet would eventually recall that scrap of conversation and track her down. Perhaps she has always known she would not have been able to keep the baby. In the passing days she has become increasingly aware of what she has done.

'I would have given her back,' she calls across the widening sea to where Harriet, yellow hair streaming in the breeze, holds Laura once again in her arms. 'Oh, Harriet, I would, I would.'

Behind Harriet a woman hurries back towards the town. She can see the terrace of the Hôtel Splendide, a single striped umbrella battered by the wind, pastel-coloured houses leaning against each other, all receding, growing smaller, 'All I wanted was to see what it felt like to be ...' she begins, and feels the sea plunge itself into her, fill her, possess her as she sinks again beneath its surface. Paul, Peter, somewhere they wait for her; the pain of their loss has never, in all this time, abated. Tears fill her eyes and mingle with the salt of the sea.

Once again she erupts into bright air, water clouding her vision. Near at hand there are white birds, seagulls, landing on the water's surface: she sees how they arrange their wings, how they tent them above their backs before allowing them to lie flat. Far away, Harriet stares in her direction. There is horror in her face. Nights at home return, icicles made of tears, the roar of the winter wind under the eaves, shingle in the wet street; she feels the rats gnaw again at her womb, her brain, her heart.

I am drowning, she thinks, as the sea currents rush her away from the land. *I am dying.*

Her spinning thoughts float free to hang above her head. Conor is dead too, lovely Conor who might have given her what she wanted; but he did not die like this, not in salt water with the wormwood bitterness invading his body; Conor, pinned, suffocated by leaves, fading through green mystery to death, just as Denis had eddied through the warm Spanish night, receding from her into oblivion, eyes still astonished as he hit the edge of the concrete planters and death broke him. She remembers the way his drink sprayed from the glass he still held, catching the light in a hundred diamond sparks.

A wave smacks against her face and forces her under once more. She bobs up again, lungs seared with lack of air. She remembers those telephone calls, standing breathless in the call-box across from Harriet's flat, waking her, hearing her sleepy voice, hoping somehow, some way, to drive her into incompetence, even insanity, so that she herself could take the baby. She remembers whispering down the line to Conor's mother, telling her of Harriet's pregnancy, and, later, of Laura's birth, intending in some way to — to what? She leans back against the solid water and wonders now just exactly what she had expected.

Miles away, gulls flap above the head of a golden-haired girl, pretty as an angel, who looks straight into her eyes. Who is it? She knows the name so well — as well as her own. Harriet? No, Angélique, Angélique, with the little town sparkling along the foreshore behind her, her white dress blowing about her like mist; Angélique, blue-eyed, pink-cheeked, loving, uncritical, shining now, waving, waving ...

Christina lifts an arm and waves back. *I am drowning*, she thinks again, *just as they drowned*. 'Peter, Paul, wait for me, my beloved brothers', she calls and feels their big hands reach out for her, their arms enfold her, their warm bodies enter hers as they used to long ago before she sinks for the last time beneath the surface of the barren, implacable, hungry sea.

PART FOUR

· 33 ·

Snow fell during the night. Harriet awoke to find the bedroom filled with gaunt white light, the ceiling blanched and hard. She got out of the old-fashioned four-poster bed and walked over to the windows which led out onto a balcony. Snow glittered unblemished towards the pine-trees, a flat field of icy brightness; in front of the house the big cedar drooped, its branches meringued. There were bird-marks along the balcony rail, skeletal impressions in the deep-piled snow. Icicles hung like the teeth of some glass monster from the roof above.

She walked quietly, so as not to waken her sleeping husband, across the polished pine boards towards the door; they were warm beneath her feet, and solid. Listening, she could hear downstairs the rumble of her father's voice as he moved about the kitchen, and answering chirps from Laura; the dark smell of coffee hung in the stairwell. In the looking-glass her hair hung in an untidy cloud around her face; looking for a suitable scarf with which to restrain it, she pulled open a drawer. Something rolled heavily about behind the pile of folded silk. Reaching in, she brought out the glass egg.

The glass egg: she held it in her hands, remembering the comfort it used to bring her. It had seemed then to be a metaphor for her own life, trapped as she had been behind the walls of confusion and grief, able to see others but not to join them. She held it up against the window and saw how the pure cold snow-light was transmuted through its swirling colours into warmth.

The kitchen still smelled of the cinnamon buns she had baked yesterday. Laura was sitting in the high-chair which had once belonged to Tom's father; she was watching her grandfather and banging a spoon. Harriet put the glass egg down on the table and kissed her daughter's shining face, before taking a coffee-mug from the pine dresser which extended along one wall.

'Snow,' her father said with satisfaction. 'A white Christmas.' He pulled a chair up to the table. 'Do you know, Anita's never seen snow?'

'Nor has Laura. I wonder what they'll both make of it.'

Noel Arden-Smith laughed reminiscently. 'I remember you, at the same age. We were spending Christmas with your grandparents in Cornwall, and I took you out to show you —' His voice died away and he frowned. He picked up the egg. 'Where on earth did this come from?'

'It was a wedding present,' Harriet said. She put out a hand and touched Laura's leg; even after a year she still had to remind herself of her daughter's presence, her physical actuality.

'From whom?'

'I don't know. Maggie and I couldn't find the card which came with it.'

'Are you sure there was one?'

Something in her father's voice made Harriet raise enquiring eyebrows. 'Not really. Why do you ask?'

'It's just that —'

'I've got some earrings too,' Harriet said. 'They came when Laura was born, though again I don't know who from. I assumed it was the same person. Some family friend.'

'The woman you told me about,' Noel Arden-Smith said slowly. 'The one who snatched Laura from that poor deluded creature — what did she look like?'

'Fiftyish, curly blondish hair going grey, one of those beautiful bony faces.' Harriet had repeated the description often enough to the French police, though in fact the details of those fraught moments on the harbour wall still eluded her.

'What colour eyes?'

'I only noticed them at the end, as she ran past me on the jetty: they were grey, very clear and ... there was something strange about them.' She tried to remember what but without success.

'Was it by any chance because she had very black eyelashes?'

Harriet stared at her father. 'Of course. With the fair hair they seemed odd — striking. How did you know?'

'I wonder ... it sounds so like Helen, so much the way she would look ...'

'Helen? You mean my mother?'

Noel Arden-Smith got up and took Harriet's hand: 'Come here a moment.' He led her to the fruitwood-framed mirror which hung beside the door into the hall. 'Look.'

Harriet saw piled fair hair spilling around the twisted silk of her scarf, high cheekbones, grey eyes surrounded by black lashes.

'You're so like her,' her father said. 'In looks, that is. Not in character. Poor Helen, she couldn't come to terms with restraint, with responsibility. She never understood the concept of children being helpless. "I'm helpless too," she used to say. "I have as much right as they do to a life." And, of course, she did. Except she was free to choose, and you and Matthew were not.'

'Just a minute. Are you saying that woman, the one who rescued Laura, was ... my *mother?*'

'It sounds to me as though it might have been.' Ruefully he shook his head. 'She was fine until you were born, but after that — I suppose you could say she simply opted out.'

'Deserted sounds more like it,' Harriet said. She tried to fit what she remembered of that windy afternoon into the vague concept of *mother* which she had manufactured for herself over the years.

'Not entirely. She used to sit for hours outside your grandmother's house when you were down there on holiday, hoping for a glimpse of you. We often saw her out there. Once I even asked her to come in, but she wouldn't. She said she'd forfeited any right to you.'

The years rolled back. Harriet recalled a church clock striking the hour, the blue skies of summer and the distant murmur of the sea, a straw-hatted woman, the scent on her fingers of crushed rosemary. 'Maybe I remember,' she said carefully, as though memory was fragile, not to be disturbed.

'She sometimes hung about outside the Richmond house, too, but she would never come in,' said her father.

'She was keeping tabs on us, was she?'

'Yes. Matthew used to complain of someone following him home from prep-school; I always thought it must be her.'

'I think she must have followed me, too. Someone did,' Harriet said. She stared back into the past, trying to reconstruct it once again. 'And someone used to telephone me, especially after I got married. They didn't say anything, but I never used to feel it was a heavy breather.'

There was the phone-call, too, after Laura was taken: the sad voice, tentative, afraid to intrude. She tried to feel something for the woman who had played so little part in her life, but failed. What a waste, she thought.

'She was an artist,' her father said. 'Very talented. She was at art school when I met her; I don't think I ever knew anyone as isolated as she was, so desperate to be alone. Like an idiot, I thought I could fill the emotional gaps, but I couldn't. She was so creative in so many ways, but she just couldn't handle commitment.' He cupped his hands around the glass egg. 'She took up glass-blowing when Matt was about three: it seemed to be the medium she felt most at home with.'

'You think she made this?'

He turned the egg over and examined it. 'Look.' Against the flat edge Harriet could just make out a minuscule letter H. 'She even signed it for you.' Once again he shook his head. 'Poor Helen.'

'What about the man she ran off with?'

'Tony Pickford? She didn't exactly run off with him, so much as go with him to the States. He offered her a ticket in return for ...' He sighed. 'I don't really know what for. Sex, perhaps. She saw him as a passport to freedom. Certainly it was never intended as a long-term relationship on either side. Helen wasn't capable of sustaining one.'

'And yet ...' Harriet lifted Laura from her chair and cuddled her. 'If it really was her on the phone, or behind me in a crowd, she seems to have tried to create one with me.'

'I don't call that a relationship,' said her father. 'Don't you think love is about shared terms rather than unilateral ones? She never gave you and Matt the chance to develop a relationship with her, did she?'

Harriet thought about Conor's mother. Next time Tom and she visited Europe, she would take Laura over to Ireland: it was only fair, even if the baby's parentage still seemed indeterminate. The terrible weeks of Laura's disappearance had changed her; with Laura safely back, she had grown more tolerant, more compassionate, unable now to take happiness for granted, and therefore relishing its presence all the more. There had been time for her to reflect on Mrs Pearse's own sense of loss and grief, to understand and accept that she had not, after all, been guilty of anything more than a desire to maintain some link, however ephemeral, with her lost son.

Outside, snow began to fall again, slowly at first, then more thickly, the heavy flakes tumbling past the kitchen window. Later that day, Amis and his family would be flying in from California to spend the holiday with his parents; they would all be coming over on Christmas Day. Matt, too, was planning to arrive later: it was to be a big old-fashioned family Christmas.

Where is she? As so often in the past, that thought inserted itself into the present. Was that really her mother, the one who had snatched Laura away from her abductor, the one who had pushed Christina to her death by water? And did those acts of rescue make up for the years of absence? Could the lack of mother love through all the missing years be compensated for in one single act of devoted courage? She was not yet competent to pronounce, but she thought not.

And later, walking through the snow with Tom to find a Christmas tree, watching Laura, bulky in a crimson snow-suit, stagger and tumble through the white flakes, laughing as Matthew swung her high into the air and caught her again, she reflected that the bridge between a child and its parents required something more than instinctual love if it was to be strong and to last.

She wondered too, whether non-commitment, the flight from responsibility, had brought contentment to her mother. Did she regret the paths not taken, the avenues deliberately left unexplored?

Standing on the edge of the sea, feet steady on the slippery black rocks, Tom's arm in hers as they watched the coldly heaving water and, far out, the black heads of seals, hearing the voices of her family about her, Harriet thought again of the mother distanced from her not only by place but by inclination, and told herself that perhaps next time the telephone rang and no one spoke, she would speak herself, she would talk gently of Laura, of Matthew, of Tom, of the new baby coming and her present fought-for happiness.

JOANNA HINES

DORA'S ROOM

The brilliant and mesmerising first novel from a dazzling new talent.

When timid unworldly Fern unexpectedly inherits the entire estate of her rich and forbidding grandfather she has to force herself to claim the family house inhabited by relatives who have never acknowledged her.

Orphaned years before by violent death and insanity, Fern has been brought up to bury the things that hurt. But Chatton Heights evokes memories of a long-forgotten childhood happiness. Searching for the source within her parents' shattered past she uncovers a tragic love story of innocence betrayed.

This is now her terrible legacy. As she struggles to reverse the past and find the elusive 'Dora', someone is trying to silence her for ever.

HODDER AND STOUGHTON PAPERBACKS

LINDA BARNES

STEEL GUITAR

A Carlotta Carlyle Mystery

Dee Willis is a star. A blues singer whose latest album was a double-platinum seller. She's a property, surrounded by a growing coterie of execs, minders, managers and all manner of hangers-on.

But Dee and Carlotta go way back. Back to pre-electric, pre-historic college days, playing and singing together, sharing friends and laughter. Until they shared one friend too many and Dee left town with Carlotta's newly ex-husband Cal.

And now Dee is back – and in trouble. A missing mutual friend, a blackmailing letter and a dead bass player in her bed.

Private eye Carlotta finds herself investigating all their yesterdays together. And finds the old hurts are all there just waiting to be reopened.

'Sensitive, gutsy Carlotta is the swordarm of feminism, the girl for the Nineties' *The Observer*

'Fans of early Warshawski will find a suitable '90's replacement in the finely-drawn form of ... Carlotta Carlyle' *Time Out*

'A heroine worth spending time with' *New York Times Book Review*

HODDER AND STOUGHTON PAPERBACKS

MARY MACDONALD BELL

THE DAYS NEVER KNOW

Already, at eighteen, Frances Rintoul resents the narrow poverty-stricken life of the small Fifeshire pit town. But now, as the express train thunders over the dizzyingly high girders of the brand-new Forth Bridge, the possibility of escape beckons. Not just Edinburgh, Liverpool or London, but beyond to a true New World: Canada and the wide-horizoned prairies.

Life in frontier Canada is to prove hard and uncertain. Frances has to grow into a strong, determined woman if she is to overcome the bitter blows the future holds in store for her but the vigorous energy and challenge of her new life offers the opportunities that are all she ever asked for.

'Tackling a big canvas, *The Days Never Know* is new-wave romantic fiction, tougher and more realistic than has been traditional. The author is terrific at evoking the pioneering experience. Frances is a tough, believable heroine.' Elizabeth Buchan, *The Sunday Times*

HODDER AND STOUGHTON PAPERBACKS